The First Chronicle of Zayashariya:

OUT OF NIGHT

By: Violette L. Meier

VIORI PUBLISHING

VIORI PUBLISHING

P.O. Box 5283
Atlanta, GA 31107

This book is a work of fiction. The characters and events
portrayed in this book are products of the author's imagination.
Any similarity to real persons, living or dead, business
establishments, events or locals is coincidental and not intended by
the author.

ISBN: 978-0-9887805-1-4

Printed in the United States of America

Cover and Interior Designed by Viori Publishing
Artwork by: Latif B. Reid

DEDICATED

...God. Thank you!

*...to all who believe in the power of imagination. It is
the only peace in
a world of chaos.*

*...to my family. I love you all more than you can ever
know. I feel blessed to be a part of you.*

The First Chronicle of Zayashariya:

OUT OF NIGHT

Chapter 1

Night, a sweltering planet void of natural light, where solitary darkness reigned as queen and melancholy whimpering was etched into the very atmosphere. Gray skies masked the planet beneath a drab, misty blanket. Jagged buildings littered the dry and rocky surface, protruding from the ground like encrusted spines. Misshapen and haggard, they reached toward the foggy heavens in heaps of twisted architecture. Between the buildings, in mammoth menacing billows, foul vapors floated up into the hot air from singed bodies as they passed through the fires of Molech. Cackling laughs flowed from the mouths of demons as they tortured souls, bound in white-hot chains, hanging from sporadic edifices.

"It is your turn," a porcine face demon grunted as she grabbed the arm of a trembling young male. The puny boy dropped to the ground, the thin cloth covering his body fell off, exposing him completely. He plopped down hard, hoping that the demon would be thrown off by his weight but the she-demon's muscled pimply arm did not flinch.

"Get up!" the demon squealed as she effortlessly yanked the boy up, slamming him into the lapping tongues of the sacrificial fire.

Appalling displays of human and animal sacrifices littered the surface of the planet like a colony of frenzied ants feasting on miscellaneous insect flesh.

The pied muddy brown, slate blue, and charcoal gray surface of the planet was divided by toothed structures, murky waters, and harsh mountains which cut the planet into two halves.

Northern Night had a baneful atmosphere, while southern Night's atmosphere was breathable but its land dwellers were tortured in the fierce heat of the callous sun.

On the northernmost point of the planet, under the surface, the city of Gehenna thrived. It was a town of caves. The air was too poisonous to breathe above ground.

Deep within the center of the city, a mammoth castle sat surrounded by row upon row of round cacti and aloe growing on rocks. The castle was nothing more than a ten-story tall rectangle, ten times as long as it was wide. Its pale walls stained with eons of splattered blood. Two wooden cathedral doors, almost as high as the front façade of the building, broke the monotony of the featureless castle. Five broken granite steps led to the door. The muffled sound of weeping slipped through the cracks and penetrated the ears of Kalpvaleim. The half man, half beast took a deep breath, attempting to relieve himself of unwanted tension, and tapped on the door three times. A strange energy flowed from the door into his hand, implanting fear in his mind. Peeling paint fell to the ground in dark flakes. Kalpvaleim brushed off the door's dandruff that clung to his knuckles and waited. A sour frown bent his lips as his breath floated from his partially opened mouth in uneasy puffs. Moments later, the massive doors silently swung open. A gust of damp wind brushed his face, blowing his pink locks backward. Uneasiness flooded him as the primordial smell of Queen Lilith's castle pervaded his nose.

"Are you Kalpvaleim, the daemon, son of Ashtoreth?" a small voice whispered. Kalpvaleim did not see anyone. "Are you Kalpvaleim?" the voice asked again. Kalpvaleim looked down. Standing a little more than knee high to him was a small impish creature.

"It is I," Kalpvaleim responded.

"Welcome," the creature said, stepping to the side and bowing. "Please come in quietly. The princess is expecting you; however, the master of this castle does not know of your presence. If the queen finds you here, there will be grave consequences."

"I understand," said Kalpvaleim, stepping into the atrium of the castle, his navy blue skin blending into the darkness appearing to dissolve into nothingness. Muffled screams floated through the air, so faint that the average ear could not detect them, but Kalpvaleim felt their vibration. A chill snaked through his bones.

"Need a light, Sir?" the small, impish creature asked. It stood about three feet tall and was covered in smooth, gray scales. Its face was snakelike in appearance with slit eyes and two nicks in the flesh of its face for a nose. It wore a thin, silk-like loincloth and a gold ring on its right thumb, nothing more.

"Yes, I would like that," Kalpvaleim said.

Being inside Queen Lilith's castle drove Kalpvaleim near insanity, but he refused to reveal to the imp how petrified he was. Against his will, Kalpvaleim perspired feverishly and wiped his forehead with his sweaty palms. He was always nervous when he set foot in the castle. Nervous was an understatement. The feeling that flowed through him was near panic. But he refused to show any fear. His pride did not approve of fear; therefore, he placed mind over matter and buried his paranoia deep within himself like a dirty secret kept for eternity. Kalpvaleim's will was phenomenal; his demeanor changing almost immediately.

The imp vanished faster than a newborn flame on a stricken match. It reappeared within seconds holding a torch. It was as if it dematerialized and materialized right before Kalpvaleim's eyes.

"Would you like to hold it, Sir?" the imp asked with a childlike voice, small and squeaky.

"Thank you," said Kalpvaleim, taking the torch from the imp. "I will go no further into the castle. I am uneasy in this place. This is base ground I stand on." Cool breezes that materialized out of nothingness whisked past him. His eyes darted to and fro. It seemed as if spirits stirred within the room. "Bring Zayashariya out to me."

"Yes, Sir," said the imp, disappearing again.

"Please hurry," Kalpvaleim whispered into the emptiness. The hairs on the back of his neck stood up. He walked over to the nearest wall and leaned against it, placing one hoof on the wall and standing on the other. Scratching his head, he let out an edgy sigh and waited. *Why am I here?* Moments later, he heard footsteps and hesitantly stood up straight, looking towards the inner door.

*   *   *

"Kalpvaleim," Zayashariya whispered from the doorway. Her bright violet hair looked shocking against her black skin. "Come," she gestured to him. Her purple eyes glowed and went dim like a light signaling her whereabouts. "Hurry! Follow me! Quickly! We haven't much time!"

She was surprised that he had actually showed up after his last experience in the castle. Queen Lilith had him whipped and thrown out on his head. Zayashariya knew how much Kalpvaleim hated Queen Lilith. Zayashariya's heart smiled. The idea that Kalpvaleim would come because of his love for her made her belly flutter but she knew that love was not the reason. Kalpvaleim did not believe in trivial things such as love, especially regarding the love of the wicked like her mother and every other inhabitant of Night. Maybe he thought he was capable of love, but never Zayashariya. Kalpvaleim was arrogant enough to feel that way, that he was the only one on the planet capable of sincere emotion. He must have sensed the urgency in her voice and appeared out of respect for their friendship. Yes, respect.

Friendship was a rarity on Night but Kalpvaleim and Zayashariya had forged one long ago. Kalpvaleim came to her aid when she was a young girl. She had run away from home. Zayashariya, weary and hungry, stumbled upon his cave and he took her in, fed her and hid her as long as he could. Queen Lilith's soldiers had finally found her and the Queen has hated Kalpvaleim since that time. The only reason he still breathes is because of Zayashariya's constant pleading for his life.

Zayashariya led Kalpvaleim through a narrow hallway and down two flights of twisted stairs. After a quick right turn, they stood before a small metal door covered with dust and draped in cobwebs. Zayashariya turned the dusty knob and wiped the residue on her thigh, leaving a gray handprint. As the door opened with a loud screech, the two entered quickly and she closed the heavy door behind them.

"What is this place?" Kalpvaleim inquired. The daemon followed closely behind the princess of Night. Gray webs hung from the low ceilings, falling upon their faces like silk veils and the sound of small scurrying feet warned the pair of the presence of rats.

A small bed sat in the corner of the room. A mahogany table with a matching chair sat adjacent to it. Two short mahogany dressers sat on each side of the slightly ajar bathroom door, opposite the bed. Everything was covered with dust.

"It is an old guest room," said Zayashariya, pulling a torch from the wall and lighting it by chanting a few words and a wave of her free hand. "It has not been occupied since my best friend Yoki died by the hand of my mother." The heartrending memory sent a jolt through her core. *Yoki.* The name flashed in her thoughts like a bolt of bright lightening against the black sky. Zayashariya willed the name back into the dark recess of her mind. It was not the time for old hurts to manifest, pulling her away from the situation at hand.

"Come sit down," Zayashariya instructed. Gray dust decorated her ebony skin in silvery strands. Her purple hair carried a nest of webs that had fallen from the ceiling.

Kalpvaleim sat in the mahogany chair while Zayashariya sat on the grimy mattress.

"What is it that you want of me?" Kalpvaleim questioned. A violent sneeze sprayed from his nose. "This room is deplorable!" His eyes admired her from head to toe. "Even covered in filth, you are beautiful," he mumbled. "Would I still be here if you were the tiniest bit less attractive?" He scratched his head and wiped his nose. "I can barely breathe in this place."

"Stop your complaining," Zayashariya laughed light heartedly. "Do you request that we meet in the queen's quarters?" His admiration of her was always flattering. She groomed for him unconsciously by running her fingers through her hair and brushing some of the dust from her skin.

"Never that!" said Kalpvaleim, twitching. "Why did you summon me?" He brushed the dirt from his hairy legs and drew circles in the dust with his hooves.

"I have a proposition for you," Zayashariya said, puckering her full plum lips, flirtatiously.

"I am listening," said Kalpvaleim, rolling his eyes. "You can save your womanly wiles for someone else. They have no power here." He placed his hand upon his belly. Butterflies did back-flips in his stomach.

"Of course they do." Zayashariya winked.

"Yes, yes they do." Kalpvaleim grinned. "But I am sure that you did not invite me to this hellhole just to seduce me; although, that may not be a bad idea." A wicked smirk curled his mouth.

"You are right lover," she said.

"Stop procrastinating, Zayashariya. I have very little patience. You know that."

"You and I are similar creatures." Zayashariya smirked.

"How so?" Kalpvaleim raised one of his pink eyebrows.

"We both abhor this God forsaken place."

"So," Kalpvaleim spat. "I know that you did not call me here to vent your frustrations. Out with it!"

"I have a way out of Night and I need you to help me," said Zayashariya, leaning forward and looking Kalpvaleim straight in the eye.

"You have my attention," said Kalpvaleim, meeting Zayashariya's gaze head on. "Out of Night? Impossible!"

"Last week I supped with Belial. As you know, his flippant mouth never ceases. During one of his verbose episodes, he began to speak about the old wizard and how he had built so many space capsules. Belial even spoke of some of the old wizard's servants who escaped in some of them and to this day have never been located."

"Why do you tell me this? I do not care what the old wizard possesses. What good does it do me? That despicable creature makes my stomach turn. My hate for him keeps my heart pumping."

"I need for you to persuade the old wizard to aid us," said Zayashariya.

"Are you insane?" Kalpvaleim hissed. Anger filled him like a dead antelope lying at the foot of a lion. "Have you no regard? My life means so little to you!" Kalpvaleim wanted to hate Zayashariya for summoning him but he could never hate her. She was not like the other demons. She had something within her that muted the evil within her and a pale light shined from her visage. "How am I supposed to persuade him to help us? He hates me like I hate him," Kalpvaleim's said. His countenance fell.

"Kalpvaleim, you are one of great astuteness and I trust your methods completely. You will find a way I am sure. Besides, we need him."

"How can you ask me to do such a thing? I hate that madman more than I hate your mother," Kalpvaleim said. "My hate for the old wizard runs deep; deeper than any canyon on this hellish planet. That soulless man marveled at the fact that daemons were neutral creatures, neither good nor evil. It intrigued him how we lived so peacefully with demons so he decided to find out, instead of simply asking us, what matter of beasts we were. With trickery and traps, he abducted many daemons. First certain individuals came up missing and then entire colonies disappeared," said Kalpvaleim, sick to his stomach. "Why am I telling you this?" he asked angrily. "You know what he did to my family, my people, my species! He killed them all conducting horrible experiments for the sake of his cruel magic and malicious science!" Kalpvaleim spat, inhaled dust, and coughed. "If I stand before that man, I will kill him instantly!"

"That's the past. The daemons are gone. Accept it. The future holds greater things," Zayashariya snapped, totally unsympathetic to his feelings.

"Like what? What can be greater than me killing that sick scientist?" Kalpvaleim jumped to his feet. "My hands yearn for your neck just for asking me to debase myself! Tell me. What can be greater? I can not conceive of anything greater than seeing the old wizard vomiting blood."

"Our freedom and our escape from Night. Is that not great enough? We both can dwell on the material plane and I can forfeit my destiny and flee from the Council of Demons. Isn't that worth meeting with the old wizard?" Zayashariya stood. "Sit." She pointed to the chair. "Hear me out," she pleaded. "Please."

Kalpvaleim sat. "Are you insane woman? The old wizard will not help us! He may use our need for him against us. Should we give him leverage over us? And may I add that he has no love for Lilith and all within her house, and that includes you."

"I know these things, Kalpvaleim. But you have something that he wants," said Zayashariya, squeezing her fists.

"What is that?"

"You." Her eyes flashed bright violet.

"Me!" said Kalpvaleim, gasping. His brows furrowed. A distressed panic crossed his face. "Zayashariya, what are you asking of me?" His voice quivered. "Are you asking me to sell my soul to that animal?"

"Only for a short while. The old wizard would do anything if you would bow to him and agree to serve him," said Zayashariya, peering at Kalpvaleim with pleading eyes.

"You are a fool! Do you really think that I will be a slave to him?"

"If it means freedom, yes!" replied Zayashariya.

"How do you suppose that will happen, Zayashariya? Should I just walk in and ask him nicely?" Kalpvaleim leapt to his feet. "What can the old wizard do for us? He has no power to defeat Queen Lilith. He can not save you."

"You are wrong. Many underestimate the old wizard. He is one of the most powerful on Night. Not only is he a powerful wizard, he is an accomplished scientist and he can create things that we cannot. You forget that the old wizard is human. He does not possess supernatural powers. His powers are learned."

"What is your point, Zayashariya?" Kalpvaleim snapped.

"My point is that he can build machines that can jump from realm to realm. He has hundreds of spaceships within his castle. My powers are limited. I can only transport myself so far. The old wizard can take me out of Night's reach, out of the reach of demons. Kalpvaleim, he can get me out of this place forever."

"What about me?" asked Kalpvaleim. "He will never help me and once I submit to him, he will never set me free."

"When I reach the material plane, I will summon you."

"How will you guarantee that you will remain true to your word?"

"Trust," said Zayashariya, standing before him and caressing his cheeks with her hands.

"Trust?" Kalpvaleim knocked her hands away. "You are a demon. You know nothing of trust!"

"Yes. I am. But, you know me. I am not like the others. We are not like the others. I will summon you. I put that on my life," Zayashariya said, kissing his lips gently. A tear rolled down her cheek. "Will you go to the old wizard?"

"Yes."

Chapter 2

In a metal walled room filled with shadows, and what seemed like hundreds of dim candle lamps hanging from the ceiling like stars twinkling in the midnight sky, the Queen of Night, the mistress of bouleversement, sat at the head of a circular medieval conference table surrounded by the demonic rulers of the Nether Worlds. Every wicked eye was tattooed to her own as she opened her mouth to speak.

"The time has come again when we must place the appointed one in the thirteenth seat to complete the Council of Demons. The circle must be completed in order for us to come to absolute power and to reign across all the realms," said Lilith as she stood before the grand table addressing the demons before her. Her flame of hair leapt with every word.

"Do not flatter us, Lilith," Iblis said, leaning back against his high back chair. His snow-white skin looked like a pale shock against the red velvet of the chair. "We all know that *you* will come into ultimate power. Zayashariya is your daughter. She serves no one but you."

"We are all equals here. No one is powerful enough to overthrow the others. Each of us reigns over one of the twelve planets that make up the Nether Worlds. Zayashariya will give us the power of thirteen, the number of ill fortune for mortals and absolute domination for us," said Lilith. "She serves us all because I serve us all," Lilith rebuked Iblis. Her eyes narrowed and she hissed at him like a cobra ready to strike. "If you were not such a dim idiot, you would understand that!"

"You serve no one," Rehab interrupted. "But because you are the ruler of this land, I will honor your words," the gray haired demon nodded at Lilith. His gray skin was the color of slate and when he sat still, he appeared to be a statue, pure granite stone.

A soft cackle escaped the cherubic pre-teen face of Astaroth. He sat quietly, waiting for the drama to unfold.

Zaglofagmen stood up and clapped. His flowing black robe covered him from head to toe; only red eyes could be seen beneath his hooded cloak. "Thank you for that moving dialog Rehab. We all are touched by your pseudo pledge of allegiance. Now if everyone is finished with their wasteful banter, please continue Lilith."

Rehab's deadly gaze fell upon Zaglofagmen but it went unnoticed.

"Thank you," Lilith said. She sat down in her chair. Her skin became unified with the scarlet cloth. "We all know why Zayashariya is important to The Council. Let us not pretend that she is not needed. If I only needed her power, I would have joined with her long ago and banished you foul fools into oblivion."

"You flatter me," Beelzebub, The Lord of the Flies, laughed. "You have no power here."

Samael impatiently growled in his seat. Black smoke floated from his nostrils. No features could be detected on his pitch-black skin. Even his eyes and teeth were completely black. Like a living shadow, he sat quaking with anger.

"If all of your overweening egos could just subside for a moment, I will explain to you ignoramuses why the need for her to join us is so great!" Lilith spat between her teeth. Her eyes narrowed and her hair flashed from yellow to red then to blue flame. "I dream of the day when I can torture you like my feeble little slaves! Believe me; I would kill you all slowly and painfully if only I had the power."

"Do you ever cease with the compliments, Lilith?" Abaddon laughed. A faint glow surrounded his body. Great power pulsated from his very being. He was transparent in appearance, only a silhouette of pale light. "You have always been such a dreamer. How sweet and idealistic. Ambitious and beautiful, what more could the planet of Night want from a queen?" Abaddon leaned towards Lilith, his face severe. "I would gladly give you the chance to take my life. Futile adventures come so scarcely these days. I welcome the challenge."

Fire filled Lilith's eyes. "You demons will respect me! I show all of you homage when I visit your kingdoms, mere Cockaignes. Yet you all consistently provoke me to anger. I warn you all. You do not want me to fully abominate you. My wrath is like a roborant. The more I partake of it, the more diabolical I become and the closer you will walk near the shadow of death." Lilith hopped to her feet. A jagged dagger was pulled from her boot. So scantly clad was she, her boots covered more flesh than the rest of her clothes. Lilith wore only a skin-tight brown leather loincloth and a matching rag tied around her breast. She jammed the sharp blade into the table, her voluptuous body vibrating from the power of the blow.

"Silence fool! Enough of your cocky banter, Lilith! I grow weary of your mouth!" Asmodeus slammed his giant fist against the black iron table. The room quaked at the sound of his voice. "Garrulous dupe! Do not anger me she-demon!"

"I do not wish to war with you. I would just like to speak without interruption." Lilith sat down. "I only wish to speak!" she yelled. "I only wish to speak! I can't do that with..."

"Speak!" Babylon interrupted. Her white skin was covered in sores and swellings, each blister having an excrescence of a smaller blister on top of it. Her long jet-black hair fell over her nude body, covering her nakedness.

"Silence!" Lilith struck Babylon across the cheek. The blisters on Babylon's face popped and soaked Lilith's hand with pus. "Look what you made me do! You filthy beast! I take no orders from a lesser demon. You are not yet a member of the Council of Demons, just a lowly servant slithering your way up the ranks. Remember to whom you speak!"

Babylon sat backwards and held her aching face. Anger filled her but her life depended on her silence. She was not strong enough to overthrow the queen.

"Do not worry love," Semyaza purred. He placed his hand on Babylon's thigh and gently squeezed. "Lilith is a moody whore. If you wish, I could relieve her of some of her tension." He flicked his tongue provocatively then turned to Lilith and tried to grab hold of her hand. Lilith knocked his perverted paw away and spat in his face. His abnormally long tongue licked the spittle from his face and cooed with pleasure.

Beautiful Belial, angelic face and perfect body, laughed at the ludicrous advance Semyaza had made and nodded for Lilith to continue.

Lilith opened her mouth, paused for potential interruptions, and began to speak. "Zayashariya is different from the rest of us. Her demon blood is polluted. It is not pure and her hate does not run as deep as our hate. She has a quality within her that transcends realms. We demons are restricted to the Nether Worlds. We cannot walk with mortals unless we are summoned by one of them or given permission from a force greater than ourselves, but Zayashariya can. She can walk many realms freely. She knows this. Zayashariya has traveled many places and has remained unharmed and unaffected."

"How can this be?" Babylon questioned. Lilith's dangerous eyes fell upon her. Babylon dropped her eyes and lowered her head. "Forgive me," she whispered.

"I know Zayashariya's origins, cur! I am her mother and I know that her father is not one of us. Zayashariya does not know of him and never will as long as life is within me." Lilith looked into each demon's eye one by one. "If Zayashariya is persuaded to sit with us on this great council, we will receive access to walk the realms freely and the power to pound all mortals into submission, to obey our wills, to become victims to our twisted imaginations, and to satisfy our lust for chaos for all times. We all can create our own version of hell and rule over it on every plane. Can't you see the beauty of it?" Lilith rubbed her hands together. "You must share my vision!" She licked her lips. "Can't you taste it? Can't you feel how close victory is?" asked Lilith. "Maybe one day our power will exceed the master's. Maybe we can enslave that arrogant angel and worship him no more," Lilith guffawed, "and I will be the queen of all the Hells and Nether Worlds and you all will rule with me on high."

"You forever play the fool, Lilith," snapped Asmodeus. "You are doing nothing but filling your head with folly with all of your ineffectual gibberish. You will never be an apotheosis in this life or the next. Furthermore, I will not exchange one hated ruler for another I hate even more."

Lilith cut her eyes at him but remained silent for the moment.

"What can we do to make this vision come to pass?" Astaroth asked, bewitched by Lilith's prophecy of ultimate bedlam.

"You all can help me convince Zayashariya that she needs to join us. Her tainted blood will not let her join us without careful consideration; or shall I say, careful manipulation and maybe mutilation," cackled Lilith, rubbing her hands together. The thought of various tortures aroused her. She flicked her tongue on the roof of her mouth and sighed. "Thus far all of our attempts to force Zayashariya to be a part of us have failed. She has no fear of us. Death has no hold over her. Her hatred toward me has grown and I fear that soon she will try to escape. I have placed her personal maid as a guardian over her and I trust that Sarai will prohibit Zayashariya's departing at all costs. Sarai fears me and will never cross me."

"Servants always betray dreadful masters," Abaddon replied. His words lingered in the air, reminiscent of a past experience.

Mephistopheles nodded his canine head in agreement.

"What can we do to make this vision come to pass?" Astaroth asked again.

"We must seduce her with evil. We must sway her with everything we can muster. We must prey on her weaknesses. We must rip her apart and rebuild her into a diabolical demon of the highest possible magnitude."

Chapter 3

Massive. Plain massive was the octagon room. Each of the eight pale painted walls was adorned with art, weapons, and shelves with potions and powders sitting on them along with innumerable books. There were books everywhere, books on the shelves, the floor, even the on the edge of the bed.

In the center of the room was a round bed with a brass frame and gold satin covers and pillows. A black marble and brass nightstand was on each side of the bed with twin brass lamps wearing golden shades shaped like lilies. The floor was covered with plush green carpet and gold pieces of art was scattered throughout the room. There were no windows in the dim room.

The old wizard slept soundlessly. His gray whiskers fluttered with every exhaled breath. He lay upon the golden bedspread balled up like a cold child, his legs tucked tightly within his arms. He slept in a galaxy print robe and matching cap. His head rolled backwards and his cap fell to his side. A quiet snore rumbled from is nose.

"Wiz," a voice whispered. "Wiz."

The old wizard opened one eye. There was no one in the room. The old wizard accredited the voice to his imagination. He closed his eye and tried to go back to sleep.

"Wiz," the voice whispered again.

The old wizard opened his eyes, rolled onto his back and looked suspiciously around him. There was no one there. *I know I heard something. Maybe I was just dreaming.*

"Wiz. Oh great wizard whose name cannot be mumbled. Whose name bears the curse of all who speak it," a heckling laugh floated through the air, vibrating so hard that it seemed tangible enough for the old wizard to reach out and grab the creepy cackle.

"Maybe I'm still sleeping," the old wizard said, wiping his eyes and yawning. The laugh echoed through the room once more, this time more menacing.

The old wizard could not ignore the laughter any longer. "Who is there?" he questioned. He sat up straight, eyes searching the room frantically. His beard flapped as he turned. "Answer me or I'll turn you into a cockroach!"

"It is I," the invisible being whispered.

"Who are you?" the old wizard asked, leaning over the side of the bed and turning one of the brass lamps on. "Where are you?" the old wizard demanded. "Show yourself!" The old wizard jumped to his feet and began to wave his arms around, threatening to cast a spell. "I am warning you intruder. Don't force me to scatter you to the winds!"

"Here I am," the voice whispered.

"Where?" The old wizard looked around seeing nothing. He lifted his arms higher than before. This time a small pink spark lit up his fingers. "I am warning you!"

"Here I am," said the invisible being. A swirl of light appeared before the old wizard, startling him. He stepped backwards. The light twisted and turned in a serpentine motion.

The old wizard put his arms down. The light slowly took form and an angel, appearing before him wearing the deepest shade of red. He stood directly in front of the old wizard with a wicked smirk on his face. The angel had chalk white skin and small red horns protruding from his forehead. His face was handsome and statuesque with large round eyes and a sharp nose. Red and white tipped black wings extruded from his back. The wings were about six feet tall and six feet wide each. He wore a floor length red robe with bell shaped sleeves.

"Lucifer? Is that you?" The old wizard squinted his eyes. *It couldn't be!*

"In the flesh," he answered. The angel smiled. His eyes flashed blue.

"Old Luci! How are you? I'm surprised that you are even allowed to leave Sheol to visit me," the old wizard said, laughing uneasily. He sat back on the bed, crossed his legs and displayed an insincere smile. "Good old Luci. What do I owe this pleasure? Surely you know I do not deal with the devil." Like a pounding fist, his heart thumped within his chest. The old wizard found it hard to believe that the ruler of the Hells and the Nether World was sitting before him. He grinned again, careful to block his thoughts because Lucifer could easily read minds. The old wizard was truly worried. Showing the devil fear was like putting the noose around your neck for the lynch mob. So, the old wizard channeled his fear into laughter and let his petrified chuckles freely fly from his throat.

"I dare you laugh! Do not force my wrath upon you!" the devil roared. His pale eyes wrinkled at the corners. "I have been loosed for a season, if it is any of your concern."

The old wizard felt a tinge of sensitivity on the subject and stopped laughing. Some of his fear diminished. The old wizard huffed, "What do you want? You disturbed my rest." He picked up his cap and placed it back on his head. "Surely, you know you are not welcome here."

"I came to make a deal," said Lucifer. The evil angel grinned.

"I don't deal with the devil!" The old wizard looked into the angel's eyes and frowned. *Why is he here?* He thought. *Something must be terribly wrong. Anytime Lucifer pays a visit, something is terribly off balance.*

"Ha!" Lucifer laughed. "You deal with me everyday. All that you do is evil. You are a male witch! A warlock! A sorcerer! A conjuror of tricks. A caster of spells. A mojo man." Lucifer laughed. "For goodness sake man, you live on the planet Night!" He threw his hands into the air in disbelief. "I am the source of your magic, fool!" he snapped. Lucifer floated closer to the old wizard and placed his finger in his face. "Remember, if something is not of God it is of me. Contrary to popular belief, there are no shades of grey when it comes to good and evil."

The old wizard gasped. "Point understood." Sweat began to form into beads on his forehead. "What do you want?" He swallowed. A cold chill ran down his spine.

"May I sit?" Lucifer asked abruptly.

"Yes, as if you need my permission," the old wizard answered. He winked his eye and a chair appeared in front of the devil.

"Thank you," Lucifer replied arrogantly. He walked to the front of the chair and his wings folded behind him until they were no longer visible, disappearing beneath his robe. He was remarkably humanlike in appearance and would be easily mistaken for one if it was not for his horns and his pale complexion. At will, his horns could be made invisible and his skin a bit livelier; but, he did this only when walking among mortals. Lucifer sat.

"I understand that Lilith's kingdom is slowly collapsing. Zayashariya has escaped her obligation to me to sit on the Council of Demons."

"Yes," the old wizard answered uncomfortably. "That is all true." He swallowed. "But what does any of this have to do with me?"

"I want you to pretend to help Zayashariya," Lucifer paused, placing a smooth finger to his cheek. "Do what you must to keep her within your reach at all times." He paused again, thinking. "She needs her mother's wickedness to corrupt her and then I will be able to mold her into the fiercest demon in my legions. Keep her from fighting Lilith one on one. Zayashariya would win. She is stronger. She just does not realize it yet. For some odd reason, she has a light hidden deep under her killer exterior. I can not understand how that demon child manifests even the tiniest amount of goodwill." Lucifer shook his head. An uncommon look of mystification crossed his face. "Especially, after Lilith made her drink of my blood." Lucifer paused, immersed in deep thought. Frustration contorted his pleasant face temporarily into something grotesque and frightening. The old wizard winced.

"I can not control her," continued Lucifer, closing and reopening his eyes in disappointment. "Lilith will go after her but I want you to help Zayashariya escape her grasp. Lilith is being much too forceful with the girl. Zayashariya's nature is a delicate one. Lilith is turning Zayashariya away from Night and fueling her hatred. Lilith thinks that torturing her daughter will make the girl stronger but Lilith is a fool. She thinks that ultimately she can overthrow me," laughed Lucifer. "Her logic is full of folly." He shook his head. "She does not realize that Zayashariya is unlike us," he said then paused. "Wizard, arrange for Zayashariya to vanish for a while. Maybe her anger will cool and she will return. She is nursing many wounds now. But if her repletion of hate for Lilith festers more..." Lucifer's mouth spread wide in a horrible grin. "Keep her away. If you cannot, aid Lilith in destroying her. It would be better on your behalf to send Zayashariya to a place where she can easily be destroyed if she does not change her heart and return to Night. Send her to a place where she will have no allies. When the people find out what matter of creature she is, they will annihilate her. I cannot be humiliated by her mutiny. If she succeeds in escaping without punishment, others will try to gain their freedom also and I cannot have such division in my kingdom. Any kingdom divided against itself will fall," said Lucifer, leaning forward. "The daemon will come to you. Accept his offer. Do whatever he asks of you. He will give himself for the girl's freedom. Wizard, if you do my bidding, I will make your magic stronger tenfold," he said, grinning. His teeth were perfectly even and of the purest white. The devil was a breathtakingly beautiful creature. "I promise."

"How can I trust you?" the old wizard snapped. "You are the father of lies!"

Lucifer stood up. "You have no choice! You either do my bidding or I will destroy you!"

"You have no power over me!" The wizard stood firm.

The devil walked over to the wizard and bent down face to face with him. His breath was freezing. Chill bumps covered the wizard's face like hives.

"You are mine and I can do with you as I wish. The time will come when you will join me in the fire. I just choose to let you live. You can be of service to me. God will not help you. You are one of the damned. Remember well wizard, you committed the eternal sin," he said. "You can not be saved," the devil laughed and vanished. His voice echoed long after he left.

The old wizard sat upon his bed trembling and staring at the empty chair before him, his face frost bitten. Warmth came to his cheeks again after frantic rubbing.

"What will I do?" the old wizard muttered.

He winked and the chair that the devil sat in, only moments before, disappeared. The old wizard stood up and began to pace.

"How can I help? How?"

Chapter 4

"Where are you going mistress?" Zayashariya's servant, a frail old woman questioned. Her skin was smooth and brown, her hair short and kinky, her face round and very pretty for her age. She limped over to Zayashariya. "Why are you gathering your things?"

"I am leaving this God forsaken place, Sarai. I cannot remain here any longer," said Zayashariya, grabbing her hip pouch and filling it with various items. She grabbed her black fur cloak and wrapped it around her shoulders.

"But how, that is impossible? Where will you go? The queen will find you and punish you more than you could ever endure. Don't go," Sarai pleaded.

Zayashariya rushed past Sarai and grabbed the doorknob. Sarai grabbed Zayashariya's arm and pulled her close.

"Tell me child, where will you go? There is nowhere you can hide in the Nether Worlds. Queen Lilith will find you and when she does, you will pray for death."

"She will not find me. I am leaving the Nether Worlds."

Sarai gasped. "How can that be?"

"I found a way, Sarai. I can leave this place," said Zayashariya, seizing the older woman's hand. "Help me," she said, squeezing it tight and kissing Sarai's cheek softly. "I need you." Zayashariya smiled. "You are more of a mother to me than my own."

"What can I do? I am nothing more than a damned soul living out my punishment as your servant. Serving you has been a privilege. I could have been thrown under Queen Lilith's floor but you chose me as your own. I thank you for your kind-heartedness. You are nothing like the queen and I will do anything to help you; even if helping you means me losing my life."

"You can cover for me. You can ensure my escape from this castle," Zayashariya answered.

"I fear for you," sobbed Sarai. "The queen already thinks that you may escape. She has come to me for information. She is watching me."

"Don't fret, Sarai. All I ask for is your silence," said Zayashariya. "Nothing more," she added. "Are you able to look the other way?" Zayashariya placed her hands on the old woman's shoulders. "I would never ask for you to do more. I treasure your life."

"I will," said Sarai. A tear gathered in her right eye. "I will help you in anyway I can. You have been the only kindness I have known in this place of horrors."

"Thank you." Zayashariya hugged the woman. She slowly let her arms drop, smiled and walked to the door. She opened it and asked, "Sarai, where is my mother?"

"She is meeting with the Council of Demons. She has been occupied with them for hours. Now is the time to go. Leave now and never return. If anyone asks for you tonight, I will tell them that you are in bed in a terrible fit of pique and you do not want to be disturbed."

A tear fell from Sarai's eye and rolled down her mahogany cheek. The thought of Zayashariya leaving felt like fire shut up in her bones. *What will become of me?* She knew that she would be punished for letting Zayashariya escape but she knew in her heart that she would never be freed from Night. Maybe she would be granted death and perpetual damnation would be no more.

"Go now princess. I will always remember you," Sarai cried. She gave Zayashariya a peck on the forehead. Sarai brushed the violet locks from Zayashariya's face and pinched her chin. "A demon with a heart; who knew?" Sarai smiled. "I will miss you."

"And I you." Zayashariya embraced Sarai one last time and fled the castle.

*   *   *

Outside of the castle, Zayashariya could see no one. A sigh of relief exited her mouth. She quickly ran until she arrived at the nearest busy road. To hide her identity, she pulled her hood over her head and stood on the corner. A rickety rickshaw pulled by filthy sweaty humans stopped before her. A monstrous toothless demon with red hair and eyes and yellow skin grunted and dropped the reigns.

"Where are you headed?" he growled. His hand toyed with the handle of a huge club which was leaning against his tree trunk of a leg.

"To the old wizard's castle," said Zayashariya, avoiding his face. Under no circumstance could she be recognized. It would mean the end of her.

"What business do you have with the old wizard?" the gigantic demon croaked.

"My business is my own, stupid creature," barked Zayashariya, pulling herself up into the rickshaw. "Pick up your reigns and take me to my destination. Do not force me to lay hands on you."

"GO!" the demon yelled to his beasts of burden, slobber flying from his fat lips.

Zayashariya sat quietly, careful to avoid the eyes of the juggernaut driving the rickshaw.

Demons were crafty creatures and they always looked for ways to destroy others. Evil was as vital to demons as food and water. The driver would be overjoyed if he only knew who he was escorting to the old wizard's castle. Turning her in would make his day and destroy her life.

"You friends with that old menace?" the demon asked, looking forward and whipping the backs of the humans pulling the wagon. He chuckled under his breath every time he heard them wince in pain.

Zayashariya did not answer.

"You hear me?" the demon growled. He turned and looked at her but she remained unresponsive and pulled her hood down lower. The demon turned forward and grimaced. He made a complete volte-face. "You hear me, strumpet!"

"I owe you nothing. Take me to the old wizard and cease talking to me. I am in a foul mood and it will only give me pleasure to thwack you with your own club."

"You are a feisty wench," the demon laughed. "Your tongue is untamed. You have no fear."

Zayashariya remained silent. She had a qualm about this demon. He would not stop aggravating her until he provoked her wrath. He longed for confrontation.

"I do not like to be ignored," the demon grumbled.

"Drive. Say nothing more or you will force my hand," Zayashariya warned.

"Force your hand?" the demon cackled. He pulled the rickshaw to the side of the road and brought it to a halt. "I think I may need you to force your hand."

The demon climbed out of the wagon and pulled Zayashariya out by the leg. She hit the ground, falling heavily on her buttocks. Her hood flipped backwards and revealed her scowling face.

"Get up!" he spat, recognizing her immediately. "Princess," he cackled. "Imagine what I can do with you. Wait until your shrew of a mother hears of this."

The demon kicked her thigh so hard that a knot appeared and darkened. Ignoring the pain, Zayashariya jumped to her feet and punched the demon in the stomach. He laughed. She swung again but he caught her fist and tried to crush it under his strength. A loud cry fell from her lips.

"You like that?" He squeezed.

Pain jolted through Zayashariya's arm. Her eyes flashed. Anger flooded her face like crimson waters escaping a damned dam. She pulled his hand to her mouth and bit down. The demon fell to his knees and bellowed in pain. With his free hand, the demon grabbed the wagon. His fingers reached desperately for his club but Zayashariya tightened her grip and pulled him backwards. A howl thundered from his belly. Blood dripped down her face, covering his yellow hand in crimson. The beast howled until he fell silent, then still, then dead. Zayashariya let go of his hand and the demon plopped to the concrete. She wiped her mouth, savoring the bitter twang of his blood, and jumped into the wagon.

"Go!" she yelled. "To the old wizard. Hurry!"

Zayashariya arrived at the old wizard's castle within half an hour. She was met by the wizard and escorted inside. The old wizard led her down a winding staircase to a tall stained glass door.

"Welcome to my toy room," said the old wizard, grinning. He took off his pointy hat and tipped it towards her. He opened the door and she followed behind.

Motorized vehicles, spaceships, bicycles, and rocket boards lined the room in every shape, size and color imaginable. The room looked like a factory complete with tools, assembly lines, and workers hard at work.

Zayashariya was in awe.

"Which one is mine?" she asked, running her fingers across the cold metal as she walked through the room. Each machine was made uniquely and with fine craftsmanship. A strong feeling of freedom flowed through her. To prevent herself from doing flips throughout the room, she had to contain the feeling and remain calm. She could not appear desperate to the old wizard. Zayashariya did not want him to feel that he had more power over her than what he possessed. She would do anything to obtain freedom but he did not need to know that.

"That one." The old wizard pointed at a bubble shaped ship. It was very small, about the size of a twin bed. "Come," he gestured, opening the door to the ship.

Zayashariya sat in the ship and placed her hand on the controls. They were chilly to the touch. The old wizard explained the functions of the ship. She understood easily and adjusted herself comfortably. Her stomach felt weak when she thought of blasting off. Her entire life flashed before her eyes in vivid scenes. The face of her mother spun in her head. Now was the time to leave her past behind. There was no room for second thoughts. *I can do this. I can do this.* She sat back and exhaled.

"Good luck," said the old wizard, bidding her goodbye.

"Thank you," said Zayashariya, grabbing the door. "You will deal fairly with Kalpvaleim won't you?"

"He is no longer your concern," the old wizard hissed. "You got what you wanted. Now go!" The old wizard slammed the door down. Zayashariya started the space shuttled and vanished.

Chapter 5

It was an enormous castle. Black in color. Bold in design. It sat alone on a hill on the edge of Night secluded from the rest of civilization. It was carved out of the very planet, made of pure stone and clay. It was a remarkable structure. The castle was a structure that was suitable for a descendant of an earthling, very Earthen in design with its many windows and large doors.

The daemon dropped his backpack to the ground and stared at the gigantic structure. He could hear the polluted water splashing in the moat that surrounded the castle like a crescent. Kalpvaleim stood on the edge of the moat under a barren tree and looked around for some sort of device that would lower the drawbridge. He saw nothing. The land around him was leveled ground covered with drying grass and dying trees. The daemon looked at his watch. He knew that he was at the right place and it was the right time. Days ago, Kalpvaleim had sent a message to the old wizard regarding his arrival. He and the old wizard struck a bargain; the old wizard would help Zayashariya and he would serve the old wizard. The old wizard had done his part, now it was time for Kalpvaleim to accede. An irrefragable feeling of resentment toward Zayashariya and loathing toward the old wizard conflated into a trenchant headache.

There was no sign of the old wizard or the person he said that he would send. Kalpvaleim sat down on a nearby rock. His navy blue skin was hot from his long travel. He took off his shirt and freed his well-formed arms and chest from the confinement of the thick fabric. His body was stunning; tall, slender, and very muscular from his broad shoulders right down to his hoofed feet. He could pass for an average humanoid if not for his goat-like feet.

Kalpvaleim was growing impatient. He dropped his head into his hands and mumbled a few unsavory words under his breath. Not only was there no sign of the old wizard, there was no any sign of life anywhere. He was not looking forward to a season of doing the old wizards bidding. He was no one's slave. It was no telling what the old wizard would have him doing. He could be subjected to all kinds of belittling assignments but he realized that a deal was a deal and he was a man of his word, most of the time anyway. Kalpvaleim smiled. Little did the wizard know about deals. Kalpvaleim had his hopes riding on Zayashariya. He leaned back on the rock and waited. Silence began to hurt his ears. Whistling a melancholy tune, to pass the time and break the monotony of the quiet, he created paltry entertainment for himself. Soon his throat dried and he prayed for a cool drink of water.

Minutes turned into hours and he could hear his stomach growling like a mad lion, rumbling like two dwarves wrestling in his belly. He rubbed his belly and sighed. He still saw or heard no one. But he knew that something had to live nearby and that something would make a sufficient meal. Out of his backpack, he pulled a slingshot; then, collected a few pebbles off of the ground around him. Kalpvaleim rolled up his pant legs exposing his dynamic calves, his small ankles, and his hoofed feet. He turned his head sideways, listening to his surroundings, his pink hair falling into a cascade of curls into his pretty boy face. Hastily, he tossed his hair backwards and quickly braided it into a ponytail and continued to listen. Leaves rustled. *Life.* There was a twig breaking nearby. Kalpvaleim stooped, preparing his sling for action. Leaves were rustling. He froze. His pointy ears stiffened. Something was behind him. Kalpvaleim fell upon his back and rolled onto his belly. He aimed the sling at the small gray creature standing before him.

"Please don't shoot," said the gray fur ball, whispering in a voice as light as the wind. "The master sent me," the fur ball, with eyes almost twice its size, said. Its mouth, ears, arms, and legs were invisible.

Kalpvaleim pulled himself to his knees and put his sling into his back pocket. "Who are you?" he asked, focusing his eyes, trying to get a closer look. *What a peculiar creature,* he thought to himself as he tilted his head like a curious kitten.

"I am Shayla," whispered the fur ball. "The master told me that you were handsome." She giggled.

"Thanks," Kalpvaleim responded to the compliment, a blush of embarrassment flooding his cheeks. He hoped that the fur ball wasn't interested. "I thought the old wizard was sending a woman." He smiled a crooked smile. "No offense."

"I am a woman" snapped the fur ball, obviously insulted. "Look."

The fur ball stretched itself like a furry ball of rubber. It pulled and popped and stretched and molded until it was a short furry woman about three feet high. She was very slender with short gray dreadlocks. Her face, the only part of her body that was fur free, was very pretty.

Kalpvaleim was impressed. He stood up and walked over to the rock to pick up his backpack. Nothing in the Nether Worlds surprised him anymore. All sorts of strange creatures existed in the bowels of these dark worlds. He was not the average looking creature himself so who was he to judge.

"When do I see the old wizard?" he asked, staring into her big gorgeous eyes. Her eyelashes were abnormally long.

"Now," said Shayla, walking up to him and grabbing his hand. She barely stood tall enough to reach his hip. Shayla walked him to the edge of the moat and looked into his eyes. "Do not look away. Not even for a moment," she instructed. They locked eyes and the two of them began to levitate. Kalpvaleim felt like a feather as he floated in midair. He could see by his peripheral vision that they were very high in the air. There were flying creatures zooming past them. He could see clouds floating beside him. He adverted his eyes just a bit.

"No!" Shayla yelled. "Look at me!" She gripped his hand with all her might. "Do not look away. Do you understand? Do not look away!"

"Okay," said Kalpvaleim, looking at her. She was so close. He could feel the tickle of her fur on his chest. He wanted desperately to scratch, to look around, to move. Kalpvaleim could not resist. He looked down and suddenly began to fall.

"Help me!" he screamed as he reached for Shayla's floating form. "Help me please!" He was falling so fast that his breath was being ripped from his lungs.

"Look into my eyes!" Shayla yelled at him as she descended into arms length, her gray eyes changing into a kaleidoscope of designs. "Look into my eyes, Kalpvaleim!"

He looked up at her. He could not focus. He knew that he would die.

"Look into my eyes," she shouted.

Kalpvaleim stretched his eyes wide open and tried whole heartily to ignore the air raging in his ears and drying out his eyes. He did not want to die like this.

"Look into my eyes."

Kalpvaleim focused. He stopped with a jerk and began to levitate toward her. He grabbed Shayla's out stretched hand and they soon landed on the opposite side of the moat.

"Our master will see us now," Shayla spoke in a quiet voice. She knocked on the castle door and waited.

"I have no master," Kalpvaleim huffed.

"You do now," said the old wizard, suddenly appearing in front of Kalpvaleim as if he was already there. His long white beard touched his toes. He wore a floor length gown and a pointy hat decorated with moons and stars that were constantly changing colors and positions. He looked like a traditional storybook character. The old wizard pointed at the door and it opened. The three of them walked inside and the door closed fast behind them.

"You are at my mercy. Have no misunderstanding about who the master is. Be obedient and nothing too horrible will happen to you." A wicked smile bent the old wizard's lips.

Kalpvaleim was maddened. "You are not my master! I am only at your service for a small season," Kalpvaleim said forcefully, growing angrier with every breath he took. "I will never have a master!"

"Tsk tsk tsk." The old wizard shook his finger. "I own you." He smiled. "I own you for a season. You are my property for now. A deal is a deal, urchin." The old wizard grinned. "First and foremost, I want you out of those clothes and into these." The old wizard wiggled his finger and a puff of smoke covered Kalpvaleim. When the smoke vanished, Kalpvaleim was wearing a royal blue body suit and a bright red cape. A golden belt was around his waste and his pink hair was cut on the sides creating a flowing mohawk.

Shayla wiggled her nose and a floor length mirror appeared in her hands. She stood in front of Kalpvaleim.

Upon seeing his reflection, Kalpvaleim felt as if his entire body would spontaneously combust. His stomach wambled. His hands yearned to embrangle itself within the old wizards beard and wrap it around his neck until he breathed his last breath.

"That is more like it my boy," said the old wizard sniggering, his red nose wiggling uncontrollably. He sneezed. "Excuse me." He smiled. "Off to the laboratory." He walked down the dark stone hallway, lit poorly by torches.

"Zayashariya. Please remember me," Kalpvaleim whispered to himself as he followed the wizard wearing his ridiculous slave uniform.

Chapter 6

The cold wind wrapped around the legs of Zayashariya. Icy air nipped at her calves as if it was a hungry entity that possessed razor sharp teeth. The ebony-skinned woman pulled her cloak tightly around her robust yet perfectly formed body to fight away the battering wind. She had been walking for many days. Her destination was unknown to her, yet she had faith that she would encounter life somewhere. The deserted road she walked on seemed endless. It seemed to fade into the very sky; like staring at the horizon, being lost in a helpless state of purgatory. Her keen eyes could not detect any signs of intelligent life in any direction. She walked on. The dust of the road painted her boots with a tan film, sprinkling her heels with dark speckles of dirt. Suddenly the road was no longer a barren wasteland. Vegetation began to sprout many miles back, now it grew into an intense forest. Twisted and tangled vines and branches surrounded her from every side. She was engulfed in emerald brush and quickly became swallowed into their depths. The distant sound of winged insects and small animals hummed in her ears although they were too far off for her eyes to detect them.

Zayashariya brushed the bracken from her path and continued her slow and restless journey. Her eyes turned towards the heavens and she witnessed the sky change from periwinkle to pink to peach to plum purple. The breathtaking spectacle brought to her soul an overwhelming feeling of freedom. The colors were awesome. The sky was a miracle before her eyes. Never had she seen such beauty. Where she came from, sunsets and sunrises were only figments of the imagination. They were obsolete on her shadowy planet. Therefore, she took a minute to absorb the scene and moved on.

Zayashariya could not see a town or an advanced life form in sight, only plants. She walked alone in silence, trying with all her power to be patient, her breath rising and falling like the ocean waves grabbing at the sea shore but being pulled back by the possessive moon. Zayashariya was weary and she feared that she would not make it to shelter. Panic slowly crept into the crevasses of her subconscious. Hope of finding civilization seemed moot. The uneasy feeling was quickly dismissed. Negative thoughts had no place in her mind now. She would not let them breed and fester within her like a powerful parasite waiting to eat her alive. Her knees ached and her legs were becoming weaker by the second. Thoughts of home flashed through her mind. She was beginning to think that she had not made a wise decision to run away. Anything was better than dying in a wasteland, or was it? Zayashariya pulled her cloak tightly around her to defend herself from the bitter cold. It seemed as if the wind had a personal vendetta against her as it whisked past her with icy force.

Time had no place on her sojourn. She walked on faith, hoping to discover a new world and praying to forget her old world. She was on the brink of starvation. Hunger pains rumbled within her firm belly like a belch of thunder erupting from the sky. She held her cloak close and walked on. She moved through the dusty path at a faster pace than before. Zayashariya had been walking for days, maybe weeks. She had lost track of time long ago.

Her spaceship was severely damaged. It lay in the midst of the desert in a heap of twisted metal. Therefore, the idea of further travel was eliminated. She walked on. The dust formed tiny tornadoes at her heels and twirled away into the void. Zayashariya cut through the brush with her bare hands drawing spider web scratches across her palms. Tree limbs flew in every direction. They yielded to her strength. The path before her became clearer. To the north, she could see the setting of the twin suns. She squinted her slanted eyes and tried to focus on the mystery before her. The pink orbs of light rested behind the most beautiful city on which she ever laid her eyes. Zayashariya was awestruck at the divine sight. Her heart began to beat a little faster, her breath to quicken. *Sanctuary at last!* She hurried her pace, eyes fixed on her destination. *Salvation!*

Before her stood eleven enormous buildings whose tops connected to one another creating a dome shaped honeycomb. The structures were all white in color with a different color light force projecting from their centers. The building in the center projected a pale yellow beam as the beams from the other buildings projected their beams towards the center point causing a bright glow to overcast the entire city.

Zayashariya continued on her path, never moving her eyes from the splendid sight ahead of her; hypnotized by its potential, its walls of refuge and its promise of food. Minutes turned into hours and the blackness of night swept through the land. The vagabond woman finally arrived at the gate of the city weary from the long walk.

The mammoth word "WILZASP" was carved into the iron bars of the gate in front of her. The word was written in an ancient script from what she recalled from her memory as some sort of lost language, like something she saw in old human history books or at a museum in her homeland. Needless to say, she was not quite familiar with such a writing style but strangely, she could read it with ease. She ran her slender fingers across the block letter writing, felt the coldness of the iron and shivered. Zayashariya removed her hand and looked around. At first, she did not see anything close by but under further evaluation, her eyes sat curiously upon living beings.

Zayashariya observed four male creatures staring down at her from a wooden post erected behind the gate. Their facial expressions did not appear very inviting. Many of their faces were twisted into frowns and others ambiguously bland. At the gate, four more soldiers stood. Two soldiers were on each side of the gate's entrance. The humanoids were all about six feet tall and had bright orange skin, the color of sun-dried apricots. She looked at them with a childlike curiosity. Zayashariya had never seen such people. Cartoon-like characters swam through her thoughts. She smiled and laughed under her breath. The humanoids reminded her of the Norps, fairytale people with orange skin, she read about as a child. The guards were strange looking yet considerably handsome. They all wore the skins of animals, snow zebras, she presumed. The skins were green and gray striped. Snow zebras were one of few animals that existed on every realm.

Upon the men's heads were fuzzy white headbands which held their peach colored afros in place. She smiled at the guards but received no reply. They stared at her like a nuisance that needed to be neutralized. Zayashariya placed her hands upon the bitterly cold bars once more, this time she attempted to push the gate open. A gust of steamy breath escaped her mouth. The gate did not budge an inch. A guard walked toward her. Zayashariya looked at the guard, waited for him to speak words that never came, and then she tightened her grip on the bars. Her dark knuckles turned a reddish brown. The cold bars shot pain through her palms. She let go, rubbed her hands together vigorously and pushed again. The gate did not budge. Frustration filled her, frustration with the guards who looked at her with an air of curiosity but refused to render aid and frustration with the gate that refused to yield to her strength. Zayashariya began to apply more force when the guard placed his hand upon hers, stopping her intrusion.

"Why are you here strange one?" he asked while placing his hand on the hilt of his dagger. He looked at her with the same intrigue that she looked at him with. He had never seen such a dark and bewitching creature. She was stunning. Her skin was the color of a starless midnight, smooth and unmarked. Her cheekbones were high and her jawbone was square with a perfect pointy chin. Her extra long violet eyelashes curled into her thick arched violet eyebrows, almost as if the two connected. Her nose was small and round, her lips full and desirable. She looked alluring yet dangerous with her wild violet hair and intense violet eyes. A feeling of quiet lust and confused repulsion welled up inside of him. Although her cape covered her body from head to toe, the lines of her body hypnotized him. He detected voluptuous curves and imagined how angelic her figure must be. The guard averted his eyes from her and rubbed the back of his neck to relieve the tension he felt building inside of him. Quickly he calmed himself and looked upon Zayashariya with un-hungry eyes. He felt no immediate threat from her because she appeared to be weary beyond reason so he removed his hand from his dagger.

"I am seeking a place to reside. I am lost in this strange land," Zayashariya replied, looking into his sand colored eyes. She pulled her cloak closer to her body and trembled as the cold air ran its fingers through her hair. Her lips were chapped and dry. Her tongue ran over them leaving a wet shine that quickly dried up.

"State your name and from where you came," another soldier said in a deep voice. He was dressed a little different from the others and he was a lot more muscular. A leader, she assumed. He walked over to the soldier at the gate and stood beside him. His eyes stared at her peculiarly. He had not seen anyone quite like her. Her beauty was both stunning and horrifying, unparalleled. A slight frown crossed his otherwise emotionless face. He stepped closer. His stance was almost threatening. "Your name?"

"My name is Zayashariya. I came from a far away land called Gehenna. My ship crashed in the middle of the wastelands and it seems that I have been walking for months," she stated. She stared into the questionnaire's eyes. Nothing could be read within the vague depths of their faces.

"You may not have heard of my land. It is located on the planet of Night. I have traveled very far." Zayashariya trembled harder to persuade them to give her shelter from the cold. "I would really appreciate your hospitality," she said. The warm air inside the gates of Wilzasp brushed her face. It was amazing how the atmosphere inside the gate was a total antithesis to the air outside the gate. Zayashariya could not fathom how the gate separated hot from cold.

"It is very cold out here, not to mention very dangerous for a female to be wondering around alone. I am sure that your town is one of great kindness. I implore you kind sir, grant me refuge from the bitter cold." Zayashariya was growing impatient. Sincerity was absent from her voice. She had traveled too far to be turned away by anyone. She would fight first and she was sure that she would win.

The soldiers looked at each other and fell into an uproar of laughter. They could not believe her preposterous reply. Zayashariya's face did not bear any emotion. She stared at them quietly. Their laughter continued, provoking her rapidly growing irritability.

"Sir, my ill circumstance is hardly a laughing manner. I am in a dire situation here," said Zayashariya, searching their eyes for answers.

"The Land of the Dead!" the soldier next to her laughed. "I suppose that you are an apparition, right?!" He lifted his hands over his head imitating a haunting spirit. "Oooooh!" he sang. The soldier held his stomach from laughing so hard. Tears began to form in the corners of his eyes. His stomach began to cramp. It had been such a long time since a stranger had come to Wilzasp and this stranger was the strangest of all. The soldier observed his men roaring with laughter.

"What must she think of us? Are we soldiers or are we clowns?" he said under his breath. "Lady, if you want shelter, you better refrain from your foolish imaginings and become serious," he said. "Stop entertaining us with your fairytale." The guard grew suddenly serious. The smile fled from his face. He realized that he was behaving inappropriately in front of his men. Giving them all the evil eye, his men quickly regained their composure and stood at attention. "Tell me, from where did you come! Make no fool of us!" he snapped. Anger shined in his eyes. A long wrinkle danced across his orange forehead. He placed his hand on his dagger and fondled the blade with his tangerine fingers. His eyes showed a definite threat.

"I am from Gehenna like I told you before," said Zayashariya, standing firm. "It is much too cold to try to entertain you sir. I am from where I am from." She grew impatient with the gatekeepers. Her face was still emotionless as she stood before them with folded arms. "If I am not welcome here, inform me now and I will continue my journey elsewhere, otherwise let me through." Her hair blew into her clearly vexed face. She brushed the violet locks away quickly.

The soldier looked into her purple, slightly slanted eyes. He realized that she was really serious. It saddened him to think that insanity had claimed such a beautiful woman. The Land of the Dead was nothing more than a mere myth. No one had ever been to Gehenna. It was the largest city on the imaginary planet of Night. It was a place in ancient legend where dragons, demons, witches, wizards, and vampires lived among other horrible monsters of lore. It was a world ruled by Lilith, the Dark Goddess and queen of all of its inhabitants. No one believed in her anymore. No one really believed in gods anymore. After the scientific advancements of all human and humanoid kind, there was no need for gods.

Gehenna was a fantasy world where mothers told their children they would go if they were disobedient. It was a place that people made jokes about and scholars called ridiculous. It just wasn't real. It was as real as ancient tales of the boogeyman or heaven and hell. It wasn't real in this galaxy or any other galaxy. Her story was ludicrous but if she believed it, who was he to persuade her way of thinking. She may have been a loon but even loons needed shelter from the bitter cold of the wasteland. The soldier shook his head in pity and turned to his men. He placed his dagger back into his belt and raised his bright orange hand. He turned his back to Zayashariya and addressed his men.

"Open the gate Zed. Inform the king of a visitor Cledom. Escort this woman to the Inn Gredly," he instructed, pointing to each of the men. His voice was stern and baritone. It had the sound that commanded great respect and authority.

"Yes Quedoff," the men all said in unison.

"Thank you," said Zayashariya, bowing to the soldier, opening her cape in a curtsy, and quickly wrapping it back around her.

He nodded. A look of embarrassment crossed his face.

All of the soldiers did as they were instructed to do and Gredly took the hand of Zayashariya. She accepted his strong hand and they began to walk through the gate hand in hand. The heavy gate closed hard behind them with a thud. Their eyes surveyed the path ahead and they began their short journey to the Inn.

Zayashariya was in awe. The town was a pulchritudinous artistic masterpiece. Strange icicle shaped multi-colored crystals were hanging from everywhere. In some places, they seemed to dangle from the very sky. *This is what is giving the town its glow*, she thought. The two walked down the tar road. She could feel the soft warmth escaping from the glowing crystals.

Every tavern was filled with the vociferous voices of the inebriated. Babies cooed as they twirled their plump fingers through their mother's dangling locks and blew spit bubbles out of their heart shaped lips. Young men blew kisses at their lovers as blossoming girls blushed the color of strawberry sunsets. Taverns were alive with laughter as huge goblets of ale were raised in the air in lighthearted toasts. Old women sat on nearby benches, buzzing like frenzied bees, as they exchanged fruitless gossip. Rowdy men wrestled one another in the street to settle childish disputes. Thieves crept through the crowd like wisps of wind unloading unsuspecting people's pockets of their valuables. Liars stumbled over their words as they attempted to explain their whereabouts the night before.

Suddenly, the happenings of everyday Wilzasp came to a halt and everyone's attention was given to the odd couple walking down the busy street. Humanoids stood on the sidewalks, peered out of windows, and peeked from behind their merchandise stands to watch the bizarre couple walk through the luminous city. Faint whispers danced in the air, too secretive to understand. Muffled giggles and gasps of surprise fell from the lips of silly children and pretentious old women.

Zayashariya observed how all of the bright colored humanoids all looked basically the same. All of the men she saw wore the same peach afros, but in various lengths. All of the women she saw wore their hair cut in the same mid-length style. All of the adults of Wilzasp were about six feet tall. Their faces were structured about the same, high cheekbones, short noses, and voluptuous lips. The only difference between them were their body shapes; some were sensuous, some scrawny, some plump, and some puny. They all had different eye colors.

"Where am I?" Zayashariya asked, while examining the town with her eyes. It reminded her of primitive Earth with its plain architecture and simple market places. The town of Wilzasp looked very small and the main road seemed to circle the entire village, at least as far as she could see. Nothing but the mysterious crystals hanging from every single part of the town seemed extraordinary about Wilzasp. But the crystals were enough to make the town a unique beauty in its own right. It was amazing how the honeycomb dome that covered the city was virtually invisible from inside the city. When she looked up, all she saw was the clear sky and the bright suns. This place was magnificent, a true wonder, a magical place located in the middle of nowhere.

"Didn't you read the sign?" Gredly sardonically responded, rolling his eyes. He had an epicene quality to his personality which was very unattractive to Zayashariya.

"Yes, I did read the sign. I meant, where is this strange land located?" Zayashariya asked, as she observed a child across the street whispering and pointing at her. "No manners," she mumbled under her breath. "What planet is this? I have never been here before?"

"Well, how did you get here?" Gredly asked rhetorically in a nonchalant manner. Gradly really didn't care for her to answer. It was evident by his facial expression. He sighed and let go of her hand to rub the back of his neck. He grabbed her ebony hand once more and walked on. He took a deep breath.

"It is hard to explain," Gredly said, pausing for a moment. "You are familiar with the destruction of the earth, right?" he asked in a condescending tone.

Zayashariya did not answer.

"Well?" he asked again looking at her like she was mildly slow witted. She nodded for him to continue.

"Well, if you were to map out the old solar system, we are close to where the Earth's moon used to be. Earth is no more. This planet, Neoearthmoon, and our sister planet Neotsion were formed from the debris of the explosion of the Earth and the moon. This phenomenon happened thousands of years ago. One could say that a miracle occurred, if you believe in miracles. Not many around here do. We believe that there is a logical explanation for what happened. We just have not found it yet," Gredly said pretentiously.

"Explain further please," Zayashariya urged, truly interested in his tale. "I am not familiar with the history."

"When the Earth exploded, the moon was destroyed along with it. The other planets in the solar system remained intact and a new sun appeared. It is a lot less powerful than the original sun that it orbits around and a lot less warming but it makes a more beautiful sunset. We got a few moons out of the deal too." Gredly smiled. "Neoearthmoon and Neotsion were formed in a supernatural amount of time. The debris of earth and the moon miraculously came together like a big clump of hot rock and cooled instantly. All of the elements needed on a planet in order for life to survive were present on the new planets automatically. Overnight it seemed that plants and animals evolved out of nothing. Everything happened as if a superhuman force spoke it into being. Six days it took for Neoearthmoon to come into being. Six days! Can you believe it? To this very day, scientists cannot explain how this miracle occurred. All they knew was that they had a new planet to live on so they inhibited it. Scientists say that Neotsion did it all within a day. Neotsion is a very mysterious place. Only humans live there. Not natural homosapiens but more like supernatural humans, transformed into pure spirit beings." He paused. "It's complicated. People say that they are immortal. The atmosphere of Neotsion will not allow others to enter it but they can exit the planet if they wish to never return and to become mortal once more." He took a deep breath. "A lot of myth and mystery surround that place but I don't believe the hype," he said, rolling his eyes up and sighing. Gredly looked into Zayashariya's attentive eyes and said, "Before the explosion, the technology of mankind became so advanced that they began to travel through space. They found new lands to conquer and new planets to inhibit. So the destruction of the planet Earth did little to prevent the life of humankind from striving. Most of them were gone before the explosion anyway. They had found new places to ruin, new people to harass. Norps, our people, are descendants of Earthlings and Norpsongants."

"What are Norpsongants?" Zayashariya asked. Her eyebrows rose. The warm air was heavenly against her body. She loosened her cape but kept it closed.

"Norpsongants are humanoids from the Planet Norpucry. It is located outside of the planet Pluto. It was the planet that the Earthlings called Planet X when they suspected there was another planet in their solar system beyond Pluto. Obviously, they were correct. For a long time Earth's scientists dismissed Pluto and Planet X as a moon and ignored them. Little did they know about the rich planet of my ancestors. Norpucry was full of natural resources. It had three times the amount of gold, oil, gemstones, and coal found on Earth. Not to mention new minerals, metals, and other resources never before known to man." Gredly smiled, very proud of himself for his extensive knowledge. "How did you get here?"

"I was bored with my homeland. I wanted to experience something new and a friend arranged for me to be warped to another galaxy and I ended up here simply by chance," Zayashariya answered, avoiding his eyes.

"Warped?" Gredly asked.

"Yes. That means that I was placed in a machine that transports things to other places throughout space," Zayashariya answered.

"Oh," he said, nodding his head. "I've heard of those machines. I never really thought they worked well. From what I heard, people could not control where they landed very well and had a difficult time returning home. And from what I see, my speculations about those warping machines were correct indeed. They are virtually worthless and dangerous." Gredly laughed. "Where is your ship?"

"It is in the center of the wasteland, broken. It is nothing more than a pile of rubble. I ended up here, in the middle of nowhere, and I have been walking for weeks maybe even months. I am not sure. I am just glad that I found civilization," Zayashariya said, realizing that he was not as annoying as she had perceived him to be. She enjoyed their conversation. So far, he seemed to be a nice man, a little too girly in his ways but nice.

"What is your name?" Gredly asked her.

"Zayashariya. Yours?"

"Gredly," he answered as he looked around him. He began to feel awkward. The town's people gawked at them. Zayashariya opened her mouth to speak but he motioned for her to remain quiet by placing his finger in front of his lips. He decided that they had talked enough. Her thoughts of him were reconfirmed. He was annoying.

The two walked the rest of the way in silence. She discounted his unpalatable demeanor and continued her sight seeing. Zayashariya was hypnotized by the newness of the city. She was not used to seeing such wondrous things like laughing children and crisp blue skies. Her life at home did not display such pulchritude. Thoughts of home clouded her mind and her countenance fell.

* * *

Home.

The smell of death floated through the air like fog. Deep moans of abominable pain escaped the lips of the imprisoned. Zayashariya was apprehended by two foul smelling ghouls. With her hands tied behind her back, she was forced to walk forward. Any normal person would vomit at the sight of these creatures. Both were short, slime covered beasts with pale white skin. Dark green fangs protruded from their lipless mouths and a constant putrid odor was secreted from their pores. The ghouls were both around three feet tall with immense physical strength. They were lean creatures with muscles twisting all over their bodies like millions of snakes wrapped around trees. They pushed her forward into the chamber.

The rectangular room was dark with faint glowing red lights pulsating in the far corners. The energy source was unknown. Zayashariya had been there many times before but never under these conditions; yet, she could never get used to this literal hellhole. The ghouls continued to force her forward as fingers reached through the floor trying fruitlessly to grab her boots or any part of her that they could grip. She tried hard to avoid crushing the fingers under her heels but the number of fingers reaching through the floor was innumerable. They looked like they grew through the floor like flesh colored grass. There were so many people down beneath her, crying through the iron bar floor that they seemed to mesh together and form one gigantic creature.

Queen Lilith had this floor prison specially constructed so that she could occasionally pour hot tar down upon the inmates or allow the prisoners to see their ultimate fate by watching her annihilate other victims.

Zayashariya walked forward, breathing in the stench of the ghouls and the unclean humanoids beneath her. Her head swam with dizziness. The trio came to the center wall of the chamber. In front of them was a high back throne. The back of the chair was facing them. Nothing could be seen past it. The throne had to be at least ten feet tall and a weird mix of pale peach, brown and green, the color of rotted filth, flesh, and blood. One of the ghouls let go of her and walked over to a black iron pole coming out of the far wall of the room with a red button protruding from the end of it. He pushed the button and walked back over to help subdue Zayashariya. The ghouls forced her to her knees and both of the hideous creatures stood a few steps behind her. The fingers beneath the floor were rubbing Zayashariya's bare legs and their voices were crying louder for help. The princess of Night yearned to ignore the galling sensation, but it was not possible. Fingers fondled every inch of her exposed flesh. The ghouls stomped on the fingers nearest to them, mashing the flesh like soft potatoes. Zayashariya looked at the throne as it spun around slowly. A bright red glow beamed from the throne, casting the room in crimson light. The ghouls and Zayashariya both squeezed their eyes shut until the glow dimmed and their eyes were able to adjust.

Upon the humongous throne sat Lilith, Queen of Night, an evil demon creature that ruled the planet of Night with unimaginable force. She was the mother of all abominations. Upon the throne she sat, dressed in a red leather leotard scarcely covering her near naked flesh. Her skin was deep scarlet and as fresh as infant flesh. She had the perfected smoothness of a marble statue. Her skin was flawless, free from all blemishes and human imperfections. She sat upon her throne wearing an evil smile like a mask which seemed to cover her entire face. Her hair was a single red-yellow flame, sometimes transforming to blue, that leapt as if the wind was threatening to extinguish it and it was going to go out within seconds. The flame was large compared to her head, crowning her head like a fallen angel's former holy glow. It gave off a neutral temperature, only threatening to sight.

Lilith's body was unnaturally long. She was very tall and robust. Pure muscle, you could see it in her masculine formed legs and overdeveloped abdominal muscles. She sat upon her throne smiling like a naughty child. She opened her mouth and a gigantic serpent's tongue came from her behind her teeth, reflecting the light of her hair, and licked Zayashariya's face. Zayashariya wiped the stinging drool with her shoulder, regrettably spreading the unpleasant sensation, and stared at the queen. Hatred was embedded deep within Zayashariya's unbreakable stare.

"Daughter," Queen Lilith laughed, her heckling voice echoing through the otherwise empty chamber. "Why hast thou forsaken me?" She laughed again.

Zayashariya was silent. She stared at the pure madness that was her mother in utter disgust.

"You know you hurt my feelings when you wipe away my kisses." Lilith's flaming eyes gleamed.

"Mother, what do you want of me?" Zayashariya asked between her teeth, trying hard to ignore the rotting fingers molesting her legs.

"You defied me!" the queen hissed. "I dare you to disavow my kingdom! Do you really think that your birthright is an option? You have no choice! You must not reject your place in the order of chaos. I will not have you humiliate me once more before the Council of Demons!" Lilith jumped to her feet. Her flaming hair glowed a fierce indigo. Pea sized fireballs shot from her eyes and burned a few of the badgering fingers that were irking her daughter. A sharp wail permeated the air. "Silence!" Lilith screamed. Silence fell. She turned back to the dark princess. "Don't defy me Zayashariya. I created you. You are my flesh. Do what is required of you!"

"Mother I want no part of this," Zayashariya calmly stated. Her face was stern. "I care nothing for your evil. I want out," Zayashariya told her mother.

"You want out?" Lilith smirked. "Out you say? Out is never an option. What do you think this is my dear daughter? You and I are not creatures of the light. Our way is a simple way. We rule and we wreak havoc." A soft menacing chuckle erupted from her throat. "You will die first!" she screamed. "Is that what you wish? I am not above mutilating my own flesh. In many ways the experience may be invigorating."

"So be it!" Zayashariya yelled back fearlessly. "Death would mean peace. A peace that I will never find here! I am willing to accept my fate. Are you willing to accept yours?"

Queen Lilith sat back upon the stagnant throne. She crossed her thick scarlet legs and placed her hands upon her knee. She looked like a mock impression of a "lady." Her long black fingernails were shining in the effulgence of her hair.

"You will change your mind. I am sure of it," Lilith said, running her fingers up her thighs, her nails tickling her smooth flesh. Lilith cooed with perverse pleasure. "I will give you time to think." She licked Zayashariya's cheek with her slimy tongue. This time the sting from Lilith's saliva was so intense that it forced a tear from the captive woman's eye and left a red swollen trail down Zayashariya's cheek. "You will change your mind," said Lilith, leering. "I am sure of it."

"Never!" Zayashariya belched in pain.

Queen Lilith gave a deep gruntal cackle. "I like your determination daughter. Your hate is deep. It will make you a supreme ruler. You are just as I am. We are one."

Lilith's words stabbed into Zayashariya's flesh harder and sharper than any weapon could have. "I am nothing like you! You are a sick and twisted demon who only loves torture and misery!"

"And you are not? Don't deceive yourself," said Lilith.

"Nothing like you!" Zayashariya spat.

"Of course you are daughter. You love death, murder, and violence as I do. You are evil dear. It is your nature. A bad tree cannot bring forth good fruit. It is what you are. You are the seed of me, spawn of my corrupted womb. Accept this and you will know peace. You are an unconquerable evil to any poor soul that falls in your path. Do not fool yourself. Any person who crosses your path will perish no matter how virtuous your intention is. Righteousness doesn't dwell in the devil's heart you fool!" Lilith's voice echoed.

Zayashariya spat at the queen.

"Cute my dear; but, you know you have to do better than that," said Lilith, shaking her flaming head of hair. "Stupidity always amuses me. Believe me. You don't have to behave like a fool just because you are stupid. You will obey me and do just as I ask. It is up to you how you want to handle this situation. You can do it by your own will or I will bend you to mine. It is your choice. Now make it!" she yelled.

Zayashariya remained dudgeon, the look on her face defiant.

Lilith giggled, amused by the girl's insubordination.

"Let me go..." Zayashariya was quickly cut off by a wave of Lilith's hand.

"Silence! I have had enough of you! You disgust me!" Lilith's face transmogrified. She opened her mouth and blew a dark cloud into Zayashariya's face. The fog enveloped the helpless woman and quickly dissipated.

"Pick her up and take her to the torture chamber. Be careful not to harm her. She is my child. Leave the discipline to me," she instructed the ghouls. Lilith sat wide-legged with her back hunched over and one hand touching the floor as if she was about to pounce in any minute.

"Yessssss Madammm," the ghouls said in unison as they bowed low and lifted Zayashariya's limp form from the floor and turned toward the direction they came.

"By the way," Lilith cooed.

"Yesssss Madammm," they said and looked back over their shoulders at the queen.

"If I see one scratch on her flesh, even the minutest injury, you die." Lilith smiled, her perfect white teeth shining. "Understand?" She leaned back, chin in hand.

"Weee understandddd."

"Now be gone foul curs!" Lilith screamed as she watched them hurry out of the room, careful not to drop the sleeping princess and squashing the wiggling fingers as they walked. The howling captives were restless. "Silence!" she screamed at the humanoids under the floor. "Or you all will die this night!"

The chamber fell tacit. The gory throne spun around slowly and the dim glow of the chamber went dim.

*   *   *

"Miss," Gredly called out. "Miss." He squeezed Zayashariya's ebony palm. His voice was deep but quiet. His voice was a distant thought in her ear. Gredly did not want to attract more attention to them. He was very uncomfortable with the town's people staring at him as it was. He was the type of person who weighed other's opinion of himself higher than his own. Gredly squeezed Zayashariya's hand even harder. His display of strength was feeble. She did not flinch. Zayashariya did not even acknowledge his presence. Vexed and a little overexcited, he let go of her hand and shook her shoulder. Amazed at the softness of her ebony cloak; his palm lingered on her shoulder a moment longer than necessary. Gredly wondered what kind of animal possessed such luxurious fur and why his wardrobe was lacking such a luxurious item. He made up his mind to go shopping as soon as he left her at the Inn.

Zayashariya snapped out of her trance. Visions of home evaporated before her. She looked into Gredly's eyes puzzled. "Yes," she responded, wondering what this tight mannered humanoid wanted now. *Had I missed his message already?* She was enjoying her observations. She was transported in thought. *What could he possibly want?* Zayashariya smiled at him to lighten her mood. "I am sorry. What did you say? My mind had completely wondered away."

"I see." Gredly's mouth curled upward in one corner. "Here is the Inn." He pointed to the door directly in front of them. Gredly looked into her eyes and was suddenly smitten by their amethyst luster. He felt uncomfortable, as if his adoration of her was a sin. Gredly turned his eyes from her and walked toward the door.

She smiled at him, feeling a bit ridiculous because of her selfish thoughts a moment before. Zayashariya looked at the tall white building. There were pale blue and yellow crystals hanging all around the building making it look like a preternatural scaly creature, like a wise dragon she knew long ago. The sight was breathtaking. She walked to the door and placed her hand on the cube shaped doorknob.

"Thank you, sir, for your pleasant company and for escorting me here. I am very appreciative," said Zayashariya, opening her cloak, reaching into her hip pouch and retrieving three gold coins. Zayashariya placed the coins into Gredly's hand and proceeded inside. Suddenly she halted. She was frozen by his stare. *What could be wrong now?* She pondered to herself. *Did I insult him by giving him such a large amount of money?* It was just an extemporaneous gesture of kindness. Zayashariya was not familiar with his customs and she was much too tired to stand outside any longer worrying about his emotions. She gripped her fur cloak, pulled it tightly around her, and raised her plum colored eyebrows. She raised and dropped her shoulders and let out a quiet sigh. He placed the coins back into her ebony hand. Now she was really confused. Zayashariya rolled her eyes and took a deep breath.

"Is something wrong?" Zayashariya asked, curiously annoyed by his repulsive expression. She held the coins back out. "Was this not enough?" She reached back into her hip pouch. He stopped her by grabbing her hand. Zayashariya was set aback by his grip. She jerked her hand away.

"What are you wearing beneath that cloak?" he forced the words through his teeth trying not to be too loud.

Self-consciously, his eyes darted around trying to see if anyone heard him. Gredly had already turned a few heads close by. He pointed to her body. He prayed that his eyes had deceived him. The lines in his face traced his frown as his eyes narrowed in bewilderment.

Zayashariya placed her hand on the guard's shoulder. Her calming touch erased the desolate expression from his face. His eyes were still laced with the tiniest bit of worry. The dark woman opened her cloak. Underneath it, she wore a black leather leotard which blended perfectly with her skin. She wore black leather knee-high boots with silver chains around her calves. Several silver armbands circled her curvy arms and a pair of leather gloves met the bands. A thick silver choker with an odd symbol on it shaped like a crescent moon with rings around it, hung around her neck.

"What is wrong?" she asked. Zayashariya knew. She always knew what ignorant people assumed. People were the same no matter where she went. They were innately negative. Knowing this made her existence a lot easier. She was a master at knowing the nature of humanoids but a novice at knowing her own nature.

"I apologize, my dear. I thought that you were naked." The orange man blushed. His assumption shamed him. Gredly forced a counter-factual smile to his face.

"That is quite all right. I am sure that animals like me debate daily whether or not to put on clothes before I interact with superior beings," Zayashariya laughed.

"No. No. I did not mean to insult you. It just looked like you were nude and I was flustered by it."

"If I was, would it be any business of yours?" asked Zayashariya, grinning.

"I guess not. Please except my apology."

"I do. Here, take this. Thanks again for your help." Zayashariya handed him the gold coins and walked into the Inn.

The inside of the Inn was covered with the same strange glowing crystals that brightened the city. The crystals made up the walls and ceilings of the Inn. It glowed a pale pink. The lighting was dull but it was sufficient. Zayashariya walked to a big rectangular counter which sat in the center of the room. On each side of the counter was a spiral staircase that led to the upper levels. An older bright orange woman with her peach hair pinned to the top of her head sat in a rocking chair behind the counter. The old lady stared at the strange visitor with her thick peach eyebrows raised high. Her expression changed when she realized that Zayashariya was wearing clothes.

"Missy, I suggest a brighter color," the old woman said, laughing. Her face glowed in the pale light. Kindness shined in her eyes. She had the smile of a young girl but she looked at least eighty years old in human years. Wrinkles were engraved deep in her skin and her teeth were starting to yellow. Her shoulders were slightly hunched over and her arms thin and veined.

"What?" Zayashariya responded, not understanding the nature of the comment muffled by hearty giggles. All she heard was a comment about color. *Did she insult me?* She wasn't sure so she decided not to react negatively. She realized that her defenses were high. After all, she was used to dealing with the worst of the worst.

Zayashariya was always ready for battle. Most of the time, she looked forward to it. Although she took great pride in herself for seeking out beautiful and serine things and adamantly separating herself from the demons she was spawn from, she had to admit that she was nothing more than a lesser evil. She was not disillusioned enough to mistake herself for good, but viewed herself as more of a neutral creature. Knowing herself well, she realized that maybe the people here meant her no ill will. Zayashariya relaxed. She said, "I am sorry ma'am. What did you say?"

"Brighter color clothes," the old woman suggested. "You look nude." The lady pointed at Zayashariya's leotard with her skinny fingers adorned with chewed to the flesh fingernails.

Zayashariya gave the woman a half smile and disregarded the comment. "Do you have any rooms available?" She leaned on the counter trying to be cordial. She was unimaginably tired. Sleep was consuming her. She knew that she would not be able to fight it for much longer. At this point in time, she would be lucky if she could make it up the stairs. Zayashariya covered her mouth and let out a yawn.

"Of course, dear. How many rooms do you need?" The old woman placed a box on the counter that read "Room Keys."

"Just one." *How many people do you see?* She thought to herself. Zayashariya smiled. *Be Nice.*

"All right young lady. Here is your key." The old lady handed the key to Zayashariya. "May I ask you a question?" she asked in a curious voice. Her eyes squinted nearly closed as she leaned her head to the side and looked Zayashariya up and down.

"Sure," Zayashariya said politely. She fondled the shiny gold key with her fingers, awaiting the funny looking woman's question.

"What are you and where are you from?" the old lady asked, eyeing Zayashariya rudely. The old woman was trying to be as polite as possible without offending the pitch colored woman standing in front of her. She found Zayashariya quite queer, downright bizarre to be frank.

"I was about to ask you the same thing!" Zayashariya sneered as she turned and walked away towards the stairs. She could not believe the people in this place. They were so uncouth. Some demons had better manners. She would never ask a person a question so rude. Not in that manner anyway. After all, they looked just as strange as she did. She had never even heard of an orange race and she had traveled across many realms over many centuries. The people of Wilzasp were a new race to her and probably to the rest of the universe too. And, they had the gall to treat her as if she was a circus freak. Irritated, she walked faster trying to let out her frustrations. *Maybe I am overreacting. I am just tired.*

The old woman sat back in her chair and shook her narrow head. "I only asked a question. Such strange creatures shouldn't be so testy," she said to herself as she closed her eyes for a quick nap.

Zayashariya climbed the spiral stairs to the fourth floor. She walked down the glowing green hallway until she arrived at her room. It was the door at the very end of the narrow hallway. Taking the small golden ring shaped key, she opened the black iron door by pressing the end of the ring into a small crescent shaped lock. The dark stranger stepped inside of the glowing red room. "What an interesting color." She smirked as she observed the room around her. "Mother would love this," she said, shivering at the thought.

The room was shaped like a right triangle. Her bed protruded from the ninety-degree angle of the room. There were two windows, both on the longest wall of the room. Velvet cloth covered the bed and the windows. The cloth was made of old ornate lace. It looked hand made and very antique as if it was born in a different century. The lace was made of velvety roses and leaves connected by scarlet satin thread. It was the color of fresh blood before the air changes it dark. Zayashariya adored the color. She walked over to the bed and touched the fabric. It was so soft to her hands that she rubbed the bedspread against her cheek. The softness lulled her to sleep, her eyes closing for a brief moment. Zayashariya quickly released the cloth and observed the rest of the room.

In the other corner of the room, there was a mahogany shelf for her belongings. She had none except for her hip pouch and her panther skin cloak. She placed her items on the ornately carved shelf and walked out of the room. Zayashariya walked down the hall until she found a washroom.

The small room glowed bright yellow. There was a fireplace in one corner with a kettle of boiling water hanging over the fire. On the other side of the wall, there was a silver tub with sunflower yellow towels hanging on its edge. Bath oils sat around the tub in a rainbow of colors. The oils sat in diamond shaped crystal bottles, reflecting the yellow light, creating little rainbows on the tub and the floor. The sight was absolutely breathtaking. A full mirror was nailed to the back of the door. A mahogany table sat next to the tub covered with tortoise shell combs and brushes.

She picked up two small but thick hand mittens from the floor next to the fireplace and took the water from the fire. She poured the hot water into the tub, added cold water from the faucet to make the temperature tolerable and added blueberry bath oil then climbed into the tub. Steam rose around her like a friendly ghost offering her a welcoming hug. Zayashariya splashed her face with the hot water and dipped her head underneath. Then, with a quick splash, she emerged from under the soothing liquid. Slowly she washed, savoring the pleasant smelling lather as it covered her body. Her muscles relaxed and she laid there for what seemed like hours. After the water cooled, she drained the tub and dried with the sunflower yellow towels. She picked up one of the plush brushes and brushed her mane. Then she put everything into its proper place and exited the washroom with her garments in her hand.

Zayashariya walked back to her chamber feeling refreshed and anticipated that no one would spy her nude form walking down the hallway. She was too tired to care. She was almost positive that she was the only occupant on that floor, or so she hoped. Zayashariya had not seen or heard anyone else in the building but the old woman downstairs. Finally, she entered her room, put her garments on the mahogany shelf, and laid her weary body across the bed and fell into a deep coma.

Chapter 7

In the basement of the Inn, there was a bar and lounge with a huge dance hall where the town's people gathered nightly to have a good time. The orange people drank, danced, flirted with harlots, and made merry. The brothel glowed with a cream colored light. A few multicolored crystals hung from the ceiling. There were tables spread out all over the wide dance hall with a small section left for dancing and a bed in the corner left for the harlots' next victim. A cable holding a huge marble block was hanging from the ceiling.

On the block hanging from the ceiling, a woman wearing a sparkling gown made of silver sheer material sang, teasing the crowd with the contours of her body. Her voice was like an angelic symphony corrupted by the power of temptation. Her hair was pulled back into a bun pinned with silver sparkling hairpins. A few men played drums behind her. They were swaying to the beat like palm trees in a hurricane. The men at the tables closest to the sultry singer looked at her lustfully as their women looked upon her with jealousy and disdain. The dance floor was full of hip shaking and laughter. The bar was surrounded by staggering drunks and women trying to meet their future husbands. People partied long into the morning and many stayed most of the day. The old woman that worked behind the counter upstairs limped into the dance hall. Her dress was wrinkled and her hair a mess. A frown hung on her face like a bent wire hanger. The crowd let out a disappointed sigh in unison.

"Okay party's over. Let's go!" the old woman shouted, her voice drunken with fatigue. Her eyes were blood shot and her mouth was rank with morning breath. She waved the foul odor away and frowned. "Now!" she yelled and pointed toward the exit.

The booing crowd all stopped their merrymaking and foolishness and moved toward the exit. The music stopped and the lady in the silver dress was helped down from the block and exited into the back room. All of the people moved except for two drunken men behaving like imbeciles. They were the town's trouble making drunks, Edzab and Peckler. The two sloppy oafs flopped back in their chairs, guzzling down jars of whisky.

The old woman walked over to their table and dropped her hand down hard on the wood. "Let's go boys," the old lady yelled. "I gotta clean up," she said as she walked over to a window and opened it, letting the bright light of the twin suns shine in. The sunlight shot through the room like a bolt of lightening.

"What is ya tryin' ta do ya o' fool? Blind us?" Edzab yelled as he covered his fat squinting eyes. His dingy clothes hugged his flabby body tightly. He resembled a giant sausage.

"Let's go!" she yelled again, trying with difficulty to keep her composure. She did not want any trouble but, with these two, trouble was almost inevitable. "Don't make me put you out!" She raised her fist in the air and shook it. Her voice was on the verge of supreme irritability. The men sat, immune to her annoyance with them, as if no one had said a thing.

"Put me out!" yelled Peckler. His eyes flared dangerously. "I wanna see ya try ya o' hag!" the skinny drunk slurred. A glistening string of drool fell from his intoxicated lips. His boney fingers wiped away the slobber from his mouth as he began to present the old woman with his toothless grin. "I'm tired of ya mouf! You been bullying us every morning and today I aint gonna go no where!"

The old woman put her hand around Peckler's wrist with an iron grip. She was unusually strong for an old woman but in Wilzasp, the women were almost as strong as the men.

"This is my place and I make the rules here. Open up your own Inn and you can stay as long as you please. You got to leave here and you got to go now," she said.

The paper-thin man jumped to his feet and shoved the old woman to the floor. The remaining crowd disappeared from the hall with cowardly speed.

"Whacha gone do?" Peckler slurred, his thin body towering over the elderly woman. The hem of his pink pants brushed her trembling cheek.

The old woman tried to get to her feet but the heavy foot of Edzab landed on her frail chest knocking the air from her lungs. She coughed heavily. Tears formed in her eyes. She knew that she would suffer. She looked up at the cruel drunk men and fought away the tears. She tried to sit up again.

"Did I tell ya to get up?" He traced her face with the tip of his moccasin.

She kicked Edzab in the groin. He grabbed himself and tumbled over. He rolled on the floor moaning and laughing wickedly. He pulled himself to his knees and quickly rejuvenated. A moment later, he was back in her face smiling.

"Did I ever tell ya how sexy I find ya Kyre?" Edzab asked. He slapped her hard. Her face fell back against the cool floor.

She refused to show pain.

"I think we need to show her who the man around here is. Huh, Peckler?!" He laughed and looked at his buddy. Peckler laughed also. Edzab turned back to Kyre.

"I've always found ya sexy for an ole shrew. I've always wanted ya for myself," said the foul man giggling like a merry-andrew. "What good man don't want a nag?" He kicked her in the ribs.

The old woman tried hard to bear the pain. She held her chest tightly trying to revive from the kick. She tried even harder to catch the breath which was forced from her lungs. Fear was in her eyes as she stared at the frail man leaning toward her. Peckler reached down and ripped the front of her dress.

"Did ya like that?" he asked, smiling a drunken smile. "All women like an aggressive man, don't they?" He slapped her again, this time drawing blood.

She refused to cry aloud. Kyre scratched his face and wrapped her arms around her body trying fruitlessly to hide her nakedness.

"Do you want me Kyre?" Peckler asked, laughing as he drug his slimy hand across her old flattened breast. They looked like stuffed pancakes.

The old woman's body stiffened. Fear grabbed onto her like a pit bull ordered to attack. Her eyes stared past the two thugs and words refused to fall from her trembling lips. She wept. She wept not because of the merciless thugs attacking her but because of the atrocity she saw behind them. Her eyes stretched with horror.

The two molesters were baffled by her fearful expression. They refused to turn around. They wanted to think that they implanted such fear in her heart, but they doubted it. They knew her better than that. She feared no one. Both men cringed at the thought but hey continued stripping her despite their inner voice warning them that something was terribly awry.

Kyre refused to fight back. She was frozen with panic. Her eyes were fixed on the horrid sight standing behind the men. The two men began to worry. They stopped and turned around.

Behind the men was a terribly deformed creature. It was jet black in color with eight arms and eight legs. The face of the creature was not deformed like the rest of its ghastly body. It had the face of a beautiful woman. The creature resembled a caterpillar and a spider combined. It had tough black skin that looked like new leather, smooth and glazed. The gruesome creature had the most intense violet eyes.

The beast grabbed the alarmed Edzab with a clawed hand, and locked him, between its arms. It opened its mouth and out shot eight razor sharp fangs, four protruding from the top and four from the bottom, forming a horrid maw of slimy ivory teeth. A dark purple tongue dripping with an oily substance came out of the creature's mouth, flickering like a serpent's tongue. The horrified man screamed as the beast licked his neck clean and placed its fangs inside of his flesh, destroying every vein that rested there. His body was rendered useless. His eyes stared helplessly into nothingness. Edzab was drained of all blood. His dry, limp body fell to the cold marble floor. The two remaining humanoids watched the murder, paralyzed with fear.

The purple eyes of the creature were fixed now upon Peckler. Peckler stood in front of the beast frozen with fright as Kyre struggled to pull her torn clothes together. The beast knocked the old woman flat on the floor and stood directly in front of Peckler.

Six of its eight arms melted away and so did six of its legs. The melted flesh evaporated into thin air like mist. In the place of the limbs grew long spiked poles which entrapped the running man, digging themselves into a nearby wall forming a cage around the weeping man. The beast broke away from the poles and now appeared to be a woman. The woman walked over to the trembling man, gliding across the floor like a vicious apparition, staring deep into his blue eyes. Peckler only gazed back into her violet eyes for a brief moment before her fangs drained his body of all blood. The monster wiped her deep plum lips with the back of her hand and turned toward the old lady.

The old woman gasped at the monster's face. It was strangely familiar, a face she had seen before. A look of realization dawned on her and her wrinkled hands covered her open mouth.

The monster grabbed the woman up from the floor, suspending her in the air. Her deadly grip silenced the old woman's whimpering into a muffled whine. The beast installed her life stealing fangs and whispered into the old woman's ear as she supped, "I am what I am and I came from where you are going."

The old woman closed her eyes to the world and fell to the floor lifeless.

The vicious creature wiped the blood from her full yet perfectly formed lips and walked over to the bar. Her fiendish appearance melted away. She poured herself a jar of white wine and sat frozen in thought for a moment. Thoughts of regret floated through her head as she looked upon the dead bodies scattered across the floor like fallen trees with crude twisted branches. Guilt grabbed hold of her heart. She wept. Drowning the jar of wine, she shook the thought from her head. She had to feed. She had to live. *There is no evil in survival.* After finishing another jar of wine, she got up from the bar stool and disappeared into the light of day.

Chapter 8

The day was absolutely beautiful, splendid on a grand scale. The twin suns warmed the land as its rays bathed the plain. Emerald plant life grew up in armies around every building. The town's people marched up and down the streets like soldiers, tending to their daily duties. Noise rang throughout the entire city like a church bell at noon. Humanoid children chased one another in circles like little puppies chasing their tails. The children's pet quickomwonks, two legged catlike creatures, participated in the children's game, adding to the existing clatter in the streets. Street vendors sat under their shade umbrellas to block out the heat of the scorching twin suns. The smell of fresh fish and fruit mingled together gave the air an unique tropical aroma. Street peddlers aggravated every pedestrian that walked passed them by blocking their paths trying to sell pieces of stolen jewelry, fake inventions, and attempting to lure citizens into playing con games.

Zayashariya walked down the busy streets enjoying the pleasant weather. This place was nothing like her home. Wilzasp was vivid and picturesque. Her home was dark and gloomy. Night was a place void of natural light with no sun to fall upon her dark skin to warm her flesh pleasantly. That was the very reason why she began traveling the realms to bask in the beauty of the universe, to meet new people and to escape from the depths of foul destruction. It was also the reason why she eventually decided to leave Night. Zayashariya was weary of shadowy skies and total debauchery. Something within her longed for pleasantries, for peace of mind and kindness of heart. She knew that she could never experience true tranquility if she remained in her mother's care and on the planet of Night.

Her home was a place of magical illusion and evil wonders. Some may consider it a beautiful place, in a morbid kind of way. Strangely, beauty can be found anywhere. Even evil seemed to have a good side, a justification of acts known and acknowledged to be wrong but somehow seeming logical in certain circumstances. Isn't it the nature of intelligent beings to be attracted to what is forbidden? Well that is Gehenna, the interesting side of evil. Everyone in Gehenna wasn't necessarily evil. Many there were damned but not necessarily evil. It was difficult to survive in such a dreary atmosphere and remain a child of righteousness. That is why she enjoyed the beautiful crystals and the warm twin suns of Wilzasp. Maybe there was a chance that the beauty of this world would destroy the darkness lurking within her. It felt like a miracle just to wake up and feel the suns, to see the light. Gehenna had no such light.

Gehenna was a place hidden deep within the planet Night. The northern surface of Night was too poisonous to live on so all the forms of life that dwelled in the northern area, dwelled within the planet. It was like living in a cave that went on forever. It was dark, damp, and filled with all the horrors of Night. It was a place where prisoners from other planets were sent for torture. It was where many people died at the heinous hands of Queen Lilith, the goddess of pain and torture.

She was death itself, maybe worse. Her reputation was so renowned that she was heard of on every planet and galaxy. She and her evil minions were so infamous that many did not believe that such a thing could truly exist until they were delivered into her hands. Delivered to Night. Death.

This is why Gehenna was called the Land of the Dead. No one who ever went there ever returned. Gehenna was like a rumor. It was like an ancient myth, like the River Styx or the Corn Mother. It was a rumor too horrid to be true, but all too true.

Zayashariya walked down the street, nearly skipping, with a smile on her face. It felt good to see such marvelous things. She received many baffling looks from the town's people but chose to ignore their rudeness. She figured they would realize that she was wearing clothes sooner or later. She was surprised by their obvious stares. *They could at least pretend to be discreet,* she thought. Wilzasp suffered from a terrible case of xenophobia and Zayashariya was an alien nightmare that escaped their subconscious and sashayed boldly through their everyday realities.

At least at home, people who disliked another person made them aware from the beginning. No one put on facades. You knew if you were in danger and it was you who were responsible for your own health. It was kill or be killed and the basis of hating someone had little to do with their appearance but who they were or what they did or simply a lust for blood. Nothing was hardly ever personal.

On Night, everyone looked different. There was no uniform race. People just were what they were. All kinds of creatures: demons, daemons, humans, and humanoids lived there. The colors ranged from pitch black to glowing white and everything in between. There was no room for prejudice. Good and evil is an inner quality. It is something that only is hidden momentarily by the outer skin. The inner being is what eventually damns or delivers us. Queen Lilith herself was bright red with fiery hair and Zayashariya was the color of pitch. One could not assume that a person is a certain way by appearances. It was too dangerous to think so limited. The inhabitants of Gehenna did not whisper in corners or stare out of the corner of their eyes. Her people may be demonic by nature but at least they were honest in their intentions, a seeming paradox but true.

The foreign woman stopped at a fruit stand in the center of the street market. The exotic fruit that lined the counter of the stand intrigued her. Zayashariya had never seen things of that nature. There were fruits with black skins, purple furry bananas, green strawberries, and yellow kiwis. The smell of the fruit was like pure sugar. Zayashariya's stomach growled with hunger. The ebony woman reached for one of the fruit when an ashy voice caught her attention. She looked up at the man that worked at the fruit stand and smiled. Her happy grin soon dwindled to a disappointed smirk.

"May I hep ya child?" the old man asked Zayashariya with a disturbed look in his eyes. He wrinkled his nose and looked her up and down. He wore a blue tank top exposing his age-withered arms. His skin jiggled like a liver-spotted gelatin mold. His graying peach hair looked like orange-vanilla swirl ice cream.

Zayashariya ignored the rude expression. She forced a smile to her face once more and held up a strange pink fruit. "What's this?" she asked, trying to sound as friendly as possible.

"It's a quampanickle. It is very sweet." the old man answered, staring at her with disdain.

"How much is it?" Zayashariya was annoyed by the way the man was looking at her. She forced another smile to her face just to be civil.

"One iron coin," he said, looking at her with his mouth ajar, his face twisted in disgust.

She was fed up with the stupidity of this town already. She had never met such prejudice beings in her entire life. The nerve of these people was overbearing.

"Is there a problem, sir," she sneered. Her eyes flashed like purple lightning.

"Do you want the fruit or not?" the old man yelled, ignoring her question. Her eyes frightened him.

In his eyes, Zayashariya was a true demon. Everything about her made him uneasy. She moved as if she danced to music. Her eyes were abnormal in color and luster. The way her violet hair, eyes, nails and lips clashed against her midnight black skin, gave him the creeps.

"Make up your mind woman!" The old man pushed a couple of fruit toward Zayashariya.

She picked one up and smelled it. Her fingernails looked like mini talons.

The word *demon* flashed in his mind. He heard about her being from Gehenna. He knew that hellish place was no myth. His father was sent there a hundred and fifty years ago for treachery. He stood up and frowned at the woman. His eyes were dangerous. Why should he have to be nice to a hell spawn? He did not like any kind of being but his own. Besides, if she came from where she says, she was a demon or worse and she needed to be banished from the town. There was no place for people like her in Wilzasp especially if she claimed to be from such an abhorrent land; a place where his father is still wailing and gnashing his teeth. He would be happy the day she just packed up and left. He leaned towards her face.

"Do you want it or not?" he asked through his teeth. He looked like a lion ready to pounce. "If you don't want it, move on."

"No thank you," Zayashariya declared, putting the fruit down and walking away from the stand. She never looked back, although the old man's rude demeanor wounded her. She simply could not understand why he was so unpleasant to her. She had done nothing. It occurred to her that the people of Wilzasp's would fear her no matter what she did, simply because she was an alien. Naive, is what she was. Nothing more than a child who dreamed of a perfect world and crushed when reality hit. Zayashariya picked up her pace and tried to erase the man from her mind. For the first time in a long time, she wanted to cry.

The old man watched her walk away. A smile of relief crossed his wrinkled face. He went back into the tent behind his stand and sat in a chair next to two other men. His facial expression was vague.

"Why are ya lookin' so foolish Bleg?" a younger man asked, wearing a green and white robe. He was casually sipping on a jar of mead, dropping its contents on his shirt. He tried unnoticeably to wipe his shirt. Too late. He was noticed. No one cared.

"I saw the most peculiar creature. She was woman-like but somethin' about huh just plain spooked me. I don't like huh. I want huh out of this town. That is for sure!" The old man's voice was escalating. He was thinking about those purple eyes, the rumor of Gehenna, his father. He frowned, making his already wrinkled skin look worse. He looked like a talking prune.

"She is that gal that is stayin' in the Inn." he said. "You know the stranger the color of a tar pit."

"I heard dat she was some kind of beauty," another man said refilling his jar with fermented honey.

"She aint one of us ya idiot!" Bleg yelled. His eyes bucked and his bottom lip trembled. "For cryin' out loud she claims that she is from that place where phantoms and monsters live. What does that tell ya?" He paused to catch his breath. "She knows that she is a monster huhslef!" He took a deep breath and sat back.

"She not our kind Bleg?" Gradly responded dumbly.

"Heck naw!" Bleg yelled. "Any fool can see that!"

"I'll help ya run huh out of here." Gradly tried to redeem himself. It was important for him to have Bleg's respect. Bleg was the most successful salesman in Wilzasp and his best friend Gradly one day hoped that Bleg would teach him how to become a great salesman too. Gradly doubted it. But if that day ever came, which seemed like it never would because Gradly had been following behind Bleg for fifty years. Gradly would be the proudest man in town but in the meantime he hoped to be respected by association. Gradly sat up in his chair. "Specially if ya say she a monster."

"You aint even seen her Gradly," Flum said stupidly.

"It don't matta ya fool! Didn't you hear Bleg say that she aint one of us!" Gradly frowned. He looked over at Bleg for approval. Bleg did not acknowledge him. "I am wit

Bleg!" he yelled with his filthy yellow teeth grinning at his friend nodding like the flunky he was.

"Count me in," the young man said with nervousness in his voice. Flum's slender palms rubbed against his striped robe. He bowed his head and then rubbed his palms together. He paused. He hated when his palms were sweaty. "Did you hear about those murders?" he asked, hoping to change the subject.

"Yeah! I becha that tar demon did it! It happened when she got here!" Bleg shouted out like an irrational lunatic. "Demon she is! A demon from hell!"

"How could a woman do somethin' like that?" Gradly asked, puzzled at Bleg's statement. *To blame her for those murders is crazy.* Only a monster had the capabilities to do something like that and he did not believe in monsters. Those bodies were mutilated. Bleg wanted a reason to hurt the girl. He liked hurting people who were weaker than himself. Bleg wanted to be feared. Who was Gradly to argue? It wasn't like his opinion was respected anyway. "Do ya think she could've done it?" he asked, scratching his head and avoiding eye contact, giving his hands and feet all of his attention. His eyes reflected his discomfort. He took another sip of mead.

"Well let's get huh anyway. It don't really matta." Bleg sneered.

"I say we go to that Inn tonight and put huh out of her misery. Do ya agree boys?" Gradly said.

Bleg nodded.

Gradly smiled when he saw that he had gotten Bleg's approval.

The old feeble flunky jumped up and yelled, "We aint got room for huh kind here!"

He sat back down sucking his green stained teeth. His peach hair was like peach fuzz on his head. It looked like a hazy halo. He waved for his partners to come closer to him. A look of divine revelation glowed from his wicked eyes. The cur smiled. The men smiled smiles of mischievousness and uneasiness. Their ignorance and curiosity had gotten the better of them. They gathered closer, looking into Bleg's victorious eyes like eager boys ready to go and discover new worlds. All of the men huddled closer together to concoct a plan to destroy the unwanted visitor. Faint whispers and murmurings floated through the air like weightless bubbles. They broke free from their boy-like powwow. A knavish grin sashayed across their cunning facades.

Chapter 9

"Summon my daughter," Queen Lilith commanded as she leaned back on her bed of plush pillows and lush blankets. Her flame of hair slowly disappeared into her head leaving it bald and glistening in the lamp light. A thin silk gown hugged Lilith's strong body tightly. "Tell Zayashariya to come to me. My business is urgent." Lilith's head flopped back lazily. She let her eyes close.

A look of utter horror transformed the face of the grotesquely slender being standing by Lilith's bedroom door. The creature was at least six feet tall. Yellow skin covered its protruding bones. It wore nothing. Two small black dots for eyes and a short slit for a mouth were the only features on the creature's face. The slit moved in a wavy motion and a small echoing voice broke the silence of the room.

"I do not know where Zayashariya is," it said.

"What do you mean, Pampias?" Queen Lilith turned on her side and faced her servant. "Zayashariya can not be far. Find her." Fireballs took the place of Lilith's eyes.

Pampias stepped slightly out of the doorway into the shadow of the hall. "Master, I have not seen her. No one has," it mumbled.

"Why am I just hearing this?" Lilith sprang up. Blue flames danced upon her scalp and grew into a giant torch.

Pampias trembled at the sight of the queen. The blue flame lit up the servant's fearful face. It said nothing.

"Answer me! You lurching mongrel!" yelled Lilith, fire shining in her eyes. Her scarlet skin burned redder than ever. Her flame of hair flickered back and forth from blue to red. "Answer me or you will regret the day your pitiful soul was conceived!"

"Master, we all assumed that Zayashariya had gone off on one of her adventures."

"You assumed!" Lilith hissed, rising to her feet, her hair a blazing inferno, her face a distorted mask. "Am I not the supreme power in this place?"

Pampias quivered and dropped its head. "Yes master."

"Do I not have the right to be notified of the comings and goings in my castle?" the Queen of Night questioned, gliding slowly to the petrified creature that was frantically crying and cringing. Lilith's fists were balled tight. Blood dripped from her palms. Her nails were cutting deep into her flesh.

"Yes master," Pampias whimpered.

"Why did no one tell me that she was missing? Everyone knows the trouble Zayashariya has been causing the demon rulers!" Lilith screeched. Her voice rang through the air like the scream of a banshee. Small trinkets around the room shook and small mirrors, decorating the walls, shattered.

Pampias fell prostrate before the queen, its yellow bones like a pile of sticks upon the floor. "Please master, we assumed..."

"Who are you to assume anything? You simple-minded ball of vomit! Do you have the power or the intelligence to assume anything?" Lilith questioned, looking down at the wailing creature.

"I am sorry. Pity me! Pity me!" Pampias wailed. It trembled so hard that the clicking of its elbows sounded like a beetle with an extremely hard exoskeleton flipping on the floor.

"Of course," said Lilith, smiling. "Stand up." Lilith held out her hand and helped Pampias to its feet. "You made an honest mistake," she said sweetly. Lilith caressed the creature's chin, held her arms open wide and said, "I forgive you. Come, let us embrace."

Pampias wrapped its arms around Lilith and Lilith wrapped her arms around Pampias. A bright indigo flash filled the room. In an instant, Pampias' dry bones fell to the floor in a clean white pile. Lilith sauntered back to her bed and slumped down on the mattress. Gnashing her teeth, she spat, "Where are you, Zayashariya? You can not hide from me!" Picking up a small bell, she rang it three times. In minutes, an identical looking creature to Pampias appeared at the door.

"Legatro." Lilith spoke its name.

"Yes master." The creature bowed. Its eyes spied the bones on the floor. It tried to swallow the knot in its throat but it knew that its twin had perished at the hand of Queen Lilith and a similar fate may await it. Fear filled the skeletal creature. "I am here to do your will," it said.

"Bring Sarai to me. I am sure that she knew of Zayashariya's departure," said Lilith, throwing her legs upon the bed in one heavy swoop and staring up at the ceiling. "If Sarai knows anything, I will torture her until her tongue can not cease confessing." The flame on Lilith's head died and she closed her eyes. "Leave me. I must rest."

"Yes master," Legatro said, backing into the hall and disappearing.

Chapter 10

Zayashariya walked through the town until her legs became weary with fatigue and her stomach growled like a ghoulish beast. The stranger made her way back to the Inn where a new woman sat behind the counter in the lobby. The woman was much younger than the old lady who had sat there before her. She looked about eighteen years old. Her face was smooth and void of wrinkles. She glowed in the prime of youth like a delicate flower freshly budding. Kind dark brown eyes, the color of black coffee, assumingly very intelligent, sat peacefully on her face. Her eyes revealed a gentle nature, one of innocence and inexperience. Her peach hair was combed back from her bright orange face accenting her lovely eyes. Zayashariya looked at the girl curiously. *Pretty. Innocent and sweet. She reminds me of a girl I once knew.* The ebony beauty had not seen such goodness radiating from an individual in a very long time. Zayashariya walked over to the counter and smiled a gigantic smile.

"Hello," Zayashariya greeted the girl, flipping her violet hair over her shoulder. "What happened to the old woman that worked here before?" she asked while staring at the angel faced young lady. Zayashariya's smile dropped when she saw dysphoria in the girl's face. "What happened?" she asked with what appeared to be genuine concern.

"Have you not heard stranger?" the girl asked, looking upon Zayashariya with utter disbelief.

"No. I am afraid not. Tell me. Is there something wrong? Is the old woman ill?" asked Zayashariya, searching the girl's eyes for answers.

"I am afraid my mother was found slaughtered!" the girl exclaimed.

"Your mother? Slaughtered?" Zayashariya questioned. "I am so very sorry. Is there anything I can do to help?"

"No," the young woman whimpered. Her voice shook with anger and grief. She tried desperately to control her trembling. "There is nothing you or anyone else can do. My mother is dead. Nothing can be done to bring her back.

"What happened to her?" Zayashariya paused for a moment. "Do you mind me asking? I know this is very difficult for you to speak of."

"It happened in the dance hall. My mother was killed along with two others!" A low whine escaped the girl's throat. She tried to fight back the pain. "You should have seen it!" she wailed. "My mother and the others were sucked dry like ripe muscadine and thrown aside like useless garbage." Bereavement flooded her face.

Zayashariya gave a look of sympathy to the woman. *I'm sorry.* She reached out and put her hand upon the girl's hand to comfort her. "I am sorry to hear that. Please be strong," Zayashariya encouraged. "Do you know who or what did it?" the stranger asked, trying desperately not to shift her eyes. She attempted to comfort the girl by rubbing the delicate skin on the back of her hand. The girl's skin felt like smooth suede. Zayashariya enjoyed the feel, not in a sensual way but in a curious way. The girl's skin was abnormally soft like her own. She felt a likeness between them.

"I am afraid that I do not know who or what could have done such an act. I saw no such person or beast inside the dance hall before I left. There were no others there but my mother and the two drunkards that perished with her," the girl said. "It is my fault, I feel, because I left her in the room with those two thugs and the next thing I knew was that they all were dead. Like a coward, I went into the back. That thing probably wanted the two men but took my mother because she was there." The young woman was obviously uncomfortable. She smiled awkwardly and removed her hand from under Zayashariya's hand without offending the friendly woman. After all, she knew that the stranger was only being considerate, or so she hoped. One can never be sure. The murder made everyone a suspect and the stranger was the most suspicious character.

Zayashariya observed the woman closely as she turned her head to look for a facial tissue to wipe her dampened cheeks. The dark woman admired the very noticeable veins that ran down the young woman's apricot neck. They looked like a tree branch stripped naked by the winter cold. Her veins were the color of blue violets sprayed with drops of green dew, dark like varicose veins. The look of the blood carriers may have seemed grotesque to many but they were uniquely beautiful to Zayashariya. It was almost as if she could see the blood moving through its veins when the girl stood perfectly still. *Beautiful.* Zayashariya's tongue leapt within her mouth. She swallowed hard and imagined how warm the girl's blood must be. Zayashariya wondered if it would be sweet or tangy to the taste.

"What is your name?" Zayashariya asked while trying not to stare too intensely at the woman. She did not want to be thought of as some sort of perverse freak; although, it was probably too late already. Zayashariya forced another smile to her face while tossing her mane with her hand.

"My name is Alvian," the young woman answered, forcing a smile to her face. "And yours?" she asked, unsure if she wanted to know or not.

"My name is Zayashariya." She held out her hand. The girl accepted it and shook it firmly. "Nice to meet you. I hope that one day we could become friends. I am alone here and I have no one to talk to." She took her hand back. "Friends are always needed. Don't you agree?" Zayashariya asked.

"Sure enough." Alvian nodded. She looked at Zayashariya oddly. At a loss for words, another false smile crossed her lips.

"I must go," said Zayashariya, touching the girl's shoulder. "Take care. Everything will be alright. Your company would have been a pleasure under different circumstances. Be safe and I'll be talking to you soon." Zayashariya waved as she turned her voluptuous body towards the stairway and began to climb her way upward. Her long and curly violet hair bounced with every step.

*   *   *

Alvian sat back in her chair and thought about the conversation she had just engaged in with the stranger. Something about Zayashariya sent icy needles down her spine. Alvian began to bite her nails. She was incomprehensibly nervous. Disturbing her nibbling, a visitor walked through the front door of the Inn. Her eyes danced.

"Hi Flum! What brings you here?" she asked, placing her gnawed fingers upon the counter.

"I came to see you!" the skinny humanoid lied. He grinned, revealing his poor hygiene. His discolored teeth looked frightening and his breath wasn't the most pleasant either.

Red hues spread across Alvian's cheeks. She was mysteriously drawn to him and she didn't know why. He wasn't handsome, not even attractive. He had no style, no personality, no talent, and definitely no money. He was simply Flum and she was crazy about him. "You came to see me?" Excitement was in her voice. A smile ripped across her orange and red face. She looked like a ripe peach ready to explode.

"Of course! Why else would I be here?" Flum smiled a devilish smile. "I feel like burning some time. Let's go for a walk through the Inn." He leaned across the counter and extended his hand.

"You have seen the Inn before Flum. Even a couple of rooms." She smirked.

"Come on. It will be fun," he said. "Maybe we could see a couple of those rooms again." Flum held her hand and tickled her palm with his fingers."

"I am working," Alvian said giggling. She playfully snatched her hand away. Her cheeks were redder than ever.

"It is not like many people lodge here, Alvian. You can show me around a little. I just want to see the place. All I wanted to do was spend some time with you," he lied.

"What do you need a tour for? You can stand here and talk to me," she questioned, ignoring the invitation. Her face showed confusion.

"I am just bored. I just wanted to be alone with you." Flum rubbed the back of his neck and looked at her out of the corner of his eye. "Don't worry about it." He waved her away and paced the floor in front of the counter. "Any new guests here?" Flum stopped and stared into her brown eyes.

"Not really. The only new person that has been staying here as of late is Zayashariya."

"Who is Zayashariya?" he asked, drawing closer to the young woman staring deeply into her dreamy chocolate eyes. Flum leaned closer to her, his green and white robe pressing against the counter. He looked like a seasick bumblebee.

"You know, the town's stranger, the pretty woman whose color is as dark as midnight," Alvian stated sarcastically. "The witch from Gehenna as they call her around town." She laughed.

"I have heard about her. Is she scary?" Flum asked curiously. He leaned sideways while observing his surroundings. He could not care one way or another about Alvian's response because after tonight, Zayashariya would be no more. Flum popped his knuckles one by one and continued to look around for a way to get into the Inn without Alvian knowing. He spotted a side door with no lock on it.

"Not really scary, she is just different," Alvian answered, looking at him peculiarly. "She is quite beautiful though. A matter of fact, she is one of the most beautiful people on whom I have ever laid eyes."

"I don't like her!" Flum yelled as he rammed his hand into the side of the counter. Alvian was startled and strangely aroused at the same time. Her eyed stretched wide. Her cheeks flushed. She loved his red-hot temper. Maybe that was her strange attraction to the ragged little piece of a man fuming before her.

"You don't even know her!" Alvian yelled back, surprised by her own outburst. "She is a very nice person. She is just different," she retorted childishly.

"Are you two friends?" Flum asked frankly, staring into her eyes, trying hard to intimidate her. It worked.

"Kinda," Alvian said flatly. She looked down at her hands and back up at him. "Why, does it matter?" She grimaced. "You are too insipid to ever get the chance to know her?" she snapped. "She probably wouldn't want to know you either." Alvian's voice became squeaky and full of emotion. "Sometimes I don't even want to know you! You make me sick with your loud talk and your stupid statements!" Anger flooded through her. Although she liked him, she hated the way he upset her at times. His belittling tone made her want to peel the flesh from his face.

"I don't have to know her!" Flum waved the angry girl off. He wondered if she just insulted him. *What does insipid mean anyway?* He brushed the thought away. "Zayash... whatever her name is, is not one of us. She cannot be trusted. We don't even know what kind of evil she may practice. I heard she walks around stark naked!" His narrow face distorted into a frightening mask.

"She does not! That is stupid! Her skin blends in with her clothes! She is a very nice lady! She is my friend!" Alvian yelled naively. She sounded like a three year old. Flum always made her feel that way, simple minded and immature. He frustrated her to no end.

"Your friend! Ha! I can't believe you!" *Twit*! Flum calmed down.

"Well believe me! Zayashariya is a very nice woman and she was very understanding and comforting to me earlier," she said.

"Okay, whatever you say."

"Thank you." Alvian pouted.

"Where is she staying?" Flum asked, pointing to the stairs. He calmed down a little more. He did not want to scare her more than he had. He realized that his forcefulness had put her on alert and he did not want to keep arousing her suspicions. Flum leaned on the counter. Alvian blushed. "I'm sorry." he apologized. "I'm just having a bad day and I guess I was looking for someone to blame." He touched her cheek and softly pinched her chin. He could not help himself. He pried further, asking, "What floor is she on?" Flum kissed Alvian's lips gently. He could see that she was swooning. "Tell me."

"On the fourth floor. Why?" Alvian got a hold of herself and regained her composure.

"I just wanted to know. Be careful lover. Remember that we still haven't found the beast that killed your mother," he said with faux concern. Flum turned on his heel and exited the Inn. Alvian watched him leave, simply confused about their conversation. She lifted and dropped her shoulders and started gnawing on her nails once more. Never would she understand the complexities of his mind.

Outside, Flum waited impatiently for Bleg and Gradly to show up. He stood next to the Inn tossing pebbles at nearby children making them run to their mother's crying. Tantalizing the children and occasionally even the cursing parents, he laughed defiantly and threw more rocks. Every now and then, he would hit someone more intimidating than himself and would have to hide momentarily to avoid their wrath.

Gradly and Bleg inconspicuously crept up behind Flum.

"Did ya find anythang?" the tobacco chewing Bleg asked as dark liquid oozed out of the corner of his thick lips.

Startled, Flum jumped. He did not hear the two men walk up. Turning to face them, he cleared his throat and spoke.

"She is on the fourth floor," Flum answered, repulsed at the mouth of Bleg. He stared at his pebble-filled hands to avoid looking at the muddy mess dribbling from Bleg's chin like melted chocolate.

"Great!" The old man laughed as the tobacco juice ran down his wrinkled neck. "Let's get prepared to get rid of that abomination to humanoid-kind!" he declared self-righteously.

Gradly smiled and followed like a flunky.

The men trotted side by side down the street. The suns were beginning to set. A pair of violet eyes stared out into the coming night.

Chapter 11

Darkness fell across the land once more, draping the town in peaceful darkness and sparkling starlight. After quick admiration of the night sky's beauty, the town dwellers all entered into their homes around the same hour.

The land of Wilzasp was made of ten family homes. Each home was equal in size and identical in architecture except for one tall home that shadowed the others surrounding it. The largest house was the royal house where the King of Wilzasp and his court resided. All of the houses in Wilzasp contained a full family, including distant cousins and in-laws. Families were very close-knit clans who took care of their own people. Those who did not live in their family homes were banished from them for various reasons like abuse, insubordination, and petty crimes among other things. Because of that reason, the homeless population in Wilzasp was slowly growing.

The entire town was quite small compared to most cities and towns around the galaxy. It sat in the mist of nothingness like a lost village at the end of the world undiscovered by surrounding civilizations.

All ten family homes turned down the glow of their crystals by reciting a few words while holding hands and surrounding their homes. People entered their homes and locked their doors. The town soon fell into a deep slumber. Runaways found shelter under the remaining vender shade-umbrellas still standing. Animals went back to their homes in the nearby forest. Thieves awoke to prowl the night.

A group of homeless humanoids walked together down the street laughing and telling ill-mannered jokes. Dirt and grime decorated their animal skin garments. The men's afros were untidy and dingy and the tangled hair of the women looked like spider webs spun across their heads. Leading them was a witty gentleman named Zasp who walked ahead of his vagabond disciples.

Zasp was a philosopher, a heteroclite man of many words and Bohemian ideas. He was respected in Wilzasp despite his current living arrangements. Born into the royal family, he was banished out of the house because of his irresistible desire for the fruit of the vine (his sweet exotic grape and honey elixir) and not to mention his feral personality when inebriated, which helped in the decision to give him the boot. Zasp could not be contained within prim traditions and pointless formalities. Although Zasp was a polyhistor, he was too uncivilized to represent the royal house according to the queen. He loved life and he believed in spirituality and all things poetic and beautiful. He was declared a fool before all and promptly dismissed from the king's house.

Normally Zasp would sit on a corner and recite before the masses ancient tales of great heroes of old. The people of Wilzasp enjoyed the peddler's wise words and they supported his mead habit by dropping coins into his bowl. As of late, the town's people came to him to hear information on Gehenna. His money bowl was getting quite full daily. He was happy that the stranger came into town. It made his life a little easier.

Zasp walked down the street sipping on a jar of mead, stepping lightly with a satisfied smile on his face. His voice was slightly slurred as he spoke to his followers.

"Let us go near the forest and sleep tonight. The stars are beautiful and the trees are fragrant. The wind blows warm and I want to feel the softness of flowers caress my skin. There, I will entertain you with an in-depth narrative about a vile place called Gehenna," Zasp spoke in a very articulate voice. His muscular yet aged body was being displayed thanks to the furry loincloth that he wore. His bare feet were covered with soil and his afro carried many parasites. Without hesitation, they followed Zasp, full of curiosity and fear. The leader of the homeless led his people to an opening in the forest where they all relaxed and communicated freely.

The opening Zasp led them to was a large patch of low bright green grass as soft as pillows. The homeless circled Zasp and relaxed at the sound of his soothing voice. He spoke of the great galaxy wars and distant races. He told them about Lucifer, the master of evil and about the diabolical Queen of Night. He spoke of the history of Gehenna and the evil that resided there. He explained to the people the danger that Zayashariya imposed upon them and the possibility of what she said about her origins being true. Fantastic embellishments and imaginary battles filled in the gaps in history he could not remember. The people marveled at his every word. Their fear of the town stranger grew greater everyday thanks to Zasp and his half-truths and part lies.

The night grew longer and the homeless fell asleep one by one under the moonlight. The night was quiet. Tranquility floated through the air.

Out of the forest stepped a coal colored beast. It had the body of a great bear but the face of a bear coalesced with a face of a beautiful woman. Its fierce eyes spied the resting vagabonds and moved in for the kill. It moved with a silence so eerie that the very atmosphere could not detect its presence. It glided over to a sleeping woman. Her body was resting in the fetal position, her chest rising and falling in a steady rhythm. With razor nail paws, the beast seized her, the first victim it saw, and drained the blood from the woman's body before a scream could escape her mouth. All that the woman witnessed was the violet eyes of the beast and then unwillingly received her invitation to the land of the dead. The beast moved to the next victim repeating the same loathsome task. It drained every humanoid there with its mighty fangs one by one. No one knew the beast was coming. No one awoke until it was too late. No mercy was shown. The monster moved with death's silent wrath, quenching its thirst for crimson life, until it was satisfied. It wiped the scarlet mess from its mouth and disappeared into the forest. The great historian and his followers were no more. All that was left behind was bloody clothes covering piles of unidentifiable depleted flesh.

Chapter 12

Zayashariya entered the Inn. Her eyes were heavy with fatigue. She inadvertently ignored Alvian's greeting and headed straight toward the staircase. The stranger climbed the stairs and shuffled down the hallway until she came to her room and placed her hand on her cube shaped knob. To her amazement, her door was ajar. She pushed open the iron door and stepped inside of the chamber. She searched the invaded room with her eyes. She saw nothing. Taking a deep breath, she dropped her shoulders, yawned, and began to relax. *Maybe I just forgot to close the door,* Zayashariya thought to herself. Walking over to the mahogany shelf, she took off her cloak, quickly folding it, and placing it upon the shelf. A shadow moved behind her. She spun around just in time to feel the butt of Bleg's ax hit her shoulder. The dark stranger fell to the ground, grabbing her bleeding shoulder. Red was everywhere, like a can of crimson paint was dropped and splashed across her skin. Zayashariya stared at her blood-covered fingers, wincing in pain. She looked into the orange face of the intruder and hissed like a serpent full of wrath. Purple lightning jolted through her eyes. Then, suddenly she was calm. Penetrating him with her eyes, she lit a wild fire of fear in his heart. Pressing hard on her wounded shoulder, the blood flow was slowed. Her skin began to bond like an invisible zipper zipping her skin slowly, closing it without mar. The blood on her hand and on her shoulder evaporated into steam and faded into nothingness.

"Hey there girlie! Remember me?" the old man grimaced trying to ignore her impending eyes and the miraculous healing he had witnessed seconds before. He wore a black hooded cloak shading his wrinkled face. He waved his hand in the air, beckoning, not removing his eyes from the female on the ground raping him with her eyes. Two other men came out of hiding and surrounded

Zayashariya. Flum held his sword ready for battle and Gradly pointed his spear at the back of her neck. Both men were wearing dark hooded cloaks, resembling mad monks.

"Why are you here strumpet?" Flum yelled. He pointed his weapon near her emotionless face. His voice tottered. He could see the wound on her shoulder had completely disappeared. "Answer me!" Flum screamed louder, trying hard to regain his courage. She said nothing. Her eyes flashed. His sword pricked her cheek. A moment later, the wound was gone.

"Answer me harlot! Why are you here?" Flum yelled nervously once more. *She healed!* Fear grabbed hold to his neck like a bear's jaw. *What matter of being are you?* He wondered to himself. He put his sword to her neck, pricking her skin. His hood fell backwards exposing his timorous face.

Her violet eyes glowed with fury. She fell backwards with a loud thump, like a dead tree falling in the forest, startling the three men and causing them to jump backwards. Zayashariya laid flat on her back and began to chant. The vague words fell from her lips like curses. Slowly her body transformed from solid to liquid, like wax being melted by an invisible flame. Zayashariya's body melted onto the floor. The men looked at one another in horrific amazement, completely dumbfounded at the spectacle before their eyes. They stepped back from the spreading puddle, too curious to leave, too scared to stay.

The liquid was inky, black, and syrupy thick. It started to bubble like steaming hot tar in a deep pit, like blistering lava in the mouth of a volcano. The dark liquid then evaporated into a dark mist twisting and twirling into tornado like spirals. The mist then clumped together in a dark cloud and took form. Out of the mist a violet-eyed dragon appeared. Silver claws protruded from its hands and feet like glistening steal talons. Green mist exited from its nostrils circling its vicious violet eyes and fading into the air. Eight razor sharp fangs hung from the dragon's mouth as a serpent's tongue licked the fangs until they glistened in the pale scarlet glow of the room. The beast's tale was decorated with silver spikes at its very end, forming an arrow at the end of the tail, a sterling silver sharp point. Two bull's horns came from each side of the dragon's head like two great lances pointed and ready for joust. A pair of foot long wings fluttered upon its back, buzzing and generating a chilling wind.

The beast slivered toward Gradly. Its body moved like a coiling snake with the swiftness of a stallion. The old man fell to the floor sobbing like a child as his friends fought each other to get out of the room. The dragon grabbed Gradly around the neck with its honed claws and opened its enormous mouth. Out of the beast's mammoth mouth came Zayashariya's head. Steaming drool dampened her hair and slicked it close to her head like a child's head emerging from the womb. The woman blew purple flames out of her mouth scorching his orange face, almost melting it to his skull. He wailed, hands flapping about like a drunken bird. Steam rose from his scorched flesh. The monster pulled him to her, face to face. Gradly's heart stopped when she installed her fangs and drained the paralyzed man of all blood. The beast wrapped its tail around cowardly Bleg's body and grabbed terrified Flum with one of its claws. Sweat poured heavily from their faces as their urine soiled the floor. The beast drained Flum, threw his puny body to the floor and drained Bleg. Two dark hands reached out of the mouth of the dragon, peeling away its serpent face like a rubber mask. The scaly body folded away effortlessly. Zayashariya climbed out of the beast's mouth. Her body was damp with steamy saliva and clear goo. The heavy flesh of the dragon fell to the ground and melted into the oily tar-like elixir that it first emerged from. The woman got on all fours and licked the inky liquid off of the floor. She grew lethargic from the humongous feast and fell backwards on her behind. Zayashariya was drunk with fatigue, head spinning and stomach churning in agony. Lying limply against the wall, she soon gathered her strength and arose. The shape shifter gathered the bodies one by one and tossed them out of the chamber window. She looked out at the pale twisted corpses and shook her head. The warm outside air-dried the remaining slime from her body and hair. Zayashariya looked clean and fresh. She closed the curtains and sat upon the scarlet bed. She had given herself away. Anger, pain, and hunger had clouded her logic and she knew that there would be severe consequences for her actions.

"Why didn't I destroy the bodies?" she asked herself. She had been swept up in the moment. All logic and common sense had fled from her. Zayashariya did not know what to do next nor did she care, so she slept. The bodies would not be discovered until morning. She would worry about it then and only then.

Chapter 13

Broken shadows. Darkness. Gray movement. Darkness. Sarai tried to open her eyes wider but dried blood caked her face and the close fit of the metal torture mask she wore prevented her from seeing clearly. *Where am I?* She lay upon the floor half-conscious and damp with blood. A slow throbbing dominated her body, forcing her to lay still. Any movement she made caused pain to run rampant through her battered body. *Where am I?* Sarai questioned herself. *What happened?* Faint memories crept upon her like a teasing phantom, revealing itself then hiding, taunting her yearning for recollection. Everything was a distant blur. Then, broken scenes materialized in her mind like magnetic puzzle pieces clinging together one by one to form a horrid picture. Sarai remembered sitting in her bedroom when a tall pale-skinned man burst into her door. She recognized him as one of the queen's subordinates. It all happened so fast; Lilith's personal servant questioning her, a small thump on the back of the head, being brutally whipped, the excruciating mask being put upon her head, and now, waking up in fuzzy darkness. Sarai could feel the rusty metal of the torture mask cutting into the skin of her face, her temples pressed with an unbearable amount of pressure. Sharp iron teeth dug into her lips and the bothersome heaviness of the mask made her neck ache. A sudden noise nearby alarmed her. Sarai locked away the pain and concentrated on the sound. *Footsteps!* Once again, pain quaked through her very soul but she was too hurt to bother with fear. Nothing worse could possibly be done to her. She wished for death. She prayed for it, the first prayer she ever uttered in her life, but death did not come. Selfish life would not let go of her, its grip was too painful and suffocating.

"Stand up!" Legatro ordered the pulverized woman. "Sarai, the master calls for you."

Sarai rolled unto her stomach. *Pain. So much pain.* Placing the palms of her hands to the grainy floor, she attempted to push up but her old arms gave out before she could lift herself.

"Old woman, please get up! The master ordered me to bring you before her throne within five minutes. If you can not stand, I can not carry you and we both will perish under the master's wrath," Legatro begged, its skinny frame quaking like it was having a tiny seizure. Its yellow skin gave it a diseased appearance. "Please Sarai, must we both die? The master's tortures are cruel and seemingly endless. I do not want to suffer and you can not want to suffer more."

Sarai reached her bloodied brown hand up and Legatro grabbed it. The creature was much too weak to pull the old woman up. It fell to its knees at the head of Sarai.

"Three minutes and death will become us!" Legatro wept, his boney knees scratched by the concrete floor.

With loathsome pity and grim determination, Sarai pulled her upper body up and balanced on her knees. The weight of the torture mask set her off kilter but she quickly regained her balance by placing her hands on the wall. Finally, after two failed attempts to get up, she stumbled over to Legatro who was now standing by the entrance way anxious and hysterical.

"I need for you to support me. I cannot walk alone." Sarai dropped her arm around Legatro's puny shoulder.

"I am much too weak," the frail creature complained slouching under the weight of the old woman's battered body. Sarai's bloody brown arm smudged Legatro's pale yellow skin, leaving a filthy mark like an extra ripe spot on a banana.

"Then we both will die!" The old woman threatened to lift her arm and let her whole body fall to the ground.

"No! No! I'll support you," whined Legatro, holding Sarai's arm as tight as it could. They both limped down the long winding hallway until they reached the entrance to Queen Lilith's throne room. The two servants looked into one another's eyes and paused giving one another a silent goodbye. Sarai knew that she had reached her end. Legatro knew too. They stepped forward into the room. Immediately fingers reached through the floor, grabbing blindly at Sarai's and Legatro's feet. They kept on walking until they were at least six feet away from the back of Lilith's throne. Legatro removed Sarai's arm from his shoulder and the old woman dropped to the floor like a dead woman. The clanking sound of the torture mask hitting the metal cage floor scrambled Sarai's brain, leaving her momentarily discombobulated and startling Legatro.

Slowly the massive throne spun around, casting an imposing shadow on the wall. Queen Lilith sat upon the grimy chair, grimacing, her hair ablaze and her eyes crazed.

"Are you ready to tell me where my daughter went, Sarai?" said the Queen of Night. The sound of Lilith's voice was like thunder. It echoed through Sarai's mask, sending sharp pains through her skull.

Sarai lay on the floor quietly.

"Are you seeking death old woman?" Lilith croaked. "Alas, you will find him soon. Soon, so very soon."

Sarai lay silent, unaffected, still.

"Are you willing to be torn to shreds in order to protect Zayashariya? Do you think that she would do the same for you?" Lilith belched. "Never! You are nothing more than a damned slave; a worthless hunk of flesh waiting for me to grant you merciful death," Lilith laughed, annoyed by the old woman's lack of response and loyalty to Zayashariya.

"My fate is sealed. Zayashariya was unable to help me from the first moment my soul was banished to perdition. So it does not matter if she would do the same for me or not. I am willing to die to assure Zayashariya's freedom. I rather be chewed alive by lions than betray her to you!" Sarai's wretched voice floated through the helmet in a quiet whisper. Her body was so still that it seemed lifeless.

The motionlessness of her chest appeared to draw no breath. Her limbs were completely limp. Only her voice was proof of life.

"Your choice has been made. Death welcomes you!" Lilith hissed. Out of her fingers shot blue flames that engulfed Sarai, causing a bright conflagration. Her body turned instantly to ash and fell through the gated floor.

"Are you still here?" asked Lilith, directing her attention to Legatro's horrified face. Its dotted eyes were wide and its slit for a mouth bent downward.

"No master!" it screamed and fled from the room.

Lilith watched the yellow creature flee. She sat upon her throne, her eyes narrow and her hands trembling with anger. "I will find you dear daughter. I'll search forever. No rock will be left unturned!" Lilith yelled, her voice echoing off of the walls and through the floor prison below her, causing great wailing and gnashing of teeth.

Chapter 14

The twin suns peeked through the clouds as they reclaimed their position in the heavens. New and full of promise, the day was as beautiful as the last. Warm vapors carrying the aroma of food permeated the air in all directions. The city streets became alive again with the sound of the town's people working, buying, and going on with their daily routines. It was a warm and sunny day. The clouds looked like pale green cotton balls floating across the powder blue sky. A group of seven teenagers, four boys and three girls, walked together down the busy street on their lunch break from the Academy.

The Academy was the learning center for children and young adults. A small green building connected to the royal estate. It was a place where the town's people educated their young in all things from tying shoes to technology. Well equipped and academically advanced, it was a coed institution where children actually enjoyed going.

The teens fanned the heat of the twin suns from their soft faces as they engaged in friendly conversation.

Umon, the tallest boy among the group, led the group toward the Inn.

"Come on, I say we have some real fun!" Umon yelled to his cronies with his afro bouncing with every step. He walked backwards so he could face his young companions, looking back frequently to ensure that he would not fall. He was too cool to embarrass himself in front of his friends. His reputation was too important. A very shapely girl put her arm around Umon's waist and squeezed.

"Why, do ya wanna go to da Inn?" she asked, smiling coyly while flirting with her big brown eyes. She pulled him a little closer and winked. Licking her lips and smiling again, she rubbed her body against his.

"Akza, go jump into a lake and cool yourself!" Shamblin, a skinny homely looking humanoid yelled from behind the flirting young woman. "Why are you all over him like that in the street?" Shamblin rolled her yellow eyes. "I hope your parents catch you!" she spat hatefully.

"Shut up Shamblin! You are just jealous!" Akza, the curvy girl, yelled and then turned around and purred in Umon's ear. He laughed and shook his head at her forward advances. He knew that she only wanted to anger Shamblin. Akza kissed Umon's ear lobe and watched as tiny chill bumps traveled down his neck. She fondled his chest and annoyed Shamblin further. "You like that?" she asked as seductively as she could. He laughed and playfully pushed her away.

"Jealous of what?" Shamblin frowned. "What do you have to be jealous of?" A crooked frown disfigured her face.

"Of me, you scrawny little weasel." Akza turned and jumped into Shamblin's face. "You make me sick. You... " Akza was cut off by Broka, the peacemaker of the group.

"Shut up you guys!" Broka yelled as she pushed her friends away from each other's faces. They were almost close to blows. "Let's not have this today, okay?"

"Yeah calm down ladies. No need to fight over me," Umon laughed.

"Whatever!" snapped Shamblin, rolling her eyes. "I would never fight over someone like you! Anyone attracted to a person like Akza, doesn't deserve to tie my shoe!"

"Shut-up egghead!" Akza pointed her finger in Shamblin's face. Shamblin knocked it away. Akza giggled and turned her attention to Umon. "Come over here and give me sugar," she said smirking with slight embarrassment and winking at Shamblin. Umon put his arms around Akza and gave her a quick peck.

Shamblin spat on the ground and pushed past the two.

"Hater!" Akza yelled at Shamblin. "Envy is such an ugly thing."

"Whore!" Shamblin shrieked.

Akza's mouth shriveled up. A look of genuine hurt crept across her face. She looked like a wounded animal. Xack elbowed Umon and he pulled Akza away from Shamblin's face, which was twisted in a victorious grin.

"Let's move on." Delvinex pushed through the crowd. "Follow me," he instructed with a look of annoyance written across his face. "You two do this almost everyday."

After a quarter of an hour, the teens eventually made their way to the Inn. Umon grabbed Akza's hand and headed to the back of the building. The others were oblivious to their disappearance and continued to walk on. The young couple skipped around the corner and found a nearby wall to smooch on.

Umon kissed Akza's neck softly. Her face showed a hint of sadness.

"What's wrong?" he asked.

"Can you believe what that witch called me?" she replied.

"Pay no mind to Shamblin. You know she envies you."

"But she called me a whore." Akza's eyes dropped.

Umon lifted her chin, locked eyes with her, and said, "You are a beautiful and honorable girl. You are the kind of girl that all men want to marry. You are sexy and smart and confident." He smiled at her. "Don't let Shamblin get to you okay."

"Okay," Akza blushed.

"Now, would I do this to you if you were a dirty woman?" He kissed her lips gently. "I love you," he whispered in her ear. "I love everything about you."

Umon held Akza's arms up against the wall and kissed her wildly. Her lips met his with equal passion. The young couple explored one another's body with their hands, gripping with hungry fingers. His thick lips pressed against her smooth neck. Her hands held the back of his head and the couple began to drop to the ground slowly, her back feeling the friction between Umon and the wall. Akza's right hand felt the hardness of the concrete, then her buttocks, and then her left hand brushed up against something hard and slimy. The girl stole her lips away from Umon and looked into the eyes of the dead man lying next to her. An ear tearing scream escaped her mouth and she jumped up from the ground. Umon looked, saw three dead bodies, and let out an awful scream himself. Both teens held one another tight until the rest of the gang ran around the corner and witnessed the sight of the gruesome corpses lying on the road behind the Inn.

"Who or what could have done that?" Delvinex marveled as he grabbed the shoulder of Kommon. Delvinex was sick to his stomach. He looked away from the deteriorating corpses and felt his head whirl and his stomach twirl. Vomit poured from his mouth in a torrent of multi-colored liquid.

"I don't know," Kommon answered. "But who or what ever killed them seemed to drain them from the inside out." Kommon put his hand over his mouth to keep from vomiting himself. "Look how shriveled up they look."

Akza ran to get the attention of a guard nearby. "Sir!" she yelled. The guard spun around.

"What's wrong?"

"Behind the Inn!" Akza sputtered hysterically. "There!" She pointed.

"Calm down and tell me what's wrong," he said, grabbing the girl's shoulder but she pulled away like he had the plague.

"Dead…men…dead," the words fell from her mouth in clumsy syllables. She cried. Emotion imploded within her causing her body to quake in fear and despair. "Just come!" Akza grabbed his arm and pulled him toward the Inn. The shaken teenager brought the guard to the scene. "Over there!" She pointed.

The guard walked in the direction of the girl's trembling finger.

"What in the name of the king has happened here?" the guard asked, astonished at the appearance of the corpse. He took a deep breath and turned toward one of the young men, his eyes questioning, fear and queasiness filling his body like water fills an empty vessel.

"We don't know," answered Xack. "We just saw them here." Nervousness flooded him. He bit his bottom lip and shuffled his feet from side to side. His eyes filled slowly with tears. One trickled over the rim of his eye and made a slow trail down his cheek. He brushed it away quickly, feeling like too much of a man to cry.

The guard put his hand on the boy's shoulder and said, "It's okay. I'll handle things from this point on."

Xack stepped backwards and stood closer to his friends. The kids huddled together and stared hopelessly at the crinkled dead bodies. The soldier used his pocket alert device to call for his men by pushing two crystals together to create a loud pulsating noise. The teens held their ears until the sound stopped. Out of nowhere, at least a half a dozen soldiers came running to the back of the Inn.

Alvian saw the soldiers through the window, from the inside of the Inn, and decided to go and see what all of the commotion was about. She jogged out of the Inn, searching the scene with her eyes. *What could be going on?* Alvian turned the corner and saw a shriveled up man lying on the ground. She identified him as Flum, by the clothing visible beneath his cloak. Next to him, she saw two other men lying on the ground, in a shriveled pile, robbed of life.

"Oh my! Flum!" Alvian cried. "Who did this to them!?" she yelled, her eyes stretched wide and insane with emotion. "Answer me! Who did this?" Alvian screamed into the guard's face, sprinkling his cheek with spit. Her fists were balled tight and her chest heaving. The guards were speechless. Xack left his cronies and put his arms around her. She fell into his chest, slapping her hands against his head and neck. Aching sobs blubbered from her mouth as she yielded to his welcoming arms and wept.

The soldiers searched the scene for clues. One of the soldiers looked up and noticed a piece of torn cloth hanging from the windowpane above. The cloth was dark like the cloaks that the men were wearing.

"Who stays there?" asked the guard, pointing upward at the window.

"Zayashariya," Alvian answered with clenched teeth. Her eyes burned red.

"Who?" he questioned. That name did not sound familiar to him.

"The town's stranger!?" Alvian yelled with her voice trembling with rage. "Flum was right!" She paused. "That evil creature does not belong here! She did this! She killed the man I loved! This is also how my mother was found!" yelled Alvian. "I have to get rid of that demon! Zayashariya has taken two lives from me and now she will pay with her own!" Pulling a sharp dagger from her belt, Alvian stormed away from the gathering crowd. The crowd instantly followed after her like angry villagers carrying torches and pitch forks. The group of humanoids rushed into the Inn behind the reasonless young woman and up the steps with their weapons drawn. Alvian pulled a blade out of her pocket and placed it between her teeth so she could open the door. She took the key off of her finger and unlocked the door to Zayashariya's room. Alvian stormed into the room with both hands armed and waved for the others to follow. Everyone entered. The giant iron door slammed behind them. Darkness. A loud hissing noise put the avengers on alert. They looked around the room and saw nothing. "Where is she?" Alvian belted.

"We'll find her!" another assured as he searched the room. As they rambled and raged, an enormous transparent serpent was surrounding them. One of the soldiers walked over to the bed and kneeled to look underneath it. Out from under the bed sprang the giant head of the serpent. Fire came from the snake's mouth and set the soldier aflame. The burning man fell on his back screaming and flinging his arms. When he hit the ground, he was reduced to nothing more than a silver pile of ash. The serpent morphed into an opaque being. Now its terrifying form could be clearly seen by all. The others attempted to kill the snake by stabbing at its back but its and purple iron-hard scales were impregnable. The monster surrounded all of the intruders and squeezed them within its coils until they all were unconscious. The snake loosed its grasp on the humanoids and plopped to the ground, expired. Out of the mouth of the serpent emerged Zayashariya. She pushed back the slimy flesh of the snake. It fell to the floor in a rubbery heap. Her hands contorted in a claw-like sign language as she weaved a spell with the uttering of her mouth. All remnants of the serpent disappeared.

Zayashariya installed her fangs into each humanoid neck one by one until her monstrous appetite was satisfied. The dark stranger gathered the bodies into a pile in the center of the floor and made certain that all of their belongings were with them. She went to her shelf and retrieved out of her hip pouch a glass jar filled with dark liquid. Zayashariya chanted a few mantic words and sprinkled the liquid on the dead bodies. The bodies immediately ignited and turned into ashes within seconds. The she-demon gathered the ashes by chanting more obscure words and a small tornado appeared and placed the ashes into the dark vessel which she held in her hand. She placed the vessel on the shelf, careful not to spill its contents.

Zayashariya lay upon her bed exhausted. Her heart sang a threnody. She did not expect or want her stay in Wilzasp to turn into a killing frenzy. Zayashariya only wanted to feed discreetly and nourish herself for a short time. Death was pertinent to her survival but she never enjoyed killing senselessly. These people forced her to slaughter them. Zayashariya morphed into abominable creatures as a mechanism to petrify opponents or to hide her identity; but, these humanoids didn't have sense enough to flee from sure damnation. She prayed that she would not be forced into such a position again. She prayed hard although she knew in her heart that a demon creature like herself had little chance of gaining pity from The Most High. Zayashariya knew that God was the creator of all, the good as well as the evil, and all are humbled to Him. Maybe she could be reborn one day into an angelic creature and be forgiven for being the child of Lilith. After all, who can help who they were born to? She did not create the hunger that thrived within her. Did she? Zayashariya closed her eyes and old painful memories came to her.

*   *   *

"Zayashariya," Lilith called out. "Zayashariya, come to mommy." the queen said as she sat upon a round bed in the middle of a large chamber. The room was nearly bare. Only a bed, a full body mirror, and two doors that led to closets were inside.

"Zayashariya, come here," Lilith called out again. Her flame of hair extinguished itself and laid down upon her shoulders in a wave of dreadlocks upon seeing her daughter standing in the doorway of the room. Lilith wore a long white gauze dress with gold trim. The white cloth against her scarlet skin glowed in the pale light. Her gold earrings were large diamond hoops. She looked radiant.

"Yes mommy," the young Zayashariya answered her mother. She skipped into the room wearing a pale yellow sleeveless dress, spotted with drops of blood, and matching sandals. She sat upon the bed next to her mother.

"You are so beautiful." Lilith ran her fingers through her daughter's hair. "You look almost angelic when you dress so softly." Lilith's face was pained.

"Thank you mom," said Zayashariya smiling. "What do you need?" She took her mother's hand from her hair and held it between her hands. "What is so important that you would pull me away from my daily duties? I was doing as you instructed me to do, whipping a couple of disobedient slaves. You called me right in the middle of inflicting my favorite form of torture, pouring salt into the wounds. I was just beginning to enjoy myself." She grinned an iniquitous grin.

"Very good. I see that you gotten over being squeamish," said Lilith. "There will be plenty of time for torture my dear. You are immortal. We have an eternity to inflict pain on others. I am very happy that you find joy in such things. It makes the gift I am about to present to you all the more wonderful." Lilith stood up and held her hand out for Zayashariya to take. Zayashariya took her mother's hand and stood beside her. Lilith led Zayashariya to the closet nearest to them. The Queen of Night opened the door and walked inside of the closet. Zayashariya stood outside of the door curiously watching her mother take a dark glass flask from a safe and exit the closet.

"What is that mommy?" she asked and pointed to the mysterious bottle.

"Sit," Lilith commanded. Zayashariya obeyed. "Become as I am. Partake of the cup I chose to sip of. You must exercise your free will and summon your dark powers from within. In this bottle is undeniable power. It will make you a force so powerful; the Council of Demons will need you in order to gain full power."

"I do not understand," said Zayashariya, sitting on the edge of the bed confused.

"Do you want to possess all the power of Night and more?" asked Lilith.

"Yes," Zayashariya answered.

"Do you want supreme darkness to rule your heart?"

"Yes," Zayashariya answered nervously.

"Drink my daughter. Drink," Lilith demanded, handing her daughter the flask.

Zayashariya took the flask and sipped the bitter fluid within it. Dark red liquid ran down the side of her mouth as she took the last swallow. She wiped her frowning lips. The taste was wretched.

"Here." She handed the bottle to her mother. "What was in that bottle? I don't feel so good. Help..." A deep pain in her belly ripped the words out of her mouth. "What have you done to me?!" she screamed and fell to the floor writhing in agony. "Mommy help!" she cried as she rolled on the floor screaming and coughing. "Mommy!"

Lilith stood back and watched her daughter squirm and thrash about.

"Mommy!" Zayashariya reached for her mother. Lilith watched in amusement, refusing to lend a hand, knocking her daughter's arms away.

"The pain my child, be baptized in the pain," Lilith whispered.

"Help," screamed Zayashariya, choking on her tears. Pink foam filled her mouth. "What have I done to deserve this?" she cried out. "Mommy please take this pain away."

"Ha ha ha ha ha," Lilith laughed. Her voice hissed and croaked. "No, my dear. You must endure it. Accept it and you will be free."

Zayashariya's body fell motionless. Her eyes locked with her mother's. The dark princess sat up, not blinking or removing her eyes from her mother's. She levitated off of the ground to her feet in a featherweight movement. She grabbed the back of her mother's head. Zayashariya opened her mouth. Her top and bottom incisors grew an inch, as if her jawbone pushed them out by the root. She sank her teeth into her mother's neck. The queen laughed as her blood gushed into her daughter's mouth in ruby red splashes.

"Feed the hunger!" Lilith squealed. "Feed upon damnation! Darkness will forever rule your soul!" The queen laughed as they both fell to the floor locked in a bloody twist of passion and fury.

*   *   *

Zayashariya walked down the hall to the washroom and relaxed herself in a hot bath. *I hate you mother. I truly hate you! You did this to me!*

Chapter 15

Outside the great meeting room where the Council of Demons gathered, Queen Lilith of Night paced back and forth in front of the door wearing a wan look on her face. Her scarlet skin paled to a dull red and her flame of hair gave away to baldness.

Zayashariya was still missing and Lilith was unable to force Sarai to confess any knowledge she may have had regarding Zayashariya. Meanwhile, Lilith, promising a gigantic reward of an eternity of privileged living and the power to pound as many slaves into submission as desired, had dispatched numerous search teams but they all came back empty handed. Everyone one on the planet was supposedly ignorant of Zayashariya's whereabouts. It was as if she just vanished like a sneeze in the wind. Furthermore, Lilith had no leads, no clues, nothing. No one knew anything and now she had to go before the Council of Demons and explain her daughter's mysterious absence. Lilith imagined seeing the demons, who sat waiting on the opposite side of the door, sitting around the table, chuffed looks in their eyes, basking in her failures, and blaming her for Zayashariya's perfidy. Lilith needed a bromide. Maybe if she was sedated, everything would seem a little less nightmarish. Lilith malingered around for days but now she had to face the Council and be brutally whipped by their boorish tongues. Worst of all, if she failed to locate Zayashariya in a timely manner, Lilith would have to answer to Lucifer, the master of them all, and may be banished from Night forever. That is the least he would do if he was merciful.

The massive door before Lilith swung open. A pointy headed creature stepped from the meeting room and cautiously approached her. "The Council is waiting for you, your majesty," the lurching creature said in a baritone voice.

"They grow very impatient," said the creature, staring at Lilith's feet, afraid to lift his eyes above her knees.

"Let them wait!" Lilith snapped. "They are on my time. I am not on theirs!"

"I will relay the message," he said as he turned the doorknob.

"No!" Lilith knocked his hand a way. "I will go in now."

Lilith pushed the creature to the floor and opened the door. The creature writhed down the hall whimpering, whining, and crawling like a wounded dog, its pointy head leaning to the side as if his neck was broken.

Lilith sashayed into the meeting room, her hips rolling and false confidence exuding from her. "I am here." She plopped down into her chair and tossed one of her legs on the tabletop.

"Save the performance for the simpering idiots you control. We only want to know where Zayashariya is." Asmodeus' voice echoed through the chamber. "I grow weary of your excuses. I want to know only the facts," he said. His mammoth hands laid flat upon the table. They were at least a foot and a half long as well as wide. Asmodeus' prognathic mouth looked like he was attempting to eat his own face every time he spoke. "Do you know where your daughter is?"

"Progress is being made. I assure you. The servant Sarai gave me some very useful information," Lilith lied. "I also have a team of superior hunters searching for her at the moment. Zayashariya will turn up in a matter of days, maybe even hours." Lilith smirked.

"Codswallop!" Abaddon's ghastly form sparkled in the candlelight. "You know nothing. Your brow is heavy with perspiration and you have been fidgeting ever since you got here. I am no fool. I know that you are an incompetent ruler. Now you have sabotaged this council by driving Zayashariya away with your excerebrose thuggary!"

His transparent body waved as if wind was blowing through him.

"Zayashariya will be located," the angry words bubbled from Lilith's mouth. Her fist tightened. The thought of beheading the translucent demon danced around her mind. Her eyes spied a glistening falchion hanging against the wall on the far side of the room. Lilith smiled but stayed her hand because she did not dare arouse Abaddon's wrath. He was much too powerful for Lilith to enlist in a battle that she may not win.

"She better be found soon!" Abaddon threatened. He stood up. "This meeting is over with as far as I am concerned." He vanished from the room in a wisp of slowly fading clouds.

"Your day is coming Lilith. Bide your time," Rehab whispered into the queen's ear. "I desire your fall more than all." He kissed her cheek, leaving a clammy wet chill on her face. He walked out of the room and all of the other demon's vacated the chamber one by one until Lilith was left alone, sitting at the black round table holding her head in her hands.

"Damn you Zayashariya. You will be found and I know just the cur to find you." Lilith leaned back against the soft cushion of the chair and clapped her cherry hands three times. A tall blue girl with darker blue hair appeared. Two tiny wings were on her wrists and ankles, fluttering nonstop, generating a light wind.

"Yes." The girl bowed, her hair being blown upward by the wings on her wrist.

"Get prepared quickly. Deliver a message for me," Lilith commanded.

"Yes ma'am." The girl pulled a black scroll from her pocket and a feather pen. "What is the message master?"

"Write down what I say verbatim. The message is as follows:

My dear honorable Judas,

You owe me. I have a job for you. Find out where Zayashariya is and who her cohorts are. Report to my castle as soon as possible. I will be expecting you within a couple of days. Do not make me send escorts for you. You will receive your payment upon arrival," Lilith dictated.

"Give me the pen, let me sign my name." Lilith signed the paper and handed the scroll back to the girl.

"I will deliver it immediately my queen," said the girl bowing, turning and vanishing from the room so swiftly that nothing was left of her presence but the cool breeze that blew across Lilith.

"Judas is the best at finding out information. He is the king of befriending, gaining confidence, and betraying. Why did I not think of him sooner?" Lilith grinned. "Zayashariya will turn up and she will turn up soon. I can't wait. She will suffer long and hard. Pain will become her lover and horror her best friend," Lilith cooed. "After the Council of Demons is complete, all of the Nether Worlds and every little heinous creature that dwells within this abominable place will compose doxologies to me!" Lilith laughed. "Judas, my precious Judas, why did I not think of you before?"

Chapter 16

Since the day Zayashariya arrived in Wilzasp, forty people had perished or disappeared. Wilzasp was on alert. Every family had suffered a loss. Every person feared for their lives. No one knew for sure who or what was killing their love ones, but everyone suspected Zayashariya.

The King of Wilzasp called a town meeting. All of the citizens of Wilzasp and Zayashariya gathered together in the middle of the city. Chairs sat in front of the Inn facing a wooden rostrum where the king sat with his family. The middle-aged humanoid king stood up and began to pace the stage, with arms folded behind his back, staring at the wooden platform beneath him. His peach afro was cut close to his head. His chubby cheeks were graced with a deep dimple on each side, accented by kind black eyes reflecting the light of the twin suns. They looked like onyx reflecting fire. The king wore a small crown made of emeralds and rubies which sat upon his head like a tiara. His long flowing green robe clashed with the color of his bright orange skin. He scratched the top of his head and opened his mouth, letting out a deep breath then stopped pacing. Wilzasp's king looked deep into the crowd and took another breath. He smiled a troubled smile.

"My heart cries out in mourning; mourning of people well known and loved. I am torn asunder with grief and terror. Fear shakes me. A plague as fallen upon our humble town and no one is exempt from its wrath," said King Chucklarki pausing. "People we are in danger. A devil walks among us and we know not who it is," the king continued. He looked into Zayashariya's violet eyes. "There has been peace in our land for so long and now the reign of pure bliss has come to a halt. No one knows the source of the evil but we know that evil resides in our fair town and we know we have to stomp the very life out of that evil as soon as possible. All I can recommend for us to do is to protect ourselves. Go nowhere unarmed. Go nowhere alone. Kill anything that threatens your life." He turned his gaze away from Zayashariya to the crowd, spontaneously darting from face to face. "I will provide every woman, man, and child with weapons. My guards will train you all to defend yourselves properly. My family and I will be trained also." The king cleared his throat. He looked back at Zayashariya. "Dark one," he said waving his hand. "Come to me." He insincerely grinned.

Zayashariya got up from her seat and walked toward the stage. Her violet hair blanketed her head like a great lion's mane. It was the only flash of color, besides her eyes and lips, noticeable on her body since she was dressed in a raven leather body suit which blended perfectly with her skin. Whispers from the audience filled the air like the buzz of a giant beehive.

"Do you have any knowledge of who is murdering my people?" he asked trying to sound as indiscriminate as possible. "I am sure that you are aware of the fact that these murders started occurring when you arrived here. Please do not take offense to my inquiries. I must ask you these things because the town's suspicions of you have been on a rise. By no means are you being accused. I would like to make that fact clear. But I must admit the entire situation is rather ironic. Wouldn't you agree?"

Zayashariya looked directly into his kind eyes with a simper. *Stupid weakling*, she thought. She shook her head softly. "Why do you ask me?" Her face was hard. "Should I know? Am I not in danger like the rest of you?"

The king was shocked by her bold questioning. He opened his mouth. Nothing came out. Then he said angrily, "Lady, I..." She cut him off by raising her palm to his face. His eyes went wide.

"Do you accuse me?" she asked blatantly.

"No, I do not!" the king spoke between his teeth, embarrassed by her immodest behavior. "I only know that my people are a peaceful people and...." He was cut off again.

"So, you are accusing me," Zayashariya retorted smirking. The crowd gasped at her insolence.

"Lady, I ask that you respect me. I have given you shelter and presented you with the utmost hospitality. I will not tolerate and I do not appreciate the tone of your voice. I ask that you recognize my authority and adhere to it before this situation becomes unpleasant." The king grew angry. One of his soldiers stood up and walked behind him. The king waved him away. "My people have been dying since you graced us with your presence. That is a fact and nothing more," he spat.

"Not only is he wise, but he is also observant," Zayashariya laughed sarcastically as she curtsied.

"I am warning you lady. Do not force me to throw you in jail. Better yet, I may withdraw my welcome and send you back into the wastelands to starve to death. You ungrateful wench!" said the king, stepping so close to her that she could feel his warm breath on her face. His orange face was quite red now. His fists were balled tight and a large vein appeared across his forehead.

"Do you wish for me to leave? I have done nothing wrong in the eyes of you or your people. No one has witnessed any misdeeds on my behalf. Why do you question me? Is it because I am an alien? Do you fear me? I have no fear of you. I have not been unkind to anyone yet your people have not shown me any hospitality since I have arrived in this place. All I have received are unwelcoming stares and rude comments. If anyone is threatened, surely it is I. I only came here to seek shelter and to find food. I would have died of starvation if I had not been welcomed into your town. Is that what you want? Me to be banished and to die of starvation in the cold my noble king? Does that make you feel more powerful to know that you can send a woman away to suffer in the wilderness?" Zayashariya bowed. "Is that what you want oh stately and honorable ruler, whose vast kingdom expands across the universe like the stars themselves?" Zayashariya said, staring the King dead in the eye. Her voice sounded as loud as buildings tumbling during an earthquake. He stood in front of his people baffled and embarrassed by her actions.

"Do not be foolish woman. I wish harm on no one." He was temporarily at a loss for words. The king paused and dropped his head momentarily. Then, he lifted his head quickly with hell shining in his eyes. He pointed his finger in Zayashariya's face and began to speak again, "Remember that we welcomed you here and sheltered you from the cold. Do not insult me with your stupid words. Be gone from my face!" the king screamed. He feared this woman. No one had ever spoken to him so boldly and without fear for their life. Surely, she had no respect for his power. That fact alone bothered him. He watched her walk away and looked at the crowd and said, "Everyone is dismissed. Pick up your weapons in the Inn's lobby. The soldiers will issue one weapon to everyone except the stranger. She will not receive training and will not be allowed to bear arms! If she is caught carrying a weapon, she is to be imprisoned immediately." His face flushed with rage and he gathered his family and returned back to the royal home.

The people of Wilzasp rushed into the lobby for their weapons. Knives, swords, bows and arrows, spears, axes, guns, darts, and daggers were given to every man, woman, and child who was old enough to use a weapon properly. The town was prepared to fight and also prepared to start a fight.

Chapter 17

The entire town was alive with shouts and cheers. Boasting people jumped around practicing combat maneuvers and the acceptance speech they would give when they had succeeded in murdering the monster. The kids chased each other around the streets with spears in hand, as their mothers scolded but laughed at them because of the surrounding excitement.

Zayashariya walked alone through the heckling crowd. Tension was so great between her and the people of Wilzasp that it felt as if a force field surrounded her body protecting her from crumbling to the ground like a broken cracker. Loathsome sneers and degrading names were flying toward her from every direction. Children spat at her. Men threatened her. It felt as if she was back on Night fighting with her mother and demons. Her head began to spin. Her eyes were blind to her surroundings. She was in another world. Another time. Another nightmare. Foul memories of her past began to fly into her mind. Thoughts of the times when she repeatedly tried to escape from Night came racing back to her, haunting her brain, torturing her soul. Memories of her in the dark land of Gehenna fighting against her wretched mother haunted her. The fighting. She did not need the fighting. Zayashariya did not want the fighting. She did not want to be like her mother. She did not want to be evil like Queen Lilith birthed her to be. Zayashariya knew that the people of Wilzasp would force her to destroy more and more of them, causing her to fulfill Lilith's prophecy pertaining to her evil nature. *I am not evil!* Her inner voice rang in her head. Zayashariya knew who she was. She knew that within her lived a blood consuming creature with a bottomless hunger that would never be filled. She was at peace with her nature, at peace with her beastly desires; but, she refused to believe that she was evil. She was not evil for being who she was, for being what she was, for doing what she had to do to survive. *I am not evil. I am not evil. I am not evil....* A crowd of teen-aged boys surrounded her. Their shadows fell upon her face like dark clouds shading the sun. Malicious grins were painted across their faces. They tightened around her like a noose, seeming to cut the air from her lungs.

"Why are you here dark one?" a hoarse voice yelled at her. The owner of the voice was a pimple faced humanoid wearing a black toga. His freckled face distorted and his eyes reflected sheer malice. "Answer me quickly!" he said pointing a spear at Zayashariya's left breast. "I will gladly impale that criminal heart of yours!" he growled. Zayashariya said nothing. Her breathing stopped momentarily. "Answer me wench before I spill your blood!" His eyes prayed for the opportunity to strike. "You can not imagine the pleasure killing you would bring me."

Zayashariya's eyes glowed bright. Her curved eyebrows straightened into sharp violet lines slanting from the bridge of her nose to the edges of her forehead. She smiled a dreadful smile, a smile that would mean sudden death to anyone who provoked her. Zayashariya's face was a mask of terror. Courage fled from the boy. His eyes grew afraid.

"She is the killer!" he screamed into the crowd. "Look at her eyes!"

"Let's get her!" another boy, who was naked to the waste wearing short pants, yelled. "She is the murderer! Who else could it be?!" he yelled and pointed an arrow at the dark stranger.

A heavy hand landed on the shoulder of the boy. He was spun around by the force of the hand. The arrow flew into a nearby tree truck. A deep voice full of authority and strength said loudly, "The party is over boys."

Fital, a soldier of great stature and esteem let the boy go. He shoved the boy into the crowd behind him and dared defiance. Shame and anger filled the boy's eyes as he regained his footing and stood beside his cohorts. Fital looked into the eyes of the rest of the group.

"Go home. Leave the lady alone," Fital yelled. "Don't be so quick to judge others. Leave this place. Now!"

The boys stood at attention. They looked at the soldier hatefully. No one moved an inch.

"Don't make me repeat myself!" Fital raised his voice while waving his muscular arm in the air like a warning flag.

The boys moved away from Zayashariya while mumbling under their breath and glaring at her with vengeful eyes.

"Go on now!" Fital commanded. "Do not make me debase you before the crowd."

The young men disappeared into the crowd. They knew that Fital could and would humiliate them if need be. It was better to save face and seek out their vengeance another day.

"How can I repay you?" Zayashariya asked. *Handsome, very handsome,* she thought. Zayashariya smiled and reached into her hip pouch.

Fital grabbed her hand, motioning for her to stop. An electric current seemed to flow from his warm palm.

She was uncomfortable with him touching her. Butterflies fluttered in her stomach. *What is this strange feeling?* She moved away from him but kept an artificial grin on her lips. Her heart leapt within her chest. His face was intoxicating. She had not felt such lust since her erotic encounters with the demon Belial.

"How about dinner at the Inn tonight? That would be payment enough for a lifetime," Fital invited, flashing a stunning smile. His teeth were snow white and perfectly even. His lips were gorgeous, heart shaped and thick. Fital's eyes made her thighs burn with desire.

Zayashariya was overwhelmed. She expected a lot of things but seduction by a humanoid was not one of them. *I can not get involved with this man. It would be too dangerous for me and for him. But, he is so very attractive. I can't.* "No thank you," she responded with a surprised look on her face. The words seemed to slip out of her mouth before she could finish her thoughts. Zayashariya avoided his eyes at all costs; afraid that if he looked into them she would melt like hot butter.

"Oh come on. Everyone needs friends and I am the friendliest man I know." The flirting humanoid smiled. His teeth were absolutely perfect. Fital's eyes devoured her.

Zayashariya melted as she looked into his seductive eyes. She could not help but to blush. Thankfulness filled her. Her ebony skin camouflaged her bashfulness. Hot flashes and chills attacked her in alternating currents. She almost broke out into a cold sweat but quickly regained her calm. *Thank God! The last thing I need is to be looking like an awestruck child in front of this man.*

Zayashariya was strangely attracted to his off beat charm and flirtatious ways. She admired his slender yet muscular form. He had the elongated body of a swimmer and the muscle tone of a gymnast. His peach hair was shaven so close that he looked nearly bald. He wore two emerald hoop earrings in both ears. Fital was handsome in an eccentric sort of way with an angular face and a small but broad flat nose. *How can I resist? He is so adorable.* Zayashariya decided to take his offer.

"Okay. I will go," Zayashariya agreed, trying hard not to smile. She felt like a little girl, emotionally infantile when her eyes locked with his. Her stomach was queasy and she felt freakishly dizzy. Never in her life had a person had that effect of her. *What is this nauseating feeling? I have got to get a grip. Maybe this is a bad idea.* Zayashariya took a deep breath and fiddled with her fingers.

"Great! I can't wait." Fital clapped his hands. "I forgot the most important thing." There was that killer smile again.

"What is that?" She folded her arms. Her voice cracked. *I can't take this much longer. I think I'm going to faint.*

"Your name?" he asked.

She smiled. "Zayashariya."

Fital held out his hand. She grabbed it. He took her gloved hand and kissed it gently. The warmth of his lips penetrated the leather glove. She winced with silent delight. Fital saw her pleasure when he tickled her palm with his fingers. Zayashariya smirked and brushed his hand away.

"You are positively prime evil Fital," she giggled.

"Only if you give me the opportunity to be." His pearly teeth flashed again. "You are a ravishing woman. How can I help myself?" Fital could not help admiring her beautiful body. Her curves were ample and ultra feminine. Zayashariya's body suit was so revealing and her body was so perfect. He fought to keep his eyes from straying from her face and ogling at her frame. "A beautiful name for a beautiful woman," he said.

Zayashariya smiled. His words turned her knees into jelly. She shook her head and giggled.

"And yours?" she asked. Goose pimples traveled down her arms. His eyes were mesmerizing and the desire for her to reach out and grab him, hold him, kiss him, overwhelmed her.

"Fital," he answered.

"Glad to meet you, Fital." *Very very glad.*

"Likewise."

"I must go." Zayashariya took her hand back from Fital. "Goodbye for now," she said then waved and walked away. *That man is definitely trouble.* She looked back over her shoulder and winked at him. A little skip worked its way into her step and a switch into her hips. And, she was off.

"Tonight, immediately after dark!" Fital yelled after her. "Please don't forget! I will be waiting for you! And please don't keep me waiting long! Each moment will seem like an eon." He watched her walk away with the deepest admiration for her physical being.

Chapter 18

The suns made their way across the horizon and the moons battled for their places in the heavens. The darkness of night crept into existence like a phantom appearing in the corner of a room without warning. Zillions of stars twinkled in the heavens like tiny camera flashes. It was a warm night and the sky was cloud free.

Zayashariya dried her damp body. She had taken a relaxing perfume bath moments before and was feeling clean and refreshed. A deep breath was inhaled and she exhaled in a weary sigh. In many ways, the encounter with Fital had made her day a whole lot better. However, she did not want to get her hopes up. Maybe he was just curious about her nature and just wanted to get close to her in order to incriminate her. She could never tell the rationality of these people. The people of Wilzasp were so closed minded. It was evident to her, by the treatment she received, that they only cared about their own people. Their suspicions were understandable but they had it in for her the moment she stepped foot into Wilzasp. It really did not matter if she was a criminal or not. They were going to crucify her sooner or later anyway. At least their biases are valid.

Zayashariya walked through the hall wearing nothing but a towel. She walked slowly swinging her ebony arms forward and backward, letting the wind she generated penetrate her pores, cooling her body. The golden towel was wrapped around her like a lush strapless gown. Even in a simple towel, she was stunning. She pushed through the iron door and laid her towel on the bed, then walked over to her shelf. The shelf was becoming slightly cluttered from numerous new items that she had purchased since she had arrived in Wilzasp. Many of her clothes had to be made because no one in Wilzasp dressed as she did. Her style was pure Gehenna. Most people looked at her wardrobe with utter surprise. Many considered it too bold and down right risqué. She was lucky to find a sweet old woman who lived down the block who made her clothes with zeal. The old woman enjoyed measuring Zayashariya's body and creating unique designs for her. Zayashariya was a challenge to the woman and the old woman welcomed her with opened arms every time she entered her shop. The old woman was one of few people that Zayashariya liked. The old woman's warmth and friendliness reminded Zayashariya of Sarai. For a brief second Zayashariya wondered how Sarai was doing. Then a sad realization hit her; Sarai was probably dead by now. Zayashariya knew that Lilith would not have spared the old woman's life. Mercy was a virtue that Lilith simply did not understand nevertheless possess. Zayashariya mourned the memory of Sarai in her heart. Maybe Sarai was in a better place. After all, what greater love is there than to give ones life for a friend?

Zayashariya pulled a stack of leotards out from the right corner of the shelf. She flipped through the stack until she came to one that pleased her eye. *I wonder what they will think of this one.*

The people of Wilzasp dressed in no particular style. They wore things that surpassed centuries and millenniums. You may spot one person in a toga and another in a three-piece suit. They wore a great multitude of things from silver moon boots to B.C. dated sandals. They wore whatever made them feel good. Yet, they always succeeded in making her feel out of place with what she was wearing. Zayashariya dismissed her thoughts and begin to get dressed.

Zayashariya dressed in a black leather bikini, black leather gloves with open fingertips (revealing her long red nails), and black leather boots. *This outfit ought to get Fital's blood pressure boiling.*

She shook the water from her violet hair and toweled it dry. Her silky mane curled perfectly on its own. She walked over to the bed and fell backwards, reclining and sprawling herself across the bed in a relaxing position, staring at the ceiling. Her eyes closed and she exhaled. *Maybe this little date is all I need...* Suddenly her eyes popped open. She set up on the bed and lifted her nose in the air. A faint scent drifted into the room. *Trouble.* Zayashariya turned her head from side to side sniffing the air, inhaling the elements around her trying desperately to figure out what the odor was and where it came from. The scent of intruders permeated her nostrils. They smelled near, very near but she could not determine where. *Why tonight of all nights? I can not get a moments peace in this forsaken place.* She sprang to her feet and looked under her bed as four teenage boys pushed her cracked door open and ran toward her. Zayashariya was taken aback. One of the boys, wearing a yellow jogging suit, rushed toward her with an ax. Zayashariya kicked the ax out of his hand and punched him in the neck. He fell to the floor coughing, holding his neck with quaking hands, with tears falling from his juvenile eyes. He died. Zayashariya turned around just in time to see another boy running toward her. He ran, screaming, with a club held high over his head. He swung the mammoth stick at her head and missed. He came within a hair's length of her face. She ducked and knocked him down with a leg sweep. The club fell to the ground first and then he fell onto his buttocks. He tried to regain his footing but she quickly kicked him in the face, lifted him up over her head, and broke his back across her knee. His limp body fell to the floor like a rock. She was breathing profusely when the third and forth boy ran to her with a sword in their hands, one aimed toward her heart and the other toward her head. Zayashariya fell to the floor on all fours like a beast and sprang on one of them like a wild cat, knocking the other asunder. The dark woman held the screaming boy down and froze the other boy with a sharp piercing scream that ripped from the pit of her belly. The boy stood frozen. Nothing moved but his shifting eyes, stretched and afraid. Zayashariya turned back to the boy that she had pounced on and smiled. She held her head back and four needle-like fangs burrowed through her gums and extended themselves to her bottom lip. The boy cried like a new born as the monstrous woman installed her fangs into the soft flesh of his neck. She drained him of blood until his body shriveled in her arms. The spell wore off of the other boy. He dropped his weapon to the floor and ran out of the door. Zayashariya threw the shriveled corpse to the side and ran after him. The boy made it halfway down the hall when Zayashariya's hand jerked his body up in the air by the back of his neck. She held him by the neck and began to drink his blood. Before she drained the life from him, she stopped and turned his body toward her until they were face to face. Silence filled a moment's void between anticipation and death. She looked into the dying boy's eyes. He was terrified and crying. Tears fell from his immature eyes as he prayed silently to a nonexistent god for his life. She smiled into his pitiful face. Her finger stroked his cheek to sooth him. Hope filled his eyes. He forced a smile to his face, forcing optimistic thoughts of her releasing him to subdue his fear.

"I can not kill you slowly. Fate is kind this day. You are lucky. I have a date!" She bit hard into his chest. The sound of his rib bones cracking echoed through the hallway. Zayashariya pulled his heart out with her teeth and spit it across the hall.

"Stupid child!" she crossly forced through her teeth and threw the dead boy across her shoulder. She took the boy back to her room, and gathered the bodies of the others.

"These people forced me to kill against my will." Zayashariya justified her actions. "This is not my fault! I refuse to feel guilty about taking the lives of these young fools," she told herself, trying to free herself from the impending pressure of guilt she already felt weighing on her heavily. "I was defending myself!" Zayashariya screamed. She went into her pouch and retrieved a bottle of black liquid. Carefully, she sprinkled the black potion on the bodies and watched as the liquid transformed them into smothering ashes. She placed the ashes in the same dark vessel with the ashes of the victims she had claimed before. The dark woman picked the golden towel up off the bed and wiped her face with it. Blood and tears stained the cloth.

After regaining her composure and suppressing her inner demon, she ran down the hall to the supply closet and retrieved a few cleaning items. She cleaned her room and the hallway until it was spotless. Guilt settled over her head like an atrocious migraine headache. It pounded her brain into submission. Why did she always feel so terrible for defending her life? She kept telling herself that it was not her fault but she could hear her mother's laughter in her mind, taunting her and praising her deeds. She could hear her mother's cold voice snake through her veins uttering, "You are flesh of my flesh. You are just like me. Only I can give you what you seek."

Zayashariya tried to dismiss the thought but she could not. She wanted to believe desperately that she was just a victim of circumstance but she could not fight the fact that she was clearly baneful. She was death to these people, a plague that would slowly wipe them out one by one. She was evil, a she-demon, a devil. Zayashariya cried. She fell against the wall and wept like a mother who had lost a child. Why couldn't she control her desire to kill? Why did she feel such pleasure in other's pain? The desire to preserve life and the desire to consume life raged within her being, battling for supreme domination.

She took a deep breath, suppressed her guilt, and resumed her cleaning, not wanting her date to see any evidence that might incriminate her. The feeling Zayashariya had while she was in Fital's presence was more intoxicating than the taste of blood. She wanted nothing to impede on their meeting and she was absolutely sure that the knowledge of her being a murderer would.

"Zayashariya!" Fital called as he walked down the hall heading toward her room. "Why are you cleaning the hall?" he questioned. "There are workers who can do this."

He leaned against the wall and crossed his arms. He looked nice. He wore a shirt with a ruffled collar and a pair of blue jeans with brown boots. A gold chain hung around his neck and his gold earrings shined in the glow of the hallway.

Zayashariya smiled, placing her filled hand on her hip. Warm liquid dampened her fingers. Her smile faded. A worried look crossed her face. She realized the boy's heart was still in her hand and threw it behind a trash can.

"You are right," she said, blushing and walking into her room to get her hip pouch. On the way out, she spied the boy's heart on the floor, peeking from behind the trash can, and kicked it inside of her room into a corner. She prayed that Fital didn't notice. *I hope you didn't see that.* She looked back and smiled.

He smiled back and laughed.

Good, you didn't notice. Zayashariya thought. She figured that he probably thought she had tripped.

"I'll be out in a second," Zayashariya said.

"Take your time sweet thing but not too long," Fital flirted.

"You flatter me so," said Zayashariya grinning. She walked into the room and closed the door behind her.

Inside of her room, Zayashariya uttered a quick spell which disposed of the organ and cleansed the blood from her hands. She grabbed her pouch and came out of the room, locking the door behind her.

Fital followed behind her. He slowly drew in close and tentatively kissed her shoulder, hoping that she would not find the gesture inappropriate. After all, he could not control himself. He wanted to kiss her all over. He wanted nothing more in life but to weigh her feet down with kisses and to smother her in his embrace. She was the sweetest and the most erotic female he had ever encountered. The smell of her made his testosterone levels overflow and flood his reason with senseless yearning. This woman was enthralling. Lust bubbled up in him like carbonated water.

"You look lovely tonight," Fital said, running his finger down her arm.

"Thank you." Zayashariya smiled and issued him her hand. "Shall we go?" she asked.

"Yes, my lovely lady. We shall." Fital took her hand and they headed to the Inn's dining hall.

Chapter 19

The walls of the dining hall glowed with rainbow colored crystals. Tables were scattered all over the floor in no particular pattern. Each table was draped in a different color tablecloth and each chair surrounding the table matched the cloth. In the center of each table was a single glowing white crystal.

About seven couples were in the dining hall, smiling and flirting across their tables, seeming to enjoy the lovely night and each other's company. Faint giggles and the clinking of forks hitting plates filled the atmosphere around them. The door to the dining hall opened and in stepped Zayashariya and Fital. Every head and eye in the dining hall turned to gawk at the dark stranger and her companion. The couple ignored the raping eyes of the people and made their way to an empty table near the rear of the room. Fital pulled out a seat for Zayashariya.

"Thank you," said Zayashariya smiling and sitting down. *Why did I agree to this? These people will ruin this night for us. I can feel it in my bones.*

"You are quite welcome my dear," Fital responded. He sat in the chair across from her and picked up a glossy menu. Zayashariya did the same but Fital reached over and took hers from her while moving his chair across the table so that they could share his menu. "I hope you don't mind."

"No." Zayashariya blushed. The menu became their focus and they decided on their meal together.

A red eyed waitress walked over to the table. She wore an off the shoulder brown leather dress that fell halfway down her thigh with brown high heel sandals. Her peach hair was in a ponytail in the middle of her head and large gold earrings hung from her bright orange ears.

"May I help you Sir?" the waitress asked Fital while purposely turning her back to Zayashariya, blatantly ignoring her.

"Wait on the lady first," Fital commanded, pointing at Zayashariya, trying to keep an irritated smile on his face.

The waitress frowned at the dark stranger, smacked her thick lips, and let out an unpleasant sigh.

She could be a pretty person if her attitude wasn't so flawed. Zayashariya observed. *Hopefully she will not cause anymore problems for me tonight. I do not want anymore suffering.*

"What do you want?" the waitress asked loudly and rudely while sighing and rolling her eyes.

"Is that the way you talk to a customer Meki? You are only taking away from your tip," Fital said in a condescending manner. "If you like, we could request another waitress." He knew that she was only being rude to them because she was still bitter about their break up.

Meki and Fital had been a couple for about two years until he found out that she was having an affair with a young street vendor. Fital forgave her and they continued the relationship; but, her affair with one of his fellow soldiers was the last straw. He let her go after he found them together a few months ago. He immediately broke the relationship off and had not spoken to her since the incident.

Fital could never understand why she could not comprehend that he could not tolerate an unfaithful mate. Meki acted as if he betrayed her instead of vice versa. She accused him of not committing and running away when things got hard. Fital was enraged by her ludicrous allegation and put her away. She begged for his forgiveness but Meki's contrite apologies meant little to him. He felt in his heart that she would have no conscience about being unfaithful again.

"Please be a little more professional. I am sure that your employer would not like hearing that one of the waitresses is trying to drive away a paying customer," said Fital.

"I don't consider this thing a customer!" the waitress snapped as she pointed her nubby finger in Zayashariya's face. Meki looked at the stranger and grimaced. She could not believe that Fital would rather be with a freak than be with her. She was emotionally wounded by this outrage. Her face trembled in anger and tears welled up in her eyes.

"Remove your hand please," Zayashariya requested in a calm and rational manner. *Please don't make me kill you. I only want to have a good night. Be calm. Be calm.* "Please, I beg of you, remove your hand. I do not want any trouble." Anger flooded through Zayashariya. *Be cool. Don't crack in front of Fital. He can not know what I am capable of.*

"And if I don't? What are you going to do?" the waitress yelled.

"Meki, please calm down," Fital pleaded with her. "If you do not want to wait on us, send someone else. Better yet, we will leave." Fital pushed his chair back from the table. He sprang to his feet.

"Sit down Fital," Zayashariya commanded. "She is just a little frustrated. Maybe the young lady had a hard day. I am sure that she does not want me to get angry. If everyone would just calm down, nothing bad will happen," Zayashariya spat venomously.

"Zayashariya is right. Calm down Meki," said Fital. He remained standing. "Let's just start over. Please take our order and we all will pretend none of this happened."

"No! I want to know what she is going to do!" Meki yelled as she scratched the side of Zayashariya's face with her fingernail. "Just what I thought. Nothing!" she screamed in Zayashariya's face.

Curse you for making me do this! Zayashariya grabbed the girl's finger and literally broke it in half, causing a loud cracking sound. The screaming waitress ran to the rear of the Inn, to get help, holding her limp finger which was hanging painfully to the side like boneless meat.

"I think we better leave," Fital said as he grabbed Zayashariya's arm and pulled her from the table and rushed out of the dining hall. The couple ran out into the street and searched for an open fruit stand. A young man was just putting his fruit away when the odd couple came running toward him. The man drew his sword.

"Calm down young man! We only want fruit," Fital laughed, amused by the man's vacuous reaction.

The young man put his weapon down. He let out a deep breath and asked, "Whacha need?"

"Four of those, two of those, six of those, eight of those, and two jars of blackberry juice," Fital ordered.

Zayashariya stood quietly watching to see if anyone was after them. She saw no one. Her heart stopped pounding,

After Fital paid, the man gave them the fruit in a large basket and the couple headed back to the Inn.

"Can we eat in your room?" Fital asked, raising his eyebrows and flashing a devilish grin.

Zayashariya smirked at him. "Sure, let's go," she heard herself agree before she thought about it. She raised and lowered her shoulders and grabbed his hand. *Why not?* They walked in the warm night breeze, enjoying the tranquil moment.

When they arrived at the entrance of the Inn, they spotted the waitress and a couple of fearsome looking men standing beside her.

"Can you fight?" Fital asked Zayashariya while sizing the men up. The two men were mammoth brutes known for skullduggery. He was not sure if he would be able to defeat them alone, not even with all of his training.

"Can you?" Zayashariya responded with a slight smile on her face and a glimmer in her eye.

He looked at her, a look of buoyancy on his face. "Let's do this," said Fital.

She nodded and the couple walked bravely into the Inn. Fital put the basket of fruit on the floor near the counter and he waved for Zayashariya to come to him. The couple walked towards the stairs when a husky voice broke the silence of the lobby.

"Where do you think you are going?" one of the rugged men asked. A big scar ran down the left side of his face. His two front teeth were missing. He wore dirty blue jeans and fur barbarian boots.

"I'm going to my room if you don't mind," Zayashariya said as a matter of fact.

"Not until I say so!" the other man yelled in her face. His breath smelled like liquor mixed with feces. Spit sprayed into her eye, burning it instantly. He wore a patch over one of his eyes and all of his teeth looked rotten. "Meki, are these two the ones responsible for hurting you?" he asked the contentious waitress.

"Yes. The girl did this to me!" Meki answered.

"Gentlemen, please excuse us. My friend was only defending herself," said Fital trying to mediate as he grabbed Zayashariya's arm and attempted to push past the men blocking the stairway.

"I said no one moves unless I say so!" the bad breath brute beefed.

The man with the scar on his face pushed Zayashariya to the ground as the man with one eye punched Fital in the face. Zayashariya jumped to her feet. She round house kicked the scarred man in the face. Then she swiftly dropped to the ground and tripped him with a leg sweep. He fell down with a hard thump and she kicked him on the side of the head. Blood flew from his mouth, splattering across the floor like red wine.

Angry and more determined than ever, the man spat a mouth full of blood on the floor and grabbed Zayashariya's ankle as she aimed for his head again. He pulled her down to the floor and put her in an agonizing leg lock. Pain shot through her legs like an electric current. Zayashariya winced as the man twisted her legs backwards. He made the mistake of letting her go for a moment and Zayashariya took advantage of the opportunity. She kicked him in the neck forcing him to cough and gasp for breath. His eyes bulged out of his head as he clawed at his throat, praying for air to enter his lungs. She quickly got to her feet and her legs went to work on him, stomping him with preternatural speed.

Fital flew back from the cyclops' punch and hit the floor. His back slammed down hard. A deep throb traveled down his spine, causing a faint moan to escape his mouth. The one eyed man charged at Fital but Fital gave him a right hook from the ground. The punch landed under his chin and the man fell backwards, hitting his head against the floor. Fital got up and jumped atop of the fallen man, punching him several times in the head and kneeing him in the side of the stomach until blood spilled from his gaping mouth. The one eyed man let out a horrible moan and crumpled up on the floor like a balled up piece of paper. Fital kneed him again and stood up. Sweat trickled down his brow. He placed his hands on his knees and leaned over to take a quick rest.

Zayashariya kicked the scarred man in the ribs and stomped his ugly face into the ground. Her eyes flashed. She was engulfed in fury. The sight of the man's blood drove her into a frenzy. She began to slash him with her nails and bite him, drawing abnormal amounts of blood. She lapped up the blood, smearing it all over her face. An inhuman growl bubbled from her gut.

Fital grabbed the wild woman and shook the sense back into her. He held her bloody body close to his and stopped her from killing the man who was lying on the floor bleeding like a sacrificial bull. Fital asked her if she was okay.

Zayashariya nodded in response.

Stunned by her temporary insanity, he felt sick to his stomach. Fital had never witnessed such a craze. Zayashariya had lost her mind. But worse, she seemed to deeply enjoy the pain she was inflicting. Her lips curled with wicked satisfaction as the man's blood flowed.

With misgivings, Fital looked closely at her. For a moment, he contemplated the possibility that she may be the monster destroying his people. He held her back from him and lifted her face and looked into her damp eyes.

"No. She couldn't be," Fital mumbled under his breath. He held her close again. She was too beautiful to be a merciless monster. He squeezed her tight. Through his peripheral vision, he saw Meki, the waitress, flee. The two beaten men fumbled to their feet and left behind her, limping and dragging themselves away in pain.

Fital released Zayashariya from his grasp, picked up the basket of fruit, grabbed her hand, rushed past the awe stricken old man at the front desk, and ran up the steps to her room. When they arrived at her floor, she led him into her room. Zayashariya sat the basket of fruit on the floor. Her handsome companion sat on the velvet bedspread and let his eyes tour the room. She sat next to him.

"What happened to you down there?" Fital asked, running his fingers through her hair. "You were a wild animal."

She got up and walked away from him. "I was enraged," answered Zayashariya looking down at her body, disappointed with herself. She licked her lips. The coppery taste of the blood aroused her. Dismissing the feeling, she said, "I have to go wash up. I will be right back. Make yourself at home. There is a small folding table in the hall closet." She pointed out of the room to the hall. "Sorry for such a miserable night." Zayashariya gave Fital a pitiful smile. "I had high hopes for the evening."

"No such thing." Fital walked toward her and grabbed her hand. "I've never had such an adventure."

She pulled away from him, walked over to the shelf, and picked up a pair of shorts and a T-shirt.

"I'll be back," said Zayashariya as she walked out of the room. *I am a mess.* "Do you need a towel?" her voice echoed from the hallway.

"No thanks. Don't take too long," Fital yelled after her. He walked to the closet and opened it. The table was gone. He returned to the room, sat down, and waited patiently for Zayashariya to return. With weary arms, he took off his sweaty smelly shirt, exposing his well structured chest. He wiped his hands with it and folded the shirt and placed it on the shelf next to Zayashariya's jar of ashes.

The jar was shaped like a dragon with a skull-like head and strange wings. Fital wondered what it held. It gave him chills. Walking away from the shelf, full of fear and curiosity, he sat back on the bed. Zayashariya walked back into the room moments later.

"You are even pretty, even when you try not to be," Fital complimented her while trying to get his mind off of the gothic jar.

"Thanks," Zayashariya replied, pulling her hair back. Realizing that she had nothing to hold it with, she let it drop.

Fital couldn't help himself. "What's in the jar?" he asked, pointing to it. His curiosity was eating at him. The jar was a portent to him. Damnation reeked from its small structure.

She was taken aback. *Why is he prying?* "Ashes," Zayashariya's voice was choppy. She was not prepared to answer questions.

"Of what?" Fital pressed. "There is something eerie about that container." The hairs on the back of his neck stood up.

"People," answered Zayashariya, combing her hair with her fingers and pulling it back again, this time holding it together with a rubber band. Annoyance filled her face. She hoped that Fital would save his inquisition for another time.

"Of close friends or family?" Fital asked. He walked over to pick it up. She shot him a warning glare. He decided against it and sat back down.

Zayashariya threw her soiled clothes in a pile in the corner.

"Of people I became one with. I guess you can say they were a major part of my life force."

Her mind wandered to mysterious places in the past. Memories hunted her; memories of people she had known and people who had perished under her power. Zayashariya walked over to the window for a breath of fresh air. The night was a beautiful one.

"Life force," Fital said to himself. He didn't want to know why Zayashariya would choose those words. "Why spoil the mood?" he asked himself, deciding to drop the subject. "The table wasn't there. Do you have a blanket that I can spread on the floor so we can eat? I am famished." A crooked smile, full of discomfort and perplexity, hung sideways on Fital's lips.

"You may use my cloak on the shelf," Zayashariya told Fital, pointing to the dark animal skin. *He is such a beautiful man.*

Fital sprung to his feet and picked up the cloak. He unfolded the panther fur cloak and spread it across the floor. He took the basket and put it beside the cloak and wiped his hands on his pants. Fital took the fruit out of the basket, divided it equally, and put one jar of juice in front of himself and one jar of juice beside him.

"Come, sit here," he requested, looking up at Zayashariya and patting the space next to him.

The beautiful woman walked over from the window and sat next to the attractive humanoid.

It seemed that hours had passed. The couple laughed and ate until repletion, nearly crapulent. Fital lay backwards on the floor and rubbed his full belly and yawned.

"I am so full," Fital muttered and yawned again. "I am very tired also." He sat up and looked into Zayashariya's eyes. He was hoping to be asked to stay.

"It's late, maybe you should leave," said Zayashariya smiling slyly. *Please stay.* Her heart pleaded.

"Maybe you should make me," Fital jokingly said, smiling back. He took her hand and kissed it gently. "Tell me about yourself mysterious one."

"What do you wish to know?" she asked, her eyes were heavy. Talking was the last thing on her mind.

"Where are you from?" Fital asked as he leaned closer to her.

"You wouldn't believe me if I told you," Zayashariya responded.

"Okay. Try me," said Fital.

"Gehenna. It is the main city located on the planet of Night. It is a dreary place that holds lots of bad memories for me. Nothing I care to speak about."

"The Land of the Dead. You are right. I don't believe you," Fital laughed. "What do you like to do?"

"Travel and eat," Zayashariya answered.

"I can see that!" he chided jokingly, looking down at the fruit peels, seeds, and cores in front of her.

"Shut-up!" Zayashariya giggled and pinched his arm playfully. "You didn't exactly pick over your food either."

"Who are your people?" Fital began to gather together the mess that they had made. "Your family? Friends?

"I have no people. I am an only child, at least to my knowledge. I have a mother that I abhor and a father I do not know." A picture of Lilith popped up in her head. Hate filled her.

"Everyone has people. You have to have people. Where are you really from?" Fital asked. He stopped what he was doing and gave her his undivided attention.

"I already told you," said Zayashariya, looking away. "Why? Does it really matter?" She was weary of the conversation already. Her need for companionship was growing less important by the second. A look of displeasure crossed her face.

"Are you always this vague and full of choler?"

"Yes." *Especially when it comes to my mother.*

"Well, at least you are honest," he sighed.

"I try to be." She ate the last berry in the bowl. "Tell me about yourself," Zayashariya said.

"Well, I came from a long line of soldiers. My mother was a rich and beautiful woman of nobility. We were very close. She died. The experience was very difficult for me because she gave me life, balance, and beauty. She was a kind and extremely happy woman. She taught me how to relate to women.

My father was a famous soldier. He was pretty strict but a loving man. Everything about him had to be structured. He had little time to sniff lilacs or dance in the rain. Life for him was work, work, work.

I am the highest ranking soldier in Wilzasp, a trained assassin, and protector of the king. Isn't that comedic?" Fital laughed. "As if Wilzasp will ever have need of me in that way. All we have ever known is peace, at least in my generation." Fital shrugged his shoulders. "At any rate, I have five brothers and seven sisters. We all get along well. I have no children of my own but I have many nieces and nephews. I am very close to the king. He and my father were cronies. The king is like my father in many ways. I spend as much time or more with him as I did my father." Fital paused. "I have never been married but I have been in love too many times." Fital laughed aloud. "I think I am falling in love again." He rose up on his elbows and ran his fingers down her thigh.

Zayashariya laughed. "Tell me more about you. I care nothing about your family," she said, knocking his hand away playfully.

Fital's demeanor changed.

"A little blunt aren't we?" Fital tapped his fingers on the floor and let out an annoyed sigh. "Family is everything to me and I take great offense to you disregarding them."

"I am the type of woman who speaks my mind. If I offended you, I apologize but being blunt is my way. It is the only way I know," Zayashariya said without the slightest bit of regret.

"I see." Fital scratched his head. His anger subsided. An argument on the first date was something neither of them was interested in so he continued.

"There really isn't much to know about me. I am a very simple man. I enjoy family and I believe in love and happiness. I consider myself a strong individual. I believe in logic. I don't care much for anything that can not be proven beyond a reasonable doubt. Loyalty is very important to me. I have very little talent beyond handling my sword and art. I try to be as good and as honest as I can be. I like being respected and my word weighing as much as gold. I don't know what else to say. That is me in a nutshell."

"Well say no more," Zayashariya laughed.

"Tell me about you."

"If you insist." Zayashariya sighed.

"I do," Fital said, sitting Indian style. His abdominal muscles displayed themselves in perfect block formations.

"I love to travel and meet new people. Beauty is like fresh air to me, breathing in the sight of it refreshes my body. Searching the universe for truth, interests me. I have a battling spirit," said Zayashariya

"Explain," Fital requested.

"I am always in constant conflict with my actions. I feel my soul is teetering on heaven and hell all of the time."

"You believe in such things?" Fital questioned.

"Heaven and Hell are not matters of belief but matters of fact," Zayashariya said, looking unblinkingly into Fital's eyes. "I know such things are real. I am an unhappy being because of this. If your eyes could have seen a forth of the things I have seen in my lifetime, you would be a believer."

"I doubt it. But go on, please," said Fital.

"There really isn't much to say about me. I am not a complex person. I try to be neither good nor evil. I live life to survive from day to day. I try not to question my existence too much for fear of insanity," she said.

"Don't take life so seriously. Enjoy life. Live everyday to the fullest because when it is over it is over," Fital said.

"I guess you are right."

"Come closer." Fital beckoned her with his finger.

"Why?" asked Zayashariya smiling and licking her fingers clean of fruit residue.

"'Cause I want you too."

She looked at him, leaned to the side, and stared intensely into his eyes. *What do you want from me?* She thought to herself. What could she possibly offer this man but a few memorable nights?

"Please," he pouted playfully.

Zayashariya came a little closer. Fital took her chin in the palm of his hand and pulled her face close to his. He kissed her gently and pulled away. For a moment, he let himself fall into her violet eyes. His eyes washed over her ebony skin.

"You are so beautiful," he said. He kissed her again. The natural scent of her body drove him mad. "I wonder if you see yourself as I do. If you could, you would cease searching the universe for beauty and just invest in a looking glass."

"You are something else." Zayashariya smirked. "Your charm is irresistible."

"I try." Fital kissed her cheek then her chin. "So what brings you to Wilzasp?" He pulled away, trying to control his lust. "Tell me about your home and why you left that place."

Zayashariya smiled at him uncomfortably. Fital's curiosity vexed her. He was such a beautiful man. Full of life. So naive. She stared out into space. *Why won't he leave it alone?* Thoughts of home ravished her.

*   *   *

Home.

Zayashariya lay as still as death. The only sound heard was her own deep breathing. She opened her eyes, only darkness. Her arms and legs were chained to a wooden board beneath her. Iron cuffs cut into her wrists and ankles like heavy blades. Her flesh was raw and stinging. The room was damp and rank. She could feel the sticky moisture in the air.

"Where am I?" Zayashariya thought to herself. "How did I get here?"

She laid in the darkness, listening to the silence. Her night vision was unable to adjust. It must have been a blindness spell cast on her. She refused to panic. A cold wet liquid began to drip on her bare belly. She then realized that she was naked. The sticky cold liquid covered her body slowly like extra thick syrup being poured over pancakes. A loud buzz was humming over her. She could not see or move. She knew who it was. She laid there silently.

"Zayashariya," a disturbing voice called.

She would not answer. The buzz came closer. She felt a fuzzy limb touch her arm. A repulsive feeling flowed through her. She could barely control her reflex to vomit.

"Zayashariya, I am so disappointed in you. You are really becoming an awful young lady." The buzzing creature laughed. "You know, I was called away from governing my minions for this nonsense!" the buzzing creature yelled. "I have the whole Underworld to attend to and I am summoned away for this!"

The buzz came even closer. She could feel a million little fuzzy tentacles sticking to her.

"Speak woman!" he shouted, rubbing her face with his antenna. "Or I will make you!" He touched her intimately. She withered beneath his stroke.

"Beelzebub, please." Zayashariya swallowed hard. "My mother won't stand for this!"

The giant fly demon laughed. "I am Lord of the Flies, Prince of Demons, Governor of the Underworld and you presume, with your feeble mind, that your mother, Lilith the whore, can constrain me? You are sadly confused girl." He buzzed a song and her sight returned. "She is the one who sent me fool!" He touched her again and pulled back quickly. "You are a detestable knave and I will teach you to obey!"

Zayashariya hesitantly looked at the horrid giant fly. It was twelve feet tall as well as wide, jet black with black and silver legs and antennas. Its huge eyes were pink and ardent. Its wings were silver and gold and fluttered at an unbelievable speed. It came closer.

"You disappoint me love. You are destined to be the thirteenth on the Council of Demons and you will be," Beelzebub threatened, flying above her head. He let out a loud buzzing song and out of nowhere appeared zillions of flies covering Zayashariya until they coated her naked body completely. The insects buzzed and bit into her delicate skin. She cried out in agony as Beelzebub flew above her in circles dropping sticky fluid from his mouth on top of her. She screamed until her entire body was numb and completely covered. Blackness was the last thing she saw.

*   *   *

"Love." Fital tapped her softly. "Are you okay?" he asked.

Thoughts of home fled from her.

"Enough talking," said Zayashariya placing her finger over his lips and moving closer to him. She put her arms around him and kissed him with a fiery passion. Her ebony fingers ran over his nearly bald head. She could feel his fuzzy hair tickling the palms of her hands. His body reeked of musky sweat and sweet fruit. The smell of him made her thighs ache.

He pulled away from her grasp.

She looked at him, lips trembling with anticipation.

The aroused man stood up and extended his hand to her.

She accepted it and stood up in front of him meeting his hungry eyes, although her full height reached his shoulders.

He held her close as her strangely long scarlet tongue licked his bright orange ear. A chill went down his spine. He looked down at the beautiful woman and fell helplessly into her violet eyes. He removed her T-shirt and devoured her lushness with his soul. They undressed each other while caressing one another's lips with their own. All of their garments dropped to the floor like whiffs of clouds floating down from the heavens. Fital picked Zayashariya up and carried her to the bed. Passion and fire exploded from their very spirits as the odd couple explored one another's bodies.

Hours passed as the blissful duo enjoyed one another's bodies. The two soon fell into a sweet coma wrapped in each other's arms. The night was warm and tranquil.

Zayashariya awoke from her slumber. She looked at Fital's sleeping face and kissed his temple. *What am I going to do with you, toothsome man? Your touch is the closest I think I'll ever get to Heaven.* She removed Fital's arm from around her naked body, getting out of bed slowly, careful not to wake him and made her way down the hall to the restroom. Although she was feeling content for the moment, Zayashariya's muscles were still tight from her long journey. Being in Fital's arms felt as if the happiness of the world was within her grasp but she needed time to be alone; time to reflect on the events that led her to this small pentacle in her life. Zayashariya was embarking on whole new territory. Romantic love was an abstract idea until now and her emotions reacted in ways she never thought possible. She was not sure if she liked the weakening feeling that caused her stomach to flutter and her thoughts to go haywire. It was time to separate this illogical state of confusion from reality so she ran a hot bath and settled in slowly. Moments later, there was a light knock on the door.

"Yes," Zayashariya called out quietly. Her voice sounded seductive but scratchy from fatigue caused by their lovemaking.

"May I join you fair maiden?" Fital asked through the cracked door. His bright eyes winked at her. He pushed the door open and smiled upon her. As a physically flawless Manitou, Fital stood in the doorway as naked as a jay bird.

"Come on in," she invited. "I was getting lonely without you," she half lied.

Zayashariya did love his company but she really needed to be alone. She figured that Fital would not understand and she did not want to risk creating an opportunity for him to pry her mind.

Fital climbed into the tub. His presence soon was truly welcomed by her. They washed each other slowly, pausing to kiss, and to frolic around in the water until the water cooled. The couple dried off and wrapped themselves in towels. Fital grabbed Zayashariya's hand and they walked back to the room.

"I have to go soon," Fital said quietly. He opened the chamber door for her.

She entered.

He picked up his clothes and began to dress.

"I have to go on duty," he said.

Zayashariya watched him quietly as she leaned back on the bed letting the towel that clothed her fall free.

He paused and adored her. Fital started dressing again.

"I am a soldier you know," he said, avoiding her eyes. Guilt burdened him for having to leave her. "I wish I could stay longer but…"

"I understand." Disappointment was in her voice but she did not expect forever. But secretly she did not want him to go. After sharing her bath with him, she was hoping to share her bed again.

Fital finally looked at her, after he zipped his pants.

"When will I see you again?" he asked.

"Tonight. Sleep here again," Zayashariya demanded. *What am I doing?*

"I would love to," Fital responded. He kissed her waiting lips and left the room. He looked back and winked. "I would love to!"

"Until then," Zayashariya said, blowing him a kiss.

Fital caught it and placed his hand upon his heart and said, "Until then" and walked out of the room.

The door and Zayashariya's eyes closed.

Chapter 20

"How could you allow her to belittle you so?" harped the queen of Wilzasp, sitting on a green velvet bedspread and crossing her jewel covered hands one upon the other. She frowned at the king with disdain. "I would have never thought you, of all people, would be a mere coward!"

She stood up with her face twisted in disgust and pulled the golden pins, which were holding her diadem stable, out of her hair. The queen placed the crown on the night-stand. The faint glow of sea green crystals, which covered the chamber, glistened off of her oily orange skin.

"You are a disgrace to me and to Wilzasp!" Queen Eox spat.

She picked up a silver bell off of the night-stand and rang it three times. The chamber door flew open and three maids rushed past the dumbfounded king almost knocking him to the side. The maids undressed the queen gingerly, folding her silken robes and brushing her curly peach and gray hair until it felt like spun silk. The queen waved her hand and the maids disappeared into the hall with a light thump of the closing chamber door behind them.

"Well," she said, frowning. The fine lines of her face connected to each other like thread held between a child's fingers. "What do you have to say for yourself?" She sat on the bed wearing nothing but a gauzy slip.

He could see her nakedness clearly; every delicate curve of her body.

"Darling, please don't scorn me. I did what I thought was right. I acted appropriately," the king responded with venom.

"Weak!" Her lips trembled with anger. "You acted like a moronic weakling!" the queen spat, throwing her hands into the air. "A stupid simpleton! You let that bombastic woman humiliate you! Humiliate me! She humiliated us all!"

"No, no dear," he said. The king began to undress himself. "What would you have me to do, love?" he asked, looking into her slanted eyes. "Kill her? Have her gagged and bound?" The king was in a mild swivet. He took a deep breath and did all he could do to remain calm.

"Precisely!" the queen snapped. "When my father was king, he allowed no impiety from anyone. He learned from his forefathers not to tolerate dishonor." Her eyes were savage. "He made Wilzasp a secluded kingdom, free from terrorism and uproar! He defeated and eliminated all of the kingdoms surrounding us and after hundreds years of peace, you let in an intruder who is obviously slaughtering our people and you do absolutely nothing!" Her big slanted eyes burned through him like a blowtorch copulating with steel. "Chucklarki, you sicken me!" she spat at his feet and clinched her pearly teeth. "What kind of king are you? All these years of peace have made you soft and impotent. You invite a killer into our town and allow her to disrespect you in front of your people; then, you have the gall to not reprimand her for the sake of you being civilized. I swear, if my father wasn't such a sexist man, he would have given me the crown. Even he knew that I have more strength of a man than you!"

The king was angry now. "Do not speak to me that way! I am your husband! Your king!" he roared into her face. His hot breath battered her cheek. "I will not have you bad-mouthing me! You will not jawbone me into hunting down that strange woman just because of your lust for blood. Furthermore, I earned this crown. It was not given to me on a silver platter. Your father made me fight for this crown. I proved myself and you will not belittle me woman! Do you understand?"

"Weak!" the queen snapped.

King Chucklarki slapped her face with all of the power he could muster. She flew back against the bed. Queen Eox sat up quickly and laughed.

"You don't frighten me!" She laughed even harder. "Is that all you've got old man?" she taunted "Why didn't you slap that demon-witch?! She bad-mouthed you in front of your entire kingdom and you did nothing. She mocked you and you did nothing. She challenged you and you did nothing. She dismissed your authority and you did nothing." The queen sat up straight. Her breasts were pressing against her gossamer gown. Her dark red nipples poked through the material damp with sweat as her chest rose and fell with huffing breaths of wrath. She laughed harder. "You did nothing because you are nothing!" The queen of Wilzasp roared with laughter like a crazed lunatic.

The king leapt upon her. He slapped her again and again but her laughter would not cease. She roared like a mad woman. Her haunting laughter rang through the chamber causing it to bounce off the walls in horrible echoes.

"Stop it Eox!" he demanded, locking his hands around her throat.

She laughed on.

"Eox, stop it!" He tightened his grip. "You are driving me mad!" Red pulsated through his face. Veins bubbled up on his forehead. His teeth gnashed and his eyes bulged.

"Kill me!" Queen Eox cackled. "I rather die than to be the wife of a crotch-less king!"

He slapped her again. Blood poured from her swollen lips. Her laughter never died down. The king ripped the sheer gown off of her and mounted her. As he raped his wife, she laid there teary-eyed, staring at the ceiling, laughing nonstop. The king soon rolled over to the side and begged for death or sleep, whichever came first, to save him from her unearthly laughter. The queen laughed and laughed and laughed. He wept into the softness of his pillow. Both death and sleep refused him.

Chapter 21

Zayashariya knew she could not contain her hunger any longer. The dark stranger balled herself up on the bed and held onto her legs tight. A burning feeling passed through her stomach like a small fireball as she tried vigorously to control the pain. Her teeth ripped through her gums and retracted. Her eyes flashed and dulled. *What am I to do?* She knew that she could not go into the streets and feed like an animal. It was a moot thought to even think of such a thing, although the thought seemed like the simplest solution. After all, who was powerful enough to stop her? Zayashariya shook the thought from her mind and buried her face into her pillow. She quivered.

The dark stranger was becoming weak and she had to feed but her conscience haunted her. Images of torn and shriveled bodies flashed through her mind. She could still taste their bittersweet blood on her lips. Zayashariya winced at the painful memory. Her love for Fital and her fear of becoming a clone of her mother gave her an inexorable feeling of guilt. Guilt made it more difficult by the day to feed mercilessly on the people of Wilzasp. Pain ripped through her again. Zayashariya whimpered. She had to feed. She had to partake of the unholy communion and feed upon fresh warm life. The scarlet red room sent chills through her. Dreams of red currents of blood danced through her mind. She bit down hard on her lip. Saliva filled her mouth. Zayashariya could taste the blood slowly dripping into her mouth, caressing her tongue like a long lost lover. The coppery flavor sent her head reeling. She dressed herself as quickly as she could. The tiny sound of humming whispered in her ears. Zayashariya smiled. "The maid!" she whispered under her breath. Zayashariya quickly rushed to the door and peered out into the hallway. *Forgive me.*

A very young girl with pale peach freckles stood in the hallway. Her clothes appeared two sizes too big. They covered her like a blue and gold checkered tent. Her hair was spiked and multicolored. She wore a nose ring and four earrings in each ear. The sweet sound of her voice was ear candy as she sang to herself with intense emotion. She sang as if the lyrics were her very own and she alone knew firsthand the experiences the lyrics crooned of.

Zayashariya stared at the girl with pity in her eyes. The young maid's back was facing Zayashariya, unknowing of the danger lurking close behind. Death crept up behind the girl without making a solitary sound. Zayashariya grabbed the girl's head, broke her neck in one snap and drained her body of all blood. She cradled the limp body in her arms like a baby. Tears came. They came full of confusion; full of joy and pain all at once. Zayashariya pulled the body into her room, turned the girl into ashes, and added the girl to her jar of damned mortals. She wiped her sweaty bloodstained face with the back of her hand and sighed. Her hand rested upon the doorknob as she stood quietly in reflection. Guilt overwhelmed her.

"My hunger should be satisfied for a time," said Zayashariya, slipping out of the door. *You are just as I am.* She could hear her mother whispering in the back of her mind. The voice seemed clear and close by. A nauseous feeling filled her belly. Her head swam. Zayashariya fainted against the wall and slid down slowly to the floor. Blackness overcame her. "Not like you" left her drowsy lips as she slipped into unconsciousness.

*   *   *

"Yoki, my dear," Lilith waved her hand, calling the small humanoid to her.

"Yes ma'am." Yoki stepped closer to Lilith, with her hands folded behind her back and her fingers fiddling with one

another. Her palms were clammy and the knot in her throat grew bigger and tighter the closer she came to Lilith.

"May I ask your opinion on something? It pleases me to know what my guests think of my home and the people they encounter here," Lilith said.

"Yes. I will do my very best to answer you honestly," Yoki answered Lilith, looking at Zayashariya, her eyes questioning.

Zayashariya smiled and nodded, giving Yoki permission to answer Lilith and assuring her that all was well.

"Who is the greatest on the planet of Night; the most admirable, the most powerful?" Lilith grinned. She sat upon her throne with her legs spread open and her arms hanging off of the sides of her chair. In her eyes was dangerous intent. "Tell me lovely one."

Yoki looked at Zayashariya with doubt. Impending doom's fingers fondled the back of Yoki's neck. She feared Queen Lilith but it was in her nature to tell the truth. Yoki did not want to anger the queen because she had seen what Queen Lilith had in store for those who angered her. Yoki looked down at her hands and noticed that they were shaking. She quickly placed them behind her back and nervously smiled at the queen.

"I don't know much about your planet. I am only here visiting your daughter and I have not had the honor to meet many people here," Yoki replied and looked at Zayashariya. Her eyes searched Zayashariya's for some sort of clue, an augury or just emotional support.

Zayashariya smiled and instructed Yoki to relax and to continue. Zayashariya walked over to Yoki, placing her hands on her shoulders to comfort her, and promising that Lilith would not think of harming her because she was a dear friend.

Yoki loosened up. But, every bone in her body warned her of danger. Yet, she had complete trust in Zayashariya and she felt that Zayashariya would not allow Lilith to hurt her.

"Where are you from? You have a strange look about you," Lilith inquired.

Yoki was about five feet tall with short curly black hair and bright yellow skin. Two small feet supported her round and chubby body. She had a third eye in the middle of her forehead, a slit for a mouth, two dots for a nose, and small square ears. Her chin was pointy and her fingers were extremely long.

"I am from a distant planet called Thatruth. Zayashariya invited me here to meet you, dear queen, and to see your home. I am honored to have been given the opportunity to see a place so..." Yoki paused, searching for the right words. "...different from my own. I thank you for your hospitality."

"And what do you think of my home?" asked Lilith, staring at the girl with displeased eyes. Iniquity sang in Lilith's ear, composing horrid symphonies of torture.

"It is very different from where I come from," answered Yoki, looking at Zayashariya again. Yoki was very nervous. Her palms started to sweat profusely. She wiped them on her dress and took a deep breath. Something about the way the queen looked at her sent chills down her spine. Tiny bumps covered her skin. Her eyes darted quickly back and forth from Zayashariya to Queen Lilith. Zayashariya told her to relax. Yoki could in no way relax knowing the queen was breathing down her neck. Her fear of Lilith was too great. Yoki had witnessed first hand how evil Lilith could be. She had seen Lilith behead prisoners, whip helpless children, and throw servants into hot tar pits. Yoki did not want to meet any of those fates. She loved life way too much. Regret of coming to Night filled her. Her family pleaded with her not to go but she insisted that she would be safe with Zayashariya. They did not trust Zayashariya and did not approve of their friendship. They felt that nothing good could come from Night. But, Yoki did not want to miss the opportunity to see another planet. Now Yoki wished she had heeded the voice of her mother and stayed behind. Today her curiosity may cost her dearly.

"Go ahead," Zayashariya urged. "My mother can take the truth." Zayashariya gave Lilith a disdainful look. "Right mother?"

"Of course I can." Lilith nodded, her eyes narrowing into slits. "Tell me, what do you think of Night?"

"Like I said before, your land is very different from mine. Your customs are quite shocking to me." Yoki stumbled over her words. "I do not wish to pass judgment. I do not want to offend you."

"Out with it!" Lilith snapped and sat up straight on her throne.

"Mother, you are frightening her. Yoki is very sensitive. She isn't accustomed to our harsh ways. Please be gentle. Her comfort means much to me," Zayashariya spoke gently, careful not to alarm Yoki.

"She's a big girl. I am sure that she can handle it. We are all friends here. Everyone needs a little constructive criticism. I am sure that she could never say anything to offend me," Lilith addressed her daughter. "Speak your mind Yoki."

"Well," Yoki paused then reluctantly began again. "This place is a little harsher than what I am accustomed to. My planet is a very pleasant one. We enjoy peace and happiness. The greatest force on Thatruth is love. It is a bright planet filled with sunny days and starry nights, not noxious gas and gloomy skies. The people are kind and friendly. Our world is filled with beautiful wonders. Every morning there is a miracle. We have our problems like all of God's children but we try to solve them without violence and anger. This planet is quite the opposite." Yoki regained her confidence. "O, may I speak freely?"

"Yes. Yes. Please do." Lilith leaned closer, a snide grin on her face, secretly beckoning Yoki to evoke her twisted craving to obliterate those who oppose her.

"I feel that this ignominious planet is horrible. It is full of evil and abominations. It is immersed in shadow. The inhabitants here are cruel and full of malice. I am in continual discomfort. Fear walks with me constantly." Yoki swallowed hard. "I have never seen anything as close to what I have imagined Hell to be than this God forsaken place."

"True." Lilith nodded. "That is how my kingdom is supposed to be. It is good to know that I have succeeded in my efforts to make this place a haven of sinners."

"Yes you have." Yoki exhaled.

"Very well. Now tell me, who is the greatest on this planet?" Lilith grinned, anticipating an ego stroking.

"What do you mean? I don't quite understand," Yoki questioned.

"Who is the most powerful deity here?" Lilith asked. One of her eyebrows rose.

"With all due respect Queen, The Almighty Creator of All is the greatest on every planet. But, if you mean a humanoid or being besides "I Am," I guess Zayashariya is the greatest on this planet." Yoki smiled at her friend but a dreadful shadow was cast upon Zayashariya's face. Yoki was petrified.

"Oh really?" Lilith's voice grew hoarse. "And how did you come to that conclusion?" She peered deep into Yoki's eyes. "Your pride distresses me, Yoki. I imagine, for your sake, that your explanation will be a good one."

"Zayashariya is the only one here, that I have seen, that possesses an ounce of goodness and good always reigns over evil." Yoki looked into the queen's eyes and an ear piercing scream escaped Lilith's mouth. Instantly Yoki grabbed her ears but a burning pain stung her fingers. Yoki's hair went up in flames. She tore at her flaming head as the flesh of her hands and head melted to the bone.

"Not acceptable!" Lilith squealed.

"No!" Zayashariya screamed. The smell of burning flesh made her drunk with grief and anger. "Please leave her alone! Stop the torture now!"

Two of Lilith's ghouls rushed into the room and restrained Zayashariya. She tried to break free of the two ghouls holding her back.

"Mother please let her go! She is my best friend!" Zayashariya cried.

Lilith willed a heap of burning coals to appear. Lilith used her telekinetic powers to pick up Yoki and toss her into the hot coals.

Yoki's unconscious body fell upon the glowing balls of fire in a scorched heap of tattered and torn flesh.

"Mommy, please save her! It is not too late. She still lives!" Zayashariya wept as she saw her friend's skin melt to her bones. Yoki's skull was visible and her garments were no more. "Mommy, please stop!" Zayashariya tried to break free but the ghouls held her firm. "Yoki!"

"She insulted me! I am the greatest deity here and I will forever reign. Yoki was a fool. She uplifted you above me! I am the queen and you are nothing more but my spawn, a carbon copy of the original!" Lilith spat. "She must die like all the others. She did not recognize greatness. Foolish Yoki tried to uplift you above me, the Queen of Night. That baffles me! You over me! My kingdom will never be overthrown! I would have killed her mercifully if she would have shown an ounce of humility. Pride comes before a great fall and there she is, tumbling down!" Lilith howled.

"Mommy, she did nothing but disagree with you. She did not mean to exalt me over you. She meant that I was a nicer person than you not that I should have your throne. Those things are not great in her eyes. Don't you see, she sees what is in the heart! Please save her," Zayashariya pleaded.

"Never!" Lilith shot a fireball from her hand and burned the damned girl to a crisp. "Now you may have your precious friend," Lilith roared. "This is a lesson for anyone who wishes to defile my name."

"I hate you!" Zayashariya wept. "I hate you!" She broke free from the ghouls. Sweat covered her face. The heat of the room was unbearably high. "Yoki did no wrong. She only told the truth. You killed her because she saw how hideously ugly you were. You hated her because of her light and she brought sun rays into Night. Yoki was my friend; the only good person that I knew. You killed her despite of my love for her. I hate you!"

Lilith smiled. "This is Night! There is no room for goodness here! You speak foolishness child. I did you a favor. That fool was making you soft. Good, hate me! Maybe your hate will make you half the person I am."

"I do not want to be anything remotely close to what you are! You twisted monster! Know this, I hate you and I am no longer a part of you or this world that you live in."

"You don't have a choice!" Lilith growled.

"There is always a choice. You will see. To hell with the Council of Demons! To hell with Night! To hell with you!" Zayashariya looked at her mother with the deepest hate and smiled a vile smile. "I am nothing like you. You are a monster, a mere *blustering bully, grasping for power that you know eventually will be stripped from you. Your time will come and I will ensure that it does!"*

"Daughter." Lilith walked over to Zayashariya and traced her daughter's cheek with her finger. "*You are just as I am. When I fall, you will fall likewise."*

*   *   *

You are just as I am. Zayashariya cringed at the thought. Her eyes opened slowly. She looked around her and realized that she was lying in the hallway. Slowly Zayashariya pulled herself to her feet and dusted herself off. With sluggish and dizzy steps, she walked down the stairs. "I am nothing like you!" she yelled into the emptiness of her surroundings. Today she refused to let her guilt take the best of her. Her life was more important than the people of Wilzasp's.

Chapter 22

"What do you mean Zayashariya is gone?" Lilith hissed at the two putrid ghouls standing before her throne. "How could she be gone?" Her red skin pulsated. Her red skin tone morphed from light to dark to light again. The flame of hair on her head leapt high into the air putting bright blue flashes of light on the walls, casting frightening shadows about the room.

"Madammm, sheee hasss lefttt theee Netherrr Worldsss," they said in unison. "Theee ollld wizzzard helllped herrr gooo."

"How do you know this?" she belched.

"Weee......"

"Shut-up!" the Queen of Night screamed. "Get out and send me someone who can talk faster than you babbling fools! You two buffoons annoy me to no ends!"

"Yesss Madammm." They turned and ran out of the chamber as she blew fireballs at their heels.

Queen Lilith stood up and began to pace the platform before her throne. Hearing the sound of Lilith's pacing feet, the humanoids under the floor became restless and began to wail and moan in fear of her beginning her daily torture regimen. The smell of perspiration and filth filled the room as they moved around under the floor. Crowded bodies bumped and squeezed past one another, trying to get as far away from Lilith's throne as possible. An exasperated sigh left Lilith's lips. The ruckus under the floor irritated her to no end. Lilith looked down at the prisoner's miserable, scared, soiled faces and spat. The humanoids cried louder. Their moans were so irksome that Queen Lilith frantically covered her ears.

"Shut-up!" she yelled in a swivet of frustration and began to shoot fire from her fingertips, swiveling around crazily and burning every finger visible through the floor.

The moans stopped. "Do not provoke me to torture one of you. I want absolute silence!" she screeched.

A faint cry escaped from the floor dungeon.

"I have had it!" Lilith fumed.

She sat upon her throne and pushed a green button on the control panel located on the left arm of her chair. A square piece of floor rose, separating itself from the rest of the floor, suspended by chains. Out of the opening emerged a small humanoid child balled up on a circular platform. The platform turned sideways dropping the child on the floor and quickly disappeared back into the opening. The square was replaced and the floor appeared to be as normal as before. The bruised child whimpered. His pale green skin was scarred and bruised blue and black all over. The tattered cloth covering him was almost in thin shreds. His shirt only had one sleeve and his shorts looked like a makeshift loin cloth.

Lilith walked over to the child and grabbed him up by his arm pits. "All eyes on me!" she barked. The floor looked like a field of faces and fingers smashed against the rusty bars. Lilith looked the boy in the eyes. "Were you the one whimpering when I asked for silence?"

"Yes madam," the boy cried. His sea green eyes and emerald hair made him look like a wood elf. Refilling with fresh puddles of tears, his eyes were stretched as wide as possible. His breath exited his mouth in short fast bursts. Filled with ultimate dread, he could feel his heart beating against Lilith's palm.

"That means that you disobeyed me. Doesn't it?" Queen Lilith questioned the dangling boy, a wicked grin twisting her lips.

The humanoids under the floor gasped in fear for the boy but tried arduously to keep as silent as they could. A boyishly looking woman fainted and caused a domino effect of humanoids falling into one another. Lilith glared hungrily, eyes narrowed and teeth exposed, at the tumbling people and they quickly regained their footing.

"Sorry. I'm so sorry Queen Lilith," the boy wept. "Please don't hurt me." Tears ran down his pale cheek. It made a path down his dirt caked face revealing smooth young skin. "I'm so sorry madam. I was in pain. A man stepped on me. It hurt really badly. I couldn't smother my cries. Then, you burned me," he wailed like a blubbering baby.

"I forgive you." Lilith smiled at him, her flaming hair dancing. The boy stopped trembling. "Are you thankful?" she asked.

"Yes my queen."

"Let me see you smile," she said.

The boy smiled for her. His two front teeth were missing.

"Can I have a kiss?" asked Lilith. She winked at him and hugged his feather weight body.

"Y...y...yes," he answered reluctantly. He saw fear in the eyes of the humanoids beneath him. Slowly he leaned toward Lilith and kissed her lips. When his lips touched hers, he felt her hot breath fill his mouth and flow through his body. His entire body ignited. Lilith dropped the boy to the floor. Within a few seconds, his ashes fell through the floor into the eyes of the petrified onlookers. They winced in pain but wisely chose to remain silent.

"When I say quiet, I want quiet!" Lilith turned and sat back on her throne but before she could adjust herself comfortably, the chamber door swung open. A tall man walked through the door. He had deep olive brown skin and a full black beard. His shoulder length hair looked like black sheep's wool. He was slender and wore an ankle length robe, light sandals, and a scarf around his neck. He was very handsome, the type of man that was every woman's type. A look of displeasure was on his face.

"Judas," Lilith greeted him. "How nice to see you."

"The pleasure is mine Lilith. It has been a long time." Judas bowed as he stomped on a finger that was molesting his toes. "What is the purpose of this ridiculous floor?" he asked, stomping another finger. "It is terribly annoying." He paced from side to side, his feet in constant movement.

"They are my toys. I get bored being here all by my lonesome," she purred. "You have gotten so handsome my Hebrew haint." She licked her lips. "What's with the scarf?" Lilith cackled. "Take it off. It is quite warm in here."

Judas reluctantly took the scarf off. A dangerous look was in his eyes. He locked his jaw and gnashed his teeth. He really hated her. She always mocked him. Of course, Lilith knew why he wore the scarf. It hid the mark of his suicide. He had hung himself after he had betrayed the greatest man that had ever walked the Earth. Every time the mark was revealed, guilt and shame quaked through his being. He shunned the memory and his eyes burned with hatred for the wicked queen who caused the memory to resurface. At once, he regretted coming.

"Ooooh." Lilith twisted her face in amusing disgust. "What an eyesoar. I forgot," she said, lying through her teeth.

"Of course you did," he responded through his teeth. Judas covered the severe rope burn on his neck once again.

"Okay Lilith, let's not prolong this stupid game that you play every time you see me. Pay me and I'll give you the information that you requested," he seethed.

Judas hated when Lilith brought up the painful memory of his past. He pulled the scarf tight around his neck. He truly detested her. His suicide was what brought him to the Nether Worlds in the first place. After he killed himself, his body was resurrected and he was cursed to live forever in misery and unrest. His curse denied him rest of any kind. He was damned to keep on walking, moving, wondering, and betraying others until The Most High saw fit for his torture to end. Judas was banished to the Nether Worlds and forced to offer his employ to any despicable soul who offered him thirty pieces of silver. He would rather have a millstone tied around his neck and be thrown into the sea than to endure Night for eternity.

She didn't forget. Damn Lilith and her games!

Judas could feel his body getting hot all over. A bead of sweat appeared on his temple. He imagined placing a noose around Lilith's neck and savoring the sound of her neck snapping; the sound like the popping of knuckles. The thought brought a smile to his face. Once again, he was calm.

"How much my devilish disciple?" Lilith smiled at him. She pulled a small pouch out of a compartment hidden in the arm of her throne.

"The usual," answered Judas, crossing his arms. "Thirty pieces of silver." He abhorred her. "You know the routine."

Lilith tossed him the pouch of silver and he caught it in mid-air.

"What do you want to know?" He shuffled his feet. To cease movement caused him excruciating pain.

"Stop moving. You are making me dizzy." Lilith grinned.

"To Hell with you Lilith." Judas cut his eyes at her and paced faster. "What do you want to know?"

"Where is my daughter?"

"Who?" Judas held his hands behind his back. *If she can play the fool, so can I.*

"Don't play with me imp!" Lilith growled. So far, on the edge of her seat she sat, she appeared to be sitting on nothing at all, as if an invisible chair held her up. "Where is Zayashariya?"

"From what I hear, she has left the Nether Worlds." Judas looked around him. "Can you get me a seat or something? My legs are tired. I have been walking none stop." He smirked. "I have to be comfortable to deliver the news." *Now who's feeling a little annoyed.*

"I don't have time for your games. Don't make me...." Lilith hopped to her feet, pointing her hand at him. Flames leapt across her fingertips.

"Save the threats Lilith. You can not punish me any worse than I have been punished. I have already done the abominable. Do not delude yourself. I have no fear of you," he spat. Judas' eyes narrowed. His dark eyebrows gleamed like silken arches.

"You know the rules Judas. Your soul can not find rest." Lilith shook her head. "No more droll repartee. Proceed," she demanded, "or I'll tie you to a chair and pleasure myself by watching you writhe in pain."

"Don't flatter yourself." *Shrew!* "I just thought I would entertain you with some friendly banter since you always find the time to jest, only at my expense of course," Judas said and continued, "Well, the old wizard's apprentice Shayla confided in me, obviously she didn't know who I was. I made an appearance at the old wizard's place and I disguised myself as one of the many workers he has slaving for him. It was very easy to blend in since everyone there keeps to themselves. It was rare to make eye contact with anyone except the old wizard. He was the only one I purposely avoided.

As I snooped around the castle, I was wondering why the daemon was doing the old wizards bidding so I made the apprentice an acquaintance of mine and she began to confide in me. Females find it hard to resist me." He laughed. "That little fur ball was practically head over heels. Information ran from her mouth like water from a faucet."

Lilith rolled her eyes.

"You know that beast, the daemon, works for no one so I questioned the apprentice about why the daemon was there. The apprentice said that the daemon struck a deal with the old wizard. If the wizard would warp Zayashariya out of the Nether Worlds, he would serve the old wizard for a season." Pausing, he took a deep breath and continued. "In turn, Zayashariya would summon the daemon to the material plane when she reached safety. Of course, she would summon him without the wizard's knowledge. I received that last little piece of information from the daemon himself. I heard him mumbling under his breath when he thought he was alone. This is how I knew the apprentice's story about Zayashariya's departure was true." Judas shuffled his feet. "Don't ask me how the apprentice found out about Zayashariya's deal because I do not know. I guess it is safe to say that she always has her ear to the wall."

"Well done Judas." Lilith smirked. "Forever the perfect betrayer. I bet she thought that you were her best crony." Lilith blew him a kiss.

The fiery kiss disappeared before it touched his lips. Judas exhaled.

"When are we going to have a more intimate meeting?" Lilith said, opening her legs and letting her arms fall between them, looking boyish yet sexy. "It's not like you are busy. Plus, I promise to keep you in constant motion," she cooed, gyrating her hips, excitingly groaning, and grinding against her seat.

"I'm too busy for you!" Judas snapped. He really hated her. He was as sexually attracted to her as he was to the putrid floor beneath his feet. Judas felt that he would rather hang himself again.

"I promise to keep you moving." Lilith sucked her bottom lip and winked at him.

"I rather stop and endure the pain," he spat. A disgusted frown bent his lips.

With a wave of her hand, the scarf around his neck turned to ashes, exposing the hideous rope burns on his neck.

"To hell with you demon whore!" Judas screamed. Spit flew all over his face as he pointed at her and sped up his pace.

"Too late!" Lilith laughed, falling back against her throne. "Look around you. Hell could get no better." She laughed on.

"May I go now?" Judas asked, walking backward towards the door.

"Of course Judas." Lilith regained her composure.

He walked away.

"By the way," she said.

Judas turned around, his mouth twisted in utter annoyance and his forehead wrinkled with frustration.

"On your way out, tell those smelly imps to come back in."

"Sure." Judas walked out of the door. He hated her.

After a few moments, the two ghouls reappeared before Lilith's throne. They bowed down in unison and stood erect before Queen Lilith ready to take orders.

"Fetch me the old wizard and that deplorable daemon Kalpvaleim." Lilith's throne spun around slowly and the chamber went dim.

"Yesss madammm," the two beasts said, bowing in unison.

"Now!" Lilith's voice echoed. She was no where to be seen.

The room fell dark and the faint lamentation of the humanoids under the floor began.

Chapter 23

It was night. Night in the Land of Wilzasp was a beautiful occasion. Three moons lit up the sky like sparkling disco balls. Venco, the largest moon, glowed pale violet against the navy sky, outshining the inferior twin moons Klora and Minquos. The stars were sprinkled heavily across the heavens like powdered sugar on devil's food cake. The air was warm and dry. It wrapped around the king's body like a welcomed caress. He stood on the balcony of his palace, with his hands on the rail, taking deep breaths, swallowing the fresh air. He was tranquil. The soft air blew ripples through his floor length nightgown. The black cotton garment covered him from shoulder to ankle. His matching nightcap completed his comfortable night time ensemble.

It had been a long time since the king had a moment to himself. It seemed as if his entire life was turned inside out and he was as helpless as a wounded bear entangled within the iron jaws of a hunter's trap. He felt as if he was losing control of everything. Everything that he held dear to him was slipping through his fingers like water through a strainer. His kingdom was in a state of confusion. His people were becoming hopeless and afraid. His wife had lost all respect for him. To touch her skin was like burying his hands in snow and trying to show her any other type of affection was like tongue kissing through glass. But what disturbed him most of all was the fact that he could not put his finger on what frightened him so much about the town's stranger, Zayashariya. He had seen an unmistakable evil in the woman's eyes that chilled him to the bone. Only once before in his life he had felt that way. Only once.

It was many moons ago. The king was a very young boy around the age of eight. He was visiting his great-grandmother Anna Varly in the Land of Williamskip which was about five hundred miles from Wilzasp. Williamskip existed before the time when his future wife's forefather had destroyed all of the nearby kingdoms surrounding Wilzasp.

King Chucklarki could remember his great-grandmother's house clearly.

It was a small house made of sun dried mud-bricks. The house was created by his great-grandmother's father's hands. It was one level and about ten feet high. The roof was made of shiny black tiles and the windows were dressed in pastel colored curtains. Small flowers reigned over the front yard with multicolor splendor. A wooden bench sat on the porch next to a hard wood door that read, "MY HOME IS YOUR HOME."

Anna Varly and her family were very poor but they were noble people. She was loved and well respected by many. The royal people of the land and of nearby lands summoned her for her wisdom and advice. In return for her erudition, they ensured her that she would never starve. Although they gave her food, they never considered her family's poor status and never offered her money to improve her lifestyle. A selfless server of the people, Anna Varly was thankful for the little she received and helped anyone who needed her gladly. She never expected anything in return for her good deeds. Many times she would say that a simple life kept her honest and her heart pure.

The king smiled at the thought of Anna Varly. His thoughts were carried away with the wind and his mind was transported back in time.

*   *   *

Chucklarki sat at the kitchen table with his great-grandmother, picking through string beans. Age had turned the old woman's orange skin a deep burnt color. By looking at her decrepit form, he could tell that she was on her last leg. Death would come soon. He could see its reflection in her eyes. Anna Varly leaned towards him and grabbed his hand with her skeletal own.

"Chucklarki," Anna Varly forced out in a hoarse voice. "There is much for you to know." She leaned back against the back of her wooden chair. Anna Varly wiped her hands on her tattered apron and pulled a few string bean strings from her fingers. "There is much for me to tell you and we have to speak now before it is too late." She stood up and grabbed him by his arm and pulled him behind her like a rag doll. Her strength was amazing for a woman her age. Chucklarki struggled to keep his footing as they shuffled down the hall.

Anna Varly walked to the wall at the end of the hallway, knocked on it three times, and stepped backward. She slapped her hands together and the entire narrow wall slowly opened as clouds of dust formed at its edges. The old woman turned to him and waved for him to follow her through the opening.

Chucklarki was frightened yet curious about what was inside of the hidden passageway. He did not hesitate because his trust in his great-grandmother was unwavering. Upon entering, the door closed silently behind them. Anna Varly pulled a string hanging from the ceiling and the entire room lit up.

It was a small room containing only a table and two chairs. Bookshelves filled with old books made up the walls. The room smelled of decaying paper and pinewood. A thick blanket of dust covered the entire room. He could see their footprints on the floor.

Anna Varly took off her apron and wiped the table and chairs clean. Chucklarki sneezed. She sat down and he followed her lead and took a seat himself. Leaning across the table, with her elbows pressed hard against the old wood, Anna Varly cleared her throat. A look of compassion and concern masked her face.

"Boy," she said softly, staring into his eyes. Her skin sagged as if it would fall off of her skull and hit the floor like dripping fat.

"Yes Grandma," answered Chucklarki, looking at her with his eyes wide and full of undeniable love, giving her his undivided attention. He leaned on the table with his chin in his palms. Despite her age and the toll gravity had taken on her skin, she was still pretty to him. He smiled.

"Do you believe in God?" asked Anna Varly.

Chucklarki was shocked. "Of course not Grandma! Father and Mother told me that the belief in God was foolishness. Supernatural beings and such things are a myth. Prehistoric people used to believe in that stuff. In school, they taught me of the legends of the God of ancient Israel and Jesus, Zeus, Buddha, the Corn Mother, Osiris, Mawu-Lisa, and Thor. I know those things are all fiction," he said with his face twisted in thought, trying to think of even more names. He gave up.

"Enough!" Anna Varly cut him off, irritated by his rambling. "Well, the school is right about most of it. A lot of those things are full of folly." She stood up and walked to a shelf and pulled out a large black book. Her fingers caressed the dark leather. She held it as if it was a precious rare gem. "But, there is truth in this book," she said, laying the book on the table. "There is such a thing as good and evil." She opened the book. "A true God and a devil." She turned the pages. "And both are still among us."

Chucklarki was getting scared. Everything she said, he instantly believed. His great grandmother was not the type of woman who wasted her time with tales of fantasy. Truth and logic were the balm that nourished her lips.

"How do you know?" he asked in a tiny voice, his eyes wide, and nervously rubbing his moist palms on his shirt.

"I know," said Anna Varly, smiling wearily. She closed the book. "Take this book. Read it when you are older. It talks about who God really is. Keep it forever. Believe in it. He will give you unbelievable hope and strength." She pushed the big book across the table to him. The title was written in antaean gold letters.

"Okay Grandma," agreed Chucklarki, taking the book and holding it close to him. It was almost as big as his chest. He handed it back to his great-grandmother and asked her to place it inside of the giant pocket on the back of his shirt. She did.

"Promise me something," said Anna Varly, grabbing Chucklarki's face gently with her frail hands.

"What?" He looked into her loving eyes and blinked. "I will do whatever you ask of me," he said. A look of ultimate love was given to his grandmother. Chucklarki's eyes were sincere and chaste.

"To keep it forever," she said, kissing his forehead and dropping her hands.

"I promise."

"I know you do not believe yet but I will make you a neophyte concerning the spiritual plane." Anna Varly smiled.

"How?" Chucklarki questioned. "It is not that I don't believe anything you tell me. I do. How will you prove it?"

"There is something else I want to show you," Anna Varly said as she walked over to another shelf. She parted a row of books and pulled a cloth bag from behind them. Then, she poured the contents onto the table. Sprawled across the table was a stick of white chalk, five black candles, a jar of glowing red dust, and a small book tied with a dark ribbon.

"I am not supposed to do this but... Never dabble in the dark craft. It is pure evil. But, this is the only way I can show you proof immediately." She took the chalk and drew a large star with a circle around it and said, "Again I beg you, never dabble in the mantic arts. You may unintentionally unleash an evil you can not control." Then, she put a black candle on each point of the star and then sprinkled the glowing dust over it. "It is also forbidden by The Creator," she said and lifted her eyes to the heavens, mouthing the words 'forgive me' under her breath.

Anna Varly stepped backward and picked up the little tied book. She took the ribbon off of the book, letting the ribbon fall to the floor, and read from its crumbling pages. Her words were mumbled and incoherent to Chucklarki. The circle began to glow. It pulsated and suddenly a circle of red light flooded the room.

Chucklarki was inundated with fear, paralyzed from head to toe. He wondered if this was what death felt like. He could not move. His breath left him. Sweat covered his small oval face and his peach curly hair tightened into little fists on his head.

"Gr...gr...grandma," he stuttered. "Wh..wh..what is that?" His eyes overflowed with tears and his small frame quaked. He saw a large beast within the circle. It had scarlet skin and fire for hair, a woman with long black fingernails. The pungency of her evil radiated from her pores. She was the quintessence of an abomination.

"Grandma," Chucklarki cried, "Make her go away! Make her go away!" Fear grabbed his heart. Foreboding molested him. He fell to the floor with his hands covering his head.

"Make her go away!" he cried out as dust flew into his mouth causing him to spit wildly. "Please Grandma! Please!"

Anna Varly chanted a small phrase over and over again until the room went black. A moment later, the light was back on and everything was back to normal.

Chucklarki got up. His face was gray and caked with dust, tears, and spit. He regained his footing and sat back in his chair. Breathing slowly and heavily, he swallowed hard and exhaled.

"What was she?" he asked.

"A demon," Anna Varly answered the petrified boy as she gathered the contents of the bag together and placed it back into its hiding place. "She is an evil demon from Gehenna, the queen of a horrid place called Night. Beware of her seed..." Anna Varly heard a noise. "Come boy." She jerked him from the table and rushed him out of the room. "I hear your father." Knocking on the wall three times, the door opened and closed behind them. Anna Varly pushed Chucklarki out of the room and quickly followed him into the hallway. "Do not tell anyone of the things that I've shown you. They will not understand. Nor will they believe you. They will think your mind is unstable." She pointed at her temple and moved her finger in a circular motion. They hurried down the hall and into the closest room which happened to be the bathroom. "Come here," she demanded. Anna Varly washed the dust from Chucklarki's face and hands. "I don't know what to do about these clothes." She shook her head from side to side. Her wisp of hair hardly moved. She wiped his clothes off as best as she could.

"What are you doing Mama Varly?" a deep voice asked from the doorway of the bathroom. A tall man walked into the room from the hall and leaned over and kissed her cheek. He seemed a giant compared to her wizened form.

"I'm cleaning the boy." Anna Varly smiled. "He fell and got all dirtied up." She hated telling half truths. She kissed her grandson, Chucklarki's father, back. "He's okay now." She looked *down at Chucklarki. "Aren't you love?" She winked and kissed the boy.*

"Yes Grandma." Chucklarki kissed her back and took his father's hand. "Are you ready to go?" he asked him.

"Yes son." Chucklarki's father responded as he kissed his grandmother and walked out of the door.

Chucklarki looked back over his shoulder at his great-grandmother and lipped "I promise." He waved goodbye and so did she.

*   *   *

King Chucklarki remembered that day vividly. His great-grandmother never got the opportunity to tell him more. She died a few weeks after that incident. Zayashariya brought on the memory. She reminded him so much of the demon woman that he saw that day so long ago. Zayashariya instilled in him the very same feeling of dread and helplessness. Except now, he was too proud to fall on the ground and wallow in fear. This time he would stand and face his foe. He was determined to extinguish the demon that walked among his people.

The king walked through the sheer lavender curtains that were behind him, which led into his bedroom. His lovely wife was sound asleep in bed. King Chucklarki could hear Queen Eox breathing softly. Her breathing sounded like the purr of a tiny kitten. He approached her resting body and kissed her cheek. The queen smelled of jasmine and roses. A hint of vanilla was in her hair. She had a small scar between her bottom lip and her chin. He had given it to her the night that they had fought. He had hit her to silence her laughter. The queen's taunting laughter made him temporarily insane and he had beaten her again and again that night until she had become absolutely witless. Her bruises were long gone but the tiny scar remained to haunt him forevermore. His kissed the horrible mark. He would never ever strike his wife again. Never. He would take a blade to his wrist first before he would harm her again.

The king walked over to a painting of Eox and himself on the wall across the room. They were happy then. How beautiful she looked in the painting, an empyreal perfection of loveliness. King Chucklarki knocked on the painting three times. He knocked one time each on their faces and once on their joined hands. The painting opened like a medicine cabinet and he pulled out an oak box. He mumbled something under his breath and the box opened. The king sat it upon the desk and pulled out the book. He closed the box and put it back where it belonged, behind the painting. He left his bedroom and went to his study. Reluctantly, he pulled out his desk chair and placed the book on the plane. His fingers traced the gold letters on the front of the book, savoring the memory of him acquiring it from his great grandmother when he was a young boy. Trusting Anna Varly's word, he began to read. He knew that he would find the solution to his problems soon enough.

Chapter 24

The dining hall was busy. On very hot days, most of the town's people went to the Inn to be shielded from the outside heat. It was almost a hundred and fifteen degrees outside. It was night and the temperature was at least ten degrees higher that day. The Inn was packed to full capacity. There was only one waitress serving.

Meki, the waitress that served Zayashariya the night before, worked like a slave in the dining hall. The young woman ran from table to table until she was literally out of breath. Her bandaged finger ached. Sweat ran from her overworked body, soaking her clothes. She leaned against the wall for a short rest.

"Nan!" Meki puffed. "I need a break!" she yelled through the doors leading to the kitchen.

A voice screamed back, "Go on dear. Gekav can take your place."

Meki took off her apron and walked out of the dining hall. She was dressed in a peach toga that blended almost perfectly with her bright orange skin and peach hair. Ivory earrings hung to her shoulders and her hair bounced with every step she took. Meki turned the corner and left the Inn. Taking a short cut through a nearby alley, suddenly she came to a halt. Discomfort made her stomach queasy. The hair on the back of her neck stood up but her pride would not let her back away.

"Hello," said Zayashariya, standing in front of the stressed waitress, startling her and blocking her path.

"Get out of my way freak!" Meki snapped, a scowl on her face. She was ready to fight. Hate for Zayashariya fueled Meki's desire to thrash the dark stranger. Her jealousy and anger outweighed her fear.

"Move me," growled Zayashariya, crossing her arms.

The young woman looked into the violet eyes of Zayashariya. Her eyes seemed to glow in the darkness. Every hair on Meki's body turned to icicles. "This can not be real," she mumbled to herself, looking into Zayashariya's eyes again. They were glowing like fire now. Meki looked at her broken finger and then back at Zayashariya. Fear climbed down her back like a millipede. "I don't want any trouble," the young woman stuttered, slowly backing away. "Just leave me be."

"You wanted trouble last night and it seems to me that you wanted trouble moments ago." Choler echoed in Zayashariya's voice.

"I apologize, lady." Meki backed away. "Let's call a truce. I'll stay out of your way. You stay out of mine. I no longer have an aversion toward you."

"Maybe that's not good enough," said Zayashariya. Her fingernails reflected the glow of her eyes as she sharpened them against each other. They made a subtle popping sound.

Meki turned and ran as fast as she could. Her chest heaved with pressure and fear. Her pursuer caught up to her in a millisecond.

"Why run? I want to satisfy your curiosity." Zayashariya grabbed Meki by the back of her head and ripped one of her arms clean off. The sound of snapping bones filled the air. Blood squirted out of Meki's torso like pool water out of a drowning child's mouth. The amputated arm dropped to the ground by her feet. A low whine was forced from Meki's lips as she panicked at the sight and pain of her detached arm. Her body went into complete shock. Zayashariya's face contorted into an ill-looking mask. Her face elongated as her eyes turned into amethyst fireballs. Needlelike teeth peeked over her lips. She pushed Meki to the ground and picked up the fallen limb.

"I don't like to be disrespected," the beastly woman yelled as it installed her fangs into the severed arm. "I really hate to be insulted!" Zayashariya's body contorted. Her arms elongated to the length of her legs. She walked on all fours.

Meki had a seizure, fainted then came to. A soul shattering scream ripped from her lips.

Zayashariya pinned the waitress down, Meki howling like a wolf as Zayashariya sunk her scarlet stained fangs into the screaming woman's stomach. Zayashariya drank deeply. With each pull of liquid life, Zayashariya's eyes became cloudier and threatened to transport her into complete ecstasy.

"It won't happen again, now will it!" the she-beast yelled into the dying woman's face. Zayashariya bit into Meki's neck. Blood spattered everywhere, like crimson rain drops. Hoping one more drop could be drained, Zayashariya twisted the woman's neck like a wet towel and sucked until her mouth ached. She dropped the dead body on the concrete and left it there to rot. Zayashariya wiped her mouth and disappeared down a nearby busy road, transforming quickly back to normal.

Chapter 25

Fital stood at his post outside of the King's house. His eyes examined the dwindling crowd of people passing through town. Sorrow and despair weighed heavily on his soul as he observed how his people were disappearing. It seemed as if the population had been cut in half. He wished for the opportunity to come face to face with the monster that was killing his people. The streets were almost bare compared to how it was before the murders. Like a seltzer tablet in water, the town was becoming smaller and smaller.

Almost every home in Wilzasp had suffered a loss. Fital himself had lost a few friends and relatives to the hands of the unknown culprit. If he could only find out whom or what was doing these evil deeds, he would put an end to everything. Fital's thoughts were snatched away by a piercing scream. He ran down the street in the direction of the noise. He ran into an alley behind the Inn where he found three women and a girl screaming.

"What is it?" Fital asked one of the hysterical women.

"Look! Look!" One of the women pointed. She held the young girl's head to her chest to protect her eyes from the hideous scene.

Fital ran deeper into the alley. He saw the mutilated body of the drained waitress, his ex-lover Meki, with her arm lying beside her.

"Leave this place!" Fital ordered the women and the girl. "Now!" he yelled. They backed away slowly and then ran to tell others.

The soldier walked over to the body and kneeled down. He touched the side of Meki's face gently. Her flesh felt like soft leather. A single tear ran down his bright orange cheek. He mourned his ex-girlfriend.

"This has to end!" he screamed. "We are being exterminated." Fital grabbed his sword and stormed from the alley. "Did anyone witness this? Did anyone see anyone else leave this area? Did anyone hear anything?" he screamed through the streets. "Answer me if you fear for your life!"

"We are in pain like you are," an unknown voice answered from inside a house nearby. "Threatening us will not ease your pain or ours. Go home Fital, get some rest." An old woman stepped out of her door. Despair and hopelessness was in her eyes. "The creature will reveal itself sooner or later. But if you look closely, it has revealed itself already. You just refuse to see." The tired old woman walked back into her house and closed the door behind her.

Fital watched her disappear into her home and stood stiffly while the tears came. He threw his sword to the ground in a fit of rage and gnashed his teeth.

Nearby people stopped what they were doing and gathered around the irate man. Some offered to comfort him but he wished them away. They felt his pain but no one knew who or what was destroying the people of their small race. Everyone suspected Zayashariya but there was no proof. It could be a wild animal or maybe one of their own could have gone insane.

Everyone walked away from Fital and continued their everyday chores. Tears dressed their eyes like heavy garments. All hearts were clouded and filled with sorrow.

Chapter 26

It was early in the morning. The tweeting birds and rustling animal life in the nearby forest stirred. Sleep still possessed most of the town's people. Like two roses growing in a field of lilacs, the twin suns were pink in the lavender sky.

A small group of girls played together in the rear of one of the residential buildings near the forest. They ran in and out of the trees, chasing one another through the forest paths, unbeknownst to the eyes watching them from above.

Zayashariya leaned out of her window. The breeze whipped through her purple locks, looking like violet ribbons waving in the wind. She studied the five girls from her window and her hunger raged within her.

"I will not partake! They are mere children!" she said, trying to deny herself of blood but the temptation fueled her hunger ten times more than normal. Her hunger was uncontrollable and the beast within her could not be contained.

Zayashariya quickly dressed herself and left the Inn. She cautiously checked her surroundings and went around the back of the Inn so no one could see her. The dark woman ran deep into the forest, hoping that the leaves crunching beneath her feet would not alert anyone of her presence.

The forest was populated mostly with short bushes and narrow tree trunks. She was afraid that she had no where to hide. Her eyes searched frantically. Her stomach roared, begging for deathly nourishment. She ran further, searching desperately for a hiding spot. Suddenly she tripped, scraping her knees and landing on a tangle of tree roots. Before her stood a giant tree with a massive trunk, thick twisted roots and what seemed like millions of branches stretching up into a thick canopy of emerald leaves. She concealed herself behind the enormous tree; then, mumbled a spell to herself making the sound of her voice alter.

"Little ones, come and play with me," Zayashariya called in a sweet, high pitched voice.

"Who is there?" one of the girls asked. She stopped playing with her friends and searched her surroundings. The other girls watched in silence.

"I am a fairy. Come and see," Zayashariya called as she created a buzzing noise with her teeth. Placing her palms together and blowing through her fingers, the dark one created a ball of light that floated around the tree that she hid behind.

"Here I come!" Anniz yelled. Curiosity and supreme wonder filled the child's heart. A chance to see a real fairy was a rare privilege. Her story books were filled with the tricky creatures and she always felt that something so magical had to be true. She clapped her small hands together, extremely excited to see the light. She ran toward the bright ball of mystery with all the speed that she could muster.

"Don't go!" screamed Luv, another one of the little girls. "Remember that something bad is lurking around!" the little girl warned. "Remember that someone is hurting our people and they could be out here somewhere," she whined.

"I'm going! A fairy can't hurt us," Anniz yelled and ran into the woods. "I see fairy light! Look!" She pointed ahead of her. The light circled the tree and shined brighter and brighter.

"Don't go!" the other girls begged. Anniz ran on. The other girls ran behind her, afraid of letting her go alone.

"Wait up!" Plaula, the tallest of the girls, screamed as she tried to catch up with Anniz.

No one answered. The girls ran on.

Anniz slowed when she came within arms length of the strange light. She paused and looked at the strange light with pure fascination. She reached out her hand to touch it but it floated behind the tree and she followed it. Zayashariya caught Anniz by the arm as she peeked around the tree. Zayashariya touched her own lips with her finger then she touched the girl's mouth.

"Shhh," said Zayashariya soothingly.

The girl tried to scream. Her eyes popped out in terror.

"Shhh!" Zayashariya shushed as she put her hand over the little girl's mouth. "Sit on my lap. I won't hurt you," she said to the girl while rubbing the child's soft hair. She kissed the small child's forehead. "I won't hurt you," she whispered.

Anniz relaxed. A smile curled the young girl's soft face. She looked at Zayashariya with eyes pulled into slants by tight ponytails on each side of her head.

"Here, touch the fairy." Zayashariya placed the glowing ball into the girl's hand. When the child touched it, it disappeared. Anniz giggled.

Moments later the others came through the brush, simply surprised by the stranger's presence. Not knowing whether to run or stay, they looked at Anniz's relaxed disposition and decided not to leave at once.

"Come, sit around me in a circle. I have a story to tell and a trick to show you," said Zayashariya, smiling. "Sit. I won't bite."

The girls cautiously did as they were told. They circled the dark one and stared into her violet eyes, mesmerized by the stranger's beauty, captivated by the rich tone of her voice, and intrigued by her mere existence.

Zayashariya told them many tales and showed them many magic tricks. She spoke of magical kingdoms and princesses, wicked rulers, and exotic creatures. She transformed leaves into flowers and made rocks whistle musical tunes. The girls laughed and shouted with glee.

Night was coming soon and the dark stranger's hunger was becoming greater. She did not want to harm the children but she felt that she had no choice. Her desire for blood was far greater than her desire for peace of mind. She had no strength for sacrifice; therefore, she could not allow herself to show mercy.

"W...w...we must go now," Jigh, the prettiest girl, stuttered, realizing that the   suns were setting and that they had been with the stranger since morning. "Our parents are probably worried sick. We have been gone the entire day."

"One last trick," Zayashariya told the girls. She stood up and mumbled a few strange words and a shining ball appeared in her hand. "Do you want to hold it?   It doesn't burn. Touch it."

Luv reached for the ball. A serge of power went through her body. It made her giggle hysterically. She passed the ball to the rest of the girls. Vam was the last to receive it. Vam gave the ball back to Zayashariya and the dark woman made the sphere disappear. Suddenly all of the girls fainted.

Zayashariya went to the first girl, installed her fangs, and drained her of all blood. The dark one drained each girl one by one until her evil appetite was satisfied.

Zayashariya cried.   She wailed like a banshee holding her head in her hands.   Blood bubbled in her stomach but her hunger refused to let her vomit it out. She trembled with shame and regret. Her inimical hunger was in constant battle with her compassionate heart. She had no ken of her nature. All she knew was that she was a mephitic duende who did not deserve to dwell on any planet except for Night. Zayashariya fell to her knees and let out a painful cry that rang through the entire town like a knell.

"Damn me! Damn me back to the hell where I came from! I do not deserve life in another place! I am as Lilith made me, evil," she cried out. Suddenly, she heard the sound of footsteps nearby. *Who's there?* Her cries died and she disappeared into the darkness of the forest.

A pair of soldiers arrived at the scene of the crime. They had heard the beastly woman's monstrous cry. Quietly they walked through the woods, trying to remain inconspicuous and searching the area carefully. To their horror, they stumbled upon the   girls' lifeless bodies. Gasping in disgust and overwhelmed with anger and grief, the two men could not conceive of the idea that some sick fiend had actually preyed upon children. They could not believe that any creature with a conscience could commit such an abomination, such a twisted crime. The soldiers examined the bodies of the little girls lying on the ground. The skin of the children was shriveled to their bones like an ancient mummified corpse. Their eyes were closed and sunk deep into their skulls. A peaceful smile was on each face. Death must have come to them while they slept; when they were totally unaware of danger.

"Who did this? What did this?" one of the soldiers cried aloud. "We have to stop this! We have to do something before this situation results in total genocide!"

The other soldier, Bronson, gathered the bodies into a small pile. His heart broke into a thousand fragments. Tears traveled down his smooth cheeks like a raging river of sorrow. His body shook violently.

"I don't know who did this Calry. Whoever or whatever it is, it is going to pay with its life!" Bronson yelled. "These were children! Helpless children!" The man wailed like an abused animal. Luv was his little girl and Plaula was his niece. "That beast is going to pay!" His head dropped. Bronson looked down at the ground, his eyes fogged with tears. Quickly he dried his eyes. He saw footprints leading into the woods. Waving for Calry to come and look, he said, "Calry, I think we are on to something." He kneeled down and touched the prints. They were fresh. He looked up at his friend with a furrowed brow. Adrenaline and fear pumped through his body. Bronson wanted to kill but knew very well that his chances of being killed were greater. He was no fool. Whoever did these murders was not one of them. It was something beyond his imagination.

"It is the high heeled shoeprint of a woman. I bet it is that stranger. She is the only one around that would wear such a shoe. That alien strumpet is probably the monster responsible!" Calry yelled out in hatred.

Zayashariya hid behind a large tree about fifteen yards away. The two men were blocking the path that led back into the town's streets. She waited and hoped that she would not have to kill again. *Please leave this place.* She did not have the energy to clamber over trees and rocks, risking the possibility of being discovered and having to fight after all of her efforts to escape.

"Let's follow the tracks," Calry told Bronson.

A look of terror crossed Bronson's face. He swallowed hard.

Calry saw that his partner was hesitant and said, "Let's do it for the children."

"For the children," Bronson repeated. His voice was shaky but determined.

With renewed courage, the two men grabbed their swords and followed the footprints to the tree that Zayashariya hid behind. The soldiers heard something breathing. Bronson held his sword over his head and jumped to the other side of the tree.

Behind the tree, he saw an enormous opossum. Its pointed nose was pink and wet. Its ebony slick fur and pink thick tail shined in the light of the crystals. The opossum hissed, exposing its pin-like fangs. Bronson swung at the beast but missed. The beady eyed creature slapped the soldier across the head with its tale. Bronson fell to the ground. Calry swung his sword at the opossum's head and missed. The beast opened its huge jaws exposing eight razor sharp fangs. Out of its mouth a great gust of wind blew, blowing Calry into a tree behind him. Bark and leaves flew everywhere, covering the man in wooden fragments.

"Leave me now and you will live!" the beast screeched in a high pitched voice. Drool ran down its sharp maw. It breathed heavily and unevenly. "Don't force me to kill you!"

Bronson jumped to his feet. He ran toward the beast with his sword in front of him pointing at its chest. "You killed my girl!" he screamed to the top of his lungs. "You must die!"

The opossum lifted his foot and swung it effortlessly, scratching the man's chest with his claws. Bronson fell to the ground bleeding badly. The opossum saw the blood and its hunger raged. The wounded man tried desperately to regain his footing but the beast picked him up, squirming and wailing, and drained him of all blood.

Calry lay on the ground across from the beast unconscious.

The opossum looked at the sleeping man and crawled to him.

"Sorry. Believe me. I am so very sorry," the beast squealed as it picked the man up and drained him of all blood. The opossum threw Calry's body to the ground and it fell next to the other corpse.

A rip tore through the air. The flesh of the opossum was being torn apart from the inside out. Layers of flesh fell to the ground in thick meaty peels. Out of the rodent's belly climbed Zayashariya. She stripped the dead men naked and used their clothes to cleanse herself. The she-demon wiped the gore from her body and walked back into the city, with tears in her eyes and more blood on her hands.

Chapter 27

A heavy door slammed behind the slender guard. Fital walked silently down the twisting hallway until he came to another great door. He paused for a moment, drawing a deep breath, and placed his hand upon the knocker. He let the metal drop hard on the door creating an echoing thud through the hall.

"Enter." Fital heard a voice say from deep inside the corridor. He pushed the door ajar and peered into the dark room. It took a moment for his eyes to adjust to the dim light. He walked in slowly. Although he had been there many times before, he looked around the room in admiration. The simple eloquence of the room never ceased to amaze him. Small collectable pieces of intergalactic treasures gave the room its priceless appeal. The faint smell of pine filled his nostrils. Although the room reeked with a grandiloquent beauty, he hated being there. It reminded him of the days when his father made him sit in this very room to learn the rites of passage in order to be a true warrior of Wilzasp; as if there was such a thing now. He was trained, by the king, the art of war and with the accurate eye of an assassin.

"Ha!" Fital laughed under his breath. There were never any conflicts in Wilzasp. There wasn't anyone to battle let alone assassinate. He turned his head from side to side admiring the ornately furnished room. Walking over to a hard wood desk, he placed his palms against the plane while leaning slightly forward and waiting patiently for the one who summoned him to appear. The air in the room was stale and warm. He breathed in slow gulps, eyes adoring the murals on the walls. There were paintings and murals of old humanoid and human races that no longer existed and great wars that revolutionized the planet. On the wall directly in front of him was a scene painted so vividly that the images seemed to exist in the room with him, breathing the same stale air he fought to tolerate. He pulled out the dark chair from beneath the desk. He sat upon the cool leather seat and laid his head back upon its high leather backing.

"Are you comfortable," an invisible voice questioned.

Fital sat erect, cursing himself for being so lax. He swallowed hard. "Yes," he answered. "I am at your service." He looked around trying to locate the hidden being. "Where....where are you?" he finally found enough nerve within himself to question.

"I am here." A shadow stepped from behind a ceiling high bookcase protruding from the far corner of the rectangular room. "I am here."

The soldier stood up and bowed half-way down, showing the deepest respect. "Yes Sire." Fital stood erect once more motioning for the king's hand so he could kiss his ring. The king waved him away. Fital placed his hands behind his back. "What may I do for you?"

"Fital, why are you so formal?" the king laughed. "We are friends aren't we?" He pointed to an olive green leather couch sitting on a dark flowered area rug. "Have a seat friend. Would you like something to drink?"

"No thank you." Fital sat.

"Fital, my friend, my son, forgive me for being blunt but I need you to be completely honest with me. I have very little time to engage in small talk. I need to know, where are your loyalties?" The king sat down beside Fital. A melancholy look was in the king's eyes, a look full of sorrowful regret and pity. "Are you sure I cannot offer you anything?" He smiled at Fital.

"No thank you. May I ask, Sire, why do you ask me such a question? My loyalties are with you." Fital looked confused. "I have always been a myrmidon, obedient and faithful. Do you doubt me? Have I not served you well?"

"It is not that I doubt you but your dealing with the dark stranger vexes me. I do not understand why you protect her so. The town's people tell me that you are constantly at her side and that you have threatened all who have threatened her. Who are you to offer your services as her personal bodyguard? I can't, for the life of me, comprehend why you protect her."

"I do not understand why you do not protect her enough," Fital snapped. His forehead wrinkled. "You should see how the people scorn her and hiss at her every time she leaves the comfort of the Inn. They are full of contempt and hate. Forgive my tone but I am thoroughly disgusted by the conduct of my fellow neighbors. Zayashariya is guilty of no wrongdoings. "

The king's face was disquieted. "She is a murderer! Why can't you see that? There were no murders here before she arrived. There hasn't been a murder here for over fifty years. Don't be a fool man! Her presence here and a series of killings are more than coincidence."

"How can you assume that she is responsible for the recent tragedies that have been occurring? You have no proof. Did you see those bodies? Only an animal could be capable of sucking and ripping up bodies like that. And did you see how their skins were dried to their skeletons like all of their juices had been sucked out with a straw? How do you suppose that she did that?"

"I don't know but I do know that she has to be behind this," King Chucklarki retorted. "Be logical man. Put two and two together! Who else is capable of such things? No animal in our small forest is capable of such horrors."

"You are just bitter because you were humiliated before your people at the town meeting!" Fital snapped. His eyes were burning with rage. "Zayashariya transformed you into a craven idiot before your loyal subjects. Your pride could not take the insult and now you want to blame her for all that is wrong in your kingdom."

"I dare you talk to me in that manner!" The king slapped Fital across his face. "I helped raise you! You ungrateful brat! I can not believe you would abandon your people for that...that...that....beast!"

Fital's eyes turned into slits. His chest heaved heavily. A huge vein danced across his left temple as his face turned rose red. He was filled with anger. He stood up and walked toward the door.

"Stop! I did not dismiss you!" the king huffed. His orange face was blushed with ruby rage. He stood erect. "If you do not adhere to my voice...Fital, you will be sorry."

"I am already sorry, Sire. I am sorry and disappointed. I am angry and frustrated." Fital turned his face towards the king. "You of all people?" He was full of chagrin. "I thought you were free from petty prejudice and spite. But, I guess you can pretend to be above it all because you only have to deal with our kind. Your wife's daddy made sure of that!" Fital bowed and grinned sarcastically. "May I be dismissed?" He stood erect and looked into the king's hateful eyes.

"No you may not," the king responded in a sardonic tone. "Say what you will. It makes no difference. I have already made up my mind. I thought that we could talk this over like two intelligent men but I see that lust has blinded you. I must say, you disappoint me son. You allowed your rambunctious lust for that evil woman to stymie your intellect. Your father is clawing the roof of his casket, trying desperately to escape death in order to shake sense into your head. Your ignominious behavior is a pity." The king shook his head in shame. "You have wounded me deeply but I will not let you wallow in your iniquity. Indeed, I will save your soul." King Chucklarki smiled a malign smile. It sent chills down Fital's spine.

"I have not yet given you your assignment. Maybe you will be able to put your father's dream and my good teachings to use," said the king as he walked over to a nearby shelf and picked up a scroll. He handed Fital the onion paper document. "Now you may go." King Chucklarki waved the soldier away. "Never in my life have

I been so disappointed with you. I valued you above all men," the king said. He paused and put his hand of Fital's shoulder.

Fital moved away and the king's hand dropped to his side as if no life was in his body.

The king barked, "Be gone from my sight! You disgrace me!" He spat on Fital's boots and turned his back to him.

Fital reluctantly held the scroll. He wanted desperately to drop the thin paper to the floor and walk away but he knew that would only make matters worse. Clutching it tightly, crinkling the paper almost to the point of destruction, Fital let his temper cool. Silently, he walked out of the chamber. He clinched his fist so hard that his nails tore into the flesh of his palms. He walked down the long hallway and finally exited the building. Fital tottered over to a bench on the side of the road and sat down. He opened the scroll and read:

TO: Fital, Prime Enforcer 1, Soldier 28, Unit West
FROM: The Honorable King of Wilzasp

ASSIGNMENT OF ASSASSINATION

Prime Enforcer, you are to bring me the head of the murderous dark stranger Zayashariya of Gehenna. She is sentenced to death without trial and her head is to be delivered to the King of Wilzasp within two weeks from this day.

Immediate action is demanded.

TREASON WILL MEAN DEATH

Micheem
Master

Enforcer, Micheem

ChuckJarki

Fital rolled the scroll together and leaned back against the bench. He drew in a deep breath and screamed to the top of his lungs. Tears of frustration ran from his eyes. He screamed and screamed. Not the scream of a petrified child or a wounded woman, but the scream of a roaring beast or a soldier running unto the battle field.

Pedestrians nearby came to his aid but he forced them back with his sword in hand. They ran away from Fital, flustered by his actions.

Why would he choose me? Fital pondered. He was the peacemaker in the town. *Why me? The king must have been commanded by the people. He had to be. Why else? And why would Meecham sign it?* Fital's superior Meecham was opposed to capitol punishment.

Fital was torn between his people and the love of his life, even more; he was torn between his job and his principles. Although he had only known Zayashariya for a short while, he was madly in-love with her. Lust could not conjure up such feelings. He knew what the fire of lust burned like. This was not it. No other woman had ever moved his heart. At this point in his life, she was everything to him. He was not the type of man to fall in-love easily but this woman and her enchanting eyes had him from the first hello. How could he possibly annihilate her? He could not, would not, do it even if he wanted to. Wilzasp did not mean that much. *Oh, king! I love this stranger more than I love myself. I pray that I am making the right choice.* Fital's heart was turbulent. He knew he would give his own life for the dark stranger and to be totally honest with himself, he did not know her well enough to know unmistakably that she was not the monster who was killing his people. All he knew was that she made him feel like no other and he would not let her be destroyed. *Someone as beautiful and charming as*

Zayashariya could not be a killer. I love her too much. She loves me too much. He wept. *Does she?*

The town's people ran to his aid once more, anxious to comfort him.

"Get away from me! All of you!" Fital bellowed. "You are not my people! My people would not allow me to wash my hands in innocent blood! My people would not live blissfully in ignorance and unreasonable hate!" Fital fell to his knees and wept. The crowd surrounded him confused and baffled by his irate actions for they knew nothing of his assassination assignment. The crowd parted suddenly as Zayashariya pushed her way through. She had heard his screams a few blocks away. She continued to push through the crowd and fell to her knees in front of him.

"Why do you weep so Fital?" Zayashariya asked with the deepest concern. She smiled trying to soothe his pain. She wrapped her arms around him and he leaned limply against her breast. She kissed his cheek. Secretly she savored the softness of his skin. "Why do you weep so?" Light kisses fell upon the top of his head like raindrops.

Fital looked into her violet eyes and sat up. He was embarrassed by his demeanor, ashamed of his weakness for her. He wondered if she knew how she had captured his heart. Fital adverted his eyes. He was too dishonored to face her completely.

The crowd still surrounded the bizarre couple astonished by their intimate relationship. They were mystified by the spectacle Fital had made of himself. His actions were so unlike him. They were glad that the dark stranger's presence brought him back to his senses. But, they were always downcast in her presence. Zayashariya was never welcome.

Zayashariya kissed him again, stood up and pulled him to his feet. She wiped his tears away and held his hands tight. She turned to the crowd. "Please be on your way. You have seen enough."

"Shut-up you devil! You probably hexed him!" an old woman hissed with her finger waving in the air. "Fital would never weep before the masses!" She faced the others. "He is a strong man. A man of pride," the old woman shouted to the crowd and pointed at Zayashariya. "She caused his breakdown. She's a witch! Fital would have never shown such weakness!" The old woman spat on Zayashariya's boots. "She is the devil! A pitch black devil!" the old woman sneered. "I have lived through ages and have witnessed many things. Contrary to popular belief, the evil metaphysical does exist. You young ones think me foolish but I know what I know. Believe me, she is a demon. Nothing less!" the old woman wailed. Tears formed in the corners of her eyes, slowly trickling down her wrinkled face. "Evil! I tell you. Evil!" she blubbered.

"Yeah!" a young man yelled as he pushed his way to the front of the crowd. "Fital was my fighting master and he would have never abased himself in public!" The young man looked at Zayashariya. "Witch!" he screamed. "Witch! Witch! Witch! Witch!" He lifted his hands into the air encouraging the crowd to join him.

"Witch! Witch! Witch!" the crowd all yelled in unison, chanting witch as loud as they possibly could.

"There is no such thing as a witch!" another member of the mob yelled. "But I do believe that she is a killer."

"Killer! Killer!" the impressionable crowd yelled, eager to spill the blood of the town's stranger at any rate.

Fital held up his hands. "Stop this nonsense! There are no witches, devils or demons fools! How could you even consider such foolishness?! You should be ashamed. I am responsible for my own actions. No witch's brew or devil's curses or hoodoo woman's hex influenced me! I weep because of the sadness you people placed upon my heart with your biases! I weep for the deaths of innocents! I weep because of my love for this woman! "

The crowd gasped at his last declaration.

Fital frowned in disbelief and threatened, "I will have all of your heads if you do not depart!" He lifted is sword. "I will promise death to all of you!" His eyes were wild. "Young and old!" He even frightened Zayashariya. "Depart you idiots!"

The crowd departed with lightning speed.

*   *   *

"What's wrong with you?" Zayashariya asked, shaken by his anger.

Fital handed her the scroll. She read it and rolled it back together. She looked into his eyes. "What are you going to do?" *I am so sorry that I did this to you. If only you knew my struggles.* Looking into his eyes grew harder by the second. "This is all my fault. I should have never involved myself with you."

"Nonsense. You did nothing wrong. I believe in your innocence. You are my angel. I will not harm you." Fital could not believe that she had the nerve to ask him what he was going to do. Did she think he could kill her?

"It will mean death for you! I can not let you give up your life for mine," she said.

"No life will be given. We will leave here together. But if I had to give my life for you, I would do it gladly," Fital insured her.

"I will not allow such silly talk from you. If anyone has to leave this place, it is me. You can not leave here. Where will you go? There is much you do not know about me. You do not know what I am." *And you do not want to know.* Guilt consumed Zayashariya once more. What could she do to set things right? *Nothing. I can do absolutely nothing.*

"You make it sound as if you are sub-humanoid! What do you mean by what you are? You are a humanoid as I am. Do not anger me with lunacy. This is not the time." Fital ruffled his eyebrows. "You make me crazy with your talk about "mystical nature" and your obsession with not being understood. This is serious!"

"I know how serious this is. Don't talk to me as if I am a child. I understand more than you ever will and I know that you would never understand who I am," she retorted. Zayashariya paused to cool her temper. "To be with me would mean death in itself. I am a danger and there may be others hunting me as we speak. I will not put you in harms way. My foes are unconquerable by you and your people. And to make matters worse, my foes are also your people. You and I both know that." She looked away. "I must go soon. I can not take you with me but I can not leave here just yet. My body is still in need of nourishment. After I depart, I do not know when I will encounter food again."

Fital was confused and more upset than ever. "Explain to me!" He grabbed her arm and jerked her towards him. "Explain to me, woman, what you are talking about! Who else is after you? Don't leave me in the dark. Do you not understand what I must do?"

"Yes, I understand. Do as you must do."

"I can not kill you!" Fital's heart pumped violently. His face was like red wine.

"Why? How do you know I wouldn't kill you if I were in your shoes?" she questioned. Zayashariya stared at Fital. Her eyes glowed like purple flames.

"Because you love me!" Fital roared, ignoring the chill that trickled down his back like ice water. He accredited the abnormal glow to the crystals reflecting in her eyes.

Zayashariya laughed softly. "How do you know? How do you know when you doubt everything that isn't logical to you? Love is illogical." She looked away from him. *I do love you. I wish you only knew how much. I will not let you be destroyed along with me.* "You are so naive." She shook her head and laughed again. *I have to end this.* Her nose tingled but she refused to let the tears come.

Tears had been coming to her more than they ever had in her whole life. Fital had touched something in her soul that she never knew existed. She knew in her heart that she had to end their love affair before something catastrophic happened between them. The thought of not sharing her life with him troubled her to the depths of her being but the thought of him giving his honorable life for her wretched life troubled her even more.

"What?!" Fital grabbed her close to him. He wanted to kiss her and slap her at the same time. "Do you not understand the seriousness of the situation?" he frantically questioned, searching her eyes for understanding. Fital was at his wits end. For the life of him, he could not figure her out.

"You do not understand anything outside of what your eyes can see or your heart can feel. In order for you to understand me, you have to understand that the world contains more than the physical and the spiritual does exist. In many ways the old woman was right," said Zayashariya.

"Excuse me!" Fital grew angrier. "What old woman? No wait, are you talking about the old wench that just tried to get a lynch mob after you? You have got to be kidding me! Now you tell me that you are a demon? No. I'm sorry, a witch. Better yet, you are the devil himself!"

Zayashariya laughed at him, not to mock him but in sincere pity of his ignorance.

"Who are you to say that the supernatural does not exist? Maybe I am. What do you know?" she asked.

His eyes were filled with anger and confusion. He could never understand yet she loved him despite himself. She kissed Fital's lips. He pushed her back so hard that she almost toppled over. She shook it off and instantly forgave him. He could care less at the moment.

"There is much in this universe that your mind is too limited to comprehend," Zayashariya continued.

"Is that what this is all about? You believe in that spiritual foolishness and I don't?" Fital rolled his eyes. "Oh

yeah, I forgot, you are from Gehenna, the Land of the Dead!"
he scowled. "I suppose that you are demon-witch too?" He
threw his arms in the air in total rejection of her beliefs.
"Speaking of minds, I wonder who is really the limited one
or should I say your mind isn't limited enough."

"Because you do not believe in something does not
mean it is not true. I pray that you are not too arrogant to
see that," said Zayashariya, ignoring his sarcasm. "In time
you will believe." She walked away from him. "You will
have to in order to except me. Goodbye. Tonight my love.
Until then..." She disappeared from his sight like an
apparition.

Fital's jaw dropped, eyes popped, and heart
stopped. His pride was too strong for him to admit to
himself that he was stunned. He quickly dismissed her trick.
He had more important things to worry about than a
magician's hoax, other things like treason.

Chapter 28

The light of the twin suns shined through Zayashariya's chamber window. Warm beams of sunlight landed across the faces of the sleeping lovers. The argument from the night before did not prevent Fital from coming to her. They had promised not to talk about things and let their bodies do all the talking for them.

Zayashariya was awakened by the tepid sunbeams. She sat up and Fital's sleeping head fell into her lap. Fital slept peacefully. Zayashariya ran her fingers down the side of his face and felt joy in the feel of his breath blowing against her navel. She rubbed his head lovingly, letting her eyes drift from his handsome face to his neck. As she stared at the heavily veined neck of her new found love, an aching hunger raged inside of her. Fangs instinctively grew out of her mouth, piercing her gums as they lunged through. Tears fell from her violet eyes.

"I can't!" she screamed.

Her loud cry woke Fital. He looked up. His eyes consciously fell on her face, trying hard to ignore her nakedness.

"What's wrong?" Fital asked. He eyed her frightened face. He was fortunate not to have seen her a moment earlier. Her fangs had disappeared.

"Nothing." Zayashariya fell back on the pillow.

"Why did you scream?" Fital inquired. His hand massaged her knee and he showered her softly with kisses.

"I had a bad dream about home," she lied. "Go back to sleep. I am okay." Zayashariya kissed his waiting lips.

"Would you like to talk about it?" Fital held her close. "I am a good listener. Talking may make you feel better."

"No." Zayashariya broke free of his arms and made a complete volte-face.

"Okay love." Fital rolled over to his side and closed his eyes. "I'm going back to sleep."

"Rest my love. I will be alright." Zayashariya traced his ear with her finger. He jerked lightly at the tickling feeling and fell into slumber.

Zayashariya stared at the crystals pulsating on the ceiling. Hunger fled from her. Memories crept upon her like a ravenous animal.

*   *   *

After Beelzebub's fly attack, Belial was ordered by Queen Lilith to seduce Zayashariya. Lilith knew that Belial, with all his flawless beauty and demure charm, had the power to persuade Zayashariya to stay. He had the power of pleasure and very few could deny the temptation of the flesh.

Belial and Zayashariya quickly took a liking to one another. Although he was not able to persuade her to remain in Gehenna, they continued to have an exuberant physical affair which lasted for months. Zayashariya adored Belial's erotic perversions and his punishments became more passionate and pleasurable, but as with all demons, things became too extreme and grotesque.

Lilith caught ear of Belial's failure to persuade Zayashariya to join the Council of Demons and his continuous affair with her daughter. Lilith was not pleased. She was down right angry and insulted by Belial forsaking her orders for his own carnal cravings.

Lilith was frantic and she called in reinforcements. Belial was apprehended by Apollyon for abandoning his mission to convince Zayashariya to remain on Night and for putting his own desires above the Council of Demons. When Lilith found out about the fruitless affair, she called in Apollyon, The Destroyer, and had Belial brutally skinned and banished from Gehenna for a season.

Zayashariya was then tortured by Asmodeus and his dragon for weeks at a time. Still she would not agree to become the thirteenth demon on the Council of Demons. Zayashariya wanted to be free to make her own choices and to choose her own path in life. Besides, she wanted nothing more to do with her mother.

Lilith had done so much to hurt her. The evil queen subjected Zayashariya to all sorts of tortures for the sake of making her stronger and more demented. Zayashariya refused to endure more pain, especially for something that she found repulsive and did not believe in. Deep within her heart, she felt that she was not completely evil and she made the mistake of sharing that feeling with her mother. Her foolish choice to confide in her mother made her mother loath her more. Lilith tried to force Zayashariya to join the Council of Demons immediately. Zayashariya refused and proudly faced the consequences. Queen Lilith was furious and ashamed. She had become a mockery to the evil worlds. Lilith cringed at the thought that this atrocity could possibly reach Lucifer's ear. She would be finished forever. Lilith decided to kill Zayashariya if she refused to join. No child of her's would cause her eternal humiliation. Death would be Zayashariya's fate; a long drawn-out brutal death. She would be made an example before many.

Zayashariya heard of her mother's plot to take her life and called upon Kalpvaleim. Kalpvaleim was torn between good and evil just as she was and he agreed to help her escape the Nether Worlds. They knew that old wizard dabbled in the art of travel science and Kalpvaleim made an agreement with the old wizard to do his bidding for a small season if the wizard would warp Zayashariya out of the Nether Worlds. Her destination was not important. She just needed to disappear and be out of Lilith's reach. The agreement was sealed with a promise to Kalpvaleim that Zayashariya would summon him to the material plane when she arrived on a safe planet or realm.

The old wizard created an untraceable spaceship and put Zayashariya on the ship and warped her out of the Nether Worlds. With her, he packed a few magical supplies, a cloak, and a pouch of valuable gold coins among other things. And a few days later, she landed on a far away planet and found her way to the land of Wilzasp.

*   *   *

Fital rolled over and startled Zayashariya. She rubbed his bald head and she looked into his peaceful eyes.

"What were you day-dreaming of?" asked Fital, kissing her arm, then her elbow. He was still a bit shaken by the conversation they had yesterday. He wanted to question her more about her vanishing before his eyes but he decided against it. Fital had struggled with himself mentally for the better part of yesterday before returning to Zayashariya's room at the Inn. He cared nothing for the subject anymore. Only her.

"Home." She closed her eyes. "Home sweet home," Zayashariya replied bitterly.

Fital sat up and looked at the clock on the shelf. "It is getting late. Do you want me to bring you breakfast?" he asked.

"No thanks. I think I can manage to find that on my own." Zayashariya smiled and kissed him. "You just make sure that you are not seen leaving here. I do not want to put you in more danger."

"Will do pretty lady. I have to get out of here. I have to be at my post in about an hour." Fital got up and began to dress himself. "Will I see you tonight?"

"Maybe." Zayashariya kissed him goodbye.

Chapter 29

It was night once again in the land of Wilzasp. The town's people went into their homes, barred their windows and locked their doors. Fear was very prevalent in the land. Fear controlled the actions of everyone in town. They walked in fear. They talked in fear. And most of all, they lived in fear.

Fital left his post and began his journey to the Inn. His heart was troubled by the continuous deaths of his people and his assignment to kill Zayashariya. His mind ached with fury. Every thought that materialized in his brain fertilized the darkest meadow of his soul, giving root to a profusion of twisted thorns composed of the most diabolical imaginings of torture that he would perform gleefully to the destroyer of his race. Anger combined with sorrow controlled his former zesty attitude and his usual tranquil demeanor.

The front entrance to the Inn came into sight. He smiled in spite of his heavy heart and took a deep sorrowful breath. He slowly entered the structure with his head down and his feet dragging across the marble floor, sounding like whispers floating in the wind. Fine wrinkles caressed his eyes.

"What's wrong young fellow?" an old man asked, sitting behind the counter. He had squinty eyes and a crooked mouth.

"What happened to Alvian?" Fital asked with genuine concern. To think about it, he could not remember the last time he saw Alvian. Was his mind so clouded that he no longer noticed the people around him? He had slept in this Inn every night since he had met Zayashariya and he had not paid any attention to the worker behind the counter.

"I am afraid that she mysteriously disappeared the same day those teens did," the old man said with a bit of sadness and grief in his voice. He looked at Fital like he should have known; especially since he was dating the alleged killer.

"I am her uncle. I am next in line to run the Inn," the old man spoke slowly. He tapped his chubby fingers on the countertop as he began his story. "This place has been here since I can remember. I reckon about a thousand years." He shrugged his shoulders. "Who knows?" He grinned a scattered tooth grin. "I am only five hundred and sixty-two myself." He winked his eye trying to make light of the situation. He sighed in reverence and remembrance. "I hate that Alvian is gone. She was a young beautiful one. I miss my sister, her mother, too. I hope the thing that killed them will burn in the hells forever." His eyes became glossy.

Fital nodded his head in agreement. He felt complete empathy. Many people had perished by the fangs of some horrid enigmatic monster. The scariest thing about the murders was the fact that no one knew what was doing the killing. The beast had left no evidence or clues behind. The creature was obviously intelligent. Fital looked into the old man's eyes, then reached out and touched his hand. Fital gave the old man's hand a squeeze to let him know that he was not alone in mourning.

"Bless you Sir," said Fital, bowing to the man and turning toward the stairs.

"Be careful boy," said the old man.

Fital turned around to face him.

"Love is sometimes blinding," said the old man, waving his finger. "Try hard to keep your eyes open. The simplest solution to a problem is always the one before your eyes."

Fital nodded and climbed the gray marble stairs until he reached the fourth floor.

"My love," he whispered to himself, "please do not be who they say you are. My heart could not bear it. If only you knew how much I adore you." He walked down the hallway and tapped on Zayashariya's door. "My life means nothing without you. Please be innocent of all the accusations that my people have accused you of." Fital pleaded in his heart. He paced in a small circular motion until he heard Zayashariya's erotic raspy voice.

"Yes. Who is it?" she asked.

"It is I, your every desire," answered Fital, attempting to cloak his depression and to sound content.

The door swung open and in the doorway stood Zayashariya dressed beautifully in her birthday suit.

"Come in!" she whispered softly, fingering his chin with her pointy nails.

Fital walked into the room. The door closed behind him. He disappeared into sheer ecstasy.

Chapter 30

"Queen Lilith," an extraordinarily beautiful middle-aged woman called through the Queen of Night's cracked door. She stood in the hall waiting for the queen to give her permission to enter.

"You may enter Milmoey," Lilith said.

The woman pushed the door open and hesitantly stepped into the room. Her clear blue eyes looked like two tiny ponds in the midst of her powder white face, their sparkle laced with pain and weariness. Short blonde curls crowned her head and her rosy cheeks looked as if they were freshly pinched. Ruby red lips pursed tight to hide the gritting of her teeth underneath.

Milmoey was exquisitely dressed in a flowing cream colored evening gown decorated with sequin, beads, and lace. The grandiloquent gown was floor length and strapless. Matching shoes adorned her feet. The heels of the shoes were so high that she towered over the queen but they caused her to walk in a lumbering fashion, trying constantly to keep her balance. Her knees and ankles ached and the balls of her feet were in agony. An absurd amount of diamonds hung from her ears, neck, and fingers like painful boulders. The gems sparkled in the candlelight in a gaudy parade of twinkling radiance.

Milmoey's sin had been vanity and greed and now for her perpetual punishment she had to wear the weight of the cumbersome stones that she pined for, deceived for, and killed for during her mortal life. Now her only purpose was to slave for Lilith and submit to the unbearable weight of the beautiful stones.

"Someone is here to see you," Milmoey stated and bowed slowly, paying Lilith homage.

"Who is it vain cur?" Lilith asked with venom in her voice. She abhorred visitors; especially demon rulers who seemed to drop by on a daily basis to remind her of her failure to locate her daughter.

Lilith sat upon her bed wearing nearly nothing. Her long legs were totally exposed and one of her full breasts was peeking out of her loose fitting night shirt. The flames on her head changed into fine strands, creating a mess of indigo hair. When looked upon by a total stranger, it was said that she was absolutely striking to the eyes and tempting to the flesh.

"It is the master," the woman servant answered. "He just appeared out of nowhere. He really frightened me." Milmoey leaned against the door. The diamonds made her back and arms ache terribly.

"I don't care about what frightens you fool! Get off of my door!" Lilith growled as she watched Milmoey straighten up her throbbing body. "What does he want? Lilith snapped. She was not prepared for such a visit.

"You know what I want," a handsome angel answered, pushing Milmoey to the side. The woman fell against the wall, hurting her arm. She quickly regained her composure, rubbing her aching shoulder. Milmoey quickly stepped behind him to avoid further damage.

"May I be dismissed?" Milmoey asked Lilith.

Lilith opened her mouth to speak but Lucifer silenced her by placing his index finger to her lips.

"You may excuse yourself," he said, smiling at Milmoey. The coolness of his breath touched her face as he spoke.

A thin layer of frost covered Milmoey's face. Her cheeks went numb instantly. An imploding feeling of horror burned within her chest. She stepped backwards, turned and ran away as fast as she could, her ankles twisting every other step and occasionally tripping on her bulky gown.

Lilith stood up.

Lucifer walked over to her and placed his hand upon her exposed breast.

"I see you were waiting for me," he said, letting his hand squeeze her just a little.

"What is it you want?" Lilith spat with venom. She reached for his offending hand but his eyes warned her of the consequences. Her hand dropped.

"I hear that Zayashariya is missing." Lucifer removed his hand and sat down upon her bed. His wings folded behind him and disappeared underneath his white robe. His skin and robe looked like a continuous flow of color from flesh to fabric.

"She is under control." Lilith stood between his parted legs, a look of utter disgust and displeasure on her face.

He pulled her close to him.

She felt the deathlike hardness of his hands upon her thighs. Her eyes fell upon the tiny horns on his forehead.

"Zayashariya has been found," she lied. "She will be brought to me soon."

"You take me for a fool," Lucifer whispered. "Do you think that I do not know what is going on in my world?" he asked. He looked up into her face and scowled. She avoided is eyes. With one swift yank, he pulled her night shirt off and tossed it to the floor. Lightly he ran his forked tongue up her chiseled stomach, tickling ever so perversely. He stopped and looked straight into her eyes and said, "You will fail me and when you do, you will be severely punished."

"I will not fail," Lilith whispered. The feeling that flowed through her was disgusting yet desirable, repulsive yet full of rhapsody, sickening yet sexually supreme. She could not contain her desire for the devil any longer. Hating herself for succumbing to his charms, she removed his robe and let the cloth fall to the bed. Lucifer's broad shoulders and statuesque chest made her breath quicken. In perfect angelic and human form, he stood up and let the robe fall around his ankles. His thighs were like those of a stallion.

His arms were like hilly rock formations ending with big powerful hands. His wings spread out behind him, casting the room in shadow.

Lilith's eyes flared. She fell upon him like a frenzied beast, possessed by confused passion, lusting after abominable copulation

Chapter 31

Morning had come and gone like it always had since creation. Mourning filled the hearts of the people of Wilzasp because the murderer of their loved ones had not been found. Many stayed close to their families and spent most of their time at home. It was a quiet day. So quiet that the heartbeat of the people seemed to thump loudly and echo through the city like thunder. Vacant streets made the town look ghastly and void of life. No smells of fruit or fresh meats floated through the air this day. No sounds of pattering feet lightly hitting the concrete. No laughter. No arguing. Just abandoned food stands and empty shops stood as the town's people hid locked behind the doors of their homes hoping that they were safe. The few that walked the streets wore faces so long they looked like horses. Others were soldiers who were forced to offer security to the people by monitoring the streets. Only one couple walked through the town with light hearts.

"Let's do something exciting tonight," Fital requested as he held the dark stranger's hand as they walked through the woods. Greenery shaded them from the heat of the suns. Fresh flowers offered perfume for their noses.

"Okay. Let's go visit some of your friends and family or maybe the king and queen." Zayashariya laughed. "I bet that would be exciting."

"Hardy-har-har! You are so funny." Fital replied acidly. "I just want us to be alone and out of danger." He stopped walking and looked at her. "Out of harm's way." Fital rubbed her hair and placed a small portion behind one of her ears. "I want to protect you from the harshness of these people. Can I do that for you? Can I be your shield against the world?"

"According to the king, you are harm," said Zayashariya, folding her arms and smirking. Her ample body bulged underneath the tight red leather she wore. Zayashariya searched Fital's eyes. Love was evident. Guilt stung her heart. A choking feeling came over her. It was so intense that she felt faint from the lack of oxygen. She took in a deep breath. Fital loved her so much. If he ever found out that she was feeding off of his people, it would be insufferably devastating to him.

"Zay," Fital said, looking at her then continuing to walk. He brought her to an open area where green grass and bright flowers grew. The area looked like an earthy bed, soft and plush, a fragrant mattress for lovers to lie upon. Fital sat the basket on the ground. He pulled out a yellow blanket and spread it out on the grass. Fital sat down and pulled Zayashariya down on top of him. "You are so beautiful," he sighed, looking into her violet eyes. "I see your beauty outside but I want to see your beauty inside." Fital kissed her neck. "Show me please."

"Wha..." Zayashariya was cut short.

"Shhh." Fital put his hand over her mouth. He sat her beside him and reached for the basket and pulled out a perfectly wrapped gift. He gave her a brown package tied with a dark chocolate colored ribbon. "For you," Fital whispered.

Zayashariya opened the package and unfolded a pair of baggy black jeans and a red and black halter top. "Thank you." She smiled, confused. "I have clothes..."

"Real clothes?"

"Fital, what are you trying to say?" She didn't know whether to be grateful or offended.

Fital laughed aloud. "Please don't be offended. Zayashariya, you are beautiful but you are naked. You can be just as beautiful with a few more pieces of cloth on. You see my love, every time I am with you, my heart is filled with lust and wanting. It is very difficult for me to focus on your mind when my eyes are hypnotized by your body. I am sure that I am not the first man who was bewitched by you. But, I most certainly want to be the last. "

"Thank you," said Zayashariya, trying hard to look thankful. But it was hard to hide the fact that she was insulted by him trying to force his will upon her. Fital was trying to change her. Men always tried to change her no matter what world she was in. She felt that it was only a matter of time before he would try to tell her what to do and her being obedient would never happen. An untamable beast she was. Zayashariya's skin crawled with that thought. She hated anyone who exercised authority over her or anyone who demanded anything from her. Zayashariya was a rebel by nature and the sheer thought of being told what to do made her automatically want to do the opposite no matter how small the request was.

"Put it on for me." Fital stroked her hair.

"Now?" She knew it! *It is beginning.* Zayashariya's face twisted in disappointment.

"Please," Fital purred and caressed her chin with his fingers. He kissed her eyelids softly. "I love you. It is such a small request that will bring me great happiness."

"Okay, okay lover boy!" Zayashariya squealed with playful glee. "You don't have to charm me anymore." She stood up and undressed.

Fital stared at her firm body with pure admiration.

Zayashariya pulled on the jeans with ease and he aided her by tying the halter top behind her neck and back.

"Thank you," Zayashariya whispered as she smoothed her hair down over one shoulder and sat in front of Fital.

"You are more than welcome." Fital pulled her on top of him. "You are flawlessly breathtaking. My, am I a lucky man." Fital kissed her lips, her shoulder, her cheek, her hands, and each one of her fingers. "Talk with me."

"About?" Zayashariya asked dreamy-eyed.

"Tell me about you. Make me understand you. You are such an enigma to me. I feel as is I am in love with a stranger," Fital requested.

"First of all, I can not make you understand anything. You will either understand or you won't. I have no power over your comprehension."

"Zayashariya, you know what I mean. Please cut the dramatics." Fital was becoming a little irked. "I want to know more about your life. I need to know."

"What is there to tell Fital? My home is a dreadful place filled with dreadful people." She rolled onto her side. "You would not believe me if I told you because you do not believe in anything greater than yourself. My world would be too illogical for you. I do not want to spill my life story into your hands and watch you drop it to the ground in dismissive disbelief."

"How dare you judge me! Arrogant I am not." Rose covered his quivering troublesome cheeks. "I have never disregarded anything you have said. I may not necessarily agree but I do listen and absorb," Fital argued.

"Sure Fital," Zayashariya snorted. "This is not the first time you have inquired about my past. If my memory serves me right, you called my beliefs foolish in so many words. You judged me. Why can't I return the favor lover?"

"Don't mock me," Fital spat.

"Let me tell you, Fital, most men love money more than women and women more than God. If God is at the bottom of the totem pole, arrogance and greed is always at the top."

"What does this have to do with me? I love you more than both," he asked.

"Very flattering but you have to believe in something greater than yourself in order to ever truly understand anything," Zayashariya said.

"Here we go again with this mess!" Fital sat up. "Just tell me! Let me be the judge of that!"

"Okay Fital. Let me ask you a few questions."

"Go ahead. My life is an open book." He was defensive. A frown adorned his face and his scowling eyes were intense.

"Do you believe in a higher power?"

"Like God?" he asked.

"Yes."

"Of course not. That is ridiculous," Fital huffed. "The belief in God or any other type of spiritual phenomenon has been erased from our culture for at least two to three hundred years." He paused. "No one believes in God anymore."

"Why?" Zayashariya asked.

"Because science proves all things and what we do not know now, we will find out soon enough."

"Yet science can not prove how everything came to be. There are countless theories on everything but no one can say where the original matter that began it all came from. No one can explain why all the elements needed for life to become an existing soul one day just decided to come together. No one can explain how this very planet you live on formed and gave birth to life miraculously and in such a short period of time. No one can explain any of this yet everyone can dismiss that there may be a higher power that willed it to happen." Zayashariya shook her head. Her purple mane moved freely. "You and your logic," she hissed. "I am living proof of the supernatural."

Fital was speechless. His heart skipped a beat. Crossing his arms, Fital sighed. He did not like being quieted. He had never thought of life that way and he was even more confused about her being supernatural.

"So you are telling me that you are a witch?" he combated.

"No," Zayashariya answered with a tiny chuckle in her throat. "I am no common witch. There is nothing supernatural about being a witch. Witchcraft is a practiced art. A witch is made by practicing potions and remembering spells. Yes, I can conjure and I can cast a few spells but I am hardly a bona fide witch. I am what I am by birth. I am natural."

"What are you then?" Fital asked. He leaned closer, his heart balancing on the edge of a cliff.

"I am a woman. A woman from Gehenna. I am different from you because I know the demon and the angel. I am what they are."

"Hold on one moment." Fital looked her directly in the eye. His face twisted with disbelief. "This is a bit much. I can buy the God theory but now you are telling me that you have seen real demons and angels?" He laughed sarcastically. "Get real!"

"Okay, you win Fital. You win." Zayashariya threw her hands up. "I'll tell you only what your restricted mind will allow you to understand and be comfortable with."

She was finished with trying to convert him. A proselyte he would never become.

"To make it plain, I am, correction, I was the princess of Gehenna and I wanted nothing of my mother's kingdom. She could not accept no for an answer so I escaped with the aid of a friend. My ship was wrecked not far from here. I walked and walked until I spotted Wilzasp. Now I am here with you, on a blanket, explaining my life." Zayashariya leaned backwards. "Happy now?"

"That's not very hard to comprehend. You should have said that in the first place. I believe you like to ruffle my feathers a bit," Fital said. Calm and relief rested upon him. He was glad all of the supernatural talk had ceased. His mind could not wrap around such things. Logic was his natural element.

"Of course, isn't that a woman's nature?" Resentment was in her voice. Zayashariya's heart was wounded. Fital would never understand her and never would he try.

"Tell me about your family," Fital requested with his face twisted in discomfort. "And please make it plain. I have lost the desire to debate with you any more today."

Zayashariya turned her face away from him and stared at the beautiful emerald leaves and multicolored flowers surrounding her. The smell was intoxicating. Nothing would take this precious moment from her. She saw so few of these natural wonders in her life and soon she knew that she would have to leave this place.

"I have no family. I have a mother who shows love by destruction. My father is pure evil, I am sure, whoever he is. If he is not, he would not have allowed my mother to raise me. I have never had the pleasure of meeting him."

The soft petals were heavenly against her skin. Immense enjoyment cradled her entire body.

"Tell me about you. Enough about me." Zayashariya closed her eyes and savored the warm breeze.

"As you know, I came from a long line of soldiers. My forefathers were always close to the kings. They were the commanders and chiefs of Wilzasp. I am Military royalty I guess. Although my mother was very privileged, she was happy being a humble housewife. She was the most beautiful person I have ever known. She died when I was in my early twenties. Her death was horrible and untimely. She was killed in an unfortunate accident. A rock, thrown by a naughty child, took her life. With her death, she took a large part of my heart. I have not loved a person with all of me since. Not even my father. Until now." Fital's eyes grew sad. He looked up at Zayashariya. He saw no feeling there. Fital, disappointed, averted his eyes and than continued. "I told you about my siblings already." Still no emotion showed in her eyes. He paused and quickly continued.

"Painting was my first love as a child then I fell head over heels for sculpturing. I wish that I could take you to my house. It is decorated exclusively with my paintings and carvings." Fital suddenly felt apologetic about not being able to take his lover home to his family but she knew as well as he did that it would be disastrous. Fital pushed the thought away and continued. "I have many educational degrees..."

"And you are just a soldier?" Zayashariya asked jokingly.

"Yes." Fital tickled her. "This is what I was born to be. Who am I to change tradition?"

"Are you happy this way?" Zayashariya asked.

"Most of the time." He traced her navel with his thumb. "I don't like being ordered around with no right or say so in the matter." Fital kissed her arm. "I loved my job until I met you."

"Sorry." Zayashariya's eyes closed. Her head dropped a bit.

"It's okay. I love you," he said. *If only you knew how much.* Fital kissed her hand and held it between his.

"I don't even know what love is. Where I come from, love does not exist. I had a friend once that I thought I loved but I guess I didn't because I failed to prevent her death. I knew in my heart of hearts that my mother had ill will toward my friend and I allowed them to meet. My mother is an evil being in every sense of the word. There has never been any love in her heart and I allowed my friend to fall prey to her." Zayashariya opened her eyes and looked in Fital's. "If this is how love feels, the way I feel about you. If it's the compassion that's in my heart not the lust in my loins, I love you too." She hugged him. "Let's just enjoy the time we have together. I know it will soon end."

"It will end only if you let it," he responded.

"As you will soon see, I will have no choice in the matter and neither will you."

Chapter 32

King Chucklarki sat at his desk as still as a lifeless lump. His eyes closed and reopened. He yawned. Slowly he closed the book that he was reading and held it close to his bosom. In reflection, the King of Wilzasp allowed his mind to wander freely; to meditate on what he had read. He sat the ancient book upon the desk and stood up to stretch. The king rolled his head around and lifted and dropped his shoulders. Then, he turned toward the old hickory clock hanging on the wall. He had been reading for sixteen hours straight.

The King of Wilzasp looked at the ancient book on the desk with a troubled heart and a lowly mood. Somehow, deep within his spirit he knew that what he read was not folklore or myth. The book before him held power. Power unknown to him, not of his world or his understanding. The sacred book held a strength that commanded respect and deep devotion by those who were brave enough to believe in its words. If only he could conquer the concept of faith. It seemed so far fetched. To actually believe, to know, that this thing, force, spirit, ubiquitous creature, was responsible for his existence. This "God" had all power to create and to destroy, to love and to hate, and most of all, the power of divine mercy and forgiveness. How could such a thing exist in his world? His world was a world where such a concept was as ridiculous as talking clothes and walking clouds. King Chucklarki sat back down and rubbed his eyes. He picked up a thimble sized bell and rang it three times. He leaned backwards and closed his heavy eye-lids.

"Yes Sire," said a painfully thin man peeking through the door of the king's study. He opened the door wider and stepped in.

"Sire," he called out. The king did not respond. The man closed the door behind him. He scratched his shaggy beard and walked closer to the king. He poked the king's arm.

"Sire," he called. No response. He shook him. "Sire."

The king stirred and fell back into silence.

"Sire," he called again.

"Yes," the king answered, opening his eyes.

"You rang Sire."

"Oh. Oh yes." The king sat up straight and let out a monstrous yawn. He rolled his head around and stretched his arms wide. He looked at the peasant and shook his head. The man was genuinely ugly. The king shook his head once more.

"Sire." The man twisted his face. "Are you all right?"

"Yes Vlad. I am all right."

"We all have been worried about you Sire. Even the queen asked about you." Vlad dropped to one knee and kissed the king's ring. "Even the queen," Vlad repeated.

The king couldn't help but laugh. The servant's voice sounded so child-like coming from a man nearly twice his age.

"Get up Vlad. Stop fawning." King Chucklarki pulled his hand away from the bony man. "I am fine. I have just been reading."

"Good Sire. Education is very..."

"Enough Vlad." The king smiled. It was like sunshine on his face. Smiles were rare occurrences in his home, at least lately.

Vlad smiled back nervously and the king laughed again.

"Get up Vlad and grab a chair."

"A chair?" asked the weird skinny man, baffled.

"Yes a chair." King Chucklarki grinned. "Come and sit with me. I want to talk."

"Talk?" Vlad's eyes widened.

"Yes talk." The king picked up another bell the size of a tea cup and rang it three times.

Vlad pulled up a chair and sat in front of the king. A knock on the door sounded. "Come in," the king's voice echoed through the room.

A very pretty young woman walked in. Her apron was tied tight around her waste and her hair was a very round afro. It was like a gigantic halo on her small head. She wore large hoop earrings and many rings, bracelets, and necklaces. She wore a white gauze blouse that revealed a white brassiere underneath it and a pair of white slacks. Her feet were bare.

"Nella, please bring Vlad and I some food and a nice bottle of mead."

"Yes Sire," she said bowing and walking out.

"What a pretty girl," the king spoke below his breath.

"Yes Sire, very pretty." Vlad shifted in his seat. He was visibly uneasy.

"Relax Vlad. I just want to talk man to man."

"Man to man?" Vlad asked.

"Yes Vlad, man to man. Please relax." The king patted the older man's shoulder. "I want to talk." The king paused and leaned forward. He looked Vlad in the eyes. "During our conversation, we are equals. I want you to be honest. I promise you my life that nothing you say will be held against you and nothing said will leave this room."

Vlad started to perspire. He wondered what matter of business this was and why he was involved in it.

"Relax!" the king demanded.

"Yes Sire." Vlad swallowed.

"Don't call me Sire! Call me Chuck." The king was getting angry. "Please just relax," he spat.

"Okay Sire." Vlad tried to relax to no avail. "What do you wish to talk about?" Vlad crossed his skeletal legs.

"God," the king replied. "I would like to talk about God."

"God?" Vlad was confused. "God?"

"Yes, God," King Chucklarki responded and began to clear the desktop for the food that was coming."

"Sire, I mean Chuck. I can do that," Vlad said, standing and attempting to pick up something off of the desk.

"No, let me," the king said. "Thank you for offering, friend."

Vlad sat back and relaxed. The tension was easing. Hearing the king call him friend soothed him. He leaned back for a moment until the door swung open and Nella emerged from the hallway with a tray of hot sandwiches and a bottle of warm mead. She pulled two small cups out of her apron pocket and sat them on the table next to the tray.

"Anything else Sire?" Nella asked.

"No pretty lady. That is all." The king winked and smiled. Nella nervously bowed and hurried from the room.

"Sire." Vlad picked up a sandwich and took a hearty bite. "Why do you ask about God?" Food fell from his hungry lips unto his pants, appearing disgusting to the king.

The king cringed and tried to ignore the spectacle before him. He poured them both a cup of mead and handed Vlad a cup. The hungry man gulped it down in one swallow.

Do I really starve my subjects or is he just a hungry nincompoop? The king thought. He rolled his eyes and started on his meal.

"We will talk after lunch okay," he said.

"Okay," Vlad managed to mouth while gobbling down the food like a famished hound.

After the small lunch, Vlad stretched out on his chair with one leg thrown over the chair's arm and his arms falling limply to its side.

"So Sire," Vlad mouthed while sucking meat out of his teeth. His head was a little light with mead. Vlad had a nice little buzz and he was feeling good. "What is this you ask about God?"

King Chucklarki folded his arms and closed his eyes. He did not wish to see Vlad any longer.

"Have you ever read about God?" the king inquired.

"Which God?" Vlad slurred. "Zeus, Ra, Thor, Baal, Buddha, Indra..."

"No. God!" The king's voice was low. "The God of ancient Israel on Earth. The God that is and always will be."

"Oh. God." Vlad straightened up. "The real God." Vlad laughed. "Yes, I know Him. Why?"

"Today I was filled with the deepest sadness and I walked the castle in search of relief. Something told me to come to my study and pass the time with reading. I searched my shelves and this book," the king pointed at the ancient book lying on the desk, "caught my eye and I have been reading for almost the entire day. I came here at dawn and now the suns have veiled themselves." He sat back. "Do you believe?" The king cleared his throat. He felt foolish. "In God?" The king opened his eyes once more and looked at Vlad. His voice was even lower.

"Yes." Vlad nodded.

"Then why do I not know this?" The king took a deep breath. "Why do I not know Him?"

"Sire, no one wants to hear about God in our world. No one respects their maker. God created life. Life in turn destroyed God, or the belief in Him rather. Humankind and humanoid-kind alike is arrogant. We don't worship. We want to be worshiped." Vlad shook his head. "He is still here like He always was and He will always be. He is."

"How can you be so sure?" the king asked.

"My parents worshiped Him. My great-great-great-great-great-great-great-grandchildren still worship Him today. We all were forced to worship in silence, since the belief in supernatural beings was deemed stupid and insane by the last rulers of Wilzasp. Please forgive me for saying this but your father-in-law and his father started the anti-spiritual revolution." Vlad sobered up and sat up. "I have read the holy book and all of its prophecies have been fulfilled. The Christ came back to Earth and the Earth was destroyed and yes, God provided man with a new heaven and earth like He promised. Do you think that it was a coincidence that our sister planet is named Neotsion (New Zion)?

Neotsion is a planet of pure peace. Only the elect of the creator of all can live there. Only they can leave. My father left there when he was a young man. He thought that he could spread the gift of eternal life to others but it was not his gift to give. He lost his immortal nature and became flawed flesh again. Eventually he married my mother, a native of this land. After a long happy life, he died and she died and someday I will die too. You see, death does not exist on Neotsion. There is no pain. There is no sin. There is no night. There is no sorrow. There is only life everlasting full of pure bliss.

Because man was given the option to leave paradise, man was able to integrate so many planets. The planets that held oxygen and water were given to mankind as new promise lands and the new Jerusalems. I believe man lived in peace on those new planets for thousands of years. Because they removed themselves from grace, man rebelled once more." Vlad paused. "That is what we are doing now. We are still rebelling. Everything is starting over and I believe every planet, except for Neotsion, will face judgment. All will be destroyed and created once more." Vlad clapped his hands together and held them tight. He raised his hands into the air and shook them gleefully. "I feel Him. He answers my prayers. How else do you think I have managed to live so long?." Vlad smirked. "I am nearly a thousand years old despite my father's exodus from the holy land. I have no real skills yet I have always been able to provide for my family. My health is good and my family is happy. I am madly in love with a woman I have been married to for five hundred years. The average humanoid here lives only four hundred years. My wife has been blessed with long life as well. Overall, my life has been a good one. I am overly blessed. Only God bless those who serve Him." A joyful glow, so brilliant and powerful, it could hardly be contained, surrounded his jovial face.

"But you are just a servant and a poor one at that. I hardly call your life blessed," said the king.

"You see! Arrogance. Do you think that money is everything? It cannot buy happiness and it is useless after death. I am very old and I have seen many things. I have seen many men's births and many men's deaths. Rich men with power and many of them were unhappy souls. Yes, I am a lowly servant in your eyes. But you do not see my joy. I am rich in spirit. I am warm and fed and my family never struggled for anything. I know love and have relationships that people would die to have. God is peace of mind. If you knew God, you would not be in the fix that you are in now, if you do not mind me saying. Get to know Him and ask for His peace to be poured upon you. I promise you would gladly want my life if only you knew how happy I am."

"Where is God now?" the king questioned. He was afraid to inquire about Vlad's impossible life span. *Could someone really live that long? Maybe it was the mead talking.* The king found it difficult to look into Vlad's face after his admittance.

"He is everywhere and in all things holy. Call upon His name and He will answer. Praise Him and He will be your salvation. Pray to Him and He will answer you!" Vlad claimed with joy in his voice and a smile on his face. "You just have to have faith. Believe, no, know that He is and He will know you and reveal Himself to you."

"How?" King Chucklarki's eyes searched Vlad's for an answer.

"Believe."

"How?" A look of helplessness paralyzed the king's face.

"Just believe with all your heart, mind, and soul."

"Just believe." The king sat back and closed his eyes. *Could it really be that simple?* "That is all Vlad. You are dismissed."

"Yes Sire." Vlad got up and brushed the crumbs from his black jump-suit. He started toward the door like a walking twig. He was so crooked and frail.

"Vlad." The king opened his eyes and looked at him.

"Yes Sire."

"This is between you and I," King Chucklarki whispered. "Tell no one. I mean absolutely no one about our conversation."

"Yes Sire." Vlad opened the door.

"Vlad," the king called.

Vlad turned around and answered, "Yes."

"Thank you."

"You are welcome. It was my pleasure." Vlad smiled. "God bless you Sire."

"God bless you Vlad," the king replied with his orange fingers tracing the large letters on the cover of the holy book. "May God have mercy on us all."

Chapter 33

"You men hear about the latest murder?" a plump man asked as he put his left foot up on the bench next to him. He unbuttoned his shirt and pulled the damp cloth off, discarding the garment by tossing it on the floor. Musty vapors escaped the sweaty top offending every nearby nose. The man unbuckled his belt and stepped out of his tight gray pants. He sat upon the wooden bench in his underwear letting his bloated belly fall between his legs like a heavy bag of rocks.

The men's lounge in the soldier's headquarters was full of half dressed men that were just getting off duty and was getting ready to go home to their families. Sounds of showers running drowned out the plump man's voice. He sat still for a moment waiting for the last man to finish his shower. He rubbed his hairy chest and belly with rough burly hands. He looked like a big orange bear, furry and untamed. The plump man sat back against a wooden pole that extended from the floor to the ceiling.

The entire lounge was made of wood with wooden benches and wooden closets lined around the walls. Shower stalls were in the far right corner of the rectangular room.

The chubby man sat up. He heard the showers stop.

"You men hear about the latest murder?" he asked again, looking from man to man.

All of them shook their heads.

Fital walked over to the group drying off with a towel. He sat between two mean looking soldiers.

"Well, that "unknown" monster has killed four little girls and two soldiers." The portly man leaned forward with his elbows on his knees. He looked at Fital. "That one there found them." He pointed at Fital and all of the men looked at him.

"Is that true?" asked a very young man sitting near Fital. He was extremely innocent looking and handsome with kind eyes. A look of perplexity and empathy filled his face.

"Yes, I am afraid so," Fital responded while toweling his head dry. "With my own eyes." He sighed. "It was a horrible sight," he murmured in reflection. "Truly horrible."

"Do you know who could have done it?" the boy inquired innocently. "Surely there had to be some sort of clue."

"I have no idea Bentist." Fital dropped his heavy hand on the boy's shoulder. "If I was fortunate enough to find even a small clue, I would have pursued the murderer myself."

"You know who did it Fital! Don't lie to the boy! We all know!" the chubby man spat out. "You know and you have been aiding her!"

"Fital?" Bentist looked at Fital, his eyes questioning. "What is he talking about?"

"I know no such person!" Fital stood up and walked over to the big man. "Are you accusing me of plotting and executing my own people Naffar?!" Fital was an inch away from the man's face, ready to strike at will. "I can rip your throat out with my teeth! Don't you ever accuse me of such things," Fital roared.

"Take it how you like traitor! All I know is that you are bedding that witch and since she has come here, only death has been fruitful in Wilzasp!" Naffar stood up in Fital's face. His chubby cheeks were bouncing as he growled. "Now, if you want to fight, I will fight. I can crush your bald little head between my palms like an orange," he growled.

"I would like to see you try." Fital stepped closer to Naffar.

"Stop it Naffar!" shouted Bentist, pulling the men away from one another and turning toward Fital. "Explain yourself."

Fital looked at Bentist with surprise.

Bentist picked up Fital's hand and placed it upon his heart. The warmth of Fital's palm penetrated Bentist's shirt, paining him with the sincerest of emotions and said, "Please explain, Sir. I know that whatever you say is the truth."

"Boy you are a fool!" Naffar yelled at Bentist. "Fital is bedding a bloody murderer!"

"I know no witch!" Fital snapped. "If you are speaking of Zayashariya, I have seen no evidence that insinuates that she is a murderer. Maybe it is you Naffar! I see you have gained a few pounds. Maybe they were your last few meals!" Fital pointed at Naffar's fat stomach.

The men laughed.

"Why, I'll kill you!" Naffar yelled and pushed Fital. Fital slapped him across his face and Bentist jumped between them holding the two angry men apart.

"Stop it!" Bentist yelled at the two men. His palms pressed hard against each of their chests. "We are brothers." Flailing arms wind-milled around Bentist in a battering assault of fists and fury. Bentist shoved them harder. "We are brothers. Don't let this horrible situation tear us apart!" he pleaded.

"I am no brother of a murderer!" Naffar slobbered.

"Accuse me again and it will be your head!" Fital warned.

"It will be no violence!" Bentist scolded the men.

"Let 'em fight!" one man yelled from the back of the crowd.

Fital and Naffar were now surrounded by all of the men in the lounge.

"Please calm down," Bentist pleaded. "Please be rational." Desperation filled him for a fugacious moment.

"I am through being rational! I am tired of senseless deaths!" Naffar screeched.

"Do you really feel that I am a murderer Naffar?" Fital asked calmly, letting Bentist's hand drop. "Me? I taught you everything that you know. You and I have been cronies since our boyhood. I have protected Wilzasp since the time I was old enough to become a soldier. My forefathers protected this place. They built this place. They fought wars. And you accuse me? I have been nothing but a gentlemen and a loyal servant to the King and this town. I am injured beyond repair by your words."

"I know you did not kill but you keep company with the one who kills. That makes you just as guilty. You condone it! You are a murderer by association!" Naffar calmed down inconsiderably. "You might as well have killed!" He swung at Fital but Bentist caught his fist and threw it back at him.

"I agree with Naffar," concurred an older man, stepping through the crowd.

"Myin?" Fital's heart plummeted like a volant bird whose wing had been   ripped violently from its delicate body. "How could you say such a thing?" His eyes watered. "How could you?"

"Fital," said Myin, the older man, holding Fital by the shoulders. "You are blinded boy. That witch has you under her spell. It is obvious to everyone but you that she is responsible." Myin sat Fital down. He gave Naffar a baneful look and the borderline obese man sat down.

Bentist sat next to Fital and all of the other men found a seat.

"You have been deceived," Myin said.

"No! You have been deceived by hearsay and rumors in which nothing is based on evidence!" Fital screamed at Myin with tears in his eyes. "How could you say this to me?! I am no fool! Do you not think that I have a good judge of character?" Fital ripped himself away from Myin's grip. "You are the one who taught me to get to know a person's heart before judging their appearance and now you...you...hypocrite! You judge someone you do not know or ever tried to know! You are my mentor and trainer! Ha! You judge her because she is different and she does not fear you or your king!"

"My king?" Myin questioned. "Now you do not have a king?" He smirked evilly.

"Don't patronize me!" Fital could not believe that his uncle of all people was turning against him. *Is there anyone who believes in Zayashariya's innocence but me?*

"No! You stop thinking with your second head and start using the one that has a brain! That woman is pure evil! She is poison in your veins. You are bewitched and dumbfounded!"

"She..." Fital started.

Myin slapped Fital hard.

"Quiet! I do not care about her! I care about you and the good people of Wilzasp." Myin's face flushed crimson. "I am so sick of you defending that woman! I was there when you disregarded the king's authority and spoke to him like a common peasant!" Myin snapped and slapped Fital once more. "The king was like your father. I, my dead brother, and your family think that you are despicable for teaming with that...that...thing you call a woman!"

Fital sat there unmoving, eyes cold and deadly.

"I was the one who advised the king to issue you the assignment of assassination," Myin spat. "It is for your own good boy."

"You what?" Fital stood up and looked at the older man with unadulterated hate in his eyes.

"Sit down!" Myin snapped his fingers and two men approached Fital.

Fital sat down.

"I am not the king. You will respect me! Or I will make you," threatened Myin.

"I despise you! I will never respect you!" Fital spat in Myin's face. "Never!"

Myin wiped away Fital's spittle and scoffed.

"Foolish, foolish boy." he smiled. Pity and anger mingled within him like a molesting poison. "Just kill her," Myin commanded, leaning back on one arm and crossing his legs. "It is better for her to lose her head than you to lose yours." He sat up and looked past Fital. "Bentist," he called.

Bentist walked to a nearby closet and opened the door. He pulled out a giant poster and unrolled it. He tacked it to the wall and walked back over to Fital.

"I am sorry," Bentist whispered dropping his head and avoiding Fital's pained eyes.

Fital looked at him. Words could not form on his lips. The execrable actions of all the men he knew and loved gravely wounded him.

"It was not my wish to do this. I love you Fital but Wilzasp comes first," Bentist mumbled and walked out of the room.

The men walked over to the poster and read their orders. They were informed of Fital's order to destroy Zayashariya and also their order to destroy Fital if he doesn't execute the foreigner within a specified amount of time.

"Kill the girl," Myin commanded. "Or we will kill you."

Chapter 34

Bubbling potions and colored steam filled the laboratory. Glass and metal lab equipment littered all of the table tops. The smell of strange chemicals floated through the air. Toxic vapors spotted the air with faint colors like floating clouds. The room was brightly lit by seven metal lamps hanging from the ceiling, spread evenly across the room. Glass cabinets lined the rear wall of the rectangular room like a massive crystal partition. Doors lined the wall on the right side of the room and shelves lined the wall on the left side. Upon the shelves sat lab equipment. Inside the glass cabinets were many specimens, chemicals, powders, and all kinds of unidentifiable odds and ends.

The old wizard stood in front of a table in the back of the room. He poured a yellow liquid into a beaker filled with red liquid bubbling on a burner. An orange puff of steam filled the air around him. He stepped backwards coughing and covering his mouth.

"Kalpvaleim!" the old wizard screamed. "Kalpvaleim! Where are you?" He coughed uncontrollably while covering his mouth with the back of his hand. Vapors forced tears from his eyes and his grey whiskers, fully absorbed by the odors, made him cough more hysterically. "Get here now!" the old wizard screamed.

The daemon walked into the room towards the old wizard.

"Yes Sir," Kalpvaleim answered thoroughly annoyed. The old ignoramus had been calling him all day and he had been toiling hard all afternoon. All he wanted to do was to rest his weary bones. He leaned his mop against the table. "You called?" Kalpvaleim whined. Spots of sweat were all over his body suit, giving it a polka dot design.

"I told you to bring me blue ox blood!" The old wizard held a container in the air. "This liquid is sea snake plasma!" He hurled the container against the wall and it shattered. "You could have killed us both! Now re-label the containers in the glass cabinets, imp, and do it now!" He walked closer to Kalpvaleim. "Don't let it happen again!" The old wizard pointed his finger in Kalpvaleim's face. "Do you understand?" he scolded.

"I understand" Kalpvaleim stared into the old wizards eyes. "I understand perfectly!" He picked up the mop and knocked all of the lab equipment off of the wizard's table onto the floor. "I understand that you are the stupidest alchemist in the universe. Whoever heard of making gold using animal byproducts?"

"You mutt-breed imbecile! What do you know about science? I have discovered something no man has thought of!" The old wizard fumed. "I ought to turn you into a frog!" He lifted his arms into the air in spell casting position. The old wizard's bell shaped sleeves fell backwards exposing his wrinkled elbows as his boney hands twisted in a unanimous motion. "Now, I give you three minutes to clean this mess up. If you don't, you will be in search for a princess to kiss you!"

"Do it yourself you old..." Kalpvaleim was hit in the back of the head. His body fell to the floor unconscious.

"What do you want?" The old wizard choked over his words. He stepped backwards and leaned back against the table.

"We want you!" an ugly voice howled. The being's appearance was twice as hideous as its voice.

"You have no business here!" the old wizard growled as he began to move his arms in a steady rhythm. He tried to cast a spell before the brutes seized him.

"Grab him!" the horrible looking demon Babylon ordered. Two short blue creatures grabbed the wizard. They were like blobs of jelly with arms and legs. Each of them had four eyes and no ears, nose, or mouth. One of the blobs picked up Kalpvaleim and took him out of the room.

"Let me go! I have done nothing to you or your fiendish queen!" The old wizard squirmed. *What would the queen want with me? She knows nothing of my dealings with Zayashariya and Kalpvaleim would not dare report to Lilith. Why would Lilith send Babylon here?*

"Oh no?" The creature laughed. Babylon's white skin was covered with pulsing blisters. "You aided the princess." She smiled. Two blisters adorned each corner of her extra wide mouth. Her deep black eyes shined in the lamp light. "Where is the girl?" Babylon asked, wrapping her long white fingers around the old wizard's neck and lifting him from the floor.

Her hands were covered in pus filled blisters. Some were yellow bubbles. Others were erupting volcanoes. The old wizard felt the infection drip upon his skin. A tingling sensation flowed through him. He was nauseous at once.

"How do I know where Zayashariya is? I have no dealings with her." The old wizard closed his eyes. The sight of the blisters made his skin crawl. "Release me! I know nothing!"

"Don't play with me!" Babylon slapped him and punched him in the stomach.

The old wizard coughed and let his body fall limp for a moment. Babylon's strength was immense. Pain flowed through him like his life's blood. He managed to suck air into his lungs. Her grip around his neck was so tight. The feel of her pus dripping on him was beginning to burn. His stomach ached from his pelvis to his ribs.

"What makes you think I know where she is? I have no dealings with the princess. What would I possibly get out of helping her?" the old wizard mouthed breathlessly.

"Must I hurt you old man?" Babylon sucked some of the mephitic phylum from her throat and readied her mouth to spit the burning fluid in his face.

The old wizard winced at the thought.

"I put her in an ultra mundane space shuttle." The old wizard's legs kicked wildly. "Let me go!" he demanded

Lilith's henchwoman. "I will not say more until you let me down."

"Oh please old man." Babylon squeezed the old wizard's neck tighter as he fought to swallow. Her long black hair rose and spread like a fan on her head, leaving her nude blistering body in full view. "I am sure you know how to find her." Her hair stiffened and became solid and blade sharp. "Where is the girl?" Babylon flashed her razor sharp black teeth.

"I...I...I really don't know," the old wizard stuttered nervously while staring at the potentially perilous hair. "I can try to trace her." He dodged her hair as she tried to cut his flailing wrist. "I could try to trace her essence." He squirmed. "Let me go! I can't help you if I am dead!"

"True," Babylon cooed. Her hair fell back down like before, hiding her breast and intimate parts. "Find her or death will find you!"

"Where is Kalpvaleim?" The old wizard looked past her for his indentured servant. "Please let me down."

"That is none of your concern." Babylon dropped him to the floor. "Just find her."

Chapter 35

Morning came with all certainty. A new day had begun. Another day of fear was born into the world, like an ailing child, full of bleak expectations and utter grief. The setting up of street stands could be heard throughout the city. The town's people moved around the town in a very slow, sloth-like pace. Woe and despair hung like vexatious chains around their necks. Tears flooded every eye. Sadness reigned as king.

Across the street from the Inn was a young couple sitting on a bench in front of one of the town's homes. They held hands under the warmth of the suns and gazed into one another's eyes. The woman let out a small pitiful sigh and looked into her lover's face. She searched his eyes for a resolution, a reason to be strong in their time of suffering. Nothing.

"Oakreyau, what is to become of us?" The lady blinked her dark circled gray eyes. Worry forced crow's feet to decorate them, causing her youthful age to be ignored and for her to be mistaken for a woman in the prime of her life.

"Juv, I have the slightest idea. Our people are dying and there is nothing we can do about it." Oakreyau grabbed both of her hands and put them to his heart. "I love you Juv. Let us get married tonight at the Inn. We know not when our final days are upon us. At least this way we will be together and our love will be bound by eternal commitment. I want nothing more of this life but to be your husband," he said, leaning over and kissing her quivering lips.

"I will marry you Oakreyau," exclaimed Juv, putting her arms around him and holding on for dear life. "Maybe we can escape." She held him closer. "We can leave this place and find peace elsewhere." Wild ambition filled her face. A crazed tremble took over her voice. "Don't speak of the end. We are just beginning our lives."

"But how can I not?" he questioned. "I had a dream last night, a terrible dream. I saw us both dead. We were in our wedding garments and bloody upon the floor." Oakreyau paused. "I am not afraid. I know our time will be at an end soon. You and I both know that my dreams hold truth. They always have." Oakreyau kissed Juv's hand and dropped it softly on her lap. "I do not want to be afraid anymore. There is no way to escape the inevitable."

"We will find a way," Juv cried. She bit into her bottom lip. "If that creature can get in, we can get out."

Oakreyau kissed her forehead, wiped her weeping face, and said, "I promise we will find a way."

Juv looked into his eyes. She knew he did not believe in his words.

"All that matters is that we are together," she whispered softly.

"Yes, that is all." Oakreyau kissed her passionately and slowly pulled away. "My love for you will never cease to be," he confessed. Juv rested her head upon his shoulder and felt comfort in the warmness of his arms.

The couple sat on the bench for hours watching their neighbors carry out their daily duties. A man with clear irises walked over to the bench where the couple sat.

"Hello lovebirds," greeted the jolly man smiling. "Don't look so gloomy. What's wrong?"

"We are getting married," Juv responded forlornly.

"And that is something to be sad about?" the jolly man asked with a confused expression on his face.

"Of course not." Oakreyau smiled. "We are sad because of the deaths of our friends and families. When is the madness to stop?"

"Who knows dear boy? Maybe it is our destiny to perish. No one can control fate. Why try? Just be happy with the time you have on this planet. Everything else we should not worry about." The old man put his hand upon Juv's shoulder and kissed her cheek. "So when is the wedding sweet child?" he asked.

"It is tonight. I would love for you to be there. Please invite Farrish, Javid, Maloy, Brevis, Luttved, and Dragol for me. I only want them to come. Invite no one else please. Oakreyau and I wish to have a small ceremony. It will be tonight in the dining hall of the Inn," Juv said. "Sir Wilfrev, will you marry us?"

"Of course I will child. Of course I will. Just tell me what time to be there," the jolly man said. "And of course, I'll invite my children for you. I am sure that the will be pleased that you thought of them. They will be very honored to witness your sacred union."

"Be there at dusk," Oakreyau muttered.

"Until then children," said the old man, waving his hand and vanishing into a crowd of people nearby.

Juv and Oakreyau waved goodbye to Sir Wilfred and stood up and kissed.

"Until we meet again my love," Oakreyau said.

"Until we meet again," Juv replied.

The woman and man went their separate ways to prepare for tonight's event.

Chapter 36

"Hello sweetheart," King Chucklarki said while stroking his wife's peach hair.

Queen Eox did not respond. Her back was turned to him as she lay under the plush blankets on the bed, ignoring every word that he said.

Old memories of their happy life together ran rampant through his head. Images of her frolicking around the bedroom with a childlike smile painted across her face made him sigh with longing. He remembered her dancing with him in the wee hours of the night and kissing him gently. His wife could be an angel and a demon in one breath. King Chucklarki loved that about her. The way she could charm him and chastise him within the time span of an eye wink; it kept him on his feet.

"Honey, will you be angry forever?" The king kissed his wife's shoulder. "I love you." He turned her onto her back and she stared into his eyes quietly. He kissed her. "I promise that I will make things right. Please trust in me." He kissed her lips again. This time his kiss was featherlike and tender. The king buried his face into her neck and breathed in the sweet natural perfume of her body. "You are my life. Without your love I am nothing."

She did not respond.

He looked into her face with his lips full of wanting and his heart full of desperation and begged, "Forgive me please. I love you so much and I was a fool. My pride impaired my senses. Your words that night wounded me deeply and I wanted to punish you for them. I was wrong. What I did was terrible. I hate myself for violating you," King Chucklarki cried. "You have to believe me! I am a different man now. I promise to never harm you again. Just speak to me. Even if you no longer love me, say so! Your silence is deadlier that any word you can utter."

Queen Eox turned away from him and said nothing. His head dropped. The king got up from the bed and grabbed his robe from the bedpost, covering his naked body as he walked out of the room.

The hallway was very dark. King Chucklarki walked down it slowly until he came to the door of his study. He rested his head on his hands and took a deep breath. The entire house was un-naturally quiet. Silence seemed so loud. He paused for a moment and attempted to focus his eyes in the darkness. The king saw or heard nothing. Complete silence settled over the house like a thick invisible mist. King Chucklarki placed his hand on the doorknob. It was cold to his touch. He opened the door and walked inside. Clumsily he made his way over to his desk. Although the floor was clear and he knew the room like the back of his hand, his clouded mind made it difficult to focus. Putting one foot in front of the other to simply walk was a difficult task for him. Faith had not brought him peace just yet. The king was a man of worry and frustration. He picked up a lighter from the inside of his desk drawer and lit the lantern sitting on his desk. King Chucklarki pulled the holy book from the bookshelf and began to read.

Minutes turned into hours and he closed the book and pushed it across his desk. The room was very cool. Not cold but an eerie cool that penetrated his bones and sent light chills down his spine. He got up from his chair and picked up a few logs, placed them into the fireplace, and lit the fire. The king blew out the lantern and sat in front of the warm flames. The crystals surrounding the fireplace reflected the dancing light of the fire on the walls and the furniture, creating a plethora of color. King Chucklarki got on his knees and folded his hands. Golden light danced across his troubled face. He opened his mouth. First, there was no sound; then, suddenly a deep moan rumbled from his mouth. Perspiration accumulated on his brow.

"Lord," King Chucklarki cried aloud. "All mighty God, hear me please. I realize that I have never recognized you before now and I am not worthy to call upon your holy name but the book says that if I ask you for anything it will be given, if I seek you, I will find you and if I knock on your door it will be opened unto me." He held his hands so tight that his orange knuckles turned white. Tears fell to the floor like raindrops.

"God of ancient Israel, hear my prayer. Please help me stop the violence that is plaguing my town. Lord, have mercy. I have no other way to turn. I am cornered and too weak to do battle. Fight for me Lord. Fight for me! I believe that nothing is too impossible for you to do," he pleaded. "Lord, I have sinned against my wife. I have desecrated the temple of her body and mind. Forgive me and allow her to forgive me also. I promise my own life that I will never bring her unhappiness again. Help me!" King Chucklarki wrapped his arms around himself and wept. He fell over on his side and suddenly a deep coma overcame him.

There was a loud rapping at the king's chamber door. The king awoke with a start and wiped the cobwebs from his eyes. Startled by the noise, he sat up.

"Who would knock like that? Something grave must have occurred," the King of Wilzasp said to himself. Panic grabbed his heart. "My wife?" He bolted to his feet. "My kingdom?"

The rapping came harder and louder; then, without warning, the rapping stopped. King Chucklarki bolted over to the door and opened it. There was no one there. He stuck his head out of the door and looked down the hall.

"Anyone there?" his voiced bounced off the wall and fell into silence.

The hallway was as clear and as dark as before. He closed the door and turned around. Before his eyes stood the most beautiful creature he had ever seen. King Chucklarki was simply awestruck.

The being was human in appearance with dark brown skin. He had thick raven hair that curled below his ears. Raven eyebrows rested above his penetrating eyes. His eyes were deep set, black, round, and very kind. His face was strong, very masculine, and relatively pleasant looking. Moderately tall in statue, maybe six feet tall and an inch or two taller, the being was dressed in flowing silver robes that covered him from his neck to his toes. The metallic fabric reflected the dark mahogany color of his skin and the light of the fire which burned across the room. A pair of black, silver-tipped wings protruded from his back. He held in his right hand a sword and in his left hand a book.

"Who are you?" The king trembled. He fell to his knees and covered his face. The presence of this being strained King Chucklarki's eyes. A glow seemed to pulsate from the beings face in a faint white light. "What are you?"

"An angel. A holy messenger. Be unafraid," the angel spoke in a harmonious voice. It was sweet and deep, soothing to the ears. "I was sent here to aid you. The Almighty heard your plea and He has sent me to tell you that He is with you." The angel's wings fluttered. The silver-tipped feathers shined in the light. His face was emotionless.

"Th...th...thank you," the king managed to force from his throat. He lifted his head from the floor and looked at the angel. "You are so beautiful." The King of Wilzasp admired the creature from head to toe. A feeling of jubilation filled his body. He clasped his hands together in order to contain his desire to leap up from the floor and shout out in pure thankfulness to be in the presence of such holiness.

"All are beautiful in the Lord's eyes. We were all made in His image," the angel replied emotionlessly.

"What do I do?" King Chucklarki's voice quavered.

"Wait on the Lord. He will be your rock and your fortress. He will aid you when you most need Him. Wait on the Lord," said the angel.

"Wait?" The king sat up on the floor in Indian style, arms akimbo. Fear had left him. "But what do I do in the meantime?"

"Wait on the Lord. Have faith. He will be there. The Lord never lies. He will never forsake you." The angel began to fade. "Wait on the Lord," his voice echoed through the room.

"Please wait!" the king begged.

The angel faded into nothingness.

The king grabbed at the air but there was nothing there. He walked over to the desk and picked up the holy book. He hugged the book close and placed it back on the shelf. He threw ashes on the fire and walked out of the room. King Chucklarki closed the door and walked back down the hall to his bedroom. He disrobed and climbed into the bed next to his wife, wrapping his arms around her sleeping body and falling slowly into the world of dreams.

Chapter 37

"If I told you once, I've told you a thousand times," Queen Lilith growled as she kicked Kalpvaleim across the face. "Don't defy me daemon!" She spat smoke into his eyes.

"Damn you Lilith!" He wrenched in his chains. Kalpvaleim was chained by his wrists and ankles to a cell wall. Blood and filth clung to his scraped up skin. He had been flogged and dragged from one place to another and back.

"Damn your pitiful soul!" he yelled.

His hooves were filed down to a stub from the constant dragging on the concrete floor. He could hardly balance himself.

"You will regret this. I promise you that!" Kalpvaleim hissed.

"Don't curse your master boy!" roared Lilith. She was furious. Fire shot from her eyes and burned tiny circles in his chest.

Kalpvaleim winced and screamed, "Ouch you jade!" He tried to spit at her as he jerked around, confined within his chains.

She was too far away for his spittle to soil her.

"I'll kill you for this!" he threatened.

"Sure you will." Lilith walked closer to him. "Sure you will." She kneeled down and made a ball out of some tar on the cell floor. "I will destroy you," Lilith promised as she took the tar ball and melted it with the flame from her fingertips. "You will die for aiding my insubordinate daughter." The Queen of Night smeared the melted tar on Kalpvaleim's chest as he contorted in misery. "I dare you to humiliate me before my peers! I can not believe that your ridiculously simple mind persuaded you to conjure up the audacity to help Zayashariya escape!" She scratched him across the face with her thorny nails. "Do you really think that Zayashariya will summon you?" Lilith laughed. "In what realm will you belong besides the Nether Worlds? Who would treat a half ass like a humanoid! I mean literally half ass," Lilith huffed and pointed at his hoofs. "Be serious fool. You will be shunned in any place except this one and why would Zayashariya risk ridicule for befriending a mutant such as yourself?" Lilith huffed. "You are truly unbelievable Kalpvaleim. I mean really unbelievable!"

Kalpvaleim hung suspended in chains, achy, miserable, and blurry eyed. He had been wondering why Zayashariya had not summoned him yet. Did Lilith's word contain truth? Would Zayashariya ever summon him or would he die in the hands of the horrible demon queen? His eyes overflowed with tears.

"She will come for me," he whispered. He looked into Lilith's eyes and scoffed. "I know that she will come," he said louder full of false confidence.

Lilith disregarded his wishful proclamation. "I admire your pseudo-optimism but it will do you no good. I will kill you slowly. Death will not come to you soon enough. I will show you who I am and the extent of my diabolical imagination. If you will not honor me in life, your tattered body will in death."

"You are more of a fool than I ever imagined. You are nothing, Lilith, and I do not fear you. The entire Council knows that you are a sanctimonious idiot. You control no one. You can't even control your own child. Rest assure, your tortures and your threats of death do not phase me. I will never fear you. That is who I am," Kalpvaleim replied boldly.

"You are mere bait. If Zayashariya does contact you, you both will be at my mercy," said Lilith, turning and leaving Kalpvaleim's cell. She disappeared into thin air.

"Flog him!" her voice echoed throughout the dungeon.

Two smelly ghouls came into Kalpvaleim's cell, each carrying a whip and a spiked belt. They positioned themselves on opposite sides of Kalpvaleim and began beating.

Chapter 38

The old wizard quickly led Babylon and her two imps through his castle to his private quarter, careful to take intricate turns and twists so that the way there could not be remembered. He led them quickly through long hallways, short staircases, and various hidden passageways. The demons impatiently followed him, constantly complaining and growling until they finally reached a giant gray door fastened with four locks. The old wizard uttered a secret password and each lock magically unlocked. The giant door opened with a tiny squeak.

The old wizard's private quarter was a small room with very little furniture. The walls were bare and the lighting was very dim. A gigantic crystal sat in the middle of the room held up by metal claws coming out of the wooden floor. The ball was full of fog and swirling mist. There were seven chains circling the crystal ball, all were held together by iron claws which protruded from a podium. A book was positioned on the podium before the ball. The room was eerily silent.

"Move!" Babylon pushed the old wizard through the door. The old wizard stumbled but quickly regained his footing. "Find Zayashariya now before you find death!"

The old wizard entered. The demons followed with caution.

"Take a seat. Patience is a virtue dear woman." The old wizard pointed to the chairs as he walked over to the crystal ball and began to rub his fingers across the crystal orb. He took a deep breath and opened the big book on the podium. The pages of the book crumbled a little under the wizard's fingers and dust flew into the old wizard's eyes, causing them to water as he flipped the pages.

Babylon and her jelly imps looked on in silence.

The old wizard found his page and read silently.

"Wizard hurry or I'll have your head as a trophy!" Babylon warned. Patience was not one of her better qualities.

"Quiet! Fool you unnerve me to a degree you cannot comprehend," the old wizard shouted. "I can not focus with your wretched voice breaking my concentration." The wizard cut his eyes at her. "Woman beast, calm yourself!"

"Hurry!" Babylon shifted in her seat. Her skin bubbled with pus. "Hurry before the pain comes back old man!" she sneered. "If I feel pain, you feel pain." She nodded to her jelly imps. "Be sure that you understand my minions will be more than glad to torture you."

"Quiet I say!" the old wizard commanded. "I do not fear you! You are in my domain. Humble yourself or I will humble you!"

"On with the show!" Babylon squealed.

She knew that the wizard's power was supreme within his secret chamber. She hoped that his fear of Lilith would keep him obedient.

"Be careful and look closely. Zayashariya has the ability to change her appearance, especially when she kills. Shape shifting is her camouflage when she is in strange lands. She does it so that the inhabitants will not connect her to any murders she may commit. Her violet eyes are the sign that a strange creature may be her in disguise," said Babylon.

"I know these things you idiot! Quiet yourself and let me work," the old wizard snapped.

The old wizard rolled up his sleeves and began to chant. The crystal ball lit up and the mist inside began to clear. A face appeared. It was very blurry. The old wizard chanted louder and faster, his voice rising to an ear piercing pitch. Babylon covered her ears and her goons seemed to bury their blob-like heads into their bodies. A flash of lightening came out of the ball and everyone in the room fell to the floor. After a few moments, they all returned to their places and the wizard finished his chant. The face inside of the crystal ball came through clear. It was Zayashariya.

"Where is she?" Babylon screamed. She shifted uncomfortably. Her boils were stinging and pouring over with infection. She needed her salve and she had left it behind. Pain covered her body with horrible ease.

"Where is she?" the old wizard asked the crystal ball. "Come closer," he directed Babylon and her creatures.

The ball showed Zayashariya's surroundings. No one recognized the area.

"Where is that place?" Babylon shouted. "I have never seen such a place." She walked closer to the ball. "It is so bright there."

She touched the crystal and jerked her hand back in pain. Babylon looked at her hand. Terror consumed her eyes as her mouth curled backwards in misery.

"Ahhhhhhhh!" Babylon screamed. Burned smelly skin hung from her badly injured palm. She licked the charred flesh and sat down.

Served you right! The old wizard looked at the putrid she-demon and frowned. He wanted to laugh at her pain but he did not wish to anger her. He looked back at the ball. He picked up a small pointed stick and scrapped the burned flesh from the ball. It curled and flaked off like plastic.

"Show me the land's inhabitants," commanded the old wizard.

The crystal ball showed an orange skinned person with peach hair.

"Looks like a Norp." The wizard looked closer. "Norp and human," he said.

"What?" Babylon questioned.

"That humanoid is mixed with Norp and human." The wizard pointed. "Look at the skin tone and height. That is definitely Norp." The old wizard scratched his chin. "She must be either on Planet X or the new planet where old Earth used to be."

He scratched his chin. Doubt clouded his mind. *A demon on the material plane, so far from the Nether Worlds, without being summoned or given divine permission? I don't know. Maybe those humanoids are wraiths. No. Couldn't be! How could she have landed there? I warped her off of this planet but expected her to remain in the supernatural realm or at least on the nearby material planes where she had always been able to travel freely. Her demon nature should have prevented her from going that far. How can this be? Is Zayashariya a full demon?* He thought. The old wizard puzzled over the situation. Suddenly thoughts of her origin filled his mind. He could not recall who Zayashariya's father was and he wondered why it was so important for her to be on the Council of Demons. No other demon was forced into the position. *Who is she really and what is her significance?* The old wizard looked intently into the crystal ball.

"How can you be sure?" Babylon licked her burned hand again.

Her jelly imps sat quietly. Their eyes were closed and their limbs were invisible. They appeared to be two lifeless lumps of goo.

"I am only taking a guess," the old wizard said, pondering over the image. "I haven't seen a Norp in ages."

"You better do better than that!" Babylon turned her head to the side and vomited pus. The pus on the floor sizzled and evaporated leaving a foul sticky odor. She wiped her mouth with the side of her hand, and said "And you better hurry." Her sores began to pulsate like millions of volcanoes bubbling with yellow and green lava.

The old wizard twisted his face in revulsion. "Would you like some unguent?" he asked trying not to vomit himself. "I can conjure some up in moments," he offered not out of the goodness of his heart but out of the desire not to be thoroughly repulsed.

"Please," Babylon croaked. "Anything! Give me anything! The pain is coming." Babylon started to convulse.

The old wizard whispered a few words and a dark jar appeared in his hand. He gave the salve to the abomination before him. She snatched the jar from him quickly and rubbed the ointment on her body. Healing began quickly. Babylon's blisters closed instantly and the pus flaked and fell from her body. She became calm once more.

The old wizard was instantly sickened by the scabs and flakes resting in his floor and chair. He let his fingers dance as he whispered a spell. The disgusting residue caught fire and burned into nothingness.

"Thank you," Babylon snapped. "Now find the girl!"

"Where are you?" the old wizard asked the crystal ball. An image of the town was shown. The gate of the city was shown briefly. "Show me the gate again," he commanded the crystal ball. It showed the rear view of the gate. The old wizard could not decipher the wording on the gate. "Show me the facade of the gate." The gate had WILZASP written across it. "Wilzasp," the old wizard whispered to himself. "Well I'll be."

"You'll be dead if you don't get on with it!" Babylon hissed. "Where is she?"

"Near old earth." The wizard smiled. "She is on the material plane."

"What does that mean?" she grunted. Babylon stood up and her hair began to move with a life of its own.

"It means that you can't go there," he chuckled. "A demon or daemon has to be summoned by a mortal to walk the material plane." The wizard laughed. "The only other way for a demon to walk on the material plane is to be granted permission from the creator, which almost never ever happens or to have old Luci's okay."

"Well how did Zayashariya get there?" Babylon asked.

"I guess she is more human than demon after all," said the old wizard. He snapped his fingers and the crystal ball went dim once more. A smug look of satisfaction was on his face. He fondled his beard and raised his eyebrows, a sly grin on his cunning face.

"Don't mock me old man. Everyone knows that she is a full demon," the demon snapped. Babylon walked toward him and tried to grab his neck.

"Leave me be witch! You have no power here!" The old wizard shot lightening from his fingertips. "Don't make me destroy you! I would receive too much pleasure in the thought of it."

Babylon and her imps hurried from the room. She knew that they could be easily destroyed. Babylon was aware of the wizard's power when he was near the crystal. She was also aware that he had had enough of her thuggery so she decided to leave before she was done with. She ran from the castle and headed to Queen Lilith to report the news.

The old wizard watched, from his window, Babylon and her blobs run.

"I hope she catches that demon Zayashariya and they all destroy each other! That is, if they can get to her." *Like I considered, she may be more human than demon after all*, he thought. A smile crossed his face as he pulled a pouch filled with pieces of silver from his pocket. "I think I have an inkling of who her dear daddy may be."

Chapter 39

Zayashariya and Fital awoke in each other's arms. The morning was bright and clear. Zayashariya's room glowed pale red in the bright light of the twin suns shining through her window. She sat up in bed, pulling the covers up over her breast, her head lying against the bedpost, and stared at the crystal covered wall.

Fital saturated his eyes with her smooth black skin and imagined the bliss he had experienced the night before. He put his hand on her arched leg, feeling the silkiness of her. His bright orange skin seemed to glow when touching her charcoal colored skin. With small kisses, he showered her leg. She relaxed with each engaging peck. Serenity filled the room for the first ten minutes. A lazy sigh escaped from the plum colored lips of Zayashariya.

"What are you thinking about?" Fital asked. He laid his head in her lap and looked up into her sparkling eyes.

"There is so much you don't understand about me. You would never understand." A sadness was in her voice.

"Try me." Fital kissed her navel.

"I am not like you."

"Really? I didn't know that." Fital laughed sarcastically. "Be more specific my love. No two people are truly alike."

"I am not like any humanoid. I am different entirely." She looked into his confused eyes. "Forget it. You wouldn't understand." Zayashariya pulled the cover over her head, trapping Fital beneath also.

"If you are concerned about how others perceive you because you are different, to the hells with them! You are beautiful," Fital yelled as he pulled the cover from her face.

"Do you think I care what others think? These simple minded people mean nothing to me! They are just a means of survival, nothing more! They are as worthless as farm mammals."

"What?" Fital asked with a touch of anger in his voice. "You speak of them as if they are food." He grabbed her arm tight. "Please don't tell me that the others are right about you!"

"Be careful. I do not take kindly to force." Zayashariya jerked her arm free and rolled her eyes.

"Is that a threat?"

"Take it as you wish," she retorted.

Fital's eyes transformed into slits. He sat up straight and pulled her close to him.

She looked him in the eye.

"What do you mean, woman?" he questioned.

"Never mind." Zayashariya pulled away and attempted to stand up but Fital pulled her back upon the bed and climbed on top of her, pressing her arms against the bed and sitting on her thighs.

"Talk to me." Fital's face hovered over Zayashariya's.

"Like I said, you would not understand." Zayashariya freed one of her hands and ran her fingers through her hair and locked her eyes on the wall. "My sins are many. I have lived a life that you would not care to know of." She paused. "Why do you care anyway? Our love affair is nothing more than a momentary tryst. You will forget about me soon. After I am gone from this place, you will find a new love. Maybe marry her and reproduce like normal people do. That could never happen between you and me. We are too different. Why care about something so temporary?"

Fital pulled her toward him.

"Look at me," he demanded.

She did.

"I care because I love you woman!"

Zayashariya was thunderstruck at the sincerity in his eyes. Times before when he declared his love, she dismissed his romantic notions as fascination tainted with lust but now she knew that his love for her was unfeigned. The dark stranger put her arms around Fital's neck and whispered softly into his ear, "I love you too. But my love isn't strong enough to make you understand me."

"I understand enough. Let me show you." Fital kissed her lips while massaging her back and neck with his strong hands.

The couple fell into each other's arms once again and returned to the world of unimaginable pleasure. A world in which they discovered in each other's eyes and a world that strived in each other's caress.

Chapter 40

The day grew old like the withering bones of a decrepit soul. The twin suns were completing their daily journey across the sky. The fluffy green clouds slowly floated across the powder blue sky reflecting the pink rays of the twin suns.

Fital sat on the edge of Zayashariya's bed and dressed himself.

Zayashariya stood at the window looking out into the town beneath her. A severe hunger escalated deep within her being. Her violet eyes flared. Her teeth began to sharpen and break free from her plum gums and protrude from her mouth.

"Please leave!" Zayashariya desperately pleaded with Fital, her voice hysterical, refusing to face him. Her arms shook under her weight.

"I'll be gone in a minute." Fital pulled on his pants. "What's wrong? Why the rush?" He buttoned and zipped his clothes and sat back on the bed.

The dark stranger stood quivering. A stream of tears fell from her eyes.

"Nothing is wrong," she lied. "I just want to be alone. I am not feeling well."

Fital got up from the bed and walked toward her.

"Let me help you."

"Stop!" Zayashariya screamed as she lifted her hand behind her. "Don't come near me!" She balled her fist and dropped her trembling arm on the window pane. "I beg you Fital. Please leave. I will be okay. I promise. Leave me be."

Her fangs pierced her lips. A small drop of blood reached her tongue. Her heart quickened. The taste maddened her. A low growl rumbled within her throat. She swallowed hard to muffle the noise.

"What's wrong with you woman?" asked Fital, standing just a few feet away. "What did I do?" He began to walk toward her again until he saw her yielding hand.

"You did nothing. I am unwell at the moment. I adore you. Nothing has changed between us. I just need to be alone now. Please leave." Zayashariya choked on her words. "I still love you. I will be okay and I will see you soon. Respect my wishes and leave now."

"Zay....." Fital felt rejected. "If you are ill, let me help you. You do not have to suffer alone," he assured her.

"Just go!" Zayashariya cried uncontrollably. "Please darling."

"I'll go." He turned and walked away. Fital gathered his belongings and walked to the door. It opened with a squeak. He paused, holding the knob tight, swallowing his desire to go to her and demand an explanation for her strange behavior. With much restraint, he repeated, "I'll go,"

"Will I see you tomorrow?" Zayashariya asked, pretending that all was well.

"Sure." Fital walked out of the room confused by her actions. The door slammed hard behind him.

Chapter 41

The dining hall of the Inn was decorated from floor to ceiling. Blue lace streamers hung from the ceiling. Pink satin tablecloths were on each table. In the center of each table, a single yellow glowing crystal sat. A small platform sat in the center of the room. Flowery arches surrounded a cube shaped stage forming a hilly garden. The sweet scent of flowers permeated the room with a fresh aroma. On the stage was a small wooden podium with a single crystal on it. In the far corner of the room, a skinny woman wearing a cream toga sat in front of a golden harp. The woman pulled the harp's strings and the door to the dining hall opened. Soft music filled the room. Sir Wilfrev, the town's judge, walked through the door carrying a white crystal in both hands. He wore a white robe that hung to his ankles, exquisitely trimmed in plush silk. He walked lightheartedly to the beat of the harp's music. Behind him, the bridesmaids Farrish, Maloy, and Brevis walked side by side.

Farrish wore a pale pink toga that stopped right above her knees. Her peach hair was pulled back into a ponytail. In her hands, she held a blue crystal.

Maloy wore a powder blue toga that stopped a little below her knees around her calves. Her peach hair was curled around her face. She carried a yellow crystal in her hands.

Brevis wore a yellow toga that hung to her ankles. Her peach hair hung straight. She held a pink crystal in her hands.

After the women took their positions on the platform, the harp player played a little louder and faster. Then the groomsmen Javid, Luttved, and Dragol came in one after the other. All three men wore a pale green robe. They took their place on the opposite side of the women.

The harp player slowed her tune and the bride and groom walked in together.

Juv wore a long black dress with red roses trimming the neck, sleeves, and the bottom of the dress. Red roses were in her curly peach hair. Her lips were dyed rose red and her eyelids were tinted with a sheer black glitter.

Oakreyau wore a long black robe trimmed in red satin. A single red rose was pinned in front of his heart. Ruby studs adorned his ears.

The couple walked to the stage and faced the smiling judge. Their smiles gleamed like twinkling stars.

"Do you love her?" Sir Wilfrev asked.

"Yes," Oakreyau answered as he smiled at his wife to be.

"Do you love him?" Sir Wilfrev asked Juv.

"Yes I do," she answered with a smile as bright as sunbeams on her face.

"Do you two want to be together forever? Do you two desire only each other? Do you two understand that you will have to live faithfully and honorably for the remainder of your natural lives?"

"Yes we do," the couple answered in unison.

Juv turned to Farrish and she handed her a ruby wedding band. Likewise, Luttved handed Oakreyau a matching ruby band. Then, the couple placed the rings on one another's thumb.

Sir Wilfred wrapped a thick red ribbon around their joined hands and said, "It is done. You are forever bound by the law of the king. Kiss and dance in glory."

The couple kissed and danced cheek to cheek. The harp player played her joyful tune as the entire wedding party joined in the dance and cheered for the newlyweds. Suddenly the merriment was interrupted by a deep hoarse growl. The music stopped and everyone froze.

"What was that?" Brevis asked, her eyes rimmed with fear.

"I don't know," Juv responded as she looked around. She grabbed his arm and let her trembling palm slip down into his.

"Look!" Oakreyau pointed at the doorway. He squeezed his wife's hand. Juv could feel his palms sweating profusely. "My prophecy is being fulfilled. Our doom is imminent!"

A tremendous sized wolf blocked the doorway. The beast was at least ten feet tall. Saliva dripped from its massive jaws. Its black fur shined in the glow of the crystals causing it to appear as if it illuminated with a light of its own. The monster's purple eyes sparkled. It stood hungrily before them with its hulking chest rising and falling in grunting breaths. A low growl exited its dangerous maw.

The wedding party huddled together. The beast blocked the only way out. Tears swam from all of their eyes as many streams pouring into one great river of dread. The beast pounced upon the group and ripped them limb from limb in one single effort. It was so swift that one scream could not escape the throat of the damned. The beast gathered all of the body parts with its massive claws, pushing the mutilated limbs into one pile. With fiendish hunger, the wolf drained each piece of blood; not stopping until its crapulent feasting toppled it unto its side.

Dripping with fresh blood and twisted cruelty, the monster hobbled out of the room on its hind legs humming the tune the harp player had played before the massacre.

In the rear of the Inn, a group of children played under the light of the moon. Their parents were ignorant of their whereabouts. The children played tag and chased each other around. One of the boys, while running backwards, bumped into the beast. The monster grabbed the boy up from the ground and threw him into the other children. The beast fell down on all fours and ravished the whole group. In the midst of the feast, a strange sound echoed trough a nearby alley. Footsteps.

Fital stepped out into the opening and the beast ran off into the woods leaving bloody paw prints on the ground. It disappeared before his eyes could catch sight of it.

"My goodness!" Fital fell to his knees. "What could have done this?" He wept and ran out into the street. "Run for your lives! More have been murdered!" he cried. "Leave this wretched place if you want to survive!" He ran toward every person he saw. "Leave here!" The people ran into their homes and packed.

"Fital," Zayashariya called.

He turned toward her. "Hello beautiful one," he responded in distress. "You must leave this place. It is not safe here."

"What's wrong?" She stroked his face.

He pointed toward the alley behind the Inn unable to describe the horror he had seen. He began to vomit and she pulled him from the ground and wiped his mouth.

"It will be okay," said Zayashariya, helping him up. She walked him over to a bench nearby; sat him down and sat down beside him. She held his hands within her own.

"Where is everyone going?" she asked.

People were leaving their homes with packed bags and all the belongings they could carry. The streets were filled with frenzied humanoids, hustling and bustling, trying to evacuate the city as swift as possible.

"Away from here." Fital began to fret. He buried his face in Zayashariya's palms. "Why is this happening?" Fital moved to kiss her hands but before his lips could touch them, a strange sight chilled him to the bone. He looked at her fingers with hurt and thoughts of treachery. His eyes stretched beyond their natural boundaries as if a colossal pressure inside his skull was trying to force his eyeballs out of his head.

Zayashariya snatched her hand away from him.

"What is this?" he said. Fital grabbed her hand, inflicting pain, examining it closely, rubbing her stained dark flesh and tasting the crimson residue. Orange flesh and fresh blood was squeezed from under her nails and smeared across her fingertips.

"What is this?" He looked into her eyes. "Please answer me?!"

Tighter and tighter, he squeezed her guilty hand. Zayashariya winced but Fital's grip only tightened.

"Nothing. It is not important." She pulled her hand away and looked away. In her heart's dying moment, Zayashariya could not face him. So she lied, "I had an…um… an…um…an accident." Nervousness filled her. Zayashariya knew in her heart that her great love affair had just come to a crashing halt. She loved Fital but it would not be enough. He would never forgive her no matter how much she pleaded. Now all that was left to do was to harden her heart and face him.

Fital grabbed her face and turned it toward him.

"Don't lie to me! I asked you a question. You will answer!" he roared into her face, like a fuming wild cat, sprinkling it with saliva. His eyes were full of contempt. He grinded his teeth like a miller grinding wheat. Redness flushed his face. Tears came. Fital's nose flared.

"You would never understand if I told you," Zayashariya responded nonchalantly. She gave Fital a death chilling stare. "Never! I will not explain myself. When I wished to explain myself, you had no ear for my spiritual silliness. I owe you no explanation."

"What would I not understand?" Fital searched her eyes as he rose from his seat. *It can't be! Please. No!* "It was you, wasn't it?" Hurt was in his eyes. "My heart blinded me of your perfidy and my soul will suffer long for my stupidity. You were an aversion to all but me, but I still believed in you. I allowed the cancerous lust of my loins to fester and invade my heart. Now I am nothing more than an ignominious fool full of shame and guilt. I let so many people perish because of my benighted love for you!" Fital laughed a sad little laugh. "And you owe me no explanation? You owe me nothing?" He stepped backwards. "You are wrong. You owe me everything!" Fital could barely stand. His entire body was in the nucleus of an emotional seizure. He could barely control his rage. "I trusted you!" He pulled his sword from its sheath. "It was you." He smiled a disappointed smile. "You are right, my love, I will never understand a deceiving murderer. You are dead to me! As dead as the people you mutilated in sick perverse pleasure."

"No. It was not like that. Listen to me. Let me explain," begged Zayashariya. The ice melted from her broken heart and guilt invaded and sealed the cracks that she caused.

"No explanation is needed. You owe me nothing, remember? I have no ear for you! You made a fool of me! Everyone told me but I was too enchanted by your erotic gifts and too blinded by my love for you. You can never make me understand. I hate you!" roared Fital, tossing his blade from hand to hand trying to regain his composure. The rage within him was erupting like a volcano dormant for centuries.

"You don't mean that," Zayashariya wept. "My love for you is real. You can not mean that." She searched his eyes for a hint of sympathy. There was none. Zayashariya folded her hands across her lap and dropped her head in shame.

"Don't I?" Fital placed his sword to her neck and drew blood. "Make your peace and say goodbye. I am sure Gehenna and all its horrors are waiting for your wicked soul to return."

"Fital don't make me kill you," Zayashariya pleaded with him. She stood up to face him, his sword still at her throat. "I love you. I told you that you would not understand." She reached out to him. "I told you that I was of a different nature. I never denied taking lives. I never lied to you. Never!"

Fital slapped her hand away.

"Get away!" he growled. "Why would you do this?" He grabbed his sword tighter. He pressed the metal harder into her flesh.

Zayashariya winced. Blood trickled over the blade like small raindrops.

"I loved you! I confided in you! I defended you! I would have died for you!" Fital screamed. "You made me the fool!" His anger was uncontrollable. "Now you will pay!"

"Fital, please, I don't want to hurt you. I did what I had to do." Zayashariya pushed the sword away from her neck. Her skin healed instantly. She compassionately reached out to him and he chopped her hand off with his sword. Zayashariya picked up the writhing member and reconnected it to her wrist. The hand rejoined her body as if it had never been separated.

"Now I must do what I have to do!" Fital roared. He tossed his sword from hand to hand. Sweat trickled down his brow.

"Please Fital, listen. I need blood to survive. I do not kill for pleasure or any devilish reason that may be flooding your head. I..." Zayashariya's words were severed like her hand moments before.

"You killed my people!" he yelled, abruptly cutting her off. Fital screamed in her face trying not to show the horror he felt when she replaced her severed hand. *What kind of beast is this?* "I have no love or sympathy in my heart for monsters!" he spat. "You must die like all of the others." Fital swung at her head but missed.

Zayashariya's eyes glowed. Her fangs came from her mouth and her fingernails grew into small talons.

"You must die!" Fital charged, swinging his sword wildly and out of control. "You will pay for all of the evil you have done here. Die you foul demon!" He swung at her but missed. "I'll send you back to the hell that you came from!"

"Goodbye my love," Zayashariya said as she tried to rip Fital's head off of his shoulders. Fital jumped backwards, evading her grasp and swung his sword. A gash went across her shoulder causing a torrent of blood to pour.

Zayashariya quickly grabbed Fital by the neck. He stabbed at her leg with his sword, slicing deep gashes in her thighs. She dropped him and howled in pain. He got to his feet and tried to drive his sword into her chest. She slapped the sword sideways with her forearm and grabbed his neck once more. This time Fital could not free himself.

"I loved you," Zayashariya cried through her gaping mouth. "I would have never hurt you." She shook his jerking body. Fital laughed. Blood dripped from the side of his mouth. She squeezed his neck tighter. He kicked her in the stomach and she dropped him. Fital rolled on the ground and jumped to his feet, coughing but ready for battle.

"You have to do better than that witch!" Fital swung at her head again and missed. "Spare me your sweet lies. You do not know the meaning of love you inhuman sorceress whore!"

With lightning speed, his sword cut across her stomach, leaving a bloody line, trickling like shallow water dripping over a high edge. Zayashariya did not flinch. Fital punched her in the temple with his left hand as his right hand came up with his sword, hoping to cut her throat, but only nicked her a tiny bit below the collar bone.

"I thought that you did not believe in witches," said Zayashariya as she dodged his next blow and grabbed his neck again. This time her grip was unbreakable. Zayashariya's eyes teamed with tears, but she refused to yield. Her hand constricted around his neck like a coiling snake.

"Don't make me do this," she begged. "I would have never harmed you."

He spit in her face.

"Fital, goodbye," Zayashariya said full of regret and sadness. She installed her fangs into the back of his neck and slowly began to drink.

"I always thought death would come to me dressed in glorious robes," Fital said as he coughed blood on her wrist and laughed. The pain of her fangs were agonizing. Never had he known such pain. It intensified with every sip she took.

"Death was always welcomed. I am a soldier. War meant death." He coughed. Fital dropped his sword and with his last bit of strength, he lifted his arm. He placed his hand lightly on her cheek, rubbing her silky flesh delicately. He could feel the warmth of his blood being pulled into her mouth. Fital stroked her heavenly soft skin. Then he kissed his hand and placed it back on her cheek. His arm dropped. His saliva bubbled from his lips as he said, "But death became my only love, installing her fangs into me and stealing away the substance that gives me life. You are Death itself my dear, beautiful, dreadful and inescapable."

Zayashariya stopped drinking.

Fital looked into her teary eyes and whispered, "I love you still." Then he kissed Zayashariya with as much passion his weak body could muster. The taste of his own blood filled his mouth, making him aware of his mortality. His eyes closed slowly. He felt his spirit leaving him, like an invisible force pulling him from his body. He could feel the separation of flesh and soul. He opened his mouth and breathlessly said, "It is finished lover. Through you, I found death. Through life I found you." He coughed and lost consciousness.

"Goodbye," Zayashariya cried. She bit hard into his jugular, installing her fangs all the way to the spine. The crunching of his neck bone echoed in his ears. In deep pulls, she drained him of all blood. She dropped her lover's shriveled body to the ground and wept. Zayashariya traced his face with her finger and closed Fital's haunting eyes.

"I did love you," Zayashariya wept as she kissed Fital's lifeless lips. She laid her head on his chest and bawled. Supreme sadness filled her heart.

Silence ruled the night in the land of Wilzasp. Everything lay limply in stasis. Her soul slept in perpetual silence. The sound of breathing did not exist. Death seeped through her fangs like a dark angel, delivering its wrath, ordered by the powerful hand of the Almighty. Fital no longer lived. He no longer moved. He no longer thrived. Love strived no longer. Only abandoned dreams and soul-free bodies littered the streets of her mind like disregarded trash tossed from Death's peccant hand. Tears rained from her eyes. She took a deep breath and wiped her face with the back of her hands.

Zayashariya pulled herself together and walked away from Fital's body.

"It is finished. Time is of the essence."

She knew her time in this land was limited. It was only a matter of time before the creatures of Night would search for her. It was only a matter of time before the people of Wilzasp would hunt her down, especially now that Fital was dead. He was the only reason why they had not sought her out before. Zayashariya ran back over to Fital and bent down and kissed his lifeless lips for the last time.

"I love you," she whispered. "And I always will."

Walking backwards, she shuffled away with her eyes fixed on her slain lover, heart heavy and head pounding. Her time in Wilzasp had come to an end. Turning sadly, the she-demon scarpered into the Inn to retrieve her belongings.

Chapter 42

Zayashariya ran inside of the Inn into her bedroom and began to pack her belongings. Tears ran from her eyes like a waterfall. Sorrow had overcome her and she fell to the floor.

"Fital I am so sorry," she wailed. "If only you could have understood," she yelled into the empty air, her voice echoing off of the walls. Eager tears rolled from her eyes as her tongue quickly licked them away. "Why?" She fell flat on the floor. Her body was still wet with Fital's blood. Ripped clothing hung off of her body. Her hair was tangled and filthy with sweat and blood. Zayashariya was cut and bruised but healing rapidly. Her physical pain was tiny compared to her emotional trauma. She could not wrap her mind around the fact that her only true love was dead and that she was the one who took his life. Full of despair, she crawled into the bed and wept. Her sobbing was heavy and soul wrenching. Every window in the Inn trembled.

"Fital, please forgive..." Zayashariya pulled her face from the pillow. Her nostrils flared. A peculiar odor filled her nose. Like a feline, she arched her back. Her neck twisted upwards, holding her nose high up in the air, sniffing like a canine. Zayashariya threw her legs off the side of the bed and stood up. She smelled magic, very strong magic and it was not her own. She looked around the room overturning the bed and tossing the shelf. She found absolutely nothing. *Maybe it is my imagination.* She sat back on the bed and ran her fingers through her hair. Her hands started to glow.

"What is this?" she screamed.

The soft lavender glow moved up her arms. Zayashariya shook her arms and twirled around wildly but the glow kept moving until it covered her entire body. The scent of magic grew stronger. It was the scent of her essence. Someone was tracing her. *Who?* Lilith's magic was not efficient enough to trace her essence through planes. *Who?* Zayashariya mumbled a few words to try to counteract the spell but the glow still covered her.

"Who?" she yelled. "Who is doing this?" She pounded the wall, making a small round hole. Quickly she came to her senses. "Kalpvaleim!"

She raised one eyebrow. "No, Kalpvaleim is no wizard." She paced the room. She stopped. "The wizard!"

Zayashariya ran to the shelf that was lying on the floor, pushed it over, and picked up her pouch. She stood in the middle of the floor and sprinkled a circle of blue dust around her. Cross-legged, she sat, in the middle of the circle and began to chant. Zayashariya's body swayed from side to side in a frenzy. The lavender glow made her look like a human sized night light. Her body rose a few inches off of the floor, levitating in mid air. The circle beneath her began to swirl in a mist of cloud. Colors of all shades spun like a tornado. The floor within the circle faded and a portal opened. A dark hole lay open beneath her.

"Kalpvaleim," called Zayashariya, her voice a beckoning whisper. "Kalpvaleim, come to me," she chanted. "Kalpvaleim, come. I summon you to this mortal plane."

The portal began to flash and a bright light flooded the room. Within a second, the light faded away and the room was as it was before except for the terribly abused humanoid lying on the floor in front of Zayashariya. Her glow was suddenly gone. Her use of magic caused her essence to be lost from the one who was tracing her.

Chapter 43

Fierce hungry howls ripped through the air like cloth tearing. The smell of rotting flesh and feces was thick and heavy. It smothered Kalpvaleim like a thick blanket suffocating his senses. It was dark. It was so black that he could not see half an inch in front of him. Battered and bruised, he laid upon the filthy cell floor. Blood dried all over his depreciated body in murky scarlet puddles. His mind was a blur. He tried to lift his head but the pain was much too excruciating. He let his head fall hard against the floor. The pain was too tormenting for him to moan.

The dungeon was silent, too silent. In Lilith's castle, there was always the deafening lamentation of tortured souls and now everything was uncommonly silent. Something was definitely wrong. Kalpvaleim tried to lift his head again. *So much pain.* He forced his head up, then his upper body, then he balanced his upper body on his elbows. He realized that his chains were gone. Those gelatinous creatures and Lilith's two imps must have assumed that he would not survive their beating. *Beating.* He wondered how long he had been out. All he could remember was Lilith storming out of his cell and the gooey goblins coming in. He had passed out half way through the thrashing.

Kalpvaleim managed to sit up. It was pitch black. *Why isn't my night vision working?* Night vision was as natural to him as walking and talking. *Did the beating cripple my ability to see clearly without a light source?* Kalpvaleim was becoming angry. He grabbed the bars of the cell and pulled himself to his knees. He froze. There were faint footsteps and a slushy sound in the distance. He could not determine how far away the sound was. Kalpvaleim held his breath and listened closely.

"Make sure he is dead before you bring him to my chambers," a woman whispered. The faint sound faded away in the distance. Kalpvaleim recognized the Queen of Night's voice.

Kalpvaleim pulled himself to his feet. Literally, he was at a dead end. He was too pulverized to fight or run. There was nothing he could do. Kalpvaleim waited. The slushy noise came closer. *Maybe I could play dead.* Kalpvaleim slid down to the floor and laid on his back very still. A bright light surrounded him. He was gone.

*   *   *

"Kalpvaleim," said Zayashariya, rubbing his matted hair. His body smelled of foul filth. "Kalpvaleim." She turned him onto his back by his shoulder. "Kalpvaleim, are you all right?" Zayashariya asked, massaging his forehead and temples. His eyes flickered. He moaned.

"Zayashariya?" answered Kalpvaleim, opening his eyes. "Is it really you?" he questioned. The pain in his body was so severe that it hurt to breathe. He grabbed his chest with his battered hand and took an aching breath.

"Yes it is me," she said as she ran her fingers across his cheek. Dirt and blood soiled her fingertips.

"Where are we?" Kalpvaleim tried to lift himself up from the floor only to fall down again.

"Don't move," Zayashariya commanded as she got to her feet and walked out of the room. She jogged down the hall until she arrived at the washroom and picked up a clean towel. She wet the towel with warm water and soap, picked up a dry towel, and took them both to her room. With a sense of urgency, she placed the towels on the bed and walked over to Kalpvaleim.

"Be still now," Zayashariya said. She picked him up, cradling him in her arms, and laid him across the bed. A small pitiful moan escaped his mouth. Zayashariya undressed him and washed him. Emptying her pouch on the bed, Zayashariya sorted through the magical items left over from what the old wizard had given her and mixed them together.

"This will ease the pain. In a little while you will be as good as new." She poured the mixture on his wounds, sat beside him, and held his aching hand.

"Zayashariya," Kalpvaleim grunted, struggling to lift his head.

"Yes Kalpvaleim." She pushed him back against the bed to ease his pain.

"Why did you allow this to happen to me?" Kalpvaleim looked into her eyes. His voice was hateful and cold. "Why did you take so long to summon me?"

"I...I...I don't know," said Zayashariya trying to smile as she stumbled over her words. Fital was occupying her every thought. It was impossible for her to show concern for Kalpvaleim through her mourning. She avoided his eyes and answered, "I don't know."

She pinched his chin to make the situation lighter.

He knocked her hand away.

"This is your fault! You allowed me to be tortured!" Fire was in his eyes. "Why do you call upon me now? Why do you need my help now and why should I help you?"

"I kept my promise Kalpvaleim. You are here. I did not say when I would summon you. I promised that I would and I did." Her voice was antagonizing.

"True," Kalpvaleim agreed. He managed to sit up. Zayashariya's potions worked quickly. "What do we do now?" Kalpvaleim asked.

He could never stay angry with her. To be truthful, he was merely thanking his lucky stars that she had remembered him at all. So many others from Gehenna would have gone back on their word as soon as they were home free.

"Leave this place," Zayashariya answered.

"I just got here." Kalpvaleim stretched his arms. His wounds closed before his eyes. One by one, his bruises faded. His hooves were being made whole as if pieces of the horny sheath emerged from out of nowhere and amalgamated and formed new hooves.

"I think that the wizard is tracing my essence. He will lead Lilith to us soon," said Zayashariya, sitting upon the bed wiggling her fingers with a blank expression on her face. Fital's face was permanently imprinted in her head. Every other breath, his image flashed across her mind.

"Why would he help Lilith?" asked Kalpvaleim, realizing that he was naked. He blushed and covered his lower body with the bed spread. "He owes her nothing. He is magically stronger than her. Lilith is no threat to the old wizard."

"Kalpvaleim, you can be so naive." Zayashariya shook her head. "Why do you think he helped us? You and I together have less power than Lilith."

"The old wizard wanted me to work for him."

"Don't be stupid." She laughed. "The old wizard doesn't need you. He can easily create another like you or better."

"Then why?" Kalpvaleim propped two pillows behind his back so that he could lean comfortably against the headboard. He would be feeling wonderful if it was not for his filthy stinky hair constantly falling into his face. The stench of his hair was horrible.

"I'll wash it for you," Zayashariya volunteered. She had read his mind.

"Thanks." Kalpvaleim pushed a dirty lock behind his shoulder. "Why do you think he helped us then?" His fingers carried the foul smell of his hair. Conspicuously, he wiped his hand on the bedspread.

"You better believe that the old wizard made a deal with someone and he is getting compensated well."

"By who? Who could compensate the wizard? The old buzzard has everything already," Kalpvaleim asked. A shadow zoomed past him. He shook his head.

"What's wrong?" Zayashariya inquired.

Kalpvaleim shook his head in dismissal. "My eyes are playing tricks on me. I thought I caught a glimpse of the old wizard." The daemon grinned sourly. "I guess I became accustomed to his company."

"Maybe you miss him," Zayashariya joshed.

"Maybe you are crazier than you look." He spat. "But who could be behind it all?"

"My guess is the head of the Nether Worlds or someone who has a lot of power. The wizard helps no one without getting something in return. I would not be surprised if he made a deal with the devil."

"You mean Lucifer?" Kalpvaleim questioned.

"Yes. Who else could bribe the old wizard?"

"Then we better leave as soon as possible." Kalpvaleim was distracted by a sudden loud noise.

A large stone was thrown through the window shattering the glass. He looked at Zayashariya and she got up and walked over to the window and looked out. Insults, along with sticks and rocks, were hurled at her. The Inn was surrounded by the people of Wilzasp. They decided not to leave but decided to put the beast to rest. They carried torches and weapons. One man stepped forward holding the dead body of Fital in his arms. Zayashariya gasped.

"Come out or we will burn you out demon!" the man yelled. "You will surely die for killing this one!" He lifted Fital over his head. "Surely!"

Zayashariya gasped at the sight of Fital's limp body hovering over the furious man. She stepped back from the window and fell into Kalpvaleim's arms weeping. He could hardly hold her as she poured her pain out in torrents of tears and aching sobs. It pained him to see Zayashariya in such a state. It was clear that the dead man outside meant something to her; a lover maybe.

"No tears," Kalpvaleim demanded. "You are a pillar of power. Turn and face your foes. I am with you."

Flashing purple, Zayashariya's eyes dried instantly. Her teeth peeked from her gums, revealing themselves in all their monstrous glory.

"I love the animal demon in you!" Kalpvaleim squeezed her hand. "Be tame for no one, not even dead lovers." He turned away from her, releasing her hand and walking to the window.

Zayashariya smirked.

Kalpvaleim knew her so well.

Chapter 44

Darkness. Darkness in spirit and in mind. Dark hearts and souls surrounded a large round table like silent shadows lurking in the blackness waiting to petrify an innocent. An aura of chaos diffused the air like foul vapors from a rotting corpse. Evil eyes and faces illuminated the room with an eerie light of its own. Living death and abominable horrors sat together joined in brotherhood for one common cause.

There were thirteen black iron chairs surrounding a mammoth black iron table. A scarlet cushion covered the seat of each chair. Each chair was at least seven feet tall with a high back and arms shaped like crescent moons facing one another. All but one of the thirteen chairs were occupied.

The round table was bare except for folded hands, claws, or any other type of deformed limb a demon may possess. One pair of hands unfolded and laid palm down against the plane. She pushed her chair back with the back of her legs and stood up. Her brick red body reflected her flaming hair. All eyes fell upon her.

"Demons," Queen Lilith began in a fearsome voice. Her flaming eyes locked on each demon one by one. "We are a family, are we not?" Each one nodded so she continued, "As I thought." She nodded back. "Our family has been raped in the worst possible way. Ravished whole by a Judas." She turned around and looked at Judas pacing by the door. "No offense." She smirked and turned her attention back to the table, her face becoming suddenly serious. "We have been betrayed by one of our own. There is no crime worst, even among us. Sin is lovely in our sight." The flame leapt in her eyes. "This great sin is only punishable by torture. Death would be too kind for such a person." Lilith clamped her teeth and sat back in her chair. "I am embarrassed to admit that this traitor is my very own flesh and blood; nevertheless, she must pay the price of her betrayal. We will show her no mercy whatsoever." Lilith's hand fell down hard against the table. "And I mean no mercy! Zayashariya will be made to beg for this seat that she so carelessly abandoned! She will beg to be the thirteenth demon!" Lilith sat back in her chair trying to remain calm. Her flaming hair was in a wild heatless blaze that lit up the room like lightening. "Zayashariya will join us or perish."

"What do you propose we do?" Asmodeus asked while leaning his spiked elbows against the table. "We don't even know where she is."

Lilith belched out a blaring laugh. "Speak for yourself gremlin! Don't include the rest of us in your ignorance."

"Well, since you are so clever, why did you have to look for her in the first place?" he shot back. "If I were the ruler of Night, Zayashariya would have not escaped."

"Are you challenging me?" Lilith jumped to her feet. "I will destroy you buffoon." She placed her finger in his sinister face. "Don't you forget your place. I am the..."

"Not for long if Lucifer finds out that you let Zayashariya abandon the Council of Demons," Asmodeus cackled.

"He is already aware of the situation and I have him under control," Queen Lilith snapped and sat down. She turned her face toward Babylon. "Tell them," she ordered, making a difficult attempt to ignore Asmodeus' taunting words. Lilith knew that she had to capture Zayashariya because she could not afford to lose more respect and ultimately her throne.

"We have located the princess," Babylon spoke as pus ran from the blisters in the corners of her mouth. Even most of the demons seemed repulsed.

"Lilith, must you have this goon recite the details? She repulses us!" Asmodeus spat arrogantly.

"Enough of you!" Lilith snapped. "You will respect me or else!"

"Or else what?" He laughed.

"Enough!" Beelzebub warned.

"May I?" Babylon interjected.

Lilith nodded.

Babylon continued, "The old wizard traced Zayashariya's essence and she is located in the Land of Wilzasp. We will capture her there."

"How? That is out of our realm," Belial asked.

"We will be transported by the old wizard. First, he must materialize on Wilzasp to summon us. Then he will return immediately and place us in a transporter that transcends planes," said Babylon as she leaned back against the back of the chair. The pus filled boils all over her skin bubbled, leaving damp spots on the table. "The people there are weak and can be easily destroyed. They are a logical people. They do not believe in the supernatural. By the time they figure out what we are, it will be too late to act. Capturing Zayashariya will be no problem."

"Buzzzzzzzz. When do they leave? Buzzzzzzzz," asked Beelzebub, Lord of the Flies. "Lucifer will have our hides if you fail us Lilith. If you can not handle Night, give it to another dark lord! Buzzzzzzzzz," he shouted with his tentacles twirling around and around. One of them poked Lilith's face. She quickly brushed the filthy thing away.

"They will leave immediately," Lilith answered Beelzebub while ignoring the rest of his buzzing and rambling. "I will send only six of you." She sat back and folded her hands upon the table once more. "Do not fail me," she threatened. Lilith looked into their eyes one by one.

Silent and full of anticipation, sat the eleven.

Lilith's eyes quickly passed Abaddon's glowing form. He was too powerful.

She did not even consider Asmodeus. He sat with his mammoth hands folded in front of him, itching to pull Lilith apart. His fury burned like an eternal poisonous furnace. Asmodeus' anger was too fierce. He would probably sabotage the entire operation by trying to mutilate every being he came in contact with. Bathing in the blood of innocents aroused him.

Lilith ruled out boyish looking Astaroth. He was just as powerful as herself and Abaddon, despite his juvenile appearance.

Truly, both Asmodeus and Astaroth had more power than she. It would be an insult to consider them. They would take offense and think that she was commanding them to do her bidding like a lowly footman.

Beelzebub fell into the same category with Abaddon and Astaroth.

Samael with a baneful yet chuffed look on his pitch black face was just too irate and arrogant.

Semyaza would jeopardize the operation by his uncontrollable lust for womankind. (The last time he encountered mortal women, he fathered a mutant breed of destructive giants that ran wild and had to be annihilated by The Ancient of Days.) Semyaza sat in his chair tirelessly massaging his chest and thighs and licking his lips. It was said that he was constantly fantasizing about sexual encounters. Every now and then, he would throw his head back in rhapsody, squeezing his eyes shut and moaning like a zealous wanton woman. The contemplation of what Semyaza's deplorable mind was romanticizing about repulsed most of the demons on the council, especially the females. Lilith would never ever send him.

"I choose Babylon, Belial, Zaglofagmen, Iblis, Mephistopheles, and Rehab." Lilith pointed to the designated demons. "You will leave soon so ready yourselves for battle. Do not come back here empty handed or great punishment will fall upon us all."

Chapter 45

"Come out!" the people of Wilzasp screamed as they surrounded the Inn holding torches, axes, guns, swords, and bows and arrows.

"Your reign of death is over!" one irate man yelled, hidden within the mob. They lifted their voices in unison, hurling insults and threats.

"Today you will die!" another unknown yelled.

Zayashariya and Kalpvaleim stared out of the window. Neither of them could see a possible escape. The dark stranger looked into Kalpvaleim's eyes and shook her head, violet waves of hair falling into her delicate face.

"I am sorry that I got you into this," Zayashariya whispered as she looked back out of the window. "I have no idea how we are going to escape these people. Most of my magic potions are used up," she mumbled quietly while contemplating a plan to overcome the encumbrance before them. There was no desire to kill after she had slaughtered her true love. *There has to be another way.*

"Don't worry. We are much stronger than they are," said Kalpvaleim as he took a quick census of the crowd howling below the window. He leaned out of the window with his arms supporting his body against the windowpane. His arm muscles rippled like a disturbed pond.

"Look!" a local yelled to the others while pointing at Kalpvaleim. "Another monster!" The crowd roared.

"I know no fear." Zayashariya smirked. "I never worry." Her eyes were cold and fearless. "Never forget who we are." *Just like my mother.* Her face saddened.

Kalpvaleim looked at her suspiciously and disregarded the comment. At that point, he did not know nor did he care what she meant. "Where is their leader?" Kalpvaleim asked, unable to distinguish any kind of authority figure within the chaotic crowd. They all looked insane with anger. He wondered what she had done to these people to arouse in them this sort of hatred. Kalpvaleim was under the impression that Zayashariya had left the Nether Worlds to evade evil and chaos not to spread it to another plane. At once, he decided not to ask. This was not the time for unimportant explanations. It was time to find a way to escape. Kalpvaleim would pick her brain later.

"There." Zayashariya pointed to the king standing motionless and speechless quite far away from the crowd. "The leader is over there."

King Chucklarki stood in front of his home, robes blowing in the wind and his crown in his hand. A blank look was on his face as if he was unaware of the chaos before him.

"He looks harmless enough," Kalpvaleim said as he moved back from the window and began to look around the room. "There has to be a way out of this place." Kalpvaleim walked over to the shelf and tried to measure exactly how much magic they had to work with. It was next to nothing. He put the witch's brew down and walked back over to Zayashariya, who was stationed at the window. "I guess we will have to fight," he said as he looked down at the angry crowd once again.

"Guess so," she said flippantly.

Kalpvaleim walked away from the window, paced the floor then walked back to the window. The crowd was getting angrier and angrier. Their threats cut through the air like knives.

"Before we battle, would you mind putting on some clothes?" Zayashariya questioned, staring down at Kalpvaleim's nakedness.

He was visibly embarrassed. He covered his private area with his hands and blushed.

She picked up a pair of jeans from the shelf. She held them close to her. They were the ones that Fital had given her.

"These jeans should fit nicely." She hugged them and passed them to Kalpvaleim. "Here, put these on."

"Thanks." He took the jeans and dressed, pretending not to notice her sentimental attachment to the pants. He thought her foolish.

"Come and see," Zayashariya summoned Kalpvaleim to the window. Both of them were awestruck by the sight that they beheld.

The sky darkened. The twin suns briefly eclipsed then re-lit up the sky. All eyes rose to the heavens and witnessed a shower of colorful objects fall from the sky at such a speed that the wind screamed in pain. The objects fell from the heavens like meteors colliding with the earth. Black, white, red, and green objects fell from the sky and landed on the ground right behind the biting crowd with such a force that the entire town quaked. Small cracks split the ground. People fell from their feet and scrambled around confused and afraid. Zayashariya and Kalpvaleim held on tight to the window pane trying desperately not to fall. A warm wind wisped around them and ironically sent icecaps down their spines. They too were flabbergasted by the sudden UFO shower.

There were six round objects in all. They resembled gigantic stones covered with a glowing multicolored film. All of them were perfectly round with a jagged rock like surface. Small craters littered their surface. White smoke rose from a tiny hole on top of them.

Everyone clumsily climbed to their feet and circled the six strange stones with a childlike curiosity, being careful not to get too close.

The smell of the objects and the smoke coming from them was like sulfur. The white smoke disappeared and one of the young men in the crowd touched one of the objects with his fingers and a powerful volt of electricity shot through his hand and knocked him to the ground dead.

Zayashariya and Kalpvaleim looked at one another. Everything within their beings knew that those strange stones meant serious trouble.

One of the stones began to crack. The loud crackling sound ricocheted through the air and the other stones began to crack also.

The people were awed. In a unified movement, they stepped backwards.

The rocky shells fell open like eggshells, exposing five abominable creatures and one strangely beautiful one. The demons climbed out of their shells and the crowd fled for their lives.

"Where is Zayashariya?" Babylon yelled while grabbing a young teen by the back of his neck.

A woman ran up to Babylon screaming and begging for her child. Babylon bit the child's ear off and spat it on the ground, her infectious smile instantly paralyzing the woman.

"Where is she?" Babylon howled.

"There." The woman pointed to the Inn.

Babylon threw the child to the woman, knocking her and an old man, who was standing behind her, to the ground at the same time. The woman took the child and ran into an open home. The old man lay breathless and unable to speak. His heart exploded within him. He lay on the ground with his lifeless eyes staring skyward.

"Let's go!" Lilith's henchwoman waved and the five other demons followed behind her terrorizing and maiming every person in their path.

Zayashariya and Kalpvaleim witnessed the entire ordeal. They recognized the evil clan right off and they had to escape now for sure.

"How did they get here?" Zayashariya raged as she gathered her belongings and threw her cloak over her shoulders. She fastened her hip pouch around her waste and made sure that she had everything she could carry.

"The old wizard," Kalpvaleim responded while watching the demons coming toward the Inn. "We have to jump from the window." He looked down. It would be a nice drop. "We may be able to escape into the woods." He pointed at the nearby forest. Kalpvaleim faced Zayashariya. "Do you have a weapon for me?"

"No," Zayashariya snapped. "We have to use our heads and fight with our hands."

The door to the Inn could be heard being torn off of its hedge.

"Here they come!" Kalpvaleim grabbed Zayashariya's arm and pulled her toward the window.

"No kidding," Zayashariya responded, snatching her arm away. Her face had completely hardened. She was a complete monster, so cold that a statue had more life and vigor.

"Let's go!" She leapt out of the window, her cape flying up into the air like a great fur sail full of wind. She landed light on her feet like a feline.

Kalpvaleim leapt down after her, landing hard on both hoofs. He balanced himself and they ran into the woods. They could hear the high pitch of Babylon's voice rip through the air upon discovering their departure from the Inn.

Chapter 46

"O Lord Almighty, I need you now," the king prayed, safe inside of his home, on his knees. "I have seen true evil, O Lord. Help us." He rocked back and forth on his knees, beating his chest as he moaned a desperate prayer. "Lord, have mercy. I am humble and I beg you to save my people," the king wept. "I have faith that you will. I believe that you have the power to do all things." He choked on his tears. "Lord, have mercy." The king stood up and sat in the chair next to his desk. His study was dark and quiet. The air around him reeked of hopelessness.

He assumed that the queen was still in the bedroom sleeping or just sitting on the bed in a trance like she had been ever since the day that they fought. It was funny, at a time like this, he thought of his wife. He wanted her back. He wanted her to be well again. He would give anything to see her smile at him again or for her to just acknowledge his presence. He loved her so much. If only she knew that he was a different man now, she would gladly be next to him holding his hand. Unfortunately, she did not know that he had changed. He didn't know if she knew anything. Queen Eox had obviously had a severe mental breakdown and it was all his fault. *All my fault!*

The King of Wilzasp sat in silence. Nothing stirred but the sound of his breath rising and falling in deep loud intervals. He leaned forward, elbows on knees, and began to pray again. His eyes were heavy with tears.

"Lord, I know that I am not worthy. I know that I am impure, I...," the king's words were stifled in his throat. A blinding light filled the room. He fell to his knees and covered his head with his arms. King Chucklarki's entire body trembled uncontrollably in a frightening seizure. The light died and the king lifted his head. Standing before him, he saw six angels. All of them were tall creatures with exceptionally attractive unisex faces. They looked almost exactly alike except for small features like one angel's nose was wider and another's lips were fuller and another angel's eyes were bigger than the others. They all wore golden long sleeve floor length robes. The angels had skin the color of fine burnished brass and their hair was shoulder length, thick, and extremely curly like lamb's wool. It was silver in color. Each of them had gargantuan wings coming from their backs, black with silver and gold tips, fluttering ever so lightly. The wing span had to be at least ten to twelve feet. Each of the angels held a golden sword in their right hand, holding it across their chest. Girdling their bodies, they wore a leather strap that held their swords when not in use. The angels stood silently with their eyes looking toward the ceiling. One angel stepped forward, placed his sword in its sheath and addressed the king.

"You have been heard," the angel's voice echoed. "We are here to help you. I am Michael and with me I bring Gabriel, Uriel, Ashley, Zaynnah, and Kashyra." His face was emotionless as he looked into the king's eyes. "May the spirit be with you." A faint light left the angel's body and rested upon the king.

The king was filled with an unexplainable feeling. It was like a million tickles and a trillion chill bumps dancing over his body. It was an overwhelming of the senses. It filled his body with pure rhapsody. Heavenly elation flowed through his veins like fire shut up in his bones. Tears of joy ran down his face. He praised the Lord and danced and shouted.

"Thank you!" he rejoiced. King Chucklarki's arms swung playfully. His hands clapped and he twirled about the room, moving his feet so fast that they looked like fluttering wings.

"We must go now. We have work to do." Michael turned and walked through the closed chamber door. The other angels followed him and they all disappeared from the king's sight.

King Chucklarki quickly sprang to his feet and ran into his bedroom. He saw his wife sitting at her vanity brushing her soft peach hair. Her apricot skin looked so lovely in the dim bedroom light. He skipped over to her and kissed her cheek. Tears were flowing freely from his eyes. Surprisingly, Queen Eox turned around and smiled at him. The king wept. She held his head against her breast and rubbed his hair. Gently, she kissed his forehead and pulled him to his knees in front of her. With ultimate love, she wrapped her arms tightly around him and he did the same to her.

"I love you," Queen Eox whispered as she looked up and winked at the angel standing in the corner of the room. It waved goodbye to the queen and disappeared.

"I love you too." The King of Wilzasp buried his head in his wife's bosom. For the first time in his life, he was complete.

Chapter 47

"Where are you?!" Babylon screamed as she and her demon crew stood in the middle of the road, giant nightmarish villains come to life. "Show yourself or they all die!" she threatened and grabbed a man up by his hair. He tried to break free but she ripped his throat out before he was able to move again. She tossed his limp body to the side and licked her bloody fingers clean. Others nearby scrambled away like roaches when the light is turned on.

"You fool!" Belial chastised Babylon. "Do you think that Zayashariya cares about these people?" he grumbled. "We have to find her ourselves." He opened his cloak revealing a beautifully formed body. He wore only a tight pair of pants. His rippled chest was bare as well as his feet. "Zayashariya can not resist my charms." A smile spread across his handsome face.

Zaglofagmen laughed, his hood crinkling as his red eyes danced inside his invisible face. "You both are fools! Belial can not charm her. You already tried that and failed, remember?" He cackled. "We have to trap her and kill her."

"You can not kill the princess!" yelled Rehab. "Lilith will kill us!"

"Enough with the bickering. We have a job to do!" Babylon quieted their squabbling. "Time is of the essence. Find her!"

The demons split up and began to invade homes and to torture people for information.

Zayashariya and Kalpvaleim watched from nearby bushes, careful to remain out of view. Neither of them were prepared to fight demons. They could only hope that they would not be discovered. Each breath they took was carefully drawn and exhaled as silently as possible.

"I can not let them kill all of those people," Zayashariya whispered. Guilt commanded her words. Fital's face flashed across her mind. *I can not hurt him also in death.* Zayashariya was losing her nerve. Somehow, she needed to redeem herself. She needed to transform her spirit so that her love for Fital would not be in vain. *How?*

"What!" Kalpvaleim almost shouted too loud. He looked around to make sure that no one heard him. "What are they to us?" A look of utter confusion crossed his face. He could not believe his ears. He wondered what could have happened to change Zayashariya's state of mind. As far as he knew, she never cared about anyone other than herself.

"They are living creatures," said Zayashariya, peeking through the brush and devising a rescue plan in her mind.

"What?" Kalpvaleim barked. "They were probably nothing but food to you," he replied sarcastically, sitting on the ground with his hoofs crossed in front of him. "All I know is that I am leaving this place. After I rest a bit, I am out of here. I have no desire to battle a group of angry demons and I am sure that you don't either. So, whatever flash of humanity you seem to be overwhelmed with at the moment, get rid of it and come to your senses woman!"

"No one is keeping you! I do not remember asking you for your help," Zayashariya snapped at him with her eyes locked on the action taking place in the middle of the street. "Kalpvaleim look!"

He folded his legs behind him and got up on his knees. He peered through the brush, shocked at what his eyes beheld.

The sky became blinding white and then back to normal in seconds. Lightening flashed and in the center of the street appeared six holy angels. Everyone in town froze in their footsteps in awe of the creatures before them. Peace filled their hearts. Feelings of love and beauty flowed through their spirits. They knew that the creatures were good. Joy and rapture overcame them. They knew that they would be saved.

The angels pulled out their swords in a flash and with lightening speed, they divided up and hunted for demons.

Babylon caught sight of one of the angels. It was Gabriel. Babylon quickly and repeatedly squeezed her palm until her hand was completely filled with infection. She turned toward Gabriel and opened her palm, unveiling a yellowish ball of dripping pus. She threw the fetid goo into the angel's face. Gabriel's eyes burned with rage and pain as the putrid pus scorched his skin. Gabriel wiped his face with his robe and let out an awful war cry. He pulled his sword and swung it wildly but she threw another heaping ball at him, knocking him down to the ground. Gabriel jumped up and charged her, the goo still stinging his skin. He was off balance and unable to land a hit. Babylon struck him in the face and kicked him in the knee, forcing his leg to bend backward. A loud crack was heard. Gabriel fell to one knee. Babylon ran to him, to her surprise, Gabriel sliced her across the thigh with his sword. She gasped in pain but quickly calmed herself. She punched him in the face and turned away from him hoping to escape. The angel snapped his limb back into the socket and was in quick pursuit. As Babylon tried to run, Gabriel's sword sliced into her bane filled flesh. She fell to the ground screaming. Yellow pus ran from her wounds and Gabriel slashed her once more, but this time across the neck. Her hideous head rolled to her side as she lay on the ground convulsing and slowly melting into the dust of the road. Her head was still animated and strangled screams mingled with pus came from her mouth until the angel grabbed her by her raven hair and impaled her head on his sword. Suddenly, like a snail trapped in a shower of salt, her head melted and ran down the sword. The angel flung the goo from his hand and weapon and went off to hunt once more. A cold breeze from no where blew and a hazy form formed and separated from the goo. Babylon's spirit floated away and disappeared.

Michael swooped down from the sky and caught hold of two of the demons. Zaglofagmen, black robes flying in the air like a giant bat, got loose and hit Michael in the back of his neck with his forearm. The angel stumbled and unwillingly let go of Iblis.

The two frenzied demons, hissing and growling, double teamed Michael and knocked him to the ground with a double punch; one to the throat and the other to the chest. The demons began to stomp Michael, their feet moving with numinous speed. Michael grabbed a hold of Iblis' leg and knocked him into Zaglofagmen. Michael pulled himself up and grabbed both demons. He held Zaglofagmen and Iblis by the neck and smashed their skulls together over and over again until the two demons were delirious. The demons fell to the ground on top of one another. Michael kicked them into a juxtaposed position and began to beat Zaglofagmen with the hilt of his sword. Iblis jumped on Michael's back and choked him. The gagging angel spun around and knocked Iblis on the ground once more. A fuzzy energy pulsated around both demons. The energy haze tried to intertwine. The two demons attempted to combine their powers but Michael drove his sword into them both at the same time. Their bodies fell on top of each other as they wrenched on the ground like serpents having a seizure. The demons howled in pain as they found physical death. Their spirits left their bodies, heading for the Nether Worlds.

Michael chased after Belial but Belial covered himself with the rock-shell that he arrived in and disappeared.

Michael ran to the aid of the others.

Ashley spread her wings and took off into the air. She swooped down on an escaping demon and drove her golden sword into his back. Mephistopheles hit the ground. His wolf like body fell flat. A canine howl escaped from his sharp slobbering maw. Ashley pulled her blade free and tried to slash the monster into pieces. The beast broke free of her slashing and bit deep into the flesh of her arm. The angel screamed in agony as the demon pulled at her wing and tried to devour her limb. Ashley howled, kicked, and screamed as Mephistopheles' fangs tore deeper into her arm. Blood colored the demons maw and dripped down his heaving chest. Michael heard Ashley's cry and swooped down on Mephistopheles.

Michael hovered over the battle, whispering a prayer to the Lord.

The wolf demon's maw peeled away from Ashley's arm and Michael pulled her free. Ashley fell to the ground holding her arm. Chewed flesh and thick blood hung from her arm like wax dripping from a candle.

Michael opened his mouth. A bright flame gathered within his throat. With a mighty exhale, he enkindled Mephistopheles. The shrieking beast turned into ashes and his spirit left the material world.

Michael helped Ashley to her feet. Her arm was mangled and one of her wings was broken. Michael asked the Lord to take her up into heaven and Ashley vanished without a trace.

Zaynnah, Kashyra, and Uriel surrounded, Rehab, the last demon. Upon noticing that his demon brothers were conquered, Rehab made a half hearted effort to defend himself. In his hand, Rehab held a halberd which he swung three times, missing the angels, and dropped it to the ground. The defeated demon fell to his knees and begged.

"Please do not send my spirit away!" he cried. "I can not take the depths of Hell. Lucifer's wrath will be too great for me to bear. Send me back to Night. Let me go unpunished. Please I can..." His words were cut off as his stone like head rolled to the ground, Rehab's putrescent mouth gasping for air. His spirit left his body and blew away in the wind.

The five angels came together with a flash of light. Then, they were gone.

Zayashariya and Kalpvaleim watched the entire scene from the woods. Thankful that the angels did not search them out, they were sure that the angels had to know that another source of evil was near. Evil never goes unnoticed. Maybe it was not in HIS plan.

The two cronies stood up and walked away from the town. Fear mixed with relief filled their hearts for they knew that a damning verdict awaited for them somewhere, but judgment would not be passed today.

Many dead bodies littered the streets. All of the survivors began unpacking and unloading their carts. Awful memories of the events that transpired filled their minds. Despite it all, Wilzasp was their home and there was no where else to go. They gathered their children and belongings and headed for their homes. Rebuilding the city would be a strenuous task but there was hope. They had seen a miracle and they knew that they would soon have to change their state of mind concerning their belief system. The spirit world was indeed real and they needed someone or something greater than themselves on their side. The king and his wife led the exodus back to their homes and soon they all disappeared into the setting of the twin suns.

The she-demon and the daemon watched the people evacuate the streets and vanish quickly into their homes. Zayashariya was filled with despair and regret. *If only Fital could have lived.* She wiped the thought out of her mind. *He would have never understood.* She knew that he would have never accepted her after he found out that she was feeding on his people. But, she would give anything for his life again. Anything. He taught her that she, even with an innately evil nature, could love and was capable of being loved. Even in the minutest sense, Zayashariya felt that she was not totally evil; therefore, she was nothing like her mother. Zayashariya had hopes that one day she could change. Maybe by some miracle she could get in God's graces. After all, evil was not her choice, it was her nature and she could not be at fault for that. *Could I?*

Zayashariya knew in her heart that her battles were far from over. Lilith would still pursue her. Lucifer would definitely be involved. His pride would not let Zayashariya succeed. The angels had left her and Kalpvaleim alive for a reason. She was sure that they knew that they were there. Angels always know. Zayashariya could have sworn that Michael flew right above them, when they were hiding in the bushes, and looked right down at them and kept on flying. Therefore, she concluded, God had a plan for her. Her purpose was not yet discovered. Whether good or bad, she was willing to endure whatever the future may bring. Was there a choice to do otherwise?

Zayashariya lay on the grass supine, engulfed in the battling thoughts of her mind. Kalpvaleim grabbed her hands and pulled her to her feet.

"It is time to go," said Kalpvaleim, placing his hands on Zayashariya's shoulders. "We must leave this place." He kissed her softly. She gave no response.

Zayashariya and Kalpvaleim walked in the opposite direction of the town. They did not want to be noticed by anyone that may be wandering about Wilzasp so they quickened their pace.

"Kalpvaleim, I think that we should separate," said Zayashariya. She walked away slowly looking blankly into the horizon. A tear ran from her eye down her high cheekbone, a diamond emerging from coal. "All of this destruction was because of me."

Kalpvaleim put his hand on her shoulder. It was getting colder as the walked toward the giant gate that surrounded the town. It only took minutes for the both of them to leap over the structure.

"I will help you through your pain," he said, still curious about her experience in Wilzasp but he felt that it still was not the time to inquire about it. He erased the thought from his mind and focused on their future.

"No!" said Zayashariya pulling away from him. "I am not worthy of anyone's love or companionship." She saw Fital's face with her mind's eye. "I killed all that meant anything." All she could see was Fital's dead body looking up at her, the same body that loved her when no one else had. *I killed him!* She scorned herself.

"No. Zayashariya..." Kalpvaleim tried to comfort her but was cut off in mid-sentence.

"Leave!" she screamed. Her face began to contort. Her eyes flashed and her teeth protruded. "Leave now!" Zayashariya hissed and tore her cloak in half. She threw half to him and wrapped the other half around herself. "Leave now or perish like the others."

"I wish you well. I will never forget you. If you ever need me, I'll be there," said Kalpvaleim, kissing her bestial face and turning his back to her and running as fast as he could. He had no interest in becoming her next meal. Dust clouds hid him from her view. In no time, he was gone.

Chapter 48

"We failed you," Belial told the remaining Council of Demons, noticing that Lilith was suspiciously absent, with his head down and ashamed of his failure. "The Almighty sent his angels and they defeated us. We were not prepared to fight such unconquerable foes. We were ill prepared I tell you! Nothing we could do! Nothing! It was an anathema upon us from the very beginning. Failure was unavoidable." He paused and looked into each of the demon's eyes. "We were told that the people of Wilzasp were nonbelievers and that they would be easily terminated. I fault the old wizard. The old wizard lied to us. He told us that the people of Wilzasp had no spiritual power. But, they summoned the angels of the Lord!" Belial raged. His hand slammed into the table as he stood up and roared like a pained beast. Belial fell back into his chair with disgust in his eyes and finished his excuses. "Ha! The Almighty himself was on their side. What could we do? Nothing!" He paused again. Belial examined the other's faces to see if his speech was capturing their sympathy. "What do we do now?" Pity was not found anywhere.

"You suffer fool!" Lucifer yelled. Invisible to the Council of Demons, his voice startled them all. "You all will suffer. You will meet your defeated brothers and sisters in hell with me!" his voice echoed and faded. A giant winged shadow was cast over the room. A great quake cracked the floor in half and the table and the demons surrounding it fell into the fissure.

"What of Lilith?" Beelzebub screamed as he fell into the abyss. "She must suffer a similar fate!" the Lord of the Flies wailed as he disappeared into the bottomless pit. A tornado of flies followed him in a buzzing heap.

"She will not be forgotten," Lucifer swore, his voice vibrating through the chasm.

*　　*　　*

"Lucifer!" Lilith jumped at the sight of him. She sat up straight on her throne and uncrossed her legs. Her flame of hair died down until her head appeared shiny and bald.

"You are damned wench!" the devil croaked.

He walked toward her in long strides. His robe flowed in the wind his fast swinging arms generated with every step he took. His wings unfolded and he pounced.

"Let me explain." the Queen of Night begged, falling backwards as the prince of darkness descended upon her.

"Silence!" Lucifer spat the angry word in her face like a ball of fire. "I need no excuses. You failed me!" The devil was eye to eye with Lilith. His cold breath frosted her petrified face. He raised his hands and the whole room quaked. The devil disappeared.

"Zayashariya, you will die!" Lilith screamed. Her voice echoed through the air, bouncing off of the walls like a billion balls. She stood in the middle of her chamber with her hands raised and her fists balled tight. The walls began to close in on her. Her punishment began.

"It is not over Zayashariya! It is not over!" Lilith screamed, standing wide-legged, face twisted, and shaking her fist in the air. Her eyes searched the caving walls for an escape. There was not one. "I will find you!" The flame of hair on her head reappeared and inexplicably ignited her surroundings. Lilith howled and fell to her knees screaming in the midst of the fire. "I will find you!" she screamed once more as she disappeared beneath the flames howling in agony and defeat. "Like a phoenix driven with vengeance, I will resurrect! Zayashariya you are mine!"　　Lilith, the Queen of Night, slowly faded into silence like day into night

Chapter 49

"Wiz," an invisible voice whispered.

The temperature of the room dropped to a terrible freezing temperature. A shadow crossed the room in supernatural speed. The potions on the shelves quietly rocked and stood still once more.

The wizard looked up from his laboratory experiment. His eyes searched the room as his rubicund face produced a voluminous amount of perspiration. He felt the presence of another; a life force pulsating near him as if his ear was to the bosom of another. The old wizard put his concoction down and reached for his giant spell book. The invisible force knocked the book across the room. The old wizard's heart pounded within his chest like a sludge hammer trying to break through his ribs.

"Who's there?" the old wizard yelled into the frosty air. White clouds exited his mouth forming a momentary fog around his head. He swatted the unwelcomed miasma from his face.

"Show yourself or I will destroy you!" he threatened. In his heart, he knew who it was but his pride would not let him beg for his life.

"Who are you?" He stomped his feet like a spoiled child. His starry hat fell from his head and his wild white hair caused him to look like the mad man he was becoming.

"Wiz," the voice whispered again, a tad bit louder and with force. The evil angel appeared. "You failed me!"

His face twisted into an unbelievably ugly mask, the facade of a revolting beast born out of the twisted imagination of pure evil. His wings spreaded outward then upward with such swiftness that it was barely noticeable. A giant black shadow was cast upon the room.

Leaning against the table, the old wizard knocked his beaker to the floor and stumbled backwards. His eyes bucked and his body trembled in fear. Futile pleas froze in the pit of his belly. Speechless, he was rendered silent by the verisimilitude of perdition.

"You failed me!" Lucifer bellowed as he grabbed the wizard by the face. His long fingers wrapped around the old wizard's head like crooked tree roots enveloping a small bolder. Lucifer opened his robe and pulled the wizard into it. They both disappeared like a sneeze in the wind.

Chapter 50

The cold wind wrapped around the legs of Zayashariya. The ebony skinned woman pulled her cloak tightly around her robust yet perfectly formed body. The deserted road never seemed to end. She couldn't see a town or life form in sight. She was tired and weary. Her feet ached within her hard leather boots. Hunger and fatigue ailed her. She needed to feed herself and the gift inside of her that Fital had unknowingly given her. Lovingly, she grabbed her belly and rubbed it gently. She could feel the soft kick of the life that lived within her.

Zayashariya moved through the dusty path at a faster pace than before. Her destination was unknown, yet, she had faith that she would encounter life somewhere. The deserted road she walked on never seemed to end. It seemed to fade into the very sky. It was like staring at the horizon, being lost in a helpless state of purgatory. The dust of the road painted her boots with a tan film, sprinkling her heels with dusty speckles of dirt. The road was no longer a barren wasteland, vegetation began to sprout many miles back, now it seemed to grow into an intense forest. Twisting and tangling vines and branches surrounded her from every side. She was engulfed in emerald brush and quickly became swallowed within their depths.

Zayashariya brushed the bracken from her path and continued on her slow and restless journey. Her eyes turned toward the heavens and she witnessed the sky change from periwinkle to pink to peach to plum purple. She could not see a town or life form in sight. She walked alone in silence. Her breath rising and falling like the tides. She was weary and she feared that she would not make it to shelter.

Time had no place in her sojourn. She walked on faith, hoping to discover a new world and praying to forget her old world. She was on the brink of starvation. Hunger pains rumbled within her firm belly like a belch of thunder erupting from the sky. She held her cloak close and walked on. She moved through the dusty path at a faster pace than before. It seemed as if she had been walking for days, maybe weeks. The dust formed tiny tornadoes at her heels and twirled away into the void. Zayashariya cut through the brush with her bare hands drawing spider web scratches across her palms. Tree limbs flew in every direction. They yielded to her strength. The path before her became clearer. She squinted her slanted eyes and tried to focus on the mystery before her eyes. Her heart seemed to beat a little faster. *Sanctuary at last!* She hurried her pace, eyes fixed on her destination, her hands gripping her swollen belly. She smiled.